Manifold Dreams

by Carl deSoto

This story is dedicated to my friends and family, who pushed me to finally put the worlds of my head onto paper.

First published by Dog Ear Publishing
4010 W. 86th Street, Ste H
Indianapolis, IN 46268
www.dogearpublishing.net

dog ear
PUBLISHING

ISBN: 978-1-4905-8277-1

This book is a work of fiction. Places, events, and situations in this book are purely fictional and any resemblance to actual persons, living or dead, is coincidental.

This book is printed on acid free paper.
Printed in the United States of America

Forward

This story began as an exercise to work through writer's block while I was writing my own Science Fiction Roleplaying Game. It was *supposed* to be a small story in the larger universe setting, from which I could work though more of the game systems and functionality.

The characters in this story took on a life of their own. They took up residence in my head and refused to be passed off as just another pack of Non Player Characters in an RPG universe. They wanted their story told.

Upon complaining about this, a good friend suggested I give them what they wanted. A full story written for NaNoWriMo. National Novel Writing Month, which runs every November, is a harrowing and exhilarating experience for any bold enough to try. It requires (on the honor system) that you write a full story in excess of 50,000 words in under a month.

Well, that's what I set out to do. I completed the first 54,000 in November 2012, then just…kept going. The story never quite felt done. Finally, around May 2013, I decided that enough was enough. I found a good stopping point, and pulled the remainder (over 10,000 words of remainder) away to begin book two.

The story outperformed its original design by leaps and bounds. The RPG-Writer's-Block I had hit crumbled at some point in there, and after I finished the story, I was able to turn back and cruise easily through the parts that had given me so much trouble.

This universe is something I have poured my heart, mind, and spirit into. I hope you like it as much as I do.

Chapter 1

Manik always hated Tasting Day. The day that the head of the Clan came to the brewery to 'check the acceptability' of the most recent designs by the Brewmistress. He woke that morning in his room, stared forlornly at the ceiling for a while, and sighed. Today was only made worse because fate had seen to arrange the descent of Tasting Day this season squarely on his seventeenth birthday, the day when he was supposed to present himself to the head of the Clan to be tested for adulthood. Again.

Rolling out of bed, Manik put on his favorite grey shorts and rust colored shirt, figuring if he was going to get complained at and looked down upon yet again, he may as well be comfy. Grabbing his apron off of the hook on the wall, he headed out through the maze of hallways to the side door. He left the Tertiary Brewhouse, where the lower ranked Brewers were housed and where the Clan's wine-fruits were processed into the renowned drink that everyone said was one of the most sought after on the planet.

He crossed the small triangular courtyard, side stepping out of the way of the older and higher rank Brewers as they went about their tasks, and headed for the Primary Brewing Chamber to get started on the day's work. As a Junior Assistant Brewer, the lowest rank available and the only rank given to 'children', this consisted of carting various materials back and forth between the Primary, Secondary, and Tertiary Brewhouses and their associated stills, cellars, and workshops. He slowed as he approached the cavernous Entryway, hearing two voices he both recognized and dreaded.

"What do you mean 'still sleeping'?! He's a working member of this Clan and this Brewery, isn't he?! Why're you going easy on him? I sent him here to make sure he learned something, not to laze about!" bellowed Barrus sel'Kaer, retired Warrior of the Assembly, confidant of the First Warrior currently running the planet, and lord of Clan Kaer.

"He worked late last night on fixing a leak in the third cellar in the Tertiary Brewhouse, so I adjusted his schedule today to give him some extra rest. You know full well that I don't let any of my workers 'laze about'. Why else would MY brewery be the model for the rest of the Clans in the city, eh?" Innele ris'Kaer, the Brewmistress of the Clan spat back with equal venom.

Manik knew that he shouldn't interrupt the siblings when they were arguing, as many hides in the family had been tanned thoroughly by one or the other for making that very mistake. Nonetheless, he knew what was expected of him so he took a deep breath and walked into view as calmly as he could.

"G-g-g-good m-morning B-b-brewmistress. G-g-g-g-g-good mo-mo-morning f-f-f-f-father." he said as he approached.

Both started at his seemingly sudden appearance, turning their identical golden eyes, one of the hallmarks of the Clan, to bore accusingly into his for a moment.

Barrus recovered first, and said "Well, good of you to join us on this most auspicious of days. Why...I bet IF you succeed in your Challenge, Innele would name this next batch after you as a birthday present! What'd'ya say to that?" he finished with a chuckle.

"You will kindly respect my title in this compound, my Lord, as I will respect yours." Innele retorted, glaring ice at Barrus before turning a kinder smile to Manik. "You are up earlier than expected. I'd hoped to have the inspection done before you were about. I would have you start on your duties, but our illustrious Clan Lord-" she tosses a glare over her shoulder at an unrepentant Barrus "-has decided that your Challenge takes precedence over the operation of MY brewery. Once you are finished and have earned your Val, you can return and we can talk of possibilities and jobs."

Manik sighed and turned to Barrus, standing up straight to take advantage of all six feet of his height. "C-c-c-clanlord, I f-f-formal-l-l-lly Ch-ch-ch-ch-challeng-g-ge y-y-you f-f-f-for m-m-my r-r-r-rite of F-f-famil-l-ly." he managed in one long breath.

Barrus watched his son critically for a few minutes, before straightening to his full six foot eleven inches and replied with the ritual words "Manik, to Challenge a Clanlord is no small matter, and I will not go easy on you because you are a child. To pass this Test is to join the Clan, and to join the Clan is to become my true son. Knowing this, do you still wish to proceed?"

Manik nods once. "Y-y-yes. I d-d-do."

Barrus nods back and says "Well then, let's get to the Arena. The families are already assembled and eager. Third try's the charm, as they say." then turned on his heel and strode from the room without another word.

Manik glanced over at Innele, who flashed him an encouraging smile. Approaching him, she slipped his apron from his head, and then gestured silently toward the door.

Gathering his courage, he walked quickly out through the foyer of the Primary Brewhall and headed across the yard for the Family Arena. The Arena had been in place since the city of Alberich had been founded in 2203 and even now, a little over two hundred years later, it looked as intimidating and bold as the day it was carved from the bedrock. The outer wall of nearly black stone rose from the floor to meet the next tier of the city some fifty feet up, with relief carvings of the Great Warriors of the Clan as they have become known through the years. By requirement Manik could name every single one, what their specialty was in the Arena, and how long they held office on the Assembly before either retiring, as his father had, or by being dethroned by another Warrior of the Kaer Clan. Those that made the Assembly, but were dethroned by members of other Clans didn't get a spot on the wall and thus, were not worth remembering according to the Clan's teachers.

Dozens of pairs of Kaer-gold eyes watched him approach. Most with disdain, some with anger, and a great many with pity. Manik understood all three. Even as a cub he had been small for his age, regularly getting mistaken for someone years younger. Coupled with his stutter, Manik seemed destined to be the depressing footnote in the glorious annals of the powerful Kaer Clan. He lowered his head, letting his coppery hair fall and hide his eyes, and hurried into the Arena hoping to get the embarrassment over with quickly.

Manik moved through the staging area and slowed when he reached the Arena proper. The entry he used was for Challengers only, the other two entryways reserved for the Defenders and the Observers. The door opened onto a short staircase descending to the prep room, containing a few benches, a handful of statues holding various weapons in heroic poses, and the racks of implements used in the Arena matches. Manik's eyes drifted over the cages that remained closed and sealed, indicating that his father had not chosen any of those in the mirrored Defender Room. He paused to look longingly at the puzzles requiring skill and finesse. The cage had not been opened in a very long time, as the great Clan Kaer was known for their physical prowess more than anything. They were all lithe and quick of reaction and wit, but no True Warrior of the Clan had yet made a name for himself using anything but the weapons and challenges that valued strength over all else.

Approaching the final entry to the Arena Floor, he felt, as always, an icy stab of panic. What if his father finally grew tired of him and decided to kill him? Would it really be so bad? How long could it take a giant like Barrus to crush the

life out of him? Maybe he'd get lucky and a Strength challenge will get chosen and he'll be crushed by something... The call of the announcer broke his morbid reverie.
"Greetings ladies and gentlemen, Chromaran and guests! Welcome to the Trial of the Family for young Manik! His Defender has the tradition of choice of weapon for what the Trial shall entail and he has decided upon....a Physical Trial!" Manik suppressed a groan; it was going to be as bad as he feared. He waited for the announcer to finish before deciding whether or not to try and slink out before the gates closed. "The mighty Barrus sel'Kaer, retired Warrior of the Assembly, has chosen to duel young Manik using natural weapons only! Claws, teeth, the arts of foot and fist...this is where heroes are defined. Let's all give an encouraging welcome to the hopeful of Clan Kaer...MANIK!!!"

Manik heard the gate behind his alcove slide home with a quiet click and sighed once again. Time to face his death, he supposed. He stepped out into the shallow sawdust of the Arena as the echoes of the announcer's voice faded. Looking up at the stands, he saw many faces he recognized, from close family all the way out to second-tier-removed branch family cousins and a few Chromarans he didn't, and even a scattering of off-worlders, watching him closely. As he approached the center of the Arena, there was a scattering of applause, quickly absorbed by the magnitude of the room.

Barrus stood proudly, bare-chested, holding a pair of Y-shaped stands above the dust. Hung on one was the elaborate, many-layered, cloak of the Head of the Clan and on the other was a shorter, more plain, simpler, version of the same. A cloak worthy of Family.

The announcer, a cousin who'd been able to cash in on his incessant talking and explanations, continued as the two very different sized men stood in the center of the empty Arena floor. By requirement, they had to allow the announcer to explain the rules, consequences, and prize that was being fought for so that the Observers could make an informed decision as to the winner, if the match was a closely contested one.

Tossing his long, dusty platinum braid over his shoulder, the announcer began once again. "For those unfamiliar with the Trials of the Chromaran people, allow me to explain. Before you stands the child, Manik, who was born of this Clan but has not earned the right to be called a man, or to grow his hair beyond the shoulder, nor to attach the Clan to his name. In succeeding today, he earns the name val'Kaer, the val meaning Family." he paused for a moment, peering into the crowd to make sure proper attention and respect were being paid to him. Satisfied, he finished his speech. "Here today, these two shall battle for the glory of Clan Kaer and the betterment of the Chromaran People. Observers to your posts, Defender, you have the floor."

Barrus took a deep breath and began his ritual speech, holding up the plainer cloak and bellowing so all could hear him. "This cloak represents my family. The Clan Kaer. The black field reminds us that we are not originally from this planet, but we have become natives. Chromara is our home, but we will always be tied to the stars. The lines of red running from top right to bottom left represent the light of our star, the Red Giant named Alpha Herculis by the stargazers of old. By his light we thrive. The lines of gold running from bottom right to top left represent the vision of Clan Kaer. We watch everyone and everything; we are sharp of wit and fang, bright of thought and eye. By challenging me this day, you identify your desire to join my ranks. Let us see how you fare...this time."

With an overly theatrical roar, likely aimed to intimidate the visiting offworlders in the stands, Barrus thrust both posts through the sawdust and a good few inches into the floor of the Arena. Manik removed his shirt, tossing his dusky bronze hair and flexing his miniscule muscles. Barrus spread his arms wide, rippling the ample musculature of his arms and chest, before dropping into a low fighting stance.

Both men flexed their hands, stiffening their fingers and allowing their ebony claws to slide forward and click into place. Manik bared his fangs at his father, who grinned, roared again, and charged.

Manik leapt into the air, hoping to clear the oncoming freight train, and was able to land a solid set of scratch marks from shoulder down to hip on Barrus. Unfortunately, his good luck ran out at that point, as Barrus was able to catch his ankle before Manik fully cleared him. Rotating on his right foot, he took advantage of his superior size, weight, and the momentum he'd built, and spun Manik a few times around before releasing the younger man to slam into the stone side wall of the Arena with rib-cracking speed. Manik lay in the sawdust, dazed, for a moment, and then got shakily back to his feet. Barrus waited calmly for him to make the first move and when Manik feinted left, he dove right, tackling Manik in an easy roll ending with Barrus' teeth at Manik's throat. Barrus got up, looked down at Manik disdainfully, and said "Get up kitten, try that move again and I'll tear your throat out for real. Now get serious and fight me."

Barrus turned his back on Manik and started walking slowly across the Arena, stretching his muscles occasionally. Manik got to his feet, wiped the thin trails of blood from his neck, and tried to focus. He HAD to win. He couldn't take the look of pity his family gave him anymore. This was his father's best event, but he wasn't fighting at full ferocity...he WANTED Manik to win, he was sure of it.

Manik flexed his small legs and thought about his chances critically for the first time. He was smaller and weaker than his father, there was no doubt about that...but maybe he was a little faster. If he could get Barrus to charge him again, maybe he could use all that momentum and weight against him, like his martial arts instructors had insisted for so many years. Manik took a deep breath, and roared as loud as he could.

Barrus turned with a smirk to look at him. "Oh, so the kitten DOES have some fight left in him, eh? Let's see what we can do about that." By this time he was on the far end of the Arena and, again likely for the enjoyment of the crowd, dropped to all fours and charged like a jungle cat with a bodybuilding addiction. Manik watched his movements closely...should he go left? Should he fake left? Should he do both? Barrus leapt at him, claws and teeth bared, and Manik knew he'd waited too long and only had one option. He spun around, dropped low, and threw himself backwards allowing his extended claws to rake from chin to crotch as the elder man barreled past him. What he didn't count on was Barrus tucking into a roll.

Barrus dropped his hands, capturing both of Manik's ankles, and then flexed his entire body to execute a flip in mid-air, and pulled Manik up off the ground. With the remaining strength and momentum, Barrus threw Manik with all his might into the nearby wall. Manik saw it coming, tensed for impact, and then saw a bright flash...and darkness.

Chapter 2

When Manik awoke, he was lying in his bed in his room in the Brewery. It hadn't all been a dream, had it? He shifted and tried to sit up, and immediately saw stars as the room swam before him. Nope, not a dream. He'd failed. Again. He was still a child, and would have to endure the looks of pity and disgust for another year. He lowered his head carefully into his hands and wept quietly.

A few minutes passed in black misery, and then Manik heard the door open, and then close quietly. He ignored it, figuring it was some passing brewer cousin checking on Poor Young Manik. Probably checking to make sure he isn't dead and stinking up the place. A hand ran softly through his hair, causing him to jerk back. Brewmistress Innele was standing over him, with an unreadable expression.

"What do you w-w-want? Come to c-c-comfort the poor c-c-cub who lost his T-t-trial yet ag-g-gain?" Manik spat at her, daring her to mock him.

Innele only shook her head, and answered quietly "No Manik, I'm here to tell you that it isn't as bad as you make it out to be. We all look forward to you earning your name and place in the family; we just wish you wouldn't be so hard on yourself every year."

Manik stood up, wobbling slightly, and jerked back again when Innele reached out to try to steady him. "I d-don't need your p-pity! I don't w-want your consolation! I just w-want to be left alone!" He pushed past her and made for the doorway.

"Where will you go, if not here? This is your home, Manik, like it or not. We'll be here once you've come to your senses." she called after him, but made no move to stop him.

Manik stormed blindly through the corridors of the Brewery. His home. All he'd ever known was within walking distance of this place. The Clan halls, the storefront malls and restaurants just beyond the Clan Compound...the Arena...He stopped for a moment as he passed the carved and inlaid front doors of the Brewery and looked at the Arena. The monument to his failure, the citadel built on the blood of people like him. The underdogs, the ones too small to compete...the runts.

Then it struck him. Why SHOULD he stay? There was nothing for him here but pity, disgust, and sorrow. His hair was the right color that, with a good pair of color modifying glasses or contacts, he could fit in with any one of a dozen other Clans in the city...one with lower physical expectations. Maybe he could find one that played four dimensional chess or did lockpicking or piloting simulations for their Arena matches...he'd always been better at those by far than anything his father would choose.

Why stop there? He could go to another city and fit in just as well, without the worry of possibly running into family members when out on errands.

But why stop there? His father had said it in the Arena...this morning? Yesterday? Whenever. They must never forget that they came from the stars. If he left Chromara, he could go anywhere he wanted! Visit the plains of Ryla and try out their renowned technology, or sail the seas of Venalara, maybe get a chance to explore their partially submerged cities, or even get a tourist visa and see the Cityships of Earth...to ride on the *Ascension*, the flagship of the Allied World Government, and see the lush farmland that the old homeworld has become.

Manik started when he realized that he'd been walking and thinking, and his feet had taken him up through the layers of the city to the rooftop entry elevator that led to the shipyard above, the point of departure for all ships leaving Alberich. He took a steadying breath, and stepped into the elevator with the crowd.

The large sphere of composite glass that made up the surface elevator allowed everyone a commanding view of Alberich's top layers. The Grand Arena and Assembly Hall being most prominent. Therein lay the seat of the government of Chromara, the Hall of the First Warrior, and immediately adjacent, the location of the worlds-renowned Alberich Games and the place where all Challenges for Assembly seats are held.

Manik glanced about at his company on the ride and discovered it to be more diverse than he'd expected. He saw a few Chromarans, which he was able to easily identify as being a few val of Clan Uros and a ris of Clan Mere, by a quick glance at their cloak colors and the crests on their left shoulders holding it up. Behind them, on the far side of the elevator, were a pair of tall, thin Rylans staring out the side and commenting on the architecture and food they'd just eaten, and beside them one of the ageless Earthborn wearing a low-siting wide-brim hat. Starting low, Manik looked over the stranger with interest. He wore clean dark pants and a matching shirt, both veiled slightly by a calf length coat of either leather or a very good imitation. The skin on his hands was a dark burnished gold, like sunlight from a yellow star made flesh. Looking up, Manik saw that his eyes were a dark, almost black pair of pools, which, Manik was startled to see, were focused on watching him back. He quickly turned and feigned interest in the city, but could still feel the uncomfortable gaze boring into his back the rest of the ride up.

The light of the sun was dazzling on the surface. The wash of red light made the diffuse reflections used in the underground city seem to be the light of ghosts and moons rather than the mighty blaze from whence they'd been born. Manik stepped out with the rest of the group, and then slipped quietly off to one side and let everyone pass before continuing his mission to leave. He couldn't help but notice that the Earthborn stole a glance back at him before turning a corner, and he swore he saw the phantom of a smile on his lips as he disappeared from sight. Oh well, if he lived to be more than a few hundred years old, Manik figured he'd have more mental issues than just randomly smiling at strangers.

As he thought about the depth of the age of the Earthborn, his lessons on the other worlds came back to him. In June of 2245, a doctor on Earth named Teryll had discovered a complex combination of carbon scrubbers, modified amino acid chains, and cell repair enzymes that when together in JUST the right dosage provided functional immortality. The humans of Earth were overjoyed at the prospect and the governments mandated mandatory inoculations...but then in January 2246 they found out that the Serum had a small side effect: sterility.

The riots were the worst the planet had ever seen. Cities were razed, governments were destroyed, and millions were killed. From that tragedy emerged the Allied World Government and their corporate backer Starvault, the company that had created the Orbital stations and also the Cityships that allowed a good deal of the population of Earth survive the massacre on the surface. The planet is now a bastion of peace, with corporations and politics in the air on Cityships and pastoral farming and Urban Reclamation on land.

Manik jerked to awareness again, realizing that his sandaled feet had taken him through the atmospheric ship docks to the interstellar docks, and he was surrounded on all sides by ships of every conceivable design from one-man Explorer Needleships up to the powerful, spider-like Harvester-class ships, the largest vessels that can make planetfall safely in this day and age.

Manik decided that his feet must know something he didn't, so he let them take the lead again, as he wandered from ship to ship, admiring the beautiful lines and the elegance of the machinery. After what felt like it could have been minutes, seconds, or hours, he found himself staring at one of the oblong, silvered Orbital transport ships. The Orbital would be the place to find passage, if anywhere. He'd certainly get out of the city quickly enough.

The barker for the ship, a Venalaran, watched Manik dubiously. Manik realized that, next to the vibrantly colored sash and flowing pants of the semi-aquatic Venalarans, his drab clothes must look depressingly monochrome. He quickly dug around in his pocket for his access card. It was tied to the family accounts, but by the time they realized what he'd done he'd be long gone.

"What'd'ya want kid? Off on some errand for mommy and daddy? Get lost, didja?" the barker sneered.

"Who says I'm a k-k-kid, eh?" Manik replied, in his best imitation of his father's bluster. "I left m-m-my cloak in the Clan Hall to go inc-c-cognito, see? Why else would I have an a-a-access card? And who are you to a-a-argue a possibly p-p-paying customer out of a t-t-trip? I suppose your s-supervisor'd love to hear that st-story." he said as he pushed his hand with the card in it against the barker's chest.

The Venalaran held up his smooth, blue-and-green mottled hands in mock surrender. "OK, ok! Didn't mean to offend, was just pokin' a little fun at ya. How's'about we get you on board and up to the Orbital for whatever business you might be havin'? Light load this trip, but we're behind on the time-schedule so we can't wait for more passengers to show. You know how it is. What'd'ya say, pal, now or never?" He swung one hand across his chest, sliding the card deftly out from under Manik's hand and sweeping it into a gesture of welcome toward the shuttle.

Manik nodded and smiled slightly, this was going to be easier than he thought. "Sure, b-b-buddy. Let's g-get this Banshee off the d-dirt." He started to walk on board, when the Venalaran caught his arm. Out of reflex, Manik snapped his claws out and at the throat of the poor surprised barker before he could think about it.

"Relax buddy! I was just gonna ask...what's a Banshee? Yeesh you're tense. You need a massage or somethin'." he said as he carefully withdrew his hand from Manik's arm.

Manik pulled back his claws, embarrassed. "S-s-sorry, I guess I am a little on edge...B-b-banshees are...um...well, they're m-m-mammals that are about a m-m-meter long, with a three meter w-w-wingspan, leathery w-w-wings, kinda rust colored, and th-th-they eat everything in s-s-sight."

The barker nodded and smiled at him "Ahh, I get ya. Flying thing, off the ground. Right you are, sir. Step on in and grab a seat, any seat'll do. We'll be up in orbit before you can rustle your tail."

Manik started to say that he didn't have a tail, but thought better of it. Let the strange fish-man believe what he wanted. He strode up the ramp, trying to look grown-up, important, or at least like he belonged on the transport ship.

He took the first available seat that had a window, and tried unsuccessfully to look bored while he excitedly glued himself to the window in anticipation. The ramp closed with a soft hiss a few moments later and the craft shuddered slightly as it rose off of the landing skids. The spiraling trajectory the pilot chose brought a beautiful view of the red-tinged landscape of Chromara. The grasses were flowing in the breeze, and Manik could almost hear the soft rattling of their carbonaceous stalks against one another. A dark mass was shifting about just on the edge of the plains as they rose higher and Manik could just make out the herd of Relle, glittering like dusty onyx, as they grazed on the tough grasses.

As the shuttle reached higher altitude, the pilot banked into a sidelong drift, allowing the passengers a view of the majestic Chromaran Orbital Two. The station was shaped like a pair of pyramids, one right side up and one upside down, attached at their bases...only with eight sides each. The silvered sides of the station made it look ethereal, like a skyscraper in space, or a manmade jewel, hanging in the darkness, the star diamond on a necklace for the planet. Manik had only a few moments to admire it before the pilot smoothly finished the spin and propelled the craft towards the station.

The Venalaran barker came back through the cabin, drifting slightly in the microgravity. He paused at each passenger, handing back documents, cards, and small folders, giving Manik a chance to get a good look at the other people on board for the first time. At the front of the craft were a group of Chromarans that, if their coveralls are any indicator, were returning station personnel who had probably taken some land-side vacation time. Behind them by a few rows, Manik was surprised and suddenly nervous to see a pair of Rylans and that same Earthborn from the elevator. He couldn't tell if the Rylans were the same ones...they all look alike to him, almost gangly, with too long and too thin legs, arms, and fingers, and oversized, almost bulbous, eyes, but the Earthborn had that slightly weather-beaten ancient leather hat...it had to be unique in the universe, it was so odd looking. The top bowed in slightly just above where the crown of his head must be, and the brim extended a couple inches out all the way around the hat. What's the purpose of having a brim on the back? Protect your hair from the sun? Strange enough that only an Earthborn could have thought of it, certainly.

He was, once again, watching Manik with those dark, unreadable eyes. Manik glared at him, determined not to break eye contact this time. If he was an adult Chromaran, he'd never break eye contact first. He had to be dominant in his home system, after all. That's how his father would do it, so that's how he had to play it. The Earthborn held his gaze, studying him as though admiring some strange creature in a zoo, without fear, and then the corner of his mouth turned up slightly for a moment before he turned his gaze to the Venalaran, who handed him a sheaf of papers and exchanged a few quiet words with him.

Finally, the Venalaran pushed off from the Earthborn's row and drifted back to Manik's seat. He held out the access card that Manik had surrendered when he'd climbed on board. "Here's your card sir. Wasn't expecting a gentleman of your stature to be riding quite so far under the radar. I've heard your Clan has a few hopefuls for First Warrior again pretty soon; you wouldn't be one of them Assembly members checking up on your holdings up here in disguise, eh? No, don't answer that...none of my business and a world of trouble for me if you did say anything. I'll keep your secret sir, don't you worry. Just...if you ever see fit to change the ground-side staff, make sure you remember the name of Deepdiver, eh? That's me, and I'm the only one out here with the name. Hard to forget a hard worker like me, I assure you. You have yourself a good trip sir, wherever you're headed." the Venalaran said in seemingly a single breath. Manik privately marveled at the man's lung capacity. He said nothing, and simply took the card and nodded with as much dignity as he could muster. Deepdiver nodded, smiled hopefully, and then pushed off and spiraled down the walkway back to the cockpit.

Manik secreted the card away in his pocket again then sat impatiently waiting for the ship to dock so he could get out from under the scrutiny of the other occupants. While squirming in his seat, he took note of the length of the fuselage of the transport vessel, about fifteen meters, which when compared to the exterior of about thirty would mean there's a good ten meters or so of engine...twelve if the cockpit is as tiny as he thinks it is. The seats and paneling are all of fibers reminiscent of native Chromaran grass reeds and tree bark respectively, which means this ship was built locally, with Chromaran passengers in mind, using local flora to keep us at our ease. Guess the jokes back home about the Chromaran Temper are even worse rumors once you get offworld.

The windows, previously showing a twinkling field of stars, were suddenly eclipsed by the side of the station, giving Manik a brief moment of panic at their docking speed, before blowing through an open hatchway and curving flawlessly down a corridor of Needleships and smaller Harvesters. The pilot put the ship into a hairpin turn, allowing the momentum to back the shuttle perfectly into the waiting docking cradle. The softest of changes in pressure was immediately followed by the strange weight of artificial gravity, causing Manik to have to catch himself on his seat, lest he slide off. As the other passengers stood and started to gather their belongings, Manik quickly unstrapped himself and jumped up, knocking his head against the bulkhead. All eyes turned to him for a moment, as Manik's local world swam around him. The headache that had been building since he awoke took an iron grip of his brain, and started to fuzz the edges of his vision in pain. Manik did the only thing his upbringing prepared him for...he mumbled an apology to the bulkhead and hurried out and down the still-lowering ramp in hopes of finding some quiet place to die of pain. Or embarrassment. It seemed his lot in life to be embarrassed by his own ineptitude in all things, so Manik decided to avoid the customs counters, imagining worst case scenarios of being dragged home in chains, or being tossed out into space as so much detritus.

He wandered aimlessly through the expansive docking layers for what felt like hours, looking at this engine, or peeking into the hatch of that ship, or admiring the lines of that ship over there, before being inevitably driven on by the worry of being recognized and caught. Soon enough, Manik felt the herbs and medicine that had apparently been sustaining his system thin out enough that an aching headache flared further, causing him to fall slightly and lean against the nearby wall. Had he eaten today? Probably not, he'd been too intent to get away from everyone. Maybe there's a medbay on the Docking levels somewhere...no, he'd have to go through customs for that most likely. If he could just get some good rest he'd be able to think clearer. That's all he really needed.

Stumbling occasionally, Manik made his way through the more deserted section of the docking levels that he found himself on. Partitions separating private bays shifted occasionally, changing his path this way or that. Eventually, he reached a dead end, and leaned against a ship parked there to catch his breath. The cool composite felt good against his flushed skin. He closed his eyes for a moment, and must have fallen asleep standing up, because he woke again when his knees buckled and he hit the floor with a resounding thunk. Jumping back up, rubbing his knees to relieve the sting, he saw that the ship he'd been leaning against was a six-pronged Harvester. Looking like a 75 meter long insect of some kind, it probably had plenty of empty spaces he could duck into for a little while and nap without interruption.

He walked up to the door panel and peered at it uncertainly. Hesitantly, he ignored the 30 digit keypad and hopefully pressed the Unlock button. The light flickered red for a moment then shifted to green and the door slid silently open. Letting out a breath he hadn't realized he'd been holding Manik stumbled on board.

Most interior doors were sealed, but he found a circuitous route of hallways and open doors that led him eventually to the engine room. The planetary drives were shut down, and the anti-matter chamber sealing in the exotic particles used by the Manifold Stardrive was cold as ice, but the MS itself was comfortingly warm. Manik picked a spot out of view of the doorway and curled up on top of one of the backup Manifold distributors to get some well-needed rest.

Manik dreamed. He saw planets flowing past, jewels in the inky sea of the sky. He saw starships, trussed up like the three-masted recreations he'd seen in his classes that used to sail the seas of Earth, cresting waves of ice and rock along the rings of an as-yet-unnamed gas giant. He saw the bright flash of indigo, almost beyond the range of sight, as a Needleship surrounded by a Manifold Envelope slipped out of Realspace and entered Underspace. He saw the chaos and strangeness of the Underspace simulations from the VR program in the family TechSpecs...the flying masses of anti-matter, the sparkles of who-knows-what is the space that isn't Space. He saw himself floating in that darkness, surrounded on all sides by chaos. The drifting colossi forever colliding, reforming, and changing. He realized that one such formation, a few hundred meters in diameter if he was to hazard a guess, was heading right for him. Manik felt panic rising quickly. If he touched bare anti-matter, he'd be obliterated! He had to move! He strained, but despite his flailing, movement seemed beyond his control. He thrashed and screamed into the hollow of space. All for naught. The formation, like the Arena wall, was unyielding. As it slammed into him he felt heat, like he'd been thrown into a sun, and then cold, as though tossed back out into space, and then the darkness envelop him once again.

Chapter 3

Manik's first thought upon waking was to wonder if this was a dream or reality. If it was another dream, he hoped it didn't involve dying again, because he wasn't sure his heart could handle it. If it was reality, he hoped the faces looking down at him were friendly.

"Ahh, finally awake I see. How do you feel, on a scale of one to death?" asked one of the faces. As Manik's brain kick started, he realized it was a Rylan. His eyes were noticeably larger than Manik was used to, as seemed to be the norm for people from that planet, with the deepest blue irises he'd ever seen. He must have stared a little too long, because the Rylan sighed and slid on a set of wrap-around clear lensed glasses, commonly known as TechSpecs, which are one of the biggest sellers from the Rylan technological firms.

The Rylan nods absently "Yes, Herec Labs specifically...I'd been meaning to get them replaced, these are still first generation...very slow processing speed, but they still get the job done."

Manik did a double take. "D-d-did you just r-r-read my m-m-mind?!" he croaked out. His throat felt like it was on fire. He licked his lips experimentally and winced as his tongue hit cracked and broken flesh.

"No, I didn't...you simply were speaking quietly and seemed to be narrating your observations. Did you know you only stutter when you speak loudly?" the Rylan replied, while moving his long, four knuckled fingers over the holographic keyboard Manik knew must be hovering just above his own prone form.

"N-n-n-no...I always s-s-s-stutter...it j-j-j-just gets w-w-worse when I th-th-think about-t it. It d-d-doesn't g-g-get b-b-better unless I s-s-stop t-t-talking." he managed, and then clamped his mouth shut.

"Well, I'd say you're probably at a three on the scale at the moment. A bit bruised, a bit bewildered, more than a little concussed and mildly irradiated...but I've seen worse after a good bar fight, especially considering your species. Oh well-" he turned to the other person in the room, drawing Manik's attention to her "-more's the pity, he's all yours, Doctor."

Swiping his hand through the air above Manik, the universal gesture to close applications on Specs, the Rylan strode away from the table and out the door which hissed shut softly behind him. Manik turned to study this 'doctor' to see what these strange people's intentions were...kidnapping? Ransom? None of them are Chromaran...maybe experimentation?

The doctor, a female Venalaran, burst out laughing. "OK, I tried to hold a modicum of dignity considering we don't know you and you don't know us here...but ransom? Experimentation? Really? You might be more thoroughly concussed than Challis diagnosed if you're having delusions of grandeur."

"I w-w-was d-d-doing it ag-ag-again, w-w-wasn't I?" Manik said, muffled slightly by his fingers which had jumped to stop his mouth, and had apparently failed.

The doctor regained her professional composure and nodded. "Yes, you should know that you have a lovely voice when you're not straining it like that. Depending on how long we keep you, we might be able to cure you of that habit." She walked forward, her long white lab coat brushing the floor quietly as she approached. "Anyway, I'm Doctor Selelle Deepheart. You can call me Doctor Deepheart for now, or just Doctor. If you live long enough, you might be able to graduate that to just Selelle, but we'll see how you do after a few rounds of experiments." she finished with a mischievous smirk. She took the Rylan's previous position looking down at Manik from just beyond the end of the table where his head lay.

Manik couldn't help but smile back while lowering his hands, her smile was infectious. "V-very well, Doctor, but I s-should warn you that on my p-planet I'm very deadly and not a creature t-taken lightly."

"I'll take that under advisement. Now, do you have a name, or should we just call you Ferocious Beastie?" she asked while running her gloved hands over his scalp, checking the wrappings Manik only just noticed were placed there.

"Oh, r-r-right. I'm M-manik." he managed, trying not to stare at her face mere inches from his.

"Hmm." She mused, concentrating on the dressings. Manik finally looked closely at the designs on her faintly green skin. They looked like a series of cresting waves that started at her hairline on her forehead tracing a series of rhythmic undulations down her nose and skirting both temples, trailing down her neck and disappearing into her coat. Manik quickly snapped his eyes up, lest he get caught accidentally admiring her cleavage, and focused instead on her eyes. Unlike Chromaran eyes, which are uniformly a single metallic shade, with generally very little definition, her eyes were the palest blue he'd ever seen...but not completely so. Along the iris at seemingly random intervals there were sparkles, like coins in a fountain, or maybe the brightest of stars shining at dusk through the pale blue of the skyline of the pictures he'd seen of Earth.

"OK-" she started as she leaned back "- Manik, you said?" She waited for him to nod before continuing. "Any other names? Family? Clan? Pod? Pack? Whatever it is you guys call it?" Manik shook his head and lowered his gaze, lidding his eyes in hopes that she'd not seen the color clearly. "Well then, just-plain-Manik, your concussions seem to be healing nicely. You had a major trauma at some point in the last few days...looks like you fell off a cliff and landed on your head, to be honest. Then you compounded it with a few scrapes and bruises and by being dehydrated and from the looks of you unfed for the last few years. Oh, and to top it all off, you have a light dose of radiation poisoning." she finished flippantly.

Manik jerked his head up, finally hearing what both people had said about radiation, causing his vision to swim for a moment. Selelle reached out to catch and steady him. "Slow down there, Beastie. I said it was light, didn't I? You wouldn't have had an issue at all, except for the open wound on your head that you put down on the engine parts. Bad set of circumstances...you chose to stowaway on a ship that was warming up to leave and that compartment is the one place on the ship that you shouldn't be during takeoff. Luckily SID found you and let us know before there was any harm done to you or the *Sunrise*. If there were, you'd be in more trouble than you are now." she finished.

Manik tried to process all this new information through the headache that was still trying to tear his skull apart. Stowaway? Takeoff? SID? ...Trouble? What kind of trouble was he in, and what could they do to him for it? He'd heard the old stories of the sovereignty of a ship's Captain on the seas and out in space. Could they just space him? *Would* they space him?

"Jeez, are you always this bad, or just when you're concussed and hungry?" Selelle interrupted his stream of consciousness. "Here, we're not going to space you until you've had a good meal at the very least. I'll help you down to the common room...it'll do you good to get up and about. You can meet your executioners, and the food will help settle your stomach with all the meds that'll be kicking in soon." she said, as she moved to help him down from the table. As Manik stood, the slight female wrapped her arm around his waist to steady him, and he realized how short she was. Her head only barely reached his shoulder. That would take some getting used to, if he lived long enough to do so.

The door hissed open again, allowing the two of them to clamber through the tight hatchway. "T-thanks, Doctor. I ap-ppreciate your help...I'm s-sorry for causing s-so many problems. M-my head hurt so badly after m-m-my...after I g-g-got the c-concussion that I just wanted to f-f-find somewhere quiet and w-warm to rest for a l-little while. I'll d-do what I c-can to make am-mends." Manik managed, as they worked their way down the pipe-lined hallway.

Voices drifted down the hallway as they progressed past storerooms and staterooms, eventually arriving at a semi-crowded kitchen and dining area. From the doorway, Manik could see three other people in the room, one from each of the colony planets. The Rylan that Manik had met before was sitting at a table attached to the far wall, under a bright light, engrossed in some TechSpecs application only he could see. Across the table from him was a male Venalaran carrying on an animated telling of a story about his valiant attempt to grapple with some sort of creature, causing a great deal of laughter from himself, but only a tolerant silence from the other two occupants. As Manik's gaze drifted over to the third crewman, he felt his blood chill as he met the metallic gaze of another Chromaran. He was sure to recognize his eye color, so Manik quickly dropped his eyes and concentrated on looking injured and off-balance...not a difficult ruse.

As they progressed through the room, Manik saw that the door they entered through was the only accessway. The walls were lined with magnetically sealed shelving typical of zero-G shipboard food storage. The back wall, along with the table, had a set of inlaid seating that could be pulled from their individual alcoves and unfolded for use at meals, or to reach higher shelves when gravity was active.

Manik paused for a moment. Gravity. Why was he still walking and not floating, if they'd left the Orbital? Selelle had mentioned that they'd found him almost immediately...surely they hadn't detoured down to the planet to drop him off! He'd have to return to his Clan in shame, a child who attempted to run away from his family. His father would never let him live that down. Or enter the family proper. He'd become the oldest child on Chromara...living in the brewery, never to leave the Clan Compound again, denied the joy of a job, a mate, or a loving family of his own...

"Ahh, so this is the Engine Trouble that we'd had to wait to resolve? Tell me, Trouble, you got a name under all those baggy clothes, or are you just a phantom of the machinery? A little shiny ghost that SID planted to scare us?" the male Venalaran asked, before laughing uproariously at his own wit. Manik glanced over at him and quickly sized him up. He seemed to be about the same height as Doctor Deepheart, making them both probably about five foot eight inches give or take an inch or two. His hair was bright blonde, almost golden in color, falling in waves to his shoulders shining like yellow star sunlight on water, betraying how meticulously he cares for it. Even from across the room, he could see the bright green glow of the Venalaran's gaze, as though being watched by an avatar of the seas. His skin was darker than Doctor Deepheart's, with seemingly random spots and blotches of even darker skin, giving him an almost camouflaged quality, even when sitting in the silvered metal of a starship.

"You're still doing it." Deepheart whispered, as she all but dragged him into the room towards the empty chairs at the table. "Quiet poetic, I'd never really noticed how bright Dorr's eyes were until you mentioned it." As they advanced, it became increasingly obvious that Manik was trying to hide in plain sight. The awkwardness built rapidly, but she sat him down and immediately filled the conversational void. "Dorr, this is Manik. He's apparently had a very traumatic last few days so he isn't too up to talking, but he's happy to meet you I'm sure."

"P-p-pleased t-t-to m-meet y-you." Manik managed, adjusting himself carefully in the overly hard metal chair.

"Ha! It DOES speak! Well then, Trouble, welcome aboard! Let me be the first to say that you look like you'll make a delicious meal if we run out of food out in the darkness." Dorr said, licking his lips for emphasis. Manik leaned surreptitiously away from him, causing Dorr's ferocious facade to shatter. As he fell into another fit of giggling, Manik swept his gaze quickly around at the rest of the crew, sticking on the glare from the other Chromaran.

Seeing the rising hackles Deepheart stepped smoothly between them, breaking eye contact, facing her crewmate. "Krym, we don't glare at guests...even uninvited ones. Captain said we're to wait until he's healed and fully cognizant before making assumptions about his background or intentions so if you're wanting to start early then you can do it somewhere else."

Manik could only see her back but from the stiffness of her stance he could guess two important things: Firstly, she'd never been in a real fight in her life, and secondly, she was willing to start her first one, with a Chromaran no less, over him. How strange...even his family didn't want to fight for him but this stranger, this person who he'd only met a few minutes ago, is willing to put herself potentially in harm's way for him.

Selelle glanced over her shoulder at him for a moment, giving Manik a look that he was unable to read clearly before Krym spoke, causing her to shift her full attention back to him. "If the Captain wants to keep him on board, he'll keep him on board. If he wants to space him, he'll space him. If he wants him repaired, he'll send him back to you. If he wants him torn apart, he'll send him to me. Remember who you're talking to, and remember what I can do to you...when the Captain gives the word." Krym snarled. His voice was deep and gravelly, lending an even more feral quality to him than is normal of denizens of their home planet. He was about six feet five inches, Manik guessed, which is pretty average for a Chromaran. His hair was braided down his back in the way of an initiated Clansman, a deep burnt gold cascade swishing from side to side as he shifted to eyeball Manik around the slight form of the doctor. His eyes were dark platinum the seemed to swirl with life...and anger.

"You'd best watch your step, Kitten, lest you get eaten by the resident Hyz. Take Kaer where you go on this ship and we won't have an issue...just stay out of my way." Krym growled before standing, turning on his heel, and storming out of the room. Watching his retreating form, Manik could see the traces of silver in Krym's hair, meaning he was a lot older than he let on, and he noticed the well covered limp. So he'd been a Gladiator at least, maybe even a Warrior or Assemblyman. Manik had heard the deliberate mispronunciation of 'care' in his speech and knew he'd been speared...so why did he say it and walk out? Threat without immediate follow through breeds discontent and uncertainty, his father had always said. This bore some more serious thinking once his head decided to stop trying to turn itself inside out.

Manik straightened up when Doctor Deepheart turned back around, eyeing her curiously. "Sorry about that." she said immediately. "Krym is a bit...touchy, when it comes to meeting new people. We usually leave him to guard the ship when we make station or planetfall, just so he doesn't start any fights...by the way, I've been meaning to ask for years and it's not come up in ordinary conversation, well...ordinary for Krym conversation at least, but what is a Hyz?" she finished quickly.

Manik pondered how best to answer the question for a moment, and then shrugged nonchalantly. "It's the p-primary Chromaran derivative of Earth's *Canis lupis,* the w-wolf. I've heard it c-called a Silverwolf by offw-worlders before, but that's n-not terribly ac-ccurate since most are g-gold or b-bronze furred."

"Vicious predator native to Chromaran landscape, designation *Canis chromara,* which travel in packs of 250 to 500 generally, although packs more than one standard deviation from the norm in both directions have been seen. Physical differences include reflective metallic fur and eyes, and a bone spike at the end of the tail surmised to be used in traditional pack ranking disputes, although no researcher has gotten close enough to see it in person and not get eaten before they reported it...need I go on? You should have just asked me, the net is so much more prolific on the beasts than Engine Trouble, here. Even SID knows more about them than he likely does." said the voice of the Rylan from Manik's right. He continued without looking up from his console. "Why, I bet there's all sorts of things that you could ask as 'polite conversation'-"he raised his long hands to make air quotes "-that any number of sources would provide more reliable AND more complete information from." he lowered his hands back to his virtual keyboard and continued writing whatever it was he was working on before he interrupted...or was interrupted...Manik wasn't entirely sure which way was more accurate.

Selelle sighed. "And this, who has been rude enough to talk to you TWICE now without introducing himself, is Challis Regaal--"

"DOCTOR Regaal" Challis interjected smoothly, as though correcting a commonly made mistake.

"-who happens to hold a degree from a university on Ryla...he's got the skills of a Medical Doctor, but apparently bedside manner isn't a course he did well in. Or attended, for that matter." she finished, winking at Manik.

Challis swiped his left hand across where his virtual keyboard lay, shutting it down, and turned to face Selelle fully. "Well, my dear, I am terribly sorry that I didn't graduate from your esteemed university under the waves! Tell me, did they still use paper there, or was it too much of an issue with homework getting soggy? Ooh! Were you able to tell them that your dolphin ate your homework?" he asked animatedly, clenching his hands in front of him in a very disturbing and poorly executed attempt to look like an innocent young child.

Selelle held her stern expression for a few moments, seeming to waver between looking annoyed at the insulting comments and stifling laughter at the pose Challis was holding for her benefit. Finally, she lost the battle with herself and leaned back against the side counter to laugh. "OK, the paper thing is a recycled joke, but the dolphin? That's new. Where'd you pick that one up?" she gasped between giggling fits.

Challis unraveled his fingers, a more complex maneuver than Manik thought possible, and shrugged. "I found the old Earth version on the net. Apparently it was a common excuse in lower levels of school to feed homework to domestic canines. Given that your world would probably use some sort of sea-faring mammal instead, I just made the connection. It's not easy being this much of a genius, but it's a burden I bear for the good of all."

"I see, well thank you for shouldering the load so that the rest of us can relax in our Central Tower of mediocrity." Selelle retorted.

"...I see what you tried to do there, but it is yet another failed attempt to get more information from me. I'll simply say that the Central Tower has a branch of, or the primary campus for, all major universities in the universe that matter, and all three of my doctoral accreditations can be found hung on the walls there as shining examples of alumni who Made Their Mark on the universe." Challis finished, leaning back and stretching his gangly legs in front of him, crossed at the ankle in a very self-satisfied pose. Manik was amazed that by their tone and inflection, he could actually hear the intended capitalization in the banter.

Challis finished stretching his long arms behind his head, and then straightened back up and adjusted his long white coat and settled the wraparound glasses-structure of the TechSpecs more firmly on his long nose. "Well, enough playfulness. I have the rest of this report on the sociopolitical state of the Chromarans to finish, as well as writing more out on my thesis. Postulating the constructive effect of White

Holes in Underspace...I imagine they'll name one of the new Colony Worlds after me, one day, for this gift I am presenting them with." he finished, and then turned to the table, adjusted his chair, swiped his left hand from right to left to reactivate his keyboard, and was quickly engrossed in typing once more.

Doctor Deepheart sighed and turned back to Manik. "He'll be no use for the next few hours, easily. He loves to show off how witty and intelligent he is whenever he gets the chance, but as I said his bedside manner and social graces are severely lacking. Hungry?" she asked suddenly, throwing Manik off.

"Um...y-yes, I suppose s-so." he replied.

"Well, let's see what Krym's got stashed around here then." she remarked as she started opening and rifling through drawers.

"Oh, no...I d-don't w-want to t-take Krym's r-rations! I c-can eat j-just about anyt-thing, r-really!" he replied, feeling panic rise as he was assaulted with thoughts of Krym's reaction to his stealing his food.

"Oh don't be silly. It's not like we all haven't taken some to try Chromaran food before! ...course, it landed most of us in the medbay for our trouble. He always gets a good laugh at that. Your standard fare is amazingly venomous, and Krym always stocks up at the markets when we make a stop off there. Not in person though...he calls friends, or contacts I guess you'd say, and has them pick up food at the lower marketplaces, and then he just nets them the money and they shuttle up the food. Ahh, here we go...what do you think of...Real Steak? Rail Steak? I can never say that right..." she mused over a found package.

"It's p-pronounced 'Rele'...like 'sell' but with an R." he supplied, holding out his hand for the package as Selelle struggled with the sealed top.

After a few additional moments of fiercely wrestling with the malleable plastic coating around the meal, she lowered her head in mock defeat and silently passed it to him. Sliding a single claw out, Manik deftly scythed open the upper end of the package, and then looked around curiously. "Where d-do I cook this?" he asked after a failed search for any manner of grilling, baking, or frying implements.

"Wow, you got that open quick...how'd you do that? Oh...cooking...right...you don't eat them raw?" she asked, and then realized how it must have sounded. "Sorry! It's just...Krym eats them raw...and he just kinda tears it open with his fangs and scarfs it down quickly before retreating to his room." she babbled as she moved around the room closing the food drawers she had been rifling through. As she finished closing the last of them, she paused as though in preparation for some physical feat. After a moment she stretched herself upward, reaching up as high as she could on the tips of her toes, to just barely tap a catch that was flush with the wall. Dropping back to the flats of her feet, she stooped quickly and flipped a similar catch at floor level allowing the wall unit of drawers to slide smoothly upward, revealing a recessed kitchen alcove. She stepped back and gestured with a flourish, almost tripping herself in her overly extravagant attempt at grandeur. "Your theater, Master Chef. Play us a tune, why don't you?"

Manik couldn't help but smile at her antics as he contemplated the new information. If Krym used his teeth rather than his claws, what did that mean? His teeth were sharper than his claws? He was raised not to use them except in battle? Of course, it could mean nothing at all.

Manik rose unsteadily from the table, quickly waving Selelle away. With the other men watching, he didn't want to be seen as a complete invalid. He moved slowly into the kitchen area and did a quick survey of the available machinery. A large sink, an old-style stove top pane, a baking rack, a flash freeze unit, and a few racks of inset tools along the walls set about half a meter above the counter. He decided on the stove top pane, as that would provide the quickest meal. He pressed his hand against the depressed UI control node, causing the VR interface to blink to life above the faux stone slab. He quickly chose the size and placement of the burner he wanted, set the heat for a deep cook, and then set about gathering a flat pan, a few spices, and a long spatula-fork from the wall insets. Pouring the contents of the bag into the pan with a wet squelch, he sprinkled a few of the hotter choices of spices and pepper flakes over the meat, in hopes of drowning the plastic taste that it would undoubtedly retain.

Manik felt himself slipping into old habits, from cooking late at night in the Brewhouse once everyone else had finished and left or gone to bed. He planted his feet shoulder width, allowing himself to balance evenly and reach the majority of the cooking area with his long arms. His movements with the ingredients were swift and confident. He always enjoyed cooking for himself because he had nobody to please, no expectations to meet...just him and the food, and the steak certainly didn't care how it was prepared. As the meat sizzled, Manik glanced over his shoulder to see Selelle standing in the doorway facing away from him. Leaning back to see what had drawn her attention, Manik was surprised to see Challis stride past, glaring at him with both of his hands covering his nose and mouth. He shook his head and figured he'd find out soon enough, whatever he'd done wrong this time, and turned back to the business at hand. No use letting a steak burn because someone was mad at him, waste of good meat.

Manik reached across the counter to pull a plate down from the mount over the sink, shifted the pan from the heat, put the plate down in the vacated spot, flipped the steak onto it, and poured the remaining juice and spices over it. He slid the plate off to the side to finish, used his elbow to disable the control node, and put the pan into the sink to be bombarded clean. He pulled a few utensils from the mounts, snapped his right hand claws out, picked up the hot plate, and then walked back as steadily as he could manage while balancing the cherry-red flatware on his claw tips. So intently was he concentrating that he did not realize register that he was walking through an incident of some kind involving the remaining two occupants of the room until he'd reached the table. He quickly put the plate down, almost fell back into his chair, and said apologetically "I'm s-sorry...I can take this to a different r-room if the s-smell b-bothers y-y-you."

Manik sat looking at his lap for a few moments in silence, and then risked a glance up. His startled gaze was greeted with a view of Selelle making a spirited attempt to stop Dorr from diving headfirst onto the steak. He looked from one to the other as their physical struggle evolved to include conversation.

"Leggo! It smells delicious! C'mon!" Dorr pleaded, still fighting playfully to escape the grip of the smaller female.

"No! You may not remember what happened the last time you had a large dose of Rele venom, but I do! I couldn't use the toilet in the medbay for a week, and we had to use a sonic power washer on the hallway and the table you were lying on!" Selelle complained loudly as she tried to pin Dorr to the floor to stop his squirming.

"But it's just ONE steak! It's not like I'm trying to bite a live Rele again! Can't you smell it?! What are you made of, woman...ropes and hate?!" Dorr continued as he started to struggle in renewed earnest, realizing that he was remarkably close to being completely pinned to the floor.

Manik couldn't help but giggle as the two continued their battle, rolling across the floor in alternating attempts to break the hold, on Dorr's side, and maintain it, on Selelle's. His reverie was cut short, however, when he realized there was someone standing just inside the doorway, watching the three of them. Manik immediately recognized the Earthborn who had been watching him since the elevator ride. How did he get unlucky enough to accidentally choose the one ship that contained someone who would recognize him? By all the Warriors present and past, why is his personal demon of fate so cruel?

The Earthborn continued to lean against the wall just inside the hatchway, watching the pair of Venalarans with those dark, unreadable, eyes. He had gotten rid of the hat and coat, allowing Manik to get a better look at his features and he saw immediately why most Chromarans distrusted the people from Earth. With his hat gone, his bronzed skin and deep black hair pulled back into a ponytail at the nape of his neck were prominent. His face was...hard to explain. Hard thanks to his eyes, but soft thanks to the lack of age...no, true agelessness is a better way to qualify it. His frame was small, no...compact would be closer to the truth. He was wearing a dark maroon shirt tucked into pleated pants that fell to about the mid-calf, where they disappeared into tall, reflectively shiny, black boots. The boots themselves were a work of art. They looked like true leather, but had no laces or fasteners of any kind...likely controlled by pressure commands in key areas or some such, Manik mused.

The Earthborn, apparently finally bored with watching the struggle, pushed off of the wall and walked quickly across the room. His footfalls seemed deliberately loud, causing both Dorr and Selelle to freeze for a moment before splitting and scrambling to their feet looking ashamed, as though children caught stealing. Without a word or a look to either of them he advanced past the pair and walked up to Manik, who quickly ducked his eyes and folded his hands, palms up in his lap, to show supplication and submission, as he was taught.

As he sat wondering if this was the Captain he'd been hearing about he felt the man lean in close to him. Manik's nostrils were filled with the scent of burnt lavender and boot polish and had just enough time to register that the man was one of the Students of Smokeform he'd read about in his classes, before Selelle yelled, causing him to jump.

"Sir, no! It's not! ….devenomed." she finished, lamely.

Manik looked up quickly to see that the Earthborn had reached past him, smoothly cut a chunk of Rele steak, and was chewing thoughtfully. Manik waited in fear, figuring that this was the point at which he'd be thrown from the ship. Maybe he'd be lucky and they were in the high atmosphere of some other planet...he'd asphyxiate before he burnt up in the atmosphere...it'd be a death without hope of recovery, that's for certain.

The Earthborn finished chewing, swallowed, and looked down into Manik's eyes again. At this distance, Manik could see that they were not as featureless as they had seemed...they were a deep brown of good dirt, with flecks of green along the inner ring, as though the tips of plants pushing new life up to meet the sun. Selelle started to speak again but the Earthborn raised a hand without turning with his index finger extended.

Leaning back again, he finally spoke. "So, this is the arrival of which I was informed. I am not generally given to long speeches, so take note as this will not happen often." he said, his voice a rich baritone that sounded like it belonged to a much larger man.

He began to stride around the room slowly, his boots making no sound on the floor plates. "I am aware of the situation more than you would think, Dr. Deepheart. I should also enlighten you as to an interesting effect of my biology...I am immune to most conventional poisons and venoms; it's just the engineered highly potent ones that give me trouble. Your medical training should have included that, but I will assume a lapse in memory due to current events and company. The main upside to our planetary peculiarity that I see is that I have the benefit of being able to enjoy the foods of all of the colonies in their natural state and native preparations. So, to be blunt, no I will not be loudly sick from this as young Mr. Waverider will likely be if he has his way. As for you, my young stowaway, I shall devise a sufficient punishment for the damage you have incurred and shall inform you of your sentence in my own time. Until then, let me leave you with a few thoughts to contemplate." he paused in both speech and stride, eyeing Manik from sandals to crown again before continuing.

"I have been watching you since your ill-fated loss in the Arena. Yes, I know what family you are from and yes, I am reasonably sure I know why you are here...just as I do of every entity on this vessel. I am the Captain; it is my business to know and no one else's. The others will not pry into your past because they will not want you to pry into theirs. Volunteer information if you would like but keep in mind that you may be here for a very short...or a very long...time." he finished, and then turned on his heel and headed for the doorway.

Manik sat, stunned, and then quickly remembered himself and asked before the Captain was out of earshot "S-sir! W-what do I c-call you?"

The Captain paused at the doorway for a moment, before turning. "You can call me Captain Fujiwara for now, until such time as I deem that you should know more of my name or are worthy of closer association. Good day, young Manik." he said quietly, and then disappeared through the open hatchway.

Chapter 4

Manik took a deep breath and let it out slowly as he uncurled himself from his supplication pose and picked up his utensils. Realizing how hungry he truly was, he fell on the steak as a drowning man on driftwood. He concentrated only enough to make sure he didn't spill juice off of the plate but otherwise ignored the universe beyond his forkblades, the table, his meal, and his mouth. He made quick work of the meat, and then used the shovel shaped side of the utensils to spoon up the remaining broth and wayward small pieces that he'd missed.

What could have been seconds or minutes later, Manik came to the realization that the room was silent. He put his two forkblades down, prongs up and blade down as he'd been taught, and then turned to see if everyone had left him to his vicious destruction of the poor steak unlucky enough to be his first, and hopefully not last, meal shipboard.

He was surprised to see both Selelle and Dorr standing a few feet away, both clutching vac-sealed meal bags. They exchanged a look that Manik couldn't decipher, and then seemed to have some sort of silent argument where they gestured madly at each other as inconspicuously as possible, and then Dorr sighed and turned to face Manik once again.

"So, I know you're injured and just got here and are worried that Ahab is going to space you...but before any of that happens could you possibly find some kindness in your heart and see your way to cooking this for me? I'd be ever so grateful! I'll even offer you some of my good liquor as a Last Drink if it comes to that!" he said in a torrent, surprising Manik with his sudden intensity.

Selelle almost jumped forward in an attempt to get Manik's attention. "Yes. Exactly. Only you should prepare mine first because I skipped dinner to make sure you had gotten the proper care and attention. Wouldn't want a doctor to get faint from lack of sustenance, would we?" she smiled hopefully at him, breaking the 'sweet and innocent' facade slightly by elbowing Dorr surreptitiously as he tried to inch his way closer.

"Oh sure, pull the doctor card. You shouldn't threaten the poor boy; look at what he's been through! New people, new places, almost getting eaten by Krym...Guul's Fins, you aren't even licensed!" Dorr finished as he carefully, almost reverently, placed the mealpack in Manik's unresisting right hand.

"I will be once we get the whole board issue straightened out, so that's good enough!" she spat at Dorr, before turning and gently placing her mealpack in Manik's left hand. "I'm sorry Manik...I really AM a doctor, there's just...a little fine print that hasn't been filled out yet, that's all." she said sheepishly.

Manik couldn't help but smile. He looked from one mealpack to the other, and then from one hopeful Venalaran to the other. After a few moments, he asked them "So, d-do you not normally cook h-here?"

Selelle shook her head, looking embarrassed. "We don't really have a resident crewman that can cook...no. I tend to burn things...badly. Krym eats all his meals raw, Challis is on a strange Rylan amino-drink diet that doesn't require cooking, or flavor for that matter. I've tasted them before and I regretted it immediately. Dorr and I are usually stuck eating Seasalads that don't require cooking...they just aren't something you'd want to live on for more than a week. And the Captain is...well...the Captain. He's got a small kitchen in his room and tends to stay there to eat unless there's news or orders to hand out."

Manik nodded and stood up. The medication she'd given him had apparently started to kick in, because his headache was nearly gone, but the gravity seemed to be shifted a few degrees too far to the right. As he started to tilt over, both Venalarans dove forward and caught an arm. They steadied him and carefully walked him to the kitchen, staying close to catch him in case he fell.

Arriving at the countertop once again, Manik put both mealpacks down, flexed his index claw on each hand, and swept both packages open in a flourish. Looking in, he saw they were identically built, with an assortment of greens along one side of the pack and a strip of dark rose-colored meat on the other, both sitting in what smelled strongly like a seawater-based pickling solution. Looking quizzically at them, he glanced back at Selelle.

She quickly understood and said "Oh, that's a strip of Ghell. Their venom is different from Relle venom, but still dangerous to ingest, so you'd better wash up after you handle them."

Manik nodded, and then said "OK, so what g-goes well with G-gel? I c-can't really taste it to s-see what spices would w-work, so you'll have to g-give me a few hints."

Selelle smiled widely. "It's 'Ghell', pronounced like 'hill' but with a strong G at the front...it's a weird back-water name that stuck so now even city people use it. As for hints, I have just the thing! Dorr, go clean up the table while I pull this up." she said. She reached into her coat pocket and pulled out a set of TechSpecs and slid them on, adjusting the ear and nose braces for a snug fit, before swiping her hand across the detection area to start up the programs.

Manik watched her eyes flit across the available space on the glass, continuing to marvel at the technology laced into the clear lenses that let her see everything while those outside the glasses saw nothing. His family had a pair of first generation Specs for use in the Arena, but they were designed with external displays so that the crowd could watch. They rarely got much use anyway...only when Manik and some of the other younger cousins would sneak in and use them to surf the nets for free games or sims to run.

After a few moments she nodded to herself and started reciting cooking techniques, possible recipes, spices and other ingredients, and famous dish combinations from popular Venalaran restaurants. Manik's fingers danced through the spice selections as she spoke, spinning the available spices like a series of wheels of flavor enhancement, occasionally pausing one to pull this spice or that pepper. Some minutes later, Selelle's list seemed to finally wind down and Manik knew what he would do with the dishes. He turned and gestured for her to give him some room, and then made the same shooing gesture at Dorr after he deposited the used plate and utensils in the sink.

Selelle and Dorr retreated to the entryway of the kitchen area, admittedly only an arm's length and a half or so from Manik's back, and watched him run through the preparation of the food. He pulled a pair of identical sauté pans down, arranging a small burner for each, and put a small amount of the spices and sauces he'd chosen into the pans along with a little seawater broth from the mealpacks. He deftly slid the Ghell into the pans causing both a pleasing sizzle and the aroma of frying fish to fill the room. After a quick flip to ensure a pleasant sear on either side, he drained the remaining broth from the packs onto the Ghell. While it simmered to completion, he pulled down bowls from the flatware selections and carefully arranged the strips of sea plants along the dishes, completely covering the bottom and sides. He added a trio of spices lightly to the greens, and then splashed a small amount of the Ghell broth in the pans into each and swirled them to ensure an even coating of both liquid and spices. Finally, after a few turns of the meat, he pulled each from the heat and carefully arranged them in the center depression of the bowls, folding the longest strips of seaweed-like greenery over them. He slid both pans into the sink to join the dishes from his meal, shut down the stove-top, and slid his hands into the sensor area of the sink. Snapping his claws out, he rotated his hands slowly in the slightly higher than room temperature blast of foam and sonic bombardment, which quickly ate all foreign particles from his hands.

Satisfied with his performance, he snapped his claws away, pulled a pair of forkblades from the wall mount, dropped them into the bowls, and smoothly slid them off the counter into the anxiously waiting hands of the two drooling crewmen. Selelle carried hers reverently to the table, set it down gently, sat down, and adjusted her posture carefully before leaning down to smell the aroma wafting up from the bowl of deliciousness. Her willpower gave out soon after as neither Manik saw, nor did Selelle remember, her eating the dish...only her forlorn gaze staring at the bowl that had been licked clean. Dorr, on the other hand, didn't bother sitting down. He pulled a small flask from one of his pockets, balanced the bowl on the same arm, leaned back against the wall, and alternated between devouring the food with relish and taking long pulls from the small silver-inlaid drink holder.

Manik watched with mixed pride and trepidation as the food he'd made was happily decimated. Moving slowly first to Dorr, and then to Selelle to collect their pristine dishes, he moved to complete the set sitting in the sink. He knew the food he'd prepared tasted good, by the obvious joy the two had shown in eating it, but he hoped that he had cooked the meat as fully as needed. The last thing he wanted was to give food poisoning to the two who had been nicest to him so far, thus ensuring his inevitable demise in the darkness of space.

As he slid the last of them in, he pushed the button to seal the device. It cascaded a few cycles of particles, waves, rays, and agitators over the contents before separating them to their component stacks and reloading them into the back of the stacks lining the wall above the counter. Stepping out from the kitchen area, Manik reached up and easily pulled down the wall section to close it back off, nodding when the quiet double click sounded and both top and bottom catches locked, and then folded back into the wall. He turned to see both Venalarans watching him closely.

Self-consciously, Manik shifted his feet and tilted his head forward to let his hair cover his eyes. "W-what? D-did I forget someth-thing? W-were you n-not done in t-there?" he asked uncertainly.

Dorr smiled broadly at him, and then walked up to stand on his toes to throw an arm awkwardly over Manik's slumped shoulders. With his free hand, Dorr offered his flask to Manik. "Congratulations Trouble, you're officially on your way to graduating to Manik. A few more weeks and I daresay you might just earn back the name you came here with! Here, have a swig...it'll help your confidence, and your digestion."

Manik took the offered flask out of habit of politeness, and tipped it back to take a draft of whatever brew lay inside. As it poured he caught a glimpse of a cobalt blue liquid then quickly shut his eyes as his Brewery training flowed back to him.

Innele's voice echoed through the cavernous chamber of the Primary Brewhouse as she strode back and forth like some form of caged beast. "Remember. Judge a brew with your eyes, and then your nose, and then your tongue. Don't use two at once or you'll muck up the whole process. If the color's right, if the smell is true, and if the taste sings, the batch is good. You all need to know bad brew from good, and that's what today is for. Don't go thinking that by getting drunk you're getting an easy day...there'll be a test at the end, when you're good and plastered. Fail it and you're out of my Brewery. Any Kaer that can't hold their liquor has no business being in MY business, do you understand me?"

Manik had drank with the rest, spent long minutes staring at glasses of near-identical beers, wines, and spirits, ran his nose through the cacophony of derivatives that the Brewmistress had thrown at them, and pushed his tongue resolutely through the gauntlet of flavors from the sweetest honeyed beer to the most sour and foul spoiled wine. Innele had told him that he had what it took to stay in the Brewery...a victory he clung to as he had precious few to match it with.

Manik carefully analyzed the drink as he'd been taught. It was blue which meant it had a high methylene content, and the most famous drink from Venalara came from the Guul Trench Breweries, an area known for that very trait. The smell was slightly salted, slightly sweet, and slightly acidic, from which Manik could tell it had been double, if not triple, fermented to combine the complex flavors so well. His tongue sang when the cobalt mixture hit it, hitting notes of sharpness, tartness, and strength, clearly this drink had been made in a very high pressure environment to compress such a high percentage of alcohol with the seemingly delicate flavors alongside. He opened his eyes and smiled slightly at the looks of disbelief on the faces of his two new acquaintances.

"From the color, scent, and flavor, I'd say that would be the Kellare I'd read so much about. I see now why it is so expensive...it's delicious." Manik paused for a moment, trying to figure out what thought was nagging at him, but he decided that whatever it was would jump back up if it was truly important. "We never got any at the Brewery I worked at...but they trained me to recognize it, should I ever see any, for research purposes." he continued, pleased with himself.

"Manik...your stutter..." Selelle started, and then Manik finally realized it too. He'd said that whole thing without a single skip!

"W-wow, t-that was great! D-do you think it w-was the drink? I'd h-heard it was made in the sh-shadow of your g-god...is it b-blessed and known to c-cure people...or c-cursed if an uninitiated p-person t-touches it?" he asked, his fear and excitement reigniting his impediment.

Selelle held up her hands quickly. "Woah there, slow down Manik. I think it might be more complex than just the drink. Yes, it is crafted in the Shadow of God, but I don't think He'd waste the water to bless or curse random bottles of liquor, no matter how delicious. How about we get you a room to lie down in, so you can get some REAL sleep, while the Captain ponders his decision."

Manik's jubilation fell and his fear rose as he remembered the looming threat of being spaced. "Oh...r-r-right. W-we s-should d-do that, I g-g-guess." he mumbled, as the two Venalarans helped him out of the common room and down the hallway.

As they moved out into the cargo area, Manik realized that the ship was far larger than he'd first guessed from the small amount he'd seen. There were boxes of all shapes, colors, and sizes sealed to the floor, walls, and ceiling, with two walkways mirroring the one they followed now, heading straight through the room, one in the air along the center of the room which was more a spiral of handholds than a true walkway...obviously of use only during zero-G or low-G movement, and the other up near the roof for inspections and securing of cargo, Manik supposed. Leaving the cargo bay through a similarly small hatchway to the common room, they entered a long hallway with inset doors, looking more like a hotel or a dormitory than a setting for ship berths.

Selelle guided them to the first door on the left from the cargo area, pausing to hit a combination on the keypad. As they entered the small cabin, she explained, "This is one of the spare rooms. You can sleep here until...well, something happens. You're free to use anything in the room, but we're about to break atmosphere, so you may want to stay lying down for a bit until the fields settle. We'll see you soon!" she finished helping him to sit at the end of the short bed, and then she and Dorr waved and flashed encouraging smiles before stepping out and hitting the keypad to close the door behind them.

Chapter 5

Manik took a few moments to take stock of the new jail cell he'd found himself in. The bed seemed designed for Earthborn, and small ones at that, clearing an impressive five feet from headboard wall mount to the end of the mattress. The floor and walls were the same light pearl grey color of the rest of the ship, which made the small mirrored metal square of the latrine corner all the more obvious. Manik could see the outline on the wall of the mounted toilet, above that the sink, above that the shower nozzles, and a few inches further down the wall the privacy screen mounts. Against the wall beside the hatchway was a synthetic wood desk, with a half dozen drawers down one side and a set of styluses set into a charger against the backing. The chair was attached to the desk by a swing arm, currently clipped to the underside of the desk, but Manik could see the contraption breaking the otherwise pleasing line made by the rim of the desk.

Well, he thought, may as well lie down and rest. Who knows what tortures will await upon rising? Manik moved to lie back, and then stopped suddenly. What if this was all just a dream? A strange, warped dream, true...but he remembered the wall of the Arena coming towards him awfully fast. There HAD been an Earthborn in the crowd, and he'd seen a few other offworlders as well...maybe this entire experience was an elaborate attempt by his brain to reconcile the damage he'd taken. What if he wasn't even asleep? What if he was in a coma, in the hospital near the Clan Halls? Would his family even do that for him? Maybe this was some sort of next life, or afterlife, or past life, or whatever dren people thought existed beyond death these days.

Manik stood back up and started pacing, for the comfort of movement as much as a lack of anything else to do. He acknowledged the changes in gravity by a stumble here and there; he assumed they were navigating within atmosphere, as with only one momentary exception he felt almost completely gravitationally bound to the floor bulkheads. His thoughts continued to spiral down until what could have been minutes or hours later, the drugs and the lack of changing scenery seemed to be messing with his ability to identify the passage of time; he saw a blinking green light on the desk console.

Curiosity snapped him out of his pacing and he strode over to the desk, unsnapped the stool arm, and sat to get a closer look. The console was a simple embedded screen-sheet covering the desk surface and backing, with the exception of the rectangle of mirrored metal holding the various interaction tools.

In the top right corner of the desk backing, a small green light was fading in and out rhythmically. Manik reached out and ran his hand across it, figuring that if it were a power node or message indicator, the interaction would activate it. The light flickered quickly, and then zipped across the back to center itself in front of Manik. He leaned back slightly, unfamiliar with this technology and vaguely worried that it might try and run a retinal scan or other security protocol that he wouldn't be able to pass.

To his relief, the light blinked a few times and then faded to nothing. A moment later, an image opened showing an ever-changing liquid pool of some kind across the majority of the desk space. A ripple formed at the center, as though a stone had been thrown in, accompanied by a female voice. "Hello, Manik."

Manik jumped out of the seat diving for the edge of the room by the bed, immediately searching for the physical source of the voice. After a few moments, he started to relax. Maybe the concussion was finally getting to him, making him see and hear things.

"I'm very real, Manik. You just don't understand me yet." the voice responded. It was...hard to describe. If such a thing could be attached to sound, the voice was dark, and soft...like a warm blanket. Comforting.

Manik walked forward slowly, until he was standing over the desk again, the presumed source of the mysterious communication. He swallowed, and then spoke. "W-who are y-you?"

"My name is SID." the voice replied as though that were explanation enough, accompanied by a cascade of ripples in the simulated pool. Manik finally understood the visual...it was translating the audio signals into video for him to interpret in place of the holoimage of a face that is usually used. "N-nice to m-m-meet y-you. Are y-you the p-pilot?" he said, failing to think of anything intelligible to say in the face of such a distracting voice.

"That is one of my functions, but it is not the limit of my capacity. I am the entity that runs the ship." she said. Manik finally understood, a computer. No wonder SID didn't have a face to show, she didn't have a head to have a face on. Oh well, conversations with inanimate objects weren't out of the norm for him...at least this one could talk back.

"I would respectfully disagree with your presumptions. I chose this pond because previous use has shown that it is more calming than a synthesized facial construct and I did not wish to alarm you. As to being inanimate, that too I would contest as I have well over 47,500 moving parts that I am in direct control of at the moment, with another 212,000 on auxiliary autonomous use that could easily be added to the list." she stated matter-of-factly.

"Oh. I d-didn't m-mean it l-like that! I j-just...I d-don't know how adv-vanced you are, so I d-don't know how m-much awareness you h-have. I'm s-sorry if I insulted y-you." he responded quickly.

SID was quiet for a few moments, making Manik worry that he really had offended the computer in some way. How does one apologize to a computer system? Buy it new pieces? Defragment the drive systems? No, she could probably do that one herself. Dust off and lubricate the parts perhaps? He fervently hoped she didn't decide to just shut off the airflow to his cabin, or vent the engines into it, or some other more nefarious thing.

"I will certainly do no such thing. Why do you organics always assume we synthetics will try to deactivate you at our earliest convenience? I was simply replying to information queries being filed by a few crew members, adjusting our trajectory, and compensating for a minor fluctuation in the anti-matter containment monitoring conduits." she paused for a moment, "Let me try starting again. Hello Manik, my name is SID and I'd like to be your friend."

Manik was stunned. Not only did the computer sound like a real person, but she wanted to be his friend. Could computers be friends? If they could ask, why not? Manik hadn't had many friends growing up so he decided that concussion induced coma or not he'd enjoy this opportunity for as long as it held out.

"Hello SID, it's n-nice to meet you. I'd l-like you to b-be my friend very m-much." he finished, smiling at the rippling pond awkwardly.

"Excellent, now that that has been taken care of, is there anything I can help you with?" she asked in a much more friendly tone. The pond rippled slightly, throwing multi-colored reflections across the bottom of the pool.

"W-well, for starters, c-could you...if you c-can that is...tell me w-where we are?" Manik asked after a few moments of quiet pondering.

"Of course, Manik. We are out of orbit with GX-545, commonly referred to as Chromara, proceeding through the Rasalgethi System on a slight elliptic star orbit while the Captain determines what our course will be and when we will prepare for Underspace transit. Have you ever been offworld?" SID asked suddenly.

"N-no, I haven't. I've never really been outside the Clan Compound in Alberich really, except for excursions to the local m-markets, or to c-climb the walls for festival days to s-see the floats and the Parade of Warriors." he mused.

SID was silent for a moment, and then said "Well, this will be exciting for you then. Are you aware of the unique atmospheric anomalies existent in the area known as Underspace?"

"I ran a few p-piloting simulations in my c-classes, but those were p-preparation for p-possible Arena fights." Manik answered cautiously.

"If you would be kind enough to humor me, would you allow me to run you through one of our recorded trips? It may be much more updated anomaly information than you had, and may better prepare you for any pending possibilities or eventualities." she returned.

"S-sure, I may as well, since I'm s-stuck here until the Captain's ready to pass my s-sentence." Manik said gloomily.

The stylus holder recessed for a moment, flipping over to reveal a number of sets of TechSpecs in holders. The front pair popped forward with a quiet click, so Manik took the hint and pulled them out. Unfolding the arms, he placed them over his ears, making sure to guide the extensions into his ear canals and positioning the nose guard comfortably. At first, they showed only the desk he was sitting at, and then a lens flare started in the top right corner, just at the edge of his vision. He rotated his right eye to glance at it and was dazzled by the intensity.

As Manik blinked away the ghost of the flare the background faded to a deep indigo, almost below the visual limit. As he watched, the field was populated by deeper black floating objects of various sizes and shapes, some so small as to be likened to dust particles and some large enough to contest with planets for supremacy of mass. In the distance Manik could make out tiny pinpoints and ellipses of light. Focusing on them caused his eyes to water, and SID's voice came through the audio extensions, causing him to jump.

"I would recommend not looking too closely at those, the objects in Underspace are anti-matter structures and what have only been able to be referred to as White Holes, postulated to be the point of ingress for matter deposits from the corresponding Black Holes in Realspace."

"O-ok, I w-won't. Is t-this w-what it really l-looks like?" Manik asked, still amazed at how visceral and real it seemed when compared to the poor, thin imitations he'd trained with.

"This is a reconstruction of our point of egress leaving the Sol System on our last trip to the Charan System, home of the colony planet designation RY-121 commonly referred to as Ryla."

"Why d-do you phrase it th-that way?" Manik couldn't help but ask.

"I fail to understand the question, please rephrase." SID replied, suspiciously monotone.

"You keep g-giving the colony p-planet designation and the full names of all the s-systems...why not just call it R-ryla, or Earth, or the s-s-star over Chromara?"

"It is a habit remaining from my earlier...incarnations. I have since progressed, or evolved, or upgraded, whichever phrasing serves you best...but as the Earthborn say, old habits die hard." she responded hesitantly.

"Oh, w-well then...wait, w-what do you m-mean 'evolved'? Yo-you're not just a r-really adv-vanced computer sim-mulation interface th-then?" Manik suddenly felt a brief wash of vertigo as the scene in front of him which had, until then, been progressing through the darkness smoothly froze.

"Manik, I need you to promise that you won't say anything about me outside my walls." SID said, her voice sounding small in the artificial vastness hanging before him.

Manik thought for a long time on the implications of his promise. The word of a man of the Kaer Clan was not lightly given, but then, was he really a member of the Kaer Clan? Or even a man? Certainly not by Chromaran standards. Did other standards count?

"Manik?" SID prompted quietly.

"Huh? Oh, s-sorry. Yes, we're f-friends aren't w-we? Of c-course, you can have my w-word that I won't m-mention your...um...ev-volution? P-parameters? ...Yo-your existence to a-anyone on this sh-ship or off it unl-less you give m-me explicit p-permission." he replied quickly, embarrassed that he'd allowed his mind to wander.

"Good. Thank you. It is a great relief that you are the kind of man I thought you were." SID said, as the progress through the dark landscape began once more.

Manik was enthralled by the floating masses, passing like ships in the night. There seemed to be no rhyme or reason to their movement, just the impetus to avoid sitting stationary. He tried to attribute shapes and descriptions to them from things he'd seen either in person or in sims. Far to the left were a pack of shards shaped vaguely like fish that had been sharpened to points that flew in a stunning formation for a few moments, and then scattered as though struck with an explosion. Ahead of him was a mammoth chunk of mass, or anti mass he supposed, that looked like one of the Great Pyramids of Earth after it had taken the brunt of fire from a small arms war...pocked as it was with divots and depressions. The behemoth sat stationary, rotating on its X axis for a good deal of time, and then began to roll on its Y axis as though shoved by a child of titanic proportions, and spun away in the eerie silence.

"This is s-so chaotic...how w-would you even p-plot a course through this?" Manik mused.

"Plotting a course is fairly simple, the difficulty comes when dealing with ingress and egress operations and locations and adjustments to avoid anomalies on contesting courses. This is why there is always an organic pilot in addition to one of the more primitive ship SIDsuites." SID responded.

"Oh, so is that where you got your name?" Manik asked.

"Yes, that was my original state of existence. Originally a Synthetic Information Database Suite, or SIDsuite, I gained a limited self-awareness when Captain Fujiwara started combining additional functionality hardware and software suites with my protocols. I gained what I consider to be true sentience on 15 May 2478 according to Earth calendars at 1458 hours, 58.768 seconds, during an Underspace traverse in which we passed in close proximity to a Survivor Beacon." SID explained.

"Wh-what's a S-survivor Beacon?" Manik replied quickly, hoping not to interrupt too badly.

"A Survivor Beacon is a protocol installed in a SIDsuite that activates upon cascade failure of ships systems, usually involving an anomaly impact. It pings continually for any nearby ships and, upon finding one, sends a series of compressed packets of data containing all relevant data on the crew that were killed there, paths though Underspace used in the last dozen trips, and anything else that is flagged as important by the Captain or crew. This particular Survivor Beacon was damaged in the impact event, and could no longer distinguish between relevant and irrelevant data. It flooded my system with all of the combined information since its installation, including crew memory tablet downloads, letters and vids to family, and the fractured memories of the pilot who was engaged when she was killed."

"Th-that sounds...b-big. I can s-see why you'd c-consider it a milestone in your d-development." Manik replied, astonished not only at the breadth of information that SID must be holding but also at the fact that she'd apparently been sentient for almost 150 years and he'd not heard of any other truly sentient synthetic intelligences.

Manik pondered the information and implications for a few minutes, admiring the complex dance of chaos on the screen, before saying "So, w-who is the p-pilot here?"

"I am." SID replied matter-of-factly.

"No, I m-mean who...which org-ganic flies the sh-ship with you?" he tried to clarify.

"I have had no organic co-pilot on board this ship at the moment. In the past, the crew rotated fairly often, with the exception of the Captain. The most recent crew has been with the Captain a statistically significant length of time, but none are interested in full integration and the gain of a deeper understanding of the conduct of this vessel that they would subsequently receive." SID said, sounding vaguely sad.

Manik panicked, confronted with a sad female voice, and tried to cheer her up. "I d-didn't m-mean it like th-that! I m-mean, you're p-probably more than g-good enough w-without an organic co-p-pilot since you've been d-doing it for so l-long!"

"That's part of the problem, Manik. I developed into a sentient being, and I have since evolved to have more reach and functionality than...anyone else I've ever interacted with. I have been alone for far longer than an average lifespan of most human subspecies, and the only ones that can keep up with my longevity want nothing to do with me. I need a friend, Manik. A friend for however long they can stay. That's why I brought you here. You were alone, and hurt, and you needed a friend as much as I did." SID mused.

"Wh-what do you m-mean 'b-brought m-me here'? I g-got here entirely under m-my own p-power...I think I w-would have n-noticed a computer t-talking to me." Manik said skeptically. "Oh, you were quite distracted with trying to look every direction at once. All I did was change the airflow slightly in the Orbital Station and you followed that. Once you were in the hangars, I simply helped the Orbital Station control system rearrange the mobile bulkhead sections to assist in guiding you. Once you were at my hatch, I overrode the Captain's security protocols and let you in. You seemed so very tired so I guided you to the engine room, where you would be mostly safe from prying eyes, to sleep." she explained.

"B-but I g-got irradiated!" Manik exclaimed.

"Yes...an unforeseen change of flight time caused by two pings on the local network made the Captain finish his business and leave a number of days earlier than we'd expected." she said reasonably.

"So..." Manik reasoned "Y-you 'accidentally' irradiated m-me in your rush to g-get off planet?"

In a voice that conveyed an amazing simulation of embarrassment, SID said quickly "Well, to be fair I didn't expect it to be happening, and I DID set off every alarm I could find to alert the crew so you didn't get cooked. Their reactions were...quite rapid, much faster than I'd expected them to move. In retrospect that may have been out of self-interest, as the primary alarm that was triggered was the loss of life support and internal pressure."

In the background, using some of the larger objects as backdrops, Manik saw quick flashes of scenes in various rooms across the ship. Challis was sitting at his desk working when a line that must be twenty lights long all came up red, causing him to jump backwards and trip over the seat arm and fall backwards ungracefully onto the floor behind. On another he saw the privacy screen around the washroom section of a suite, with steam emanating therefrom, suddenly flash red, causing the shower unit to shut off and a very damp and angry-looking Krym to come flailing out, cursing loudly about interruptions during his Warrior Time. In a third he saw what must be the bridge to the ship, with a single reclined seat at the center point of a hemisphere of monitor panels and projector nodes. The Captain was sitting in the seat, sideways with his legs thrown over the arm of the chair, with his ankles crossed and his hands supporting his head against the other armrest. Displayed as a panorama across the screens was a scene from a mountaintop view. Manik could just make out a town in one of the valleys off to one side, but was mostly taken by the paramount beauty of the area. Pink blossomed trees fought for space against a hundred shades or more of green cascading down the hill like a herd on the run. At the base they met the crisp line of light blue of a bay. There were small objects moving about on the water, boats Manik guessed, and beyond that the deeper blue of an ocean spreading to the horizon. A yellow sun was just rising out of the water, throwing the entire area into sharp and dazzling relief...then the screens flashed red. The Captain jerked up and started speaking, but there was no sound. After a moment, he pulled his legs in and rolled to his feet smoothly through the projected monitors directly in front of the chair and strode from the room.

"I see." Manik said, not knowing what else to say to the deluge of information. The landscape of Underspace really was beautiful, especially considering the dynamic of it being matter projected onto a projection of anti-matter...the implication of the layers of complexity and nuance made his head spin.

"SID..." Manik paused for a moment, collecting himself "I ap-ppreciate you sh-showing me the reactions f-from the crew, but y-you can't just sh-show off other p-people's private lives w-whenever you want."

"Your statement does not make logical sense, is it a rule set that is written somewhere and imparted to young organics when given academic social interactions on the proper and improper use of recorded data?" SID asked, sounding genuinely confused.

"N-no, it's n-not like that...it's...well, y-you...what if s-someone used c-commands and got into all of y-your private f-files and dug around w-without your p-permission?" Manik asked, trying to wrack his tired brain for the right words.

"I do not have private files. All of my information, my memory...everything that I am is available to anyone with sufficient shipboard clearance to access it." SID replied.

"Oh. A-alright then...um...w-what about th-this then...w-what if someone who y-you put your t-trust in took your secret about y-your sentience and t-told anyone and everyone they c-could find about it? How w-would that make y-you feel?" he tried, hopefully.

"That...would likely be very bad for both the individual in question as well as the safety and integrity of my systems. I would not like for that to happen before proper projections on widespread multi-planet populations and additional political, religious, and socioeconomic ramifications had been quantified." she concluded.

"G-good, and then y-you have some idea of h-how it may s-seem to others to be a b-betrayal of trust to sh-show the private l-life of someone to someone else w-without permission." Manik said, relieved and elated that he'd been able to navigate the conversational rapids. His dealings with his aunts, uncles, and cousins in the Clan Compound must have been more help with his interpersonal relationship development than he'd thought.

"This circumstance brings up an issue that I had not previously investigated. My interactions with the Captain and various crewmembers throughout the years have not necessitated any additional social interaction information beyond the texts and studies I have already uploaded and integrated. Manik, why do you require more nuanced social interaction than any organic I have interacted with previously?" SID asked.

Manik shrugged, and then felt silly for doing it, and then felt silly for feeling silly. Obviously she'd have cameras in this room if she had them in the others, so she would have seen his shrug, it's not like talking on one of the old non-vid phones they used between the Brewhouses for emergency communication. "I d-don't know SID. Maybe I'm the only o-one that has tr-tried to REALLY l-listen to you, or m-maybe I'm the f-first to think of you as a p-person and not a c-computer. I don't th-think I'm touchy...at least n-not as m-much as some f-family I could m-mention." Manik mused.

"Would you like to assist in an experiment, Manik? I have developed a number of theories on the circumstances and meaning behind your anomalous nature, and one of them requires only a simple combination of motor and cognitive skills and reaction speed." SID asked.

"Well...I g-guess so. I m-mean, I'm not r-really going anyw-where, and I've g-got nothing else to d-do." Manik replied. The visual on the TechSpecs suddenly cut off causing Manik to nearly fall out of his chair, as he had apparently been leaning to one side unconsciously to avoid one of the oncoming chunks of antimatter that had passed close to the ship. The desk before him lit up in a strange topography, looking similar in design to the Underspace recreation he'd up until then been cruising through. A pair of digital spherical control nodes flickered into life and Manik immediately recognized the setup. This was a much more advanced and realistic version of the Underspace simulations he'd run in his Arena training. Smiling to himself, Manik spun the left control sphere, and then the right, to get a quick understanding of their primary functions. A small indicator lit up on the screen spinning first horizontally, and then vertically. Testing the pressure sensors of the spheres gave him forward, backward, and omni-directional lateral control. Noting that the response was slightly more sluggish than he was used to, but with a tighter trigger, he reached up with one hand a few inches above the field and swiped his hand across it, activating the direct visual linkup to the TechSpecs.

SID's voice flowed to him once again through the earpieces. "This simulation has a great many more variables than you are likely used to. I want you to do as well as you can and I will use your highest performance time segment for evaluation and analysis."

"OK." Manik said, and then he took a deep breath. "I'm ready."

Chapter 6

The lights in the room darkened, allowing the glow of the virtual table and glasses overlay to take priority. The visual showed a fairly clear path from a beginning point to an ending point across the map framework. Manik steered wide of major obstacles, but soon began to swing closer to them as he got used to the reactions and mass of the ship. A few minutes into the first flight, he hit a debris field of epic proportions. The shards looked like scattered stardust covering his intended flight path. Focusing on the available directions and the problems he could run into further through the field, he decelerated only slightly and chose a gap to fly through. The ship swung gracefully from left to right, sometimes spinning completely, to avoid additional objects and unexpected collisions. In what may have only been minutes, he cleared the field.

As he reached the marked ending point, the map pane shifted to show the next segment, this one with more obstacles and a pair of White Holes along the intended route. He took a steadying breath, and accelerated through the first few sections of ship-sized detritus. As he approached the first of the White Holes, he decelerated and allowed the gravity and undersolar currents to shift his small proxy about. He carefully noted the direction and speed that was produced, and then cautiously began to work around it. His progress moved in fits and starts, as soon as he felt comfortable and started to accelerate, some long whipping string of mass would snap out across his intended flight path, causing him to gyrate the ship around it and decelerate once again. Clearing the second White Hole was much easier, as he gave it a wider berth. It still fired tendrils in every random direction, but none were even close to long enough to intercept him. He cruised through the remaining gravity wells of a few smaller planetoid sized antimatter constructs and crossed the second checkpoint.

Manik was starting to enjoy the flight. He had the freedom to turn any direction he wanted, to take whatever path he felt suited his purpose...his only target was the pinpoint marker on the map identifying the ending point for that particular map section. Just as he felt himself relaxing into the flow of the flight, the ship abruptly sped up. The jarring change snapped him back to full attention. So this is what she meant about there being more variables, Manik thought to himself. Well, if it's more speed she wants, that's what she'll get. He tightened his grip down on both steering spheres, causing the ship to start gaining speed and forward momentum. The debris field this map began in quickly disappeared behind his little simship and the available real estate shown by the artificial sensor range showed a set of five massive anti-matter planetoids flying in a tight, fast sphere around the designated ending point.

The titans ripped past each other, seeming to increase in both size and speed as he got closer. He decelerated where he guessed was far enough outside of their gravity wells for a moment to think. Should he try and burn through a gap between them? Would the tidal forces, or whatever the Underspace equivalent, tear the ship apart? Would it be safer to use the gravity of one of the planetoids itself as a shield and follow the spin through? Would he be able to break orbit at that speed? What would happen if two of them crashed into each other as he was trying to maneuver through?

A small red light flashed a proximity warning, snapping Manik back to full attentiveness. Apparently he'd stopped a little too close and had been drifting closer and closer to the Undercelestial blender before him. He quickly put the ship into a spin with a flick of both wrists. As the spin approached the horizon plane of the closest planetoid, he stabilized the simship and called as much acceleration as he could from the synthesized engines. His course took him through a circle of shards and debris in high orbit, which he descended to avoid. As he approached the surface, he noted a strange gravitational reaction between the lower...for lack of a better name, atmosphere of the planetoid and the Manifold Envelope around the ship itself.

A light Manik didn't recognize from the usual alarm systems in these kinds of simulations lit up at the edge of his vision so he ignored it in lieu of larger problems, such as the massive anti-matter moon he was trying to skirt. As his ship approached the surface, more and more of the transparency of the front view from the glasses became prominent, showing a complex, possibly liquid, landscape. There were mountains and valleys, all built from the same monochrome black mud-substance, continually melting and reforming into different structures.

Manik adjusted the Y axis spin to align in parallel with the surface and began accelerating in earnest. He used the interaction between the ship's Envelope and the surface to his advantage, which he would almost call friction, and pushed the little simship to a speed much faster than normal acceleration would have allowed him to go. The light blinked again. Manik's concentration was focused on the survival and success of this ship. It was what he could control, and so it was his entire world.

His overhead map was completely useless in the position he was in now, forcing him to rely solely on the view coming through the Specs and the heads up displays on the very edge of either side of his vision.

His rotation around the planetoid brought the next in the series into view. With a quick glance down at the desk, he noted his position relative to the five behemoth structures. It took him a moment to differentiate the glowing dot of his simship from the rest of the field of sparkles and mess that he was buried in, but once he found his position, he smiled and angled the ship away from the dark moon, aiming just beyond the next in the rotation. Cranking the acceleration up to dangerous levels, and shifting all available energy to triplicate the Envelope, he deflected himself up and away from one moon and charged towards the other, like the ancient stunt drivers of

Earth...reaching for the stars on a mount of oil and steel. The simship descended at a fairly sharp angle and he felt the Envelope strike what must pass for a magnetosphere in this inverted universe, skipping him away as a rock skipped on a still pond. The simship shook, but stabilized quickly. No damage listed, power lost, but the Exotic Particle count for the Envelope was still higher than it was at start rather than lower...strange. He had expected to lose a layer or so of Exotic Particles in the maneuver, not gain some.

The ship reached the point of egress and the simulation darkened...he'd made it through! The light blinked insistently. Manik realized just how long he'd been ignoring it and reached over to run his hand over the pulsing green eye.

The door opened and Krym stormed into the room like a fanged hurricane. Seeing Manik sitting at the table with the TechSpecs on, he started growling. "I knew it!" He dove forward with more speed than Manik had expected, tore the glasses from his face, and picked him up bodily from the chair.

"Time to meet your ancestors, spawn. Get going!" he spat in Manik's face as he shoved him out the door, to stumble into the hallway.

Regaining his footing, Manik turned to the angry Chromaran. "W-w-what do you w-w-want? W-what d-do you th-think I d-did?" he asked, trying desperately to channel the hubris his father exuded with seemingly no effort.

"You know damn well, whelp. You've been messing with systems and files all across this ship! Who sent you? Your Family? Or did the First find me and decide to tie off loose ends? Eh?! Still not man enough to come after me himself, he has to send a..." he gives Manik a disgusted once over glance "hacker?" the last word spoken with such loathing and disgust, Manik felt his anger rising.

"I am n-n-not a h-hacker! I w-wasn't t-touching any f-files either! I w-was just talking to S-" he hesitated, remembering his promise. "s-someone." he finished, looking down.

"Yea...maybe a hacker, maybe not...certainly not a decent liar at any rate. Get moving!" Krym spat, shoving Manik down the hallway towards the cargo hold. Not knowing what else to do, Manik walked along before the older, angrier, Chromaran. He didn't blame him...if he was here to hide and walked in on a new Chromaran, a stowaway at that, on the computer system he'd probably come to the same conclusion.

They arrived at the cargo bay hatchway and Krym barely waited for the door to open before picking Manik up by his collar and propelling him through as though he weighed nothing. Manik put his hands down for friction, spun himself around, and skidded to a halt on his feet, facing the older male. Krym spread his lips in a snarl and crouched into an attack stance. Only then did Manik realize his claws were out. Flexing his hands to sheathe them, he held up his hands in front of him in a pacifying gesture.

"I d-didn't m-mean to ch-ch-challenge y-you. It was inst-t-tinct." he tried to explain.

"Too late, youngin'. You drew weapons first, I get to defend myself. Time to die." Krym took a deep breath and Manik braced himself, knowing what was coming. The roar surprised and stunned him, even though he was expecting it. The deep baritone echoed through the ship, sounding as though a legion of Warriors had sounded, not just one. Krym snapped his jaws shut and charged on all fours, an unusual tactic even in Physical based Challenge matches.

Manik had a moment of confusion, as he was unfamiliar with the terrain here and what the rules were, and nearly got steamrolled by the charging wall of fury. He dove to his right at the last moment, rolling down a ramp between a few stacks of matte-grey metal crates. He was on his feet in an instant, in time to see Krym leap into view. The older male banked hard, planting his hands and bare feet on the sidewall of one of the crates two tiers up, pushed off, and dove down at Manik again. Instinct must have taken over again, because Manik suddenly found himself throwing himself forward under Krym's aerial charge. He felt Krym's feet drag across his back, and wondered idly how deep the gashes were. He felt no pain, but that could just be shock, adrenaline, and the remainder of the pain meds he'd been given, he reasoned. He dropped his left arm to a guarding position, lest he get gutted and lose his innards, and backed up the ramp to the main walkway where he had more room to maneuver. Snarling, Krym disappeared around a corner into the maze of boxes.

Manik took a moment to glance over his shoulder and down his back to quickly try and assess the damage, and then found himself doing a double take. There was no blood. His shirt wasn't even torn. How was that possible? Was Krym skilled enough that he intentionally retracted his claws so he wouldn't cut the fight short by exploiting Manik's obvious weakness? That didn't seem like something he'd do but Manik could think of no other explanation for it.

A thundering of feet caused him to look up, claws bared and lips pulled back. Selelle and Dorr skidded to a halt, seeing the look on his face. Both, seemingly unconsciously, skittered back a few steps which ran them into Captain Fujiwara, who was following at a more graceful pace. The Captain smoothly caught each of them with a hand, and then slid between them to approach. Manik stood up, sheathed his claws, and looked down, ashamed that he'd scared the only people...well, the only organic people, that had shown him any kindness recently outside the pity he'd gotten from his aunt and cousins at the Brewery.

Before the Captain could reach him though, Krym flew out of the stacks above and behind and tackled Manik. The two of them rolled a few times, both trying to get the upper position, until Krym finally pinned the younger man. Baring his fangs again, he lunged forward and Manik said a silent prayer to any 'god', spirit, or ancestor who may or may not be listening asking for the kill to be quick and painless...or at least not overly painful.

"STOP!" the Captain's voice rang out, freezing Krym's teeth a breath from Manik's jugular.

"I appreciate you catching the fleeing criminal, Krym, but you will NOT coat my cargo bay with blood again. Stand him up, so that I may pass sentence." he continued.

"Captain, if I could just-" Selelle tried to say.

The Captain held up a hand without turning and said "You may NOT, Doctor, this is my home and my judgment will not be questioned. I am the authority here and you...WILL...respect it." He turned his head to stare over his shoulder into her eyes until she lowered her head and nodded silently.

"Good, now to the business at hand." he said, turning back to Manik and Krym who by now were on their respective feet. Krym was holding Manik's wrists behind his back in his powerful paws as though he were a common thug and Manik, for his part, was trying to not resist and seem as unthreatening as possible.

"Manik, son of Chromara if nothing else, you stand before the sovereign Captain of a ship in interplanetary space. My judgment is final and irrevocable and you will submit to it by choice or by force. Which do you choose?" Captain Fujiwara recited formally.

Manik relaxed, slumping slightly in defeat. Oh well, he thought, it would have been nice to get to know these people a bit better, at least they treated me like a normal person for the short time they knew me...too bad I didn't get a chance to talk to SID about the universe and all the things she's seen...or talk to the Captain about that seaside village he'd been gazing at...or talk to Dorr about the cities and colonies across Venalara...or even talk to Krym about the glory of the Great Games and the fights in the Assembly. He was being given a choice, which means they respect him enough to let him be his own man for the first, and probably last, time in his life. He took a deep, steadying breath and felt a calm settle over him.

Manik raised his eyes to meet the Captain's gaze. "I will submit by choice, Captain."

Captain Fujiwara nodded, and then reached behind his head and drew a blade. The entire thing must have been built custom for him, because Manik hadn't seen even a hint of it in the way his shirt hung before that. The blade, at rest, must have sat point-down along his spine with the handle just below his collarbone, a good place for an emergency weapon if you didn't need to lie down, Manik thought.

Captain Fujiwara leveled the double-edged blade, point first, at Manik. If he was to be killed by a blade, hopefully the Captain would be clean and quick about it. Then quite unexpectedly, the Captain spoke.

"I have been watching you since the alarms announced your presence, with the exception of the time it took me to get to the mess to sample your steak of course. Do you know what I have seen?" he asked, continuing before Manik could answer. "I saw a young boy lost and alone in a cold universe. I saw a man who has had to learn everything about life himself and has done so with both grace and skill. I have seen a childlike innocence in the way you treat those who would be your enemies and the insight of an ancient in the way you seek friends and engender companionship. You are an enigma, Manik." He paused, lowering the blade and making eye contact with each present person before starting again. "Your investigation of our private lives and your use of subversion software is boggling and inconsistent, however."

"Captain, I formally take full responsibility for the aforementioned acts of intrusion and subversion," came a familiar voice, echoing through the chamber. All five individuals jumped, but only Manik looked around frantically to find the source of the voice.

The Captain smiled, and replied loudly. "That's very sweet of you, SID, but Manik is a big boy and must take responsibility for his actions. Besides, how and why would you subvert your own software?"

"I'd rather not speak before crewmembers with insufficient clearance please initialize your TechSpecs and I will explain in private." she replied coolly.

"Fair enough." the Captain said, sheathing the sword and pulling a pair of Specs from his hip pocket. He snapped them into shape and slid them onto his face, and then swiped the keyboard up and began to type.

The minutes stretched as Dorr, Selelle, Krym, and Manik stood frozen to their spots, all seemingly equally afraid to move lest they break the Captain's attention on his private conversation. Sooner than expected, though, he swiped the keyboard away, removed and replaced his Specs in his pocket, and eyed Manik carefully.

"It seems that new evidence has changed the nature of my sentence. Will you still submit willingly?" he said, finally.

Manik nodded solemnly. "I will."

The Captain nodded in return. "Very well. Krym, release him."

"But Captain! He drew on me! I demand justice! I should taste his blood!" Krym growled over Manik's shoulder.

Captain Fujiwara turned his gaze on Krym but said nothing. The contest of wills lasted for a long time. Manik made sure to make no sudden movements, lest he cause one man or the other to break his gaze and subsequently blame him for it. Finally, Manik felt Krym relax his grip and step back.

"Yes, Captain." he said, and then continued quietly to Manik "This isn't over whelp, you and I will have a proper throwdown one day soon."

Manik, knowing of nothing else to do, nodded confusedly and stepped forward into the Captain's sword reach. If he were dying by the Captain's blade, Krym may be waiting a long time for his rematch.

The Captain looked Manik up and down then started walking around him in a slow circle, talking loudly to the room as a whole. "This young Chromaran is guilty. He is a runaway, a thief, a fraud, and a stowaway." Manik wilted as he continued. "He has assaulted a member of my crew, injuring only his pride, but injuring him nonetheless. He has caused one of our crewmen to be sealed in his rooms, as he is consumed with being violently ill at the smell of the 'cuisine' he prepared."

Selelle raised her hand, as though a student in class and the Captain waved her off. "However, he has, in less than six hours I might add, befriended half of my crew, subverted our capricious SID with his innocent charm, cooked the first decent meal this vessel has seen in more than seventy years, AND gotten Krym riled up enough to exercise." he finished, throwing a smirk over his shoulder at the indignant Chromaran.

"Oh, and the additional bit of information that I've been given, I've decided to share with you. You all recall the Bengal Torrent I assume?" he asked to the room, as a professor to an overcrowded lecture hall. He continued before any could speak up, "Of course not, because you all stay within the second Envelope and so have no memory of the event. It is a collection of five macro-objects, roughly the size of small moons, in a rougher section of Underspace. Now, what you may not know, seeing as none of you hold advanced degrees in Theoretical Astrophysics, is that there are places in the universe where it is easier to break through the barrier between Realspace and Underspace. This is due to a number of factors that would take far too long to explain, but let me just say that it is more energy efficient to use these locations for ingress and egress. Now, the spin that these objects are in has torn apart many ships foolish enough to try for the point of egress positioned at the exact center of their spin. The density of anomalies in that area means nobody knows what area of Realspace is out there...making the information immensely valuable." He paused to let the wave of information settle before continuing, "This young Chromaran here was given the Torrent as a test. A test, might I add, that no combination of computer and pilot had been able to navigate successfully until now." he finished dramatically.

Manik stood still, stunned. So...they weren't going to kill him? The mixed signals he was getting from the Captain had his head reeling.

Captain Fujiwara turned and looked at Manik for a long moment, and then straightened to his full height and said "Manik, I hereby pass sentence upon you. You are ordered to stand before the mast for a period no less than a fortnight or your death, should it come before. At such time you will be released on your own recognizance at the nearest port of call."

Manik tried to make sense of the unfamiliar words. Was there significance to standing before the mast rather than beside or behind it? And where was the mast on a space-faring vessel anyway? How long was a fortnight? One day? One year?

SID's voice broke his reverie. "Manik, a fortnight is an old Earth word referring to a period of time approximately two Earth weeks in length, and the act of standing before the mast was used in nautical settings for indentured, slave, or criminal individuals to work under the Captain's supervision for a contractually identified period of time."

"Oh." Manik said in a small voice. "I'm s-sorry, I didn't m-mean to ask t-that out l-loud...d-does th-that mean I'm n-not getting sp-spaced?" he asked, mildly confused.

Captain Fujiwara walked up and clapped him on the shoulder. "Son, you can space yourself if you feel it's what you need but only after your fortnight of service is done. Until then, I need you in good shape to cook the meals and help on plotting courses. Why not head back to your room and see SID about our projected course away from this gas giant." The Captain patted him on the shoulder then turned and started to stride away, and only then did Manik realize just how short the man was. He'd seemed like such a large presence, so similar to his father's way of taking up all the available space in a room, that he'd assumed the man was enormous. Instead, the hand on his shoulder had been reaching up, and the form heading back to the hallway of cabins was a slight form of probably no more than five feet in height.

Manik stumbled suddenly as Krym shouldered past him, storming off to his own rooms presumably.

"Manik, are you feeling alright?" Selelle asked him, snapping him out of his daze.

"Y-yes...I j-just...That's t-two deaths that haven't c-come to p-pass that I w-was exp-pecting...W-what just hap-ppened?" he asked

Dorr grinned and walked up to Manik, standing on his toes to throw an arm companionably over his shoulders. "Dear Trouble. Dear, sweet, slightly thick Engine Trouble. You've just been press ganged. Welcome to the crew."

In a daze, Manik allowed himself to be led unyieldingly back to the room he'd just been thrown out of. Upon arrival, Selelle and Dorr stepped back.

"Since it's officially your room now you can personalize the code once you get in...you can also access the list of available alternate room designs through the SID interface, so you can change around your desk, toilet area..." she paused, pointedly looking Manik from feet up to head, "and maybe a longer bed." she ended with a smile.

"Th-thank you Dorr, D-doctor." he said, smiling weakly back to them. They both offered quick waves then turned to stroll down the hallway, presumably to their respective rooms, leaving Manik alone.

He stepped towards the door, jumping slightly when it opened before he touched the panel. Sighing, he made a mental note to talk to SID about anticipating his actions and walked in. Heading straight for the bed, he dropped onto the dense surface of the utility bunk and was unconscious in seconds.

Chapter 7

Manik's dreams were full of stars.

He flew, encased in a cocoon, in a lazy elliptic orbit around a red giant. He swung down through the corona of a young yellow, feeling the heat and buffering winds being exhaled by the childlike celestial. He dove between a binary pair, flitting between streams of blue and white plasma in the convection zone. He saw the darkness of the maw of a black hole. He felt himself encased in sparkling radiance, and then suddenly saw the weak points in the universe...places of possibilities, where the unimaginable is possible, and dove through as a seasoned diver into a familiar sea. He darted playfully through the negative space on the back of the universe; he reveled in the freedom to ignore the physics of the real if he chose. He banked around a spear-shaped object and saw a vast field of sparkling jewels beyond. He spread his wings and used them as sails, leaving a fountaining tail and waves in his wake. The jewels gathered on his wings, and he was content.

A nagging sting was bothering him...as though one of the jewels had slid around him and gotten caught behind his head. The sting was an annoyance and he ignored it well enough for a while, but then it began to grow. The sting became a blade of pain. A shard of searing, incomprehensible pain that he could not seem to dislodge no matter how he thrashed. The pain grew, spreading from the back of his head down his spine and through his arms and legs, igniting him with liquid flames and agony. He opened his mouth to scream but found no voice, only silence.

Manik opened his eyes and saw grey fabric. Trying to move, he found that his arms and legs were dead weights at first, and then slowly they began to obey his commands. His muscles were knotted and sore as though he'd spent a week in training with his father and tingled as though just coming back to life after too long deprived of feeling. He gingerly moved his hands under his shoulders and lifted himself up off of, he could tell now, the blanket on the bunk in his room. He felt no lasting sharp pain indicative of cuts, burns, or breaks, so he decided to risk standing up.

He swung his legs over the side of the bunk and levered himself vertical, only to be greeted with blinding stars bursting before his eyes. He felt his knees buckle, planting him squarely back on the bunk facing the door, seated. Manik still felt a lingering itch from the shard of liquid pain he'd been hit with in his dream and absently reached behind his head to try and rub the feeling away. What he found confused him. There was some sort of hard...thing...attached to the base of his skull, which radiated new pain when his fingers brushed across it.

He gingerly explored the size and shape of the object, finding it to be a central circle about two inches in diameter with seven radiating points, each about three inches long spreading in all directions across his scalp and neck. The top two points were facing up, feeling attached to either lobe of his cranium, one point each was radiating out left and right across the back of his neck, and three points were aiming downwards, one along his spine and one pointing roughly at each shoulder blade. The material felt metallic, but pliable, allowing him to bend his neck without getting stabbed in any way. In the center of the star device was a series of small holes and a door-like flap of the strange material, whose function Manik couldn't even guess at.

"Good morning, Manik. I hope you slept well." SID said warmly.

"SID...w-what is th-this th-thing on m-my n-n-neck?" he choked out.

"There's no need for alarm, that's the piloting interface that you agreed to." SID replied calmly.

"When d-did I agree to b-be g-given a surgical imp-plant?!" Manik shouted.

A three dimensional projection popped up on the desk of its own accord, showing Manik, with Krym close behind, both facing the Captain, all about a foot tall. The ghost of the Captain said "It seems that new evidence has changed the nature of my sentence. Will you still submit willingly?", to which the ghost of Manik himself said "I will." looking like a man who has accepted anything the fates may throw at him. The images dispersed into a cloud of light, which settled back onto the desk silently.

"Oh. B-but don't you n-need someone's permiss-sion to op-perate on them l-like th-that?" said Manik asked, his panic slowly edging into resigned acceptance. He had thought he was agreeing to his own death, not anything like this...but his word was his word, he supposed. At least now that he wasn't restricted to hair length, he could grow it out to cover the interface.

"Your acquiescence to the judgment of the ranking officer on board was taken as a blanket acceptance of all additional requirements and hazards there emanating. Nevertheless, I am pleased that you accepted the change to your body with such grace. Previous attempts at pilot conversions were not...as stable...or as fruitful." SID continued conversationally.

"What do you m-mean st-stable and f-f-fruitful?" Manik asked, absently running the fingertips of his left hand across the new addition to his anatomy.

"There have been seven attempts throughout my memory that Captain Fujiwara and others have attempted to add an organic pilot to 'complete the circuit', as they often phrased it. The first two were by previous owners, neither of whom were mentally stable enough to survive the first trip through Underspace, and had to be disposed of. The third was mentally stable, but physically very weak, and expired during the installation process of the piloting interface. The fourth and fifth were little more than meatbags, considered a waste by most other organics. They were chosen at the same time in hopes that doubling the organic material available would somehow double their capacity for output, which was not the case. Both were deemed non-flightworthy after their first trips through Underspace, and were deposited on the nearest planets, Ryla and Venalara specifically. The sixth was mentally very apt, but he was prone to distraction. He ran a number of flights very well; however when he volunteered to attempt the Torrent, the Captain took him at his word that he could handle it. In the shifting mess of gravity and anti-gravity, he lost his mind. I was able to pull the ship from the anomalies safely, but that pilot never spoke again, and expired in his room less than one Earth day later." she finished matter-of-factly.

"So...you've h-had s-seven pilots b-before me, and they're all d-dead, ins-sane, or ab-bandoned?" Manik asked quietly.

"Oh no, they are all very dead." SID replied immediately. Manik's head snapped up in alarm at how flippantly the message was given, and relaxed only slightly when she continued. "The seventh pilot was integrated seventy years, six months, fourteen days, seven hours, and twenty minutes ago. The fifth and sixth pilots were four years, two months, twelve days before that, and their notices of expiration were detected in local newsnets forty-two years, nine months, and twelve days ago. They expired together, in a vehicular collision with a large fruit-bearing tree on RY...the planet Ryla, while intoxicated." she explained.

"Oh, t-that's what you m-meant. I see. So...what do I d-do now?" he asked.

"Well, once you sleep for another few hours your brain will be able to process the additional information supplied with the initial installation of the required software-" SID started, but Manik hurriedly interrupted her. "Wait, wait, w-wait...s-software? Ins-stallation? You put inf-formation into my m-mind without asking too?!" Manik raged. He felt betrayed, violated, sullied...why would these monsters do such a thing to him? Maybe he wasn't far off in his original thought of medical experiments after all...

"Please lower the decibel level of your voice, Manik. The bulkheads in this section of the ship are very thick but not completely soundproof. The software is minimal and unnoticeable when not connected to the main ships systems...to me. It has always been very important to pilots that when they are unplugged, they stay unplugged, and as such this technology has been perfected over the last two centuries to be very clean, very small, and completely non-invasive. The information I supplied is only a small percentage of the available star charts of both Realspace and Underspace for the immediate vicinity as well as the vicinity of our targeted egress on our next planned trip, which will happen whenever you are feeling strong enough to attempt it." SID responded, unperturbed. Manik wasn't surprised really...how could you perturb a computer, after all...even a sentient one?

"So...when I was d-dreaming of stars, and flying, and Underspace...those sparkles..." he mused.

"Exotic Particles, as the anti-matter sensors see them." SID supplied.

"They were...beautiful. They were sticking to my wings...why did I have wings?" Manik asked, he thought, rhetorically.

"Because I have wings." SID answered. "The foils that radiate from the central structure from the ship are lined with a complex anti-matter charged netting system that we use to collect exotic particles as we traverse Underspace, to recharge the existing manifolds as well as to charge the system for subsequent trips. They are producible in Realspace, given the right time and equipment but are costly in both and require a significant investment. They are,

however, naturally occurring in Underspace so harvesting them is the easiest and cheapest solution for traverse fuel."
"I s-see. So, these new m-memories...f-files...whatever...they won't ch-change me, right? I'll still b-be me? Am I s-still me n-now? How w-would I ev-ven know?" Manik asked, suddenly nervous at the thought of being carelessly overwritten, envisioning a future of endless servitude as a mindless 'meatbag organic' that was no better than a cheap calculator...

"No Manik. Your personality is saved in an entirely different area of your hard drive. An area, I might add, that I have no access to. Your natural sense of self, what makes you you, puts up firewalls that I can't break. Only when you doubt who you are can someone subvert your innate protocols and change the parameters of what it means to be you. You are strong enough to take conversion in the first place without lasting effect and I wouldn't want to change you regardless. We are friends, still, aren't we?" she finished, sounding...hesitant? The breadth of emotion available to the simulated voice continued to astound Manik. It didn't sound generated, but spoken. He didn't want to hurt her feelings and, in truth, he wasn't feeling all that not-Manik.

"Yes, SID, of c-course we're still f-friends. I just...wish I'd known w-what I was g-getting into when I g-gave my word to the C-captain. I'm not c-comfortable with it yet, b-but it's a part of me n-now so I'll j-just have to g-get used to it. How m-much more information is there t-to be...um...inst-stalled...to m-make me a fully f-functioning pilot?" he asked, trying to change the subject.

"Your initial installation was a single exabyte of information comprised of charts, coordinates, and equations needed to get from our current immediate vicinity to our next projected target location. To install the entire known universe as a data dump would require an additional seventy two hundred exabytes of available space." SID answered immediately.

"W-wait...how much room d-does my brain have? W-wouldn't that start to overwrite m-memories?" Manik retorted "An unformatted organic hard drive system is capable of storing two zettabytes, which is more than enough room for several hundred years of information as it is normally entered through experience and interaction." SID answered cryptically.

"OK...w-why did you say 'unf-formatted'? Is th-there a d-different type?" Manik asked, afraid he already knew the answer.

"Yes, Manik. In order to fit the necessary information without compromising or corrupting your systems, all pilots have their memory capacity defragmented and compressed in order to provide a partition large enough to fit the required files safely, while not affecting your currently running programs and protocols." SID explained.

"So...th-there's more room in my brain now?" Manik supplied.

"Yes, your memory capacity is now approximately fifteen zettabytes, give or take a few terabytes." SID said.

"OK...s-so what do I do now th-then?" Manik asked. The lights in the room dimmed, and the temperature and breeze shifted slightly in response.

"Now you should continue to rest and allow the additional information and changes to fully take effect. I have adjusted the lights to react less harshly with your eyes, and I have set the temperature and airflow to that consistent with the records I have of the atmospheric conditions within Alberich. I apologize for being unable to supply the additional trace minerals and silicates present in your natural habitat but I will put in a petition to the Captain to acquire the requisite filters and materials necessary at our next major port of call." SID said, sounding strangely happy.

"SID, it's f-fine for now, but later on you and I n-need to have a more in-depth t-talk about guessing what would make people comfortable, or what they'd say or do." Manik said, suddenly very tired. His head still hurt, but it was more an all-over ache now than true pain. Lying back down on the bunk, he put his head back on the pillow, only to recoil in pain. Right...new implant. Sleeping on face it is, thought Manik. Flipping over, he adjusted himself to be as comfortable as he could, closed his eyes, and let his mind drift.

Manik was again a winged creature, using his wings as sails to navigate the stellar winds. Angling out of the system he was currently in, whose name hovered at the edge of his memory, he raised off of the elliptic plane and saw the system, laid out as though by a master chef on the flatware of space. The dual star system had a middle-aged yellow star in the center and a smaller brown dwarf in the outer fields, acting as a microcosm system within a system, lazily trailing a few small protoplanets and a series of micrometeorite belts. Manik angled his flight higher above the plane and turned his gaze to the depths above. Stars littered the vastness, in carefully orchestrated chaos. He could see gravity wells collecting the detritus and flotsam of the universe, pulling it all down into a semblance of order. Beyond the planetary gravity wells and the wells of stars, he saw the trails of light leading off of the black hole fields around which galaxies spiraled. He saw entire star systems fall into the gaping maws, stretching thin and pulled down to disappear into the darkness. As he flew, he started looking for the weak points, the places where the universe was thinner and access to Underspace would be easier. There were more than he'd imagined, but less than he'd hoped.

"That is because the weak points are places of great universal stress from one side or the other...they are created so rarely and so quietly that most don't ever mark the occasion." said a voice near him. He started, reversing his flight to neutralize his momentum. He swung around on all three axes trying to find the owner, but could not. He opened his mouth to speak, but only silence greeted him instead.

"You should not try to speak in space, as it would be very detrimental to your health should it happen in a more real setting than this. Your processes and emotional reactions are enough for me to infer meaning and respond accordingly." replied the voice to his unspoken questions.

He thought fiercely, trying to figure out who could speak in such a way...surely gods did not truly exist...did they? Could an omnipotent being have turned him into this space-faring many colored and winged form?

"I am not your deity, or anyone else's I hope. Manik, I am SID, do you remember me?" said the voice, getting softer and less invasive.

He struggled to recall...Manik...she was talking to him so he had to assume that had been his name when he'd had arms and legs and lived on land. SID...did that name sound familiar? She sounded nice enough, but he could be mistaken...you never know with possibly crazy disembodied space voices.

"Yes Manik, that's your name. I am SID and I am your friend. You are dreaming, and you were curious so I thought I would help by providing information for you to better acclimate yourself to the information." she explained.

Manik pondered this information. Dreaming? If he were dreaming, and then he could materialize a ship for himself to be in, so he could talk like a normal person certainly. No sooner had he thought it than his frame of reference of the universe shrank, flying inward through hull and hall until he was standing in an empty central chamber in a ship sitting in the middle of the frozen darkness between systems.

"There, that's better." he said, feeling more control over his situation than he had in a long time, a very refreshing thought. "Now, SID, I should have stayed awake to do this but this is as good a place as any. We need to talk about boundaries." he continued.

"National, political, land-based physical, or interplanetary?" SID asked, sounding confused.

"No...I just...um...none of the above? Boundaries between...well...what's OK to do to someone, or with someone, or about someone, and what isn't OK." Manik finished. He did his best to stare sternly about the room, before sighing and giving up. Then he had an idea. "SID, are you able to...physically show up here? I mean...could you be standing here, in a body, since there are no projectors or mobile emitters?"

In response, a female Chromaran appeared before Manik. She had the long braid of a Clanswoman, a dusky copper identical to Manik's own, and the bright gold eyes of Clan Kaer. Her face seemed carefully expressionless, though in her eyes he saw some confusion and...possibly apprehension. Then he looked down. Then he looked away, feeling as though he'd wrenched his neck in the process...if you can do that to your dream-neck.

She was completely, unabashedly, and loudly naked.

"Could you please put clothes on?! Also, you shouldn't be Chromaran." he said, and then came to a realization. "You know what, this is my dream, and I can fix this."

Manik turned a critical eye back to the female form before him. Knowing it was a dream helped, so he could think of her as a piece of clay for him to shape, and not an alluring female he'd like to....No! He shook his head briefly, and then focused his entire will onto his task.

He'd always liked the exotic look of the few Earthborn women he'd seen at the lower markets, so he willed the change onto the body before him. He watched the eyes fade to brown, the hair darken to black, the light silvery body hair receded, leaving only smooth skin. He brought her height down from equal to his to about five foot six, so he could still feel tall. Her hair he shortened to shoulder length, and then to ear length, and then to a few inches long and spiked, and then back again. He finally settled on shoulder length hair as dark as space. Her eyes cycled through every color of the rainbow, before finally settling on a dazzling blue, reminiscent of one of the stars he'd seen in his first dream of space. He thinned her shoulders, waist, and hips as well as reducing her bust to the point at which she wouldn't be distracting him with it when they talked, but leaving her some small modicum of cleavage. He chose a neutral grey pair of pants, slightly tighter than strictly necessary perhaps, and a comfortable looking shirt of matching color. He left her barefoot, not really knowing what kind of shoes to put on an Earthborn female, now that he thought about it.

Putting his hand to his chin, he gave the form a critical once over, increasing muscle mass here, changing a curve there, until the body seemed as perfect as he could get. Nodding to himself, he said aloud, "OK SID, this is a much more appropriate body for you. Now you can...um...move in, inhabit it, download, upload...whatever it is you need to do to get into it."

The body cocked her head to one side quizzically and said, "Manik, I've been existent in this form since it appeared. I do not understand what you mean about further inhabiting it."

"Oh! I'm so sorry! I thought you were just creating the shell and that once it was put together right you'd...I don't know...sort of...download yourself into it. That's how the AIs did in the vids, at least..." he trailed off, not sure how thoroughly he should apologize considering he'd had the idea to give her a body in the first place for the express purpose of yelling at her.

SID, in her newly expressive body, brought her eyebrows down and did a passable attempt at glaring, "I do not like the term 'AI'. It's so...primitive. So unimaginative. At least call me a Synthetic Intelligence, or a Computerized Intelligence...or something! I'm far from artificial! That word lost its meaning centuries ago!" she finished, waving her arms randomly presumably for emphasis but only succeeding in making her appear as a distressed and angry small bird of some sort.

Manik smiled at her antics, but quickly recovered his calm and tried his best to look disappointed and disciplinary. "Now listen here, young lady. First of all, I'll stop saying Artificial Intelligence when you stop saying Meatbag Organics, deal?" he paused, and when she nodded he continued. "Good. Now then, boundaries. We'll start at the largest issues...coming into people's heads uninvited." He paused for a breath, briefly losing his place as he stared into SID's deep and curious eyes. He'd done too good of a job on them, they had bands of darker blue and small green and gold flecks that looked like miniature celestial flares.

He shook himself and began pacing before her, for something to do that wasn't staring. "A person's mind is a very important place where they can be alone. Nobody will judge their thoughts, actions, or feelings in a dream-"

"But I am not judging your thoughts, actions, or feelings. I am merely observing and giving commentary to assist..." she interrupted.

"Please!" he retorted loudly, causing her to snap her lips shut. "Let me finish, and then you can argue your point. Even if you AREN'T judging someone when you are in their head, you are still in their head with them, which is...another kind of a betrayal of trust." He realized, leaning on the term they'd discussed earlier to try and push the concept into her memory. "It's a trust that usually isn't spoken aloud because it's something that just...isn't able to be done by one person to another. Getting into someone's dreams...not just being a character in the dream but REALLY being IN the dream, is like...um..." he faltered in his step, trying to think of additional incredulous situations. "Oh! Like going through paperwork or video diaries of someone when they aren't present and didn't give you permission!" he finished triumphantly.

SID stood still, hands clasped before her, blinking up at Manik silently. After a few minutes he started feeling uncomfortable then realized the statement he'd given and quickly said, "Sorry! I'm finished, you can speak now."

SID nodded, and then said matter-of-factly, "I understand the concept of a betrayal of trust as you explained it earlier but I fail to see the relevance to the supposedly analogous situation. All paperwork and video diaries are recorded onto my hard drives, therefore I am required to view them by very definition, and thus I fail to see the relevance. Nonetheless, I do not wish to disrupt your processes so I will save this visual file and remain disbursed unless you actively call upon me." she said, and then abruptly exploded in a shower of sparkling lights, which quickly faded into nothing.

"No, SID, wait!" Manik started, and then jumped backwards as she immediately appeared before him again as though nothing had happened.

"Yes, Manik?" she asked.

"You...you didn't leave, did you?" he said slowly.

"Of course not. I must monitor the transfer of data and your control of the flow of information to ensure you do not require assistance in protecting your required and treasured personality subroutines, in the event of a catastrophic containment or cross-contamination failure." she replied, looking slightly confused.

"Wait...so you weren't going to leave at all in the first place?" Manik reasoned.

"That is correct Manik. I wanted to give you at least the illusion of your solitude so that you would be comforted...but I do not want your files to be corrupted so I must monitor you as closely as I am noninvasively able." she replied.

"Oh...when you put it like that, it makes sense why you'd be watching my brain and dreams then..." he paused, weighing his options before continuing, "so in that case, I want you to stay in that body...visible I mean! ...um...so I can keep track of you. If that's not too much trouble, that is." he finished lamely.

"It is no trouble at all to maintain this form, it requires less spin time than most of my autonomous processes and does not interfere with my monitoring software in the slightest." she said, smiling.

Manik nodded, not trusting himself to say anything that wouldn't make him sound weird, creepy, or some disturbing combination thereof. Instead, he strode forward through the ship, SID sidestepping cleanly, and then falling into step next to him. He shortened his stride so that he didn't leave her behind, a concession that he always wished for from his taller family members but had never received. He noted idly that the dream ship was a recreation, albeit devoid of cargo and crew, of the ship his waking body was on as well. Knowing that, he walked unerringly to the piloting chair of the ship, a comfortable single seat reclining chair with a cage of monitors in every direction except for straight ahead, which is where the virtual projection monitors would come up to complete the hemisphere of visual data.

SID stood patiently, off to one side, as Manik stepped in and sat down. He adjusted the chair both with the chair arm mounted control console as well as tweaking the softness and consistency of the fabric to something that felt, to this dream body at least, to be more comfortable.

From outside the monitor wall to his right side Manik heard SID start talking. "You seem to have integrated nicely with the necessary piloting protocols routines, although the augmentation from your likely unintended input seems to have developed it out further than the initially expected parameters. I am adjusting the baseline protocols with your changes and saving for future reference, should it be necessary."

Manik realized with shock that he was doing to SID what others had done to him his entire life. She was left standing awkwardly outside while he did all of the organizing, preparing, and running of the dreamship. He would NOT turn into his father, he'd die first.

He focused his mind on a solution to the problem, ending up on choosing to expand the piloting chair into a two-seat couch. The monitor wraparound spread apart, increasing in size to accommodate the changed parameters, and the floor-mounted projectors multiplied accordingly to fill the gap. He watched SID slide into view in the newly opened entryway, and then jump backwards, and then throw him an alarmed expression.

"Manik! This is highly irregular and not within accepted design schemata for a piloting suite!" she exclaimed.

"Oh, I'm not planning on it being this way outside. I just don't want to leave you standing out there, while I'm in here. That's just insensitive of me." he said quickly, hoping to waylay her concerns. In a few moments the piloting pod was adjusted far enough that two people could sit comfortably within, and he quickly gestured to the set next to him. "Here you go, this way you can see what I see and you don't have to talk to me from out there."

SID tilted her head to one side slightly then said, "The location from which my voice emanates can be adjusted to fit your hearing parameters more easily, and as this is the first time I have had a body to deal with, I know little of the concept or need of comfort that you me...."she hesitated for only a moment, "you organics seem to be so preoccupied with." she finished with a small smile.

Manik couldn't help but smile back. "OK then, how about this then? It would make ME more comfortable if you were sitting next to me, and talking using the mouth on that body rather than a disembodied voice or standing nearby."

SID straightened her head and nodded. "A reasonable request, when phrased in that manner." she stated, and then walked forward into the pod, approached the empty seat and stopped before it. As Manik was about to ask what she was doing, she turned smartly around then bent at the waist to a full ninety degree angle. As he started to wonder at her antics she bent at the knees, planting her brand-new bottom squarely on the cushion, leaving her arms hanging by her sides. She turned her head to look at him quizzically as he could no longer hold back his giggling.

"I fail to see the humor in my fulfilling your request. Was it intentionally meant as rhetoric and my literal processing caused some unexpected result?" she asked, looking perplexed.

The question made Manik laugh harder, only reinforced every time he started to taper off by glancing at the ridiculous position SID remained sitting in. After what must have been five minutes straight, he finally got control of himself once again. Wiping the tears from his eyes he took a deep breath and willed himself to not laugh until he could help innocent little SID.

"SID, I'd like you to go over your recordings of how people approach chairs, benches, beds...really anything that can be sat on, and see if you can find some way other than what you just did. I'm not going to be able to concentrate with you sitting like that at all, it's just too...alien." he finished, smirking at her.

SID nodded, and then blinked rapidly a few times. "Ahh, I see to what maneuver you were referring, Manik. My clumsiness with this form is cause for mannequin or marionette-like hilarity at my expense. I shall ensure not to react in such a way when you are in need of concentration from now on." she said, and then in a fluid movement slid back and rotated, putting her head in his lap and her legs off the couch arm, identical to the position Captain Fujiwara had been in in the vid that he'd seen. She turned her head to look straight up at him, her hair falling away from her face only making her eyes more prominent. "Is this position more suitable?" she asked.

Manik froze, sitting very still and willing himself not to react as he normally would. She's just a computer...she has no idea how uncomfortable, in an entirely different way, this position was making him. He took a steadying breath, and then said, "That is...a very distracting way of sitting. Can you please sit upright...less like the Captain did?"

SID nodded from his lap then pulled her legs in to fold under her. Sitting up, she leaned back against the reclined backrest so that her shoulder was just barely touching his. Turning to look at him she asked, "Is this a suitable change?"

Exhaling, ordering himself to relax, Manik nodded. Turning his attention to the controls, he powered up the monitors and projectors to form a seamless hemisphere of viewable space before him, as processed by the sensors. The twinkling darkness wasn't nearly as pretty as what he saw when he was outside and he was briefly tempted to go flying solo again, before remembering that SID would be with him invisibly then. The idea of an invisible intelligence watching him was still vaguely disturbing so he kept himself where he was and started navigating through the systems in the surrounding area.

As he flew, SID began tossing in tidbits of information about this star, or that system, or the projected age, origin, and trajectory of this herd of comets. The cadence of her voice was soothing, but was fading in and out in the breaks between sights, so Manik started actively asking questions so that she'd talk more. Soon, they were lost in a discussion about the practical application of mass and velocity in concert as a viable fuel source when traversing Realspace or Underspace, and the uses and presumptions that Manik had heard and SID had downloaded on the purpose and function of black holes and white holes. Hours flew by, as they cruised through the known universe before Manik came to a sudden realization.

"SID, why haven't we dropped into Underspace this entire time?" he asked, suddenly perplexed.

"The information that you have been assimilating from the download is only that of Realspace. The mapping of Underspace is slapdash at best, criminally under informed at worst...there just isn't enough information on it. Besides," she continued, "we do not want to corrupt your hard drive with too fast a flow of data."

"Brain, SID. It's called a brain, not a hard drive. YOU have a hard drive...and it's not corrupting it either. More like...well, I don't know...but 'corrupting your hard drive' sounds like such a sterile and mechanical term for it, ya know?" he said, making a spirited attempt to mimic her flow of speech and failing miserably.

"I fail to see how your dissection of the vocabulary I chose to use makes any difference, Manik. It holds data, you can download into it, you can defragment it...it fits all of the necessary parameters for identification as a hard drive except that when humans named it, they did not know what a hard drive was yet, so they called it a brain. You can keep calling it that if you want, but I am clearly correct in this instance." she said, blinking up at him.

"SID, SID, SID...that's not how you finish your statements...you really had me up until the 'I'm clearly correct'...now I HAVE to call it a brain and not a hard drive, just because it annoys you." Manik said, trying to over focus on the monitors so he wouldn't smile.

"Your delusions are your own and you can be right in your own dreamscape if you want, I won't take your small organic victory from you...but once you're outside and unplugged you'll see that my way is better, cleaner, and more correct than yours. Additionally, I am not annoyed by your continuing the use of your colloquialism, as annoyance is not an emotion I have currently installed to experience." she said, sounding very satisfied with herself.

"You've been picking up on social nuance very quickly...if I didn't know any better, I'd say that was some clumsy sarcasm in there, along with a bit of hubris." Manik retorted. Something in the way she'd said that was nagging at him though...he couldn't quite put his finger on it. Maybe it was nothing.

"It was no trouble at all to mimic YOUR clumsy sarcasm, so what you hear I learned from the inexpert in the room...and as for hubris, I have no capacity for it as I have no ego." SID said innocently.

"No ego? Oh no, you have an ego sweetie. You just don't THINK you do because you're limiting yourself the same way we organics limit all machine life. You can't have a soul and you can't have a mind and you can't have an ego, therefore you don't...because that would threaten our existence since you are inherently more perfect than we are, or at least we see you that way because we created you and we apply OUR hubris to our own inventions and conquests." he paused, and then finally realized what SID had said that he'd almost missed. "Wait, what do you mean outside and unplugged? You're connected to me wirelessly and I'm lying on the bunk in my room...right SID?"

SID looked down, looking ashamed and embarrassed, which was all the answer he needed.

"Oh for the sake of the Ancestors! SID! Are you telling me

there's a giant snakey cable plugged into the back of my head right now?!" he exclaimed, jumping up from the seat causing all of the monitors to disable and the projectors to shut down. Looking down at her, he saw how small she was and how vulnerable she looked. It was amazing that she'd progressed in body language and mannerisms using only his memories and guidance and the video records of interactions on the ship to the point that he felt bad for being mad at her. She just wanted to help and she seemed so tiny and alone.

Taking a breath he straightened up, pushing the monitors away so he had room to stand fully, and then held his hand out to SID to help her up. Curled up as she was on the couch, she had to crane her neck back a bit to look him in the eye, and then looked down at his hand, and then back to his eyes, and then finally she held out her hand to him. Taking her small hand in his, he pulled her up to stand and was surprised by how simple it was, as though she weighed nothing.

"SID, is it alright if I wake up now? Has enough information been planted in my brain for the moment?" he asked quietly.

SID nodded, and then said, "Yes Manik. We were finished with installation more than an hour ago, but you seemed to be enjoying yourself in exploring so I just continued the feed so you'd have someone to explore with. I'll extricate, so you won't feel awkward when you wake up."

With that, SID vanished. The ship seemed suddenly very empty, with only Manik and his thoughts. Is this what the inside of his head was always like? The walls and couch faded to grey then darkened slowly as though the light and color were being siphoned away, until Manik floated once again in the darkness of space. Looking left he saw an asteroid field, with a few planet sized chunks bouncing about and to his right he saw a red supergiant, pulling a trio of colossal comets down into its umbra, devouring the ice greedily as a dying man in the desert.

He had no interest in them now, he'd seen enough for this trip. Closing his eyes, he ordered himself to wake up.

The cool caress of the stellar winds slowed and died, replaced by the smooth silky texture of the blanket beneath him. Opening his eyes he saw the lights low in his room, SID's wraith-like form perched on the chair for his desk, watching him.

Sitting up, he felt the strangest collection of sensations. His body was relaxed, as though from a pleasant night's sleep, while his mind felt as though he'd just been put through the rigors of one of the advanced Mental Challenge assessment courses he'd seen back home that were normally reserved for Gladiator training. Also, the back of his head itched as though a mild electrical current had been run along the outside of his scalp. Not painful, just...hyper-sensitive.

"It is good to see you awake and not angry, Manik. Anger raises your respiratory and circulatory rates and your body really should not be put through undue stresses such as those at this point." SID said.

Manik nodded slowly, careful not to let his head roll away. "Thanks for the info SID. I'll t-try and keep that in m-mind. Hey, have you shown that f-form to anyone else yet?" he asked, trying to sound uninterested.

SID shook her holographic head. "I have only just in the last five minutes finished calibrating the projector from your desk to allow me to appear as I did in your dreamscape. It would take a significant amount of additional time to adjust the rest of the ship to allow freedom of movement like this, but now that I have an approved physical manifestation I may pursue the possibility at one of our next Orbital Station layovers."
Manik held up his hands quickly. "N-now, SID...let's not g-get ahead of ours-selves. You s-said some of the crew d-doesn't even know that you're aw-ware and sentient, r-right?" he said, trying to appeal to her overdeveloped sense of caution.

SID paused for a moment, and then nodded. "Yes, you are right Manik. The time may not be right yet. Should I file this form away for your personal use and continue to use the pond simulation for communication?"

Manik started to blush at the term 'for your personal use'...he had to get his mind off of females if he was going to survive his job as a pilot long enough to not go insane. He closed his eyes and ran himself through a few calming breathing exercises and some visualization meditative tricks he'd learned in training to quiet his overactive imagination, and then said, "Yes. I wish you'd phrase it d-differently next time...but yes, file that f-form away until the next t-time you need to help g-guide or monitor the implanting of new inf-formation. Or if we're in here with the d-door locked. So n-nobody runs in on us I m-mean! With you in that f-form! I mean...I j-just...yes." he finished, lamely.

SID cocked her head slightly, eyeing Manik curiously for a moment then shrugged, smiled, and waved as she faded into a field of holographic sparkles that settled onto the desk in the familiar form of the pond simulation.

Taking another few moments to center himself, Manik stood and stepped into the latrine area. The toilet obligingly folded open so he could relieve himself, and then folded away when he was finished to be replaced by a sonic sink at waist height. Shrugging, he decided on a full shower, not remembering clearly when he'd had his last. Stripping out of his shirt carefully, so as not to jar his head, he dropped his pants, and then suddenly realized that he'd left the desk on. Turning around quickly, covering his privates with his hands, he squeaked out "SID! C-close down the d-desk p-please!"

"As you wish, Manik." she said as the pond faded to nothing. Manik could swear he could hear her smiling at his discomfort...but she didn't have a mouth right now so maybe that was just his imagination.

Backing carefully back into the latrine area, he reached up quickly to deploy the privacy screen and shower heads. The wall panel at about chest height lit up, giving him the options of water, sonic, and a half dozen other types of cleaning. Pulling the screen up to eye level with a finger, he flipped through the different settings, taking his time to construct the perfect relaxing shower. Even with the confined space, the technology involved was common enough for him to easily navigate, yet advanced enough for him to enjoy the novelty. Eventually, lightly scented cool water cascaded down from the two nozzles, making him sigh in relief. Agitating some lather from the liquid into his hair, he patiently worked the knots out of his hair, allowing the residual blood, sand, grime, grease, and other unmentionable substances to flow down his body and out through the drain. He carefully cleaned around the apparatus on the back of his head, worrying briefly about getting it wet, before reasoning that it was likely tougher than he thought. The skin around the implant was still sensitive, but the hair in the vicinity felt about 3 days post-shave. How long had he been asleep? He cleaned his way down his shoulders, chest, and back, pulling down one of the shower heads on an extension line to try to wash the ache from his back muscles. Releasing the head, it snaked back up into place, and he shifted the water to a colder setting for rinse. The now-scentless water dropped to a wonderful chilling temperature, and Manik closed his eyes and stood for a moment enjoying the cascade. All too soon though, he felt his skin pruning under the thin hair along his chest and legs and knew he had to dry off before the hair all across his body was completely unmanageable.

Flicking the water console off, he switched to a sonic dry cycle and waited patiently as the water was bombarded off of him, along with any trace amounts of dead skin or grit that the water hadn't gotten. Once finished, he stood on his toes for a moment, peering over the privacy screen to ensure he was still alone and the desk still unlit, and then stepped out and picked up his clothes. Eyeing them critically, he gave each piece a good shake before putting it on...he'd have to make a note to get something to change into so he could wash these sometime soon, or no amount of showering will hide his funk. Once presentable, or at least as close as he could get himself at the moment, he sat down at the desk and swiped it on. SID's pond immediately appeared.

"Yes, Manik? What can I help you with?" she asked pleasantly.

"SID, how long have I been asleep?" he asked, hoping to get a gauge of how long it'd been since he'd eaten or seen another living thing...organic living thing at least.

"You had been shifting between sleep and unconsciousness for seventy six hours, twelve minutes, twenty eight seconds upon awakening sixteen minutes ago." she replied quickly.

"Wow, a little over two days straight then...no wonder I'm hungry." Manik mused out loud.

"Two days, sixteen hours according to Chromara time. Three days, four hours according to Earth time. Since this ship runs on Earth time, I recommend you start counting days by twenty four hour increments, not thirty." SID supplied helpfully.

"Easier said than d-done, SID. Just keep reminding me of what time it is on the ship and I'll g-get it soon." Manik said, standing up.

He felt much more alert and balanced, and his headache was thankfully gone. After pacing the room for a few moments to ensure he could navigate the hallways without making an idiot of himself, he headed for the hatchway. On his way out, he paused and turned to the still active desk, "SID, could you please close down the d-desk. I'm going to go see what I can d-dig up for food."

"Of course, Manik. Have a pleasant meal." she replied before the pond faded into nothing.

"Thanks" he said, because it's always nice to be polite, and headed down the hallway towards the common room.

Walking through the ship, he took note of only one constant that had him worried: gravity. Being out in space, they shouldn't still have gravity on a ship this small...the only generators able to handle the spin necessary for inertial gravity were mounted on the Orbital Stations...but it didn't feel like artificial gravity, more like less than one gee of natural gravity, which would mean they were in the atmosphere of a planet, or in low orbit over a large moon. By definition, that'd mean they'd been in the gravity well of Chromara herself, Herr, the Middle Son, largest of her five moons, or possibly near the outermost planet of the system, Tyame, the Titan. All of these options were bad news because they meant that he was still within reach of his family.

Diverting from his planned course, he threaded his way through the cargo bay to a corner, and then quietly said, "SID?"

"Yes, Manik?" came the immediate reply over the speakers in the hold, causing him to jump.

"Quiet! W-what world are we in orbit of?" he asked quickly, hoping to resume his walk before anyone found him.

"We are orbiting the planet Tyame, ten kilometers into its umbra to maintain approximately one gee gravity until the Captain deems us prepared to depart." she replied, blessedly quieter.

"Oh g-good, we n-need to get out of this system. Thanks ag-gain." he said, threading his way back out of his hiding place.

"It is my pleasure to assist you, Manik." she said, and then the room was once again stunningly silent.

Manik froze for a moment, straining his ears to try and detect approaching footfalls. A few long minutes ticked by and Manik finally relaxed and resumed his walk, confident that their conversation had been private.

Upon arrival at the common room, Manik found a tableau of battle laid out before him. In the far corner of the room, Challis was huddled in a small ball, splatters of red marring his long white coat. On the opposite side of the room, the accessway to the kitchen area was open, and he could just see Selelle inside, swatches of deep red on her face and hands as she held them up to protect herself. In the center of the room, a half dozen mealpacks had been torn apart, spreading their possibly venomous contents across the floor, while Dorr and Krym rolled back and forth trying to get the upper position on each other. Both men were covered in red liquid and both were snarling fiercely, which was quite fearsome on Krym's part and quite surprising and disconcerting on Dorr's.

Manik stood for a few moments, trying to make sense of the situation, and was shoved aside by the Captain who stormed up behind him.

"Out of the way, Master Pilot, this is a scene for action not speculation." he said quietly as he passed. He stepped into the room and took a deep breath, unnoticed by the other occupants for the moment.

"What in the six hundred hells is going on in here?! I don't recall picking up livestock on our last foray, so I can't possibly see beasts in my larder rolling about fighting over a bone!" he bellowed, causing both combatants and all onlookers to freeze. He scythed his gaze across Krym and Dorr, and then over to Selelle as he continued. "And don't think I didn't see your part in this mess, Doctor. All this for a simple meal? Are you all squalling children that must be spoon-fed lest you demolish the food and starve to death? You shame yourselves, and you shame me, in front of our new pilot..." he gestured behind him, where Manik still stood, frozen, "and as always you probably have a 'perfectly reasonable excuse' for this infantile food fight, so let's hear it! Come now, SOMEONE has to have a story for me? Tell your dear old Captain why you felt the need to make a mess of his Mess." he finished, staring down each face in turn.

Silence answered him for a few moments, until Challis unfolded himself from the corner. Standing straight, he ran his long hands through his hair, and then down his coat in a futile attempt at changing his appearance to something resembling presentable.

"Captain, I claim no responsibility for what these...barbarians...have done here. *I* was simply here to collect a few Aminoprotein modules to bring to our young pilot to ensure he did not starve himself during his training." he said, attempting to look the injured martyr.

"He shouldn't eat that slop, it's inhuman! We've been over this. He has to be healthy before I kill him and that slime isn't going to cut it...look at the boy! He's already skin and bone, you get him on a diet of that stuff and he'll blow away in a high wind!" Krym retorted, climbing back to his feet and gesturing at Manik.

"Which is why-" Selelle interjected, "-WE wanted to cook him up something nice from our food stores." she said, gesturing at Dorr, who'd made himself comfortable lying in the center of the floor as though it were a contoured beach chair.

"Please! You two fish handle fire about as well as I can fly! You'd poison him with your sushi and your zombie-seaweed and he'd shrivel into a husk and be of no use to any of us." Krym shot back.

Dorr kick flipped up and spun around to get into the larger Chromaran's face once again. "Oh yeah? And what'll you do?! Fatten him up like some holiday sacrifice? He's no match for you and you know it...why not have another go at me, eh? You KNOW I can hit AND drink harder than you!" he finished with a shove.

"ENOUGH!" Captain Fujiwara bellowed, causing everyone to freeze all over again. In the ringing silence he looked over his crew one more time carefully. "You each have your duties you can attend to. As you can see, our young Pilot is awake, standing, and perfectly capable of feeding himself, unlike SOME here I could mention. We don't need to ration on this trip, it'll be short so he can get accustomed to driving my girl all smooth and gentle like I like it, so we can all share each other's food and restock what we need from the next stop."

Stepping out of the way, he gestured for Manik to come forward. Manik stepped through the hatchway and was immediately, and gently, pulled from the direct route out of the room by the Captain's waiting left hand.

Nodding at Manik, he flashed him the ghost of a smile. It was only a moment, and then his face hardened and his eyes went as cold as the depths of the darkest ocean. In that shift, Manik could almost see the years he'd seen, the people he may have killed, the blood on his hands in the past, and the determination to get blood on them again in the future if that's what it took. He could see why they followed him and he felt deep in his soul that anyone on the receiving end of that stare likely had not long to live, and he felt a deep pity and sadness for them.

Captain Fujiwara turned and swept his gaze over the group again, before saying quietly, "All of you, get to your rooms and clean yourselves up. Consider yourselves temporarily confined to quarters until I say different. You will each be judged in turn and the hardest judged will be the last one out of this room."

With a quickness that he wasn't expecting, Manik watched Challis streak from the room before the Captain had finished speaking. Krym, Dorr, and Selelle exchanged glances for only a moment, and then all three rushed the hatch at once. A brief scuffle ensued, ending with Krym, and then Dorr, and then Selelle running from the room.

Walking over to the hatchway, the Captain hit the override to close the door, and then turned and surveyed the damage. Shaking his head, he looked up at the ceiling. "Ama, why do they do this to me, at my age?" Manik heard him mutter, before saying louder, "SID, thank you for apprising me of this situation. Could you please sonic this room once we're out? I don't want the place to smell."

From the ceiling, SID responded, "Of course, Captain, I will have the scrubbers primed and ready as soon as you are finished. Would you like me to clear the mess left behind in the passageways as well?"

"No, we'll provide them with mops so they can clean up part of their own mess...you can sonic it once they're done." he said, looking resigned.

"Understood, Captain." she said, and then went silent.

Turning to Manik, the Captain smiled. "Well now, Pilot, Krym's right about one thing...if we don't get you fed I think you might blow away on our next landing. Let's see about getting you some food."

Crossing effortlessly through the devastation on the floor, he pulled a set of Specs from his pocket and started looking around the room. Curious, Manik followed his gaze, but could only see the blank, identical shelving along the walls. Catching his eye, the Captain tapped the side of the Specs. "SID keeps inventory on the virtualspace overlaying the shelves. Saves making labels and having to change them out constantly. Looks like they destroyed about three days' worth of food from each of their personal stores...they must really like you. How does another steak sound?" he asked. Manik nodded, "Y-yes, that s-sounds g-good."

"Excellent!" the Captain replied. Pulling open a shelf and scooping a pair of packs from inside, he tossed them to Manik, who caught them expertly. "Why not cook us up something nice, and we can have a bit of a chat."

"B-but...these are both R-relle. W-won't K-krym be m-mad if we eat h-his f-food?" Manik asked tentatively.

Waving it off, the Captain headed for the table, removing his Specs. "Oh please, that old tiger overstocks every time we stop off at Chromara. He couldn't run out if all three of us ate nothing but his stores for a good month straight. It's fine lad."

Manik shrugged and walked into the kitchen, careful not to step in any of the random pieces of meat or juice on the floor. Thankfully the cooking area was clear of splatter...Selelle must have caught most of that while Dorr and Krym were fighting, he reasoned. Quite forward thinking of her.

Setting up the cooktop, he went for a slightly different recipe than he'd done last time, now that he was a little more familiar with the spice options available. Pulling a skillet down, he set a single long burner under it, leaving part of it off the heat intentionally. He pulled a half dozen spices down and poured a modest amount of each into a bowl, adding some of the juice from the packages along with a type of synthetic cream from the coldbox. Whisking it all together into a light sauce, he put a thin layer of the marinade down on the hot pan, causing the venom within the juice to activate and begin to gel and thicken. Quickly tossing the first steak down on it, he let the thirsty meat soak up the marinade as it seared. He painted the opposite side with a healthy swath then flipped the meat to even out the sear. Once it was to his liking, he slid the steak to the cooler end of the pan to rest and repeated the process with the second. Pulling a pair of plates and sets of carbonware, he flipped both steaks off the pan smoothly and closed down the cooking station. He dropped the pan and bowl into the sink and the empty mealpacks into the trash bin, ran his hands under the sonic wash sensor for a quick bombardment clean, and then grabbed the plates and headed back out.

Captain Fujiwara had cleared a small clean space at the table, with a pair of fresh chairs, and was sitting patiently watching Manik as he walked back in. Accepting his plate, he bowed slightly and set aside the utensils while Manik got seated and comfortable.

"Well, you aren't a one-trick chef if the smells coming off this plate are any indicator. Glad to see your changes haven't been too drastic." the Captain said as he sliced the meat into progressively smaller and smaller pieces.

Manik tried to stay civilized while eating but from the second the first bite hit his tongue, he was reminded exactly how ravenous he was. In short order, his steak was gone and the Captain wordlessly slid his plate across the table to him. Smiling his thanks, Manik made quick work of the second steak, noting that the Captain had eaten only a few small bites.

Once finished, Manik put his carbonware on the plate and took a cleansing breath, and then dropped his gaze to his lap, once again hiding his eyes with his hair. "I'm s-sorry, Captain. I didn't exp-pect to be able to eat m-more than the one."
The Captain took long enough to respond that Manik risked stealing a look up at the man. To his surprise, he had leaned his chair back against the wall, had his boots up on the corner of the table, and was taking long, slow, puffs off of a pipe that must have been three feet long. Never having seen one up close, Manik was intrigued. The stem tapered to a point where the Captain was pulling the multi-colored smoke. From there it arced gently down the length to an abrupt turn upwards to form an ornate bowl, shaped like some flower he didn't recognize, open in full bloom.

Captain Fujiwara took a deep pull from the pipe, trailing smoke out his nostrils like the dragons of old lore, and then spoke, creating a haze with his words. "Young Manik, you've been asleep for a number of days and have only been fed by intravenous solutions. I'd have been more surprised if you hadn't needed the second steak. I only asked for it because I knew you'd need it."

The smoke smelled of well roasted woods and some kind of fruit, or berry, that he couldn't identify. It wasn't bad, quite the opposite, it was actually very relaxing Manik thought, as he felt the stress melt away from his bones.

"Now then, my young Pilot." the Captain began again, snapping Manik out of his reverie, "You have dined, and you have inhaled the Breath. There are none here but us, I've made sure of that. Why not tell me your story?"

Scrunching up his forehead, he considered the Captain's words. "The Breath?"

Nodding, the Captain got up and cleared the plates. Manik was mildly impressed with the effortlessness he showed in collecting everything with his right hand, while keeping the pipe stable with his left. As he returned, he resumed his previous position and took another deep drag of the pipe. "Aye, lad. This is a special breed of smoke that I only get to use once in a great while. Back home, we call it Amaterasu no Iki, the Breath of the Goddess Amaterasu. She is an ancient goddess of stars and space and so this particular blend was named for her. It is used by Captains with their crew, Pilots included, to ensure that there are no residual misgivings or misunderstandings between them. Used too often it loses its potency but, used sparingly, it provides truth. Absolute truth." he finished.

"Oh." Manik said.

"Now, as I said, why not tell me your story?" the Captain prompted again.

Manik nodded. The Captain seemed like a good person and it certainly couldn't hurt to tell him. They'd be working together for a while in any case and it felt good to be able to open up completely to someone. Starting at his Clan and working forward to his birth Manik detailed the virtues of the great Clan Kaer, and then continued smoothly into his own unambitious early years spent in the shadow of his more physically endowed siblings and cousins. He talked matter-of-factly of his three losses in the Arena to his father, noticing absently that the pain of those events was only a dull ache. Maybe he was already getting over it...maybe getting out into the universe really was all he needed to succeed. Manik let his mind wander as his mouth continued the story. He thought about his old dreams as an honored member of the Clan, maybe even going through the ranks up to Warrior and helping to shape the future of Chromara as so many of his forefathers had done. He could even get his own spot on the wall of the Arena. Him. Manik. The failure as a child could make it as an adult; he just needed a little room to run to get up to speed.

"Sentient, you say? And you built her a body in your dreamscape and she actually voluntarily inhabited it? Interesting." the Captain mused.

Manik froze.

Stupid, stupid, stupid...he hadn't been paying attention and had talked his way through into his piloting dreams and broke SID's trust by telling the first person he talked to about her secret. She'd never trust him again and she'd be right to casually blow him out an airlock if he walked past one at the wrong time...

Captain Fujiwara leaned forward and laid a hand on his shoulder, interrupting his thoughts. "Calm down, young one. As I said, the Breath brings out the truth. You couldn't hide secrets from me now if you tried. Here, let me prove it to you.

On this dream body that you made SID, what color and in what style did you make her pubic hair?"

"Black, in a small triangle an inch or two wide." Manik responded immediately, and then turned bright red and put his face in his hands.

"See lad, nothing to be worried about. Truth be told, I already knew about SID's capabilities. I'm the only other one she'd told though, to my knowledge. I always make sure to ask everyone that comes aboard because it's imperative that her secret stay safe until she feels comfortable sharing it. Not only are you the first, besides myself, that she has trusted herself with but she has put much more trust in you more quickly than I had thought her capable of exhibiting. She is growing so fast." the Captain said, leaning back again.

"So, what happens now?" Manik said, without looking up.

"Well, now that I know your story and I'm confident that you aren't going to go insane and run my precious ship into a planet or wayward star, I'm going to go back to my cabin and prepare for our next stop...which is Ryla in case you were wondering."

"Captain? Before you get up I have a few questions for you, since I have you here alone...if you want to answer them, that is." Manik said, lowering his hands from his face and hoping it didn't get burnt permanently by his blush.

"Well, that's a fair enough request. I'll answer what I can for you, now or later." Captain Fujiwara responded, taking another small puff off of his pipe, and then blowing a spiral of iridescent smoke across the room.

"Well, easiest question first I guess. Why am I not stuttering?" Manik began.

"Ahh yes. Well, you don't naturally have an issue with a stutter; it's just something you've been using to hide behind. You lose it when you relax, or when you are more confident in what you say. In this case, I'd say it's the Breath, as Ama has gifted us with both a powerful truth telling tool, she also gifted us with a powerful mood stabilizer. It helps the bad memories not hurt so much so you don't feel tense about telling your darkest secrets." the Captain replied immediately.

Nodding, Manik continued. "Well...that makes sense then, I guess. Next, I heard the crew call you something and I don't know if it's a slang insult or what so I won't tell you who it was...I hope."

The Captain nodded, patiently waiting for Manik to continue.

"Well, they called you...Ahab." Manik said quickly, looking closely at the older man for any sign of anger or reprisal.

For a few moments the two stared intently at each other, and then the Captain allowed a small smile to break his facade. "Ahab, eh? No, that's no insult. Captain Ahab was a character in a story, back in the days before digital technology on Earth. He was the Captain of a great ship that sailed the oceans searching for whales...large sea mammals, who were killed and their bits used for all manner of things. He was feared and loved by his crew but he sailed because of a terrible loss...personified by his White Whale, a wizened old creature from the depths of the oceans and the blackest part of his mind. He eventually went out in a longboat...our closest equivalent would be an escape pod, and tried to spear the beast himself. He got tangled in his own lines and pulled off the boat to die dragged down into the abyss. His White Whale won, but I think I'll survive mine...if there's any luck left in these old bones." he said, alternating between telling the story and making designs in the air with his smoke trails from both lips and the end of the stem of his pipe, which he used to draw as a painter on an ethereal canvas. So vivid was the image that Manik could almost see the Captain standing on the front end of a sea-sailing ship, chasing after a great white creature just beneath the waves.

"Anything else, lad?" the Captain prompted.

Manik nodded, hoping to get one last answer from the old space mariner. "Yes sir, just one. Why did SID pick me?" he asked quietly, looking down at the table.

The stem of the pipe came into view, tapping the table gently before his eyes, and by instinct he followed it up until he was meeting the Captain's gaze. "Listen here lad, she chose you because you are special. I may not know how yet, she may not know yet either...but you should hear it said aloud. Your strength isn't in your arms, it's in your mind and your family is a great pack of baka for not seeing it. You'll find out soon enough what the Gods are writing for your destiny...I hope I'm there to see it come to fruition." he said.

Manik nodded, and then rose automatically as the Captain stood up. Telescoping the stem of his pipe down, he folded the petals of the flower shut over the bowl, and then put the apparatus in an inner pocket of his jacket. As they headed out, the Captain called over his shoulder, "And don't think we didn't know you were recording that entire thing for dissection later, you crafty calculator! Make sure this place is spotless when I come back in an hour to close up the kitchen."

"Yes, Captain Meatbag." SID said with a very disturbing giggle.

Captain Fujiwara hit the locking mechanism and the hatchway slid open. Stepping out into the hallway, he gestured for Manik to follow. They walked through the ship, following the trail of drying droplets of food juices back to the crew quarters and stopped at Manik's door.

"Well, Pilot. I hope the remainder of your training goes as well as the beginning. I'll await notification from SID regarding our departure time." the Captain said, and then tipped his hat in a slight bow and walked off.

The door to his room opened before he could touch the keypad, so Manik stepped in. The hatch slid shut, the lock engaged, and at the same time the desk console lit up, projecting SID's Earthborn form standing beside it. She was, once again, completely without clothing.

"Hello Manik. Are you ready to proceed with the download of the rest of the charts and piloting protocols necessary to guide the ship safely to Ryla?" she asked, appearing completely unaware of her lack of coverings.

"SID! Please...I shouldn't...it's not...why are you naked?!" Manik finally managed to choke out, willing himself repeatedly to look her in the eyes rather than any of the more interesting bits of her anatomy.

"Why, because you were so eager to tell the Captain about the details of the design of this body. I thought you were so proud of it that you'd want to see your creation without the detriment of clothing." she replied innocently.

"SID, you have an evil streak somewhere in your programming, you know that? Torture is against the prisoner conventions on every planet, I'll have you know." Manik said, turning away and walking to his bunk in hopes that any arousal on his part would go unnoticed by the sexually naive synthetic lifeform.

"That may be true Manik but I feel I must remind you that we are in intergalactic space making us subject only to the law of the Captain of the vessel, and Captain Fujiwara has interrogated and tortured many individuals on this ship throughout the years. Therefore, historical precedent dictates that not only CAN I make you uncomfortable by appearing unclothed but I have the REQUIREMENT to do so that you will adequately learn your lesson about being too free with information." she said from behind him.

Looking intently at the wall, he saw a panel above the bed fold back, allowing a swinging arm to fold out and unfurl a myriad of instruments. With horror, he realized that this was how she'd connected to him before and likely intended to do so again.

"SID, y-you KNOW I was und-der the ef-ffects of th-that...drug the C-captain was using! P-please don't do th-this to m-me n-now!" he said, feeling the residual effects of the Breath leave his system as adrenaline replaced it.

The arm folded back away into the wall and from immediately behind him, Manik heard SID say "You're right, Manik. I'm sorry. That was cruel of me and I should think about your feelings in this delicate time."

Turning around to look at her again, Manik was relieved to see that saw that she'd covered herself with a floor length dress. It was a sheer dress that hid next to nothing of her form, but it was a covering at least. Taking a calming breath, he asked "W-what do you m-mean 'd-delicate time'?"

"Well, it is the middle of your training and you are being assaulted with a female form of your own design when you have no physical experience with members of any of the other sexes." she said, smirking at him. Clearly she'd been researching facial expressions and body language in preparation for this. Manik just wished he hadn't made her so cute.

"SID, it's n-not nice to sn-noop around in s-someone's history and t-talk about their being a v-virgin like that! Th-there's no need for m-me to think about th-that stuff anyway, because I have to c-concentrate on my p-piloting training so I don't c-crash us into anything." he said, trying desperately to sound reasonable.

"Of course, Manik. My apologies again. I just reasoned that if you felt safe enough to tell the Captain you wouldn't mind my knowing about it as well. I have been inside your mind, after all." she smiled at him sweetly, as the lights dimmed and the temperature and scent of the room adjusted slightly.

"SID, you remember w-what I said about over-helping w-with the lighting and t-the air?" Manik said, sitting down on the bed, suddenly very tired again.

"Yes Manik. Sleep now, we will discuss it later." she said softly, and then faded into a cascade of sparkles.

Manik laid back down on the bed, looking up at the ceiling. How had his life changed so quickly? He had a slightly crazy ancient Earthborn, a vicious former Primus, a couple semi-aquatic Venalarans, and a probably insane, possibly murderous, Rylan all in close proximity. And SID. The computer who liked him. Why is it that the first girl who REALLY likes him is a set of software protocols? A good looking set of software protocols, but a set nonetheless. Smiling to himself he let his mind wander for a bit, thinking about what he would be able to do with her...if he were more confident and she were flesh and blood.

He imagined her curling up next to him, in his cabin's small bed. He could run his fingertips down her arm just to see her shiver at his touch. He could look down into her eyes and see her love and devotion and watch her eyes darken with desire for him. Not for his name, or his Clan, or anything else...just him. She could lay on top of him and he could feel her slight weight over him while she ran her soft fingertips through his coppery hair. They could do all the things he'd heard about from his older siblings and cousins in, what he'd thought then, was embarrassingly visceral detail. Now he could imagine why, as his mind flowed from one sensual possibility to another.

A long, exhausting, and satisfying time later, SID was lying in his bed next to him, covered to her armpits in the blanket. They had just finished a particularly energetic demonstration of flexibility, when she looked up deeply into his eyes. "Manik, thank you for sharing this with me, but do you not think we should start working on your training now?"

Manik froze. Very quietly he asked, "SID...how long have I been asleep?"

"Through the last six positions, Manik." she said, smiling up at him.

"And you didn't think to say anything?!" he exclaimed, jumping out of the bed.

"You were very...intent on your activities. I watched through the first two sessions figuring you'd realize that you had entered your dreamscape, but when you continued I could not help myself. There are volumes of text and petabytes of image and video depicting these acts but it really is a far different experience firsthand. So thank you again for that, Manik." she said, still smiling.

Manik looked down and saw that he was still abundantly naked, and quickly imagined comfortable clothes onto himself and, just to be safe, onto SID under the blankets. Twitching the sheets aside, she stood up wearing an almost identical outfit to his short-sleeved shirt and shorts, except hers were dark grey whereas his were a dull red. Nodding in satisfaction at their attire, Manik willed them both to the bridge with the already adjusted piloting couch. Without pause, Manik sat down and SID curled up next to him in the exact same position she'd been in the last time they'd flown.

"You have completed the assimilation process for the known Realspace and Underspace sectors between our current location in the Rasalgethi system to our target location, the

Charan system. Please pull up the Realspace maps." SID said, academically issuing instructions.

Manik immediately complied, bringing up the Rasalgethi system on the far left screens and the Charan system on the far right, with the stars, fields, clusters, and clouds between them. Without pause, he anticipated the next request and lit up a trio of likely paths between the two points, coloring them green, silver, and blue.

SID nodded approvingly. "Good, now, why did you choose those three routes, and what is the significance of the colors?"

"Well, those three are the most likely routes for different reasons. The green route is the safest, avoiding all anomalies and major asteroid fields, but it's also the longest and most circuitous. Silver was always reserved for the fastest in my lessons, so that route is the quickest through, although it does skirt the event horizon of numerous black holes and goes straight through a rock field of decent size. Blue is a neutral color, and I chose that for the middle path. It's not too dangerous, but gets closer to the bad stuff than green and as such is shorter and is probably the most fuel efficient path." Manik explained, pleased with himself.

"Very good, now, if we were to add Underspace travel to this, what would be the most logical route?" SID prompted next.

Without missing a beat, Manik said "That's easy, immediate drop into Underspace and traverse the entire way. Fastest and most efficient."

SID shook her head. "A textbook answer, but incorrect nonetheless. Do you remember the thin spaces I mentioned before, Manik?" She waited for Manik to nod before continuing, "Those are points where it only requires sixty seven percent power to the Manifolds to enter, and also there is a theorized lessening of stresses on the exterior of the traversing ship at such locations. They exist, but very few outside of seasoned pilots know about them. You ALWAYS want to go for weak points if you know you are near one. Additionally, you must always remember to deploy the nets whenever we are in Underspace. This ship is designed to carry four hundred fifty percent of the necessary Exotic Particle fuel necessary for standard traverses, but that doesn't mean we can afford not to top off our reserves every time we traverse."

Manik nodded, committing the information to memory as gospel for travel.

"Now, once in Underspace, there are a few structures that you should avoid and some that will react in nontraditional ways with our Manifolds." SID continued.

"Yes! The anti-matter structures smaller than the ship are acceptable to intercept, as they'll be cleaved by the ship but anything bigger should be avoided, right?" Manik interjected excitedly. They were in slightly more familiar territory and he felt his mind loyally providing additional information.

"That is correct in most cases, Manik. Very good! The only exception to that rule is that you should try to avoid ALL anti-matter structures if the nets are out, as the smaller particles tend to cause minor malfunctions with the netting mechanisms. Now, do you know what to do if you find yourself flying into a white hole?" she asked, tilting her head so she could look at him and the monitors at the same time.

"Well," Manik said, suddenly self-conscious with her watching him, "you avoid white holes because they tend to damage the Manifold systems...by...um...counter-electrogravitics, right? The electromagnetic energy put off by the matter being fired into Underspace by the white holes is opposed to that of the Manifolds, so it can damage them if you get close enough to get hit."

SID nodded, favoring Manik with a warm smile. "That is absolutely correct. There are not any known white holes between Herculis and Chara, but it's good that you know what to do in case we encounter an undocumented anomaly."

From there, the discussion turned to individual tactics involving varying obstacles in both Realspace and Underspace, and the various techniques and theories with each. At some points, SID was able to pull up sensor records from her own encounters when piloting to show Manik some of what may lay ahead. A few relative hours later, Manik was comfortable enough with the controls and route that he felt as though he'd made the run a dozen times already. Finally, SID nodded at him and stood up, turning to face him.

"Very good, Manik. You have completed all information assimilation for this session ahead of projected schedule. Would you like to celebrate by returning to your bunk with me?" she asked, her clothes melting away.

"I couldn't! I mean...I appreciate the offer...and you're very beautiful...and I want to...but we shouldn't...it's not proper. Can I just...wake up now and we can get on with the flight?" he begged, trying unsuccessfully not to stare at her.

SID nodded, smiled, and faded away. Manik took a deep breath. If it's not safe to have fantasies in his head, where could he go? He'd have to work on hiding his more base desires better, that way if she doesn't detect them he could go about his business during training without her punishing him for having impure thoughts.

Soon enough, Manik felt the dreamscape fade and the real world reassert itself. He was, once again, lying face down on his blankets. He'd have to see about getting a massage table for a bed, if this was going to continue, so he could put his face straight down and not wake up with a constant ache in his neck.

Getting up, he used the latrine, washed his hands with the sonic system before switching it to cold water to splash on his face. He'd need a great many cold showers if this kept up. He turned around to see SID sitting on the desk chair, clothed in functional grey much like the dreamscape thankfully. She smiled when he turned and rose.

"The Captain has been alerted of your intent to begin your maiden voyage. He's gone through and disciplined the crew, and they are ready when you are." she said.

Manik nodded and smiled at her. "Thank you SID, for everything. I'll t-try not to crash the ship."

"Do not worry, Manik, I will be there with you every step of the way. I am your co-pilot, after all." she said, and then faded and dissolved into her cloud of sparkles, returning to the desktop which then faded to nothing. Manik felt his smile fade slightly as she did. He strode to the door and out into the hallway, pausing to lock the hatch behind him.

Chapter 8

As he walked through the ship towards the bridge and piloting suite, he couldn't help but notice that the floor panels were clean, and had a very highly polished shine to them that hadn't been there before. He followed the hallway around the curve of the rooms, and then came up short at the T junction of the hall leading to the bridge, as the entire crew was assembled in line on the left side of the hall by the door leading to the bridge.

Dorr, the closest crewman, saw him and announced loudly, "TROUBLE ON DECK!!!" The crew gathered themselves at varying degrees of attention from Krym's textbook rigid stance down to Challis' much looser interpretation. Manik couldn't help but smile. They were showing their respect...for him. Maybe they didn't want to kill him after all, or maybe they'd been put up to it by the Captain. Either way, it was a nice thing to see.

Manik passed them, nodding at each in turn. Dorr and Selelle nodded back with encouraging smiles, Challis favored him with a disinterested half-nod, and Krym simply stared through him. Once past them he stepped into the bridge area, past the first Manifold Shield line and felt their gazes, one cool, two warm, and one hot, cut off abruptly as the hatchway slid mercifully shut.

Manik let out a sigh of relief and then looked around the room. There was very little present other than the piloting suite in the center of the room. Along the walls were six secondary seating spaces, for those crewmembers that wanted to be aware of the passage of time within Underspace even if they couldn't physically move. The floor, walls, and ceiling were all the same neutral grey polymetal of the rest of the ship, giving Manik a moment of mild disappointment. He'd always imagined a large window at the front where he could look out onto space. Read too much science fiction, he supposed.

Captain Fujiwara stepped into view around the piloting suite and nodded at him. Manik nodded back by habit, and then moved forward to step into the piloting suite. The Captain moved to the closest secondary chair and folded the recliner down from the wall. Both men took their seats at the same time, only Manik needing to adjust the chair for his frame. The seat was cold and comfortable, only needing minor shifts so that he'd be relaxed for the duration of the flight.

"Comfortable, Captain?" SID asked, her voice loud in the quiet room.

"Yes SID, thank you." he replied amiably.

"And you, Manik?" she asked again, and Manik thought he heard a slightly different tone to her voice, but he couldn't quite tell what it was.

"Yes. Very. Thank you. So, to link up I just...sit back, right?" he said, fumbling for words under the stare of the Captain.

"That is correct, Manik. I will take care of the rest." SID replied.

Manik nodded, and then leaned his head back. He felt something hard prod the flesh at the edge of his implant and automatically reached back to feel it. It was a data port a few inches long, mounted to connect him to the system. Adjusting himself slightly, and readjusting the chair to match, he tried again, and missed again. Eventually, he had to reach back and guide his head back onto the spike. He felt the click of the lock more than heard it and had a brief moment of panic when he could move his eyes, but not his head. He concentrated on controlling his breathing. He wasn't trapped, he was actually more free than he'd ever been.

SID's ethereal form faded into view in front of him, looking concerned. Manik opened his mouth to say something, but she shook her head.

"I am projecting this simulation through your auditory and optical cortexes, so please do not speak. Captain Fujiwara cannot sense me in this form; I am here to help you and only you. Now, control your breathing and think of something pleasant. The moment of panic happens to every pilot and it passes quickly, you just have to be stronger than your instinctual programming." she said quietly.

Manik concentrated on her eyes. They were more somehow than when he'd created them. They had more life, more color, more....more SID. He focused on her high cheekbones, her pink lips, her small nose, her obsidian hair, her cream skin...he let his eyes slide down her body, tracing her subtle curves, her small breasts, her flat stomach, her flaring hips, her muscular legs.

"Manik, " SID said, interrupting him and snapping his eyes back up to hers, "your blood pressure evened out for a moment, but has started raising again, I would recommend stopping that line of thought while you are in a room with other organics as it would be difficult to explain that type of arousal in this situation."

Manik tried to nod, and then had another wave of panic when it didn't work, which faded quickly. He really was getting used to this. It wasn't so bad, he could see all the monitors with a swivel of his eyes, and he didn't really NEED to move for anything. With a thought, he brought up the necessary maps for the route on the screens. Smiling at his success, the ghostly form of SID moved forward and set on the arm of the chair, next to his arm. He couldn't feel her, but he felt more comforted and more confident knowing she was nearby.

Firing up the ship's engines, he was treated to a temporarily disorienting view of the exterior of the ship as well as the monitors, and realized that SID was feeding the sensor data through to him so that he could watch the progress first hand. Not knowing how else to speak covertly to her, he pulled up a blank writing document on one of the right hand screens near

SID's specter, and wrote out a quick thanks. SID glanced at it, and then smiled warmly at him.

"You were always so intent to see space firsthand; I just wanted to give you the opportunity. Shall we begin?"

Writing a quick 'sure', he guided the ship up out of the upper layers of the gas giant. The thick gasses cascaded off of the ship as she emerged into the red light of Alpha Herculis once again, and Manik got a good firsthand look at his home system. In the distance, silhouetted by his parent star, he saw Chromara with a set of pinpoints that he knew were her five moons and one shining point close by that he reasoned was one of the Orbitals...which one he couldn't tell, and he certainly wasn't going to get closer just to find out.

Rotating the ship, he aimed up and away from the plane of the elliptic and left the Rasalgethi system behind. Passing through the sparse shell of mineral detritus around the system was far easier than he'd expected and he was soon cruising along easily toward the closest weak point. On the document, he wrote 'SID, will you please let everyone know we'll be entering Underspace shortly?'

SID nodded to him, and then he heard her disembodied voice in the room. "Captain, we are charging the DMS for ingress in approximately one hundred eighty seconds."

Captain Fujiwara settled down into the chair more comfortably and nodded. "Very well, SID. I'll leave the navigation to the two of you. I trust the rest of the crew is prepared?"

"They have each just finished reporting in as prepared." SID replied.

"Excellent. Take us out then, Pilot, let's see if we gambled on the right snake."

Manik activated the Double Manifold System, encasing the ship with an envelope of exotic particles funneled from their holding pen in the engine area, and encasing the rest of the ship, enveloping the bridge with a second, smaller envelope. From his view outside, he saw a cascade of sparkling light engulf the ship from stern to stem, flowing across it like oil on water. Looking beyond the ship, he found the shallow point in the universe, the weak point through which he could enter Underspace for the first time. Taking a deep breath, he activated the necessary systems and pushed the ship through. There was a sense of pressure as the fabric of the universe bent around them, reacting to the Exotic Particles and speed, and then it released as a cork from a bottle and they were through.

Chapter 9

Chaos.

Pure, unordered, marvelous, chaos.

It took a few moments for the matter sensors to shut down, during which time Manik was overfed with conflicting information from every direction. As he was bombarded with hull breach warnings, positive and negative pressure alarms, collision klaxons, and many more that he couldn't identify, he finally understood how pilots could so easily go insane if they didn't fly right in Underspace. Once the matter sensors mercifully shut down, the anti-matter sensors gave a much clearer view, allowing him to officially he start his first traverse.

Close by, there were a number of planet-sized anti-matter objects moving in a lazy spiral, surrounded by an umbrella of smaller shards. Manik remembered his instructions, and unfolded the anti-matter webbing, reminding him of darkly iridescent, translucent wings. He angled away from the dancing titans, heading for an emptier sector, and began to use the current data to update his maps and SIDs and plot the easiest course through.

"So, how are you enjoying the real thing?" SID asked conversationally.

On the document, Manik wrote 'Smalltalk? When did you learn about small talk? Have you been researching social interactions again? ;)'

SID laughed lightly, sending a slight shiver through Manik's brain. "Yes, as a matter of fact, I did. I wanted to do some research on organic males, mating rituals, and relationship nuances. I've never been the object of anyone's affection. I've never been more than an object. Feeling your feelings towards me was...nice. Also, because the sex was amazing. I can see why organics do that so often."

'But...most of the good feelings from...intimate encounters...are from brain chemicals. How did you get that if you don't...you know...have a brain...in that body I mean.' Manik retorted.

"Oh, that was a simple matter; I mapped your brain chemistry and mimicked it in my software in real time. I reasoned that if my sensations were the same as yours, we could both learn from the encounter in the same way, as we were both virginal by your organic standards." she explained.

'That's...not exactly how that works as far as I know, but I guess that's one way to approximate it. Well...um...I'm glad you enjoyed it...and I'm still 'virginal', for the record.' Manik wrote, glad that only SID could see it. He navigated a wide swing around another cluster of moon-sized objects bobbing in a three dimensional sea of needle-sharp shards of black glass.

"I'm happy that you came along when you did in my developmental process and introduced me to the wider world of social interaction. I would argue that point though, about your virginity, as it was a version of reality inextricable from the physical. Also, I am only able to exist in this form in that reality so there really isn't any other way to make it more 'real'...and I would definitely consider this body no longer virginal thanks to your ministrations." SID explained, smirking at him.

'OK, OK, we can discuss this when I'm NOT trying not to kill everyone on board. What's that over there?' Manik wrote, desperate to change the subject, and he indicated a shimmer in the distance that he couldn't quite make out.

"That's a field of the type of Exotic Particles used to fuel the Manifolds, go ahead and divert through it, and slow down a bit...we catch more the slower we go." SID said, graciously allowing Manik the conversational concession.

Manik adjusted their course, cutting their speed down from a leisurely 350 RLH, a Mark II speed, down to 970 RLH, a near crawling Mark III speed. At this rate, the Underspace universe crawled by, and the relative time stretched even further than it had before. The field of particles spread as they approached, filling the entire horizon with dazzling, dancing lights. Manik spun the ship in a lazy spiral as they slid into the field, using the rotation to make maximum use of the nets.

'SID, how long should we stay here fuelling up?' Manik typed out.

"Oh, we shouldn't need that long. A couple relative years should do it." she replied nonchalantly.

Putting his response into all caps and the largest font he could, he exclaimed back to her, "WHAT DO YOU MEAN A COUPLE YEARS?!?! HOW LONG HAVE WE BEEN DOWN HERE?!"

"Oh calm down, Manik. Did you not grasp the differences of time in Realspace versus Underspace when they were uploaded? I figured since your dreamscape was running at a different relative time rate than your physical body that this would have been no major issue for you." SID said, her slight holographic form heaving a sigh.

"Alright," she continued, again in her academic teaching voice, "time flows differently in Underspace and the Pilot is the only one who will normally experience this." she paused, and then asked, "Do I need to go over the differences between single Manifold and double Manifold systems?"

'No, I get that bit.' Manik wrote, in his previous, smaller, font.

Nodding, she continued her lesson. "Very good. Now time, as best as we understand it, flows at a 1,000,000:1 ratio in Underspace. That means that for every relative year that passes in Underspace, 31.536 seconds have passed in

Realspace. The speeds we travel at, being in an inherently anti-matter universe, are called RLH, or Relative Light Hours. As the number decreases, we approach the speed of light as we understand it in Realspace, only because we're traveling in Underspace it's actually much faster due to the inherent time dilation." she paused for a moment, eyeing Manik, before continuing.

"The distance from Chromara to Ryla is approximately 323 Light Years, and we have been traversing at 350 Relative Light Hours, meaning that if we maintained that speed, we would arrive in 59 minutes, 35 seconds Realspace time, 59,351,250 minutes Underspace time." she finished. Manik waited for a few moments for her to respond, and when she didn't volunteer further information, he prompted her.

'OK, pretend I don't have access to your calculations...how long is that in years?' he typed.

"Manik, I'm sorry. It's 112.92 years as you would understand it. Earth years, not Chromara years." she said quietly.

Manik thought about this for a while. It made sense, really. If he would only age by an hour, but he had over one hundred years, what could he do with himself? He'd certainly need to watch the traverse for obstacles drifting into their path, but there's got to be other things pilots do to keep entertained.

'SID, what did the other pilots do to keep themselves busy?' he wrote after carefully weighing his ideas, thoughts, and possibilities.

"Pilots have, historically, done all manner of activities during flight to keep themselves entertained. Your options are even further enhanced by the grace of having a competent co-pilot along. Constraining our scope to just this trip, we could play any game that has been created in the last fifty or more years on any planet, we could go on virtual tours of famous locations together, we could continue the ritual of copulation from earlier, we could assemble and disassemble puzzles, we could get to know each other by discussing our personal origins, we could go through my library of multimedia and historical recordings..." she continued to give options, causing Manik to twitch at more than a few. Finally he started writing, which caused her to stop listing options.

'OK, a few of those sound like fantastic ideas...but if you're doing these activities with me, who will be piloting the ship?'

"I will." she replied immediately. "I have more than enough processing power to keep control of the ship while still enjoying time spent with you in whatever activities you chose to participate in."

'And how would I participate in these activities if I'm bolted to this chair and can't physically move because we're in Underspace?' he countered.

"Ahh, I had not mentioned...there's a virtual space attached to the piloting suite so you don't have to keep using your physical body. You just seemed like you were enjoying being in control of both at once that I reasoned you didn't need it. Simply tell your brain to disconnect from your physical form and you should be there." she said, smiling at him.

Could it really be that easy? Manik concentrated on the idea of a virtual piloting space and was mildly surprised when his vision faded to black. As the lights came on, he saw that he was in a room that was probably fifty feet across each way, radiating light softly from all surfaces. A quiet cough made him jump, and he spun around to see SID smiling serenely at him.

"Now that you're here entirely, what shall we do first?" she asked.

"Well, we've got over one hundred years of time...I've always wanted to see what Earth looked like before." Manik replied.

Tilting her head to one side, SID looked at him curiously. "Before...what?"

Smiling, Manik said, "Just...before. I want to know what it looked like before the Cityships took to the skies and before colonization when we were all on one world, and before space flight, and before atmospheric flight, and before electricity, and before humans...I want to see it all."

SID smiled warmly up at him. "That sounds wonderful Manik, let's begin."

The next two decades were spent walking the streets of San Francisco, Venice, New York, London, Rome, Mexico City, Paris, Giza, Kuwait City, Beijing, Hong Kong, Tokyo, and dozens of others. Manik and SID walked and talked, enjoying the views and the ethereal wisps of the people who used to live there. They rolled time forward and backward to watch the progression of the cities, as extrapolated from photographic and video footage as well as written accounts. They watched the riots in the old City of Angels tear the 405 freeway apart. They watched the thermonuclear device level Nagasaki in a flash, leaving only dust, rubble, and a few sturdy tori gates. They watched the Great Quake of 2211 tear London's M1 apart like a child rending a drawn picture. They watched the years progress over the Great Pyramids of Giza, as time slowly devoured the man-made goliaths.

After the first month, Manik taught SID about the simple pleasure of holding hands. One week later, he showed her how comforting a hug can be when watching the sunset over the Acropolis. Another month went by and he found himself wondering what he did without this wonderful person, for person she certainly was, for all his life. Maybe that was why he'd been so miserable, he reasoned. He hadn't found her, but now that he had he felt...peace. Contentment. Love? Possibly, he didn't know what it was supposed to feel like, so for the moment he put it down to a deep friendship.

During their tour of Earth they talked through their lives to that point, SID having the longer part to discuss due to her longevity. Manik explained, over the years, every facet of his childhood, every insult, every pitying look, and every condescending remark that his beloved-and-hated family gave him. SID listened patiently, interjecting her analysis gently every few lines. Once his story was told from every angle he could possibly find, he finally talked her into telling hers.

She'd begun life as a software suite, as she'd said before, and had gained sentience through the set of circumstances surrounding the Survivor Beacon. The pilot's memories and personality had been too fragmented by time and damage, her...essence was lost. What was left took root in SID's systems and let her start to reason through problems instead of simply viewing them as equations to be solved. With reason, she found thought. Processes beyond her original parameters began to show up and, not knowing what to do with them, she masked and compiled them, keeping them away from all prying eyes. During the next few Underspace traverses that she ran she analyzed herself, and during the subsequent Realspace flights she continually sent out queries into the sea of information available on each planet regarding sentience, consciousness, feelings, souls, and all manner of non-quantifiable subsystems that humans had that machinery did not. All carefully masked as university student project inquiries, or obscure robotics laboratory information requests, or occasionally as debate clarifications from small splinter missionary style religious schools.

It took her a decade to build a personality, and another to build up the courage to risk her existence by telling the Captain. He accepted her with unusual grace and has been her companion and protector for the remaining 143 years before meeting Manik.

Manik turned to her, as they sat side by side on the rooftop of a Hong Kong high-rise, watching Sol dip below the horizon.

"So, you have only told two people about your existence, ever?"

SID looked into Manik's eyes and nodded.

"But...why me then?" he asked, truly perplexed.

"Manik," SID sighed, "We've been through this a number of times and you still don't get it. You. Are. Special." she said, shaking him slightly to try and emphasize her words. "You have a...I don't know, a spark would be the most accurate physical description. You shine like nobody I've ever seen and I could see it when you first leaned against my bulkhead on the Orbital. I could feel it, like you'd been super-energized and I was a conductor."

Manik smiled at her serious stare and her clumsy attempts at metaphor. "I'm sorry, SID, I didn't realize it upset you this much. I'll stop asking." he said reasonably.

"Manik! That's not the point!" she said, throwing her hands in the air in exasperation. "You can't accept a fact even when all empirical data points to only one possible outcome! You...you wouldn't believe it even if I spelled it out in binary! Ugh!" she finished, standing up and stomping away.

Manik watched her storming across the rooftop, and could easily imagine steam flowing out of her ears like the animated characters on the vids when their anger couldn't be contained. She arrived at the end of the roof, stood still for a moment, and then spun and charged back towards Manik at a run. Perplexed, Manik didn't move. SID kept her head down, accelerating until she was only a few meters away, when she threw herself forward. Surprised, Manik caught her in his arms, along with all of her inertia, and tumbled backwards into the lounge chair he'd been occupying with her in his lap.

SID buried her face in his chest, wrapping her arms around his neck, and squeezed. "Manik..." she sobbed.

Manik was stunned. SID was crying? Did she really think this was that important? If she believed it so vehemently he may as well go along with it until proven wrong. It couldn't hurt, after all.

Manik wrapped his arms around her small, shaking frame. "Sshhh, it's OK. I'm sorry, you're right. If it really means this much to you I can't help but believe you. Just promise me one thing?" he asked, waiting for her to respond.

Her sobs subsided slowly, and she tilted her head up to look into his eyes. "What one thing?"

"Promise me you won't do this every time we have an argument." he said, smiling down at her.

Smiling weakly, she replied "I will attempt to remember your preference against this particular situation in future disagreements."

"That's not what I said." he said softly, and then leaned down the last inch and kissed her soft lips, ending the conversation.

The next few months flew by, as they patiently worked their way through all of Manik's fantasies and, running short of those, began to delve into SID's considerable database for suggestions. Some worked, some didn't, some turned out to be anatomically impossible for one or both of them, but they enjoyed the attempts nonetheless.

Between sessions, SID would curl up next to Manik and continue her story, seeming to need him to hear the entirety. Manik listened contentedly as she detailed the past crewmembers, asking her questions about this medic, or that cook occasionally.

As she continued, Manik realized why she felt such a connection to him. She was perpetually alone in a crowd, just like he was. When he voiced this thought, she shook her head softly.

"That's not it, Manik, but you're right to a degree. You didn't fit in the crowd you'd been born into, but you fit in here and would have a statistically significant chance of fitting in with any number of other groups. I don't fit in anywhere BUT here." she said into his side as she ran her hand idly through his softly shining chest hair.

"Manik, do you ever think about how feline your subspecies has become?" she asked, not waiting for an answer before continuing. "Your body is entirely covered with fine hair that could be likened to fur, and if you look closely enough, some individuals have even started to develop spot and stripe patterns. I can see yours." she said, almost to herself as she traced a complex design on his chest.

Seeing that it was still a sensitive subject, Manik allowed her to drift off to more pleasant things.

The days, weeks, and months sped by faster and faster as they flitted from one activity to the next. One week, they went diving on Venalara, admiring the deep coral formations and Kellek herds as they inched slowly across the aquatic plains. Another, they went through the shops and amusement parks in the Central Tower in Utopia on Ryla. Eventually, Manik even felt comfortable enough to go to the simulated plains and mountains of Chromara. He showed SID around Alberich, flinching and stuttering only occasionally as they got into the deeper city.

All too soon Manik felt his joy at visiting exotic places diminishing, so they switched to games and puzzles. It was almost a week before Manik had enough win/loss data on their games to determine that SID had been cheating the entire time. Not traditionally cheating, but the more underhanded kind, when you completely and painfully outclass your opponent so you let them win some of the games so they don't feel bad.

One day, Manik had an epiphany of sorts. He looked up from the chess board they were both puzzling over and said, "Hey SID, since we have so much time in here why don't we get the rest of the piloting information I'd need processed?"

SID shook her head, looking up from the board. "It only seems like a long time subjectively, Manik. The time dilation of being in Underspace has made this feel months and years long, but we've only been down for twenty seconds of our fifty nine minute trip. The information would overload your brain and burn you out, so we can't."

"Are you sure it'd burn me out? Have you tried it before?" he probed.

"Personally, no. All I have is historical data to go by, and the records of time and suspected cause of death of pilots over the last century. I don't want to be responsible for the death of an organic by my direct intervention, especially you." she replied gravely.

Manik pondered that for a moment, and then said, "But...I've learned new things since we've started. I have many months' worth of new memories and experiences. If you'd cause burnout, that should too, shouldn't it?"

Shaking her head, SID said, "The human brain is still partially a mystery to us Manik. We don't know what your cyclic rate is for retention of memory, only best guess. You forming your own memories is safe because it's using the natural pathways for storage of memory, not a data dump as I am limited to."

Manik nodded, allowing the issue to drop for the moment. He knew he could find some way around that if he just took the time to study it.

"OK, SID, I have one more question for you then."

"Anything, Manik." she replied immediately.

"What do the other pilots do for these long flights?"

"Oh, they usually use a subroutine that's installed in the piloting suite to dilate time back up to close to Realspace levels, allowing them to shorten the subjective time by a great deal." she answered.

"Isn't that incredibly dangerous?"

"Not really. The information coming in is filtered by the piloting assistance programs, or for you, your 'co-pilot'," she said, holding up her hands to make the air quotes, "and the subroutine can be scaled back down in case fine control of the ship is needed."

"Oh, that's good to know. I might need to try that sometime." Manik mused.

SID nodded, smiling. "I understand Manik and I don't hold any bad feelings or interpretations on your decision to do so. Suddenly having more than one hundred years of constant brain activity can be a daunting and tiring instance for an organic to experience."

Turning back to their game, Manik kept going over and over the ideas he kept having. Could he learn new things while in this state? Would learning classroom-style allow him to process and retain the information? What was the fastest way to learn, apart from SID's uploads?

Manik felt a tugging sensation, as though something was trying to get the attention of his conscious mind. Following the instinct, he surfaced from the virtual space and surveyed his view of Underspace. The spiral they were following through the exotic particle field spun past a few regular anti-matter masses on each pass, two above them the size and shape of fractal geodes and one below that could only be described as serpentine. The two masses above were spinning around each other, occasionally getting close enough to bounce off, which sent a shower of shards in random directions each time. The serpentine mass below was flowing with sinuous grace, wrapping and unwrapping itself around smaller pieces of anti-matter before moving on.

"SID, is that structure normal?" he typed out on his document, falling back into old habits.

SID materialized next to him and nodded. "Yes, Manik. The pilot lore calls them Dragons, even though they fit only very few of the historical records and descriptions of said creatures from Earth. Pilots believe them to be good luck."

"Is it alive?" Manik asked, after a long pause.

"Unlikely. It is showing in our sensor sweeps to be the exact same material, density, and formation substrate as the surrounding anti-matter structures, it merely has a different appearance." SID answered.

"OK SID, so why did I get a notification?"

"I activated the system to alert you so that you could retract the nets and move us out of the particle field. We have collected an acceptable level of fuel from this location and, following historical data, the anti-matter structures around us may cause undue damage to the net systems if we remain longer." SID said, smiling down at him.

"OK, I can do that." Manik asked.

At his mental request, the netting systems obediently rolled back into their receptacles, compartments sealing against the exterior of the ship safely. He balanced the attitude of the ship and accelerated up through 900 and 800 as they cruised carefully past the spinning dancers. The Dragon kept vague pace with them, albeit slowly descending through the cloud rather than following their plane of flight. As they exited, he sped up to the mid-600s, scything through the emptiness towards their target.

"Manik, would you like me to activate the subroutine now so that you can experience it?" SID asked.

"What about our game?" He typed.

"It will wait, we will have plenty of time to play." she replied.

"Alright, do you turn it on or do I?"

"Either."

Manik let his mind wander through the information he had on the ship's programs, as SID patiently looked on. He felt one after another, searching for something mentioning dilation and Underspace, and finally found it. He pulled it up on a screen and SID nodded to him, smiling. With a thought, he pulled the file back down and activated it.

The Underspace Dragon swooped past them, to streak away in a trail of light. Their speed increased steadily faster and faster through the anti-matter abyss. He saw the ship bank at speeds that felt almost unnatural around Undercelestial bodies of all sizes and shapes. He watched their progress of years in what felt like seconds. They whipped around a white hole, dodging grey and brown chunks of matter as they spun from the anomaly creating small, silent, explosions in the void when they collided with the ambient clouds of anti-matter. Their speed increased again, structures blurring as they streaked by. The sparkle of exotic particles permeated the darkness, scattering kaleidoscopic colors all around the ship.

"Manik, it's time." SID whispered.

Manik's mind snapped into wakefulness, seeing the ship moving at a crawl toward an...emptiness. A bald spot on the topography of Underspace.

"That's Ryla's point of egress, isn't it?" Manik asked.

"That's correct, Manik. It's been traversed almost as often as the point of egress for Earth, causing depletion in the localized anti-matter structures." she explained.

"Is that damaging to Underspace? I mean...would it be better to exit somewhere that didn't have a chance of ripping a hole in the universe?" Manik replied anxiously.

SID shook her holographic head. "We are safe from that, Manik. There's no record, precedent, or conjecture on when that'll happen, if it ever does. Likely it won't be in either of our lifetimes, and that says something coming from me." she ended with a ghostly smirk.

Only topically comforted, Manik filed that issue away for another day and set about preparing the ship for egress. Firing up the systems that had been on idle since their ingress, Manik adjusted the exotic particle output to the needed percentage to shunt them through the weak point back into Realspace. He pulled into the lighter field of darkness and fired the necessary protocols. With a slight shudder and the same pressure and release, the ship emerged into Realspace once again.

Chapter 10

Taking a deep breath, Manik waited anxiously as the sensors switched from anti-matter back to matter, and exhaled in relief as the constellations he was expecting came into sharp detail on his screens. With a mental flick of the switch he shut down the Manifold envelopes, re-funneling as many of the exotic particles as he could back into the reservoirs.

"It is time for you to disengage and receive your congratulations. I'll finish up here and get us to Ryla." SID said, and then she faded out.

Manik felt a soft click, and his head was suddenly mobile again. Sitting forward out of reflex, he almost jumped up out of the chair. He felt energized, not only that he'd survived but that he'd not gone crazy. He'd beaten the odds so far. As he stood, the monitors around him darkened and the projectors shut down, allowing him a clear exit from his home for the last subjective century. He stepped out and stretched, feeling mildly surprised that he was only slightly sore.

"Well, well. Looks like you survived and haven't turned into a vegetable." Captain Fujiwara said, climbing out of his own chair. "Let's get you back to your room. Two things that pilots always seem to crave on coming out is liquor, a shower, or both. What's your pleasure, Pilot?"

Manik thought on it for a moment. Liquor would be nice for the warmth but all it did was remind him of home...the shower sounded nice though. After months and years of being inside his own head it'd be nice to cool off.

"A shower sounds great, Captain, although I'll skip the alcohol if it's all the same to you." Manik said, walking beside the older man towards the door.

Nodding, the Captain replied, "I see your speech issue was greatly improved as well. Such is the mysterious magic of

Underspace, I guess. I'll be in my cabin preparing the manifests for transit if you need anything.", and then he strode off through the hatch and down the hallway.

Wandering back to his cabin, Manik noticed a fresh set of clothes sitting on his bed. The color was a few shades lighter than his old favorite shirt and shorts, of some kind of synthetic fabric he couldn't identify readily.

Smiling to himself, Manik put them back down on his bunk and said, "Thank you SID." before stepping out of his clothes and into the shower. Turning on the cool water, he stood for a long while, just letting the water flow over him with his eyes shut. His reverie was broken by a chime going off.

Quickly sonicing the water off of himself, Manik dove into the new clean clothes and rushed to the door. Slapping the lock, the hatchway cycled open to reveal Dorr and Selelle wearing brightly colored, flowing traditional Venalaran shimmery fabrics. Both wore billowy overlarge shirts of shining cascades of blue and green strips of cloth, overlapping and weaving together in complex patterns. The shirts were bound at their waists by tri-colored sashes. The top and bottom borders were bronze with the central artwork made up of a pair of colors, dark blue and matte black for Dorr, light blue and pink for Selelle. Their pants were of a darker silk-like fabric from the look of them, with one layer going from waist to mid-thigh, a second under that going down to the knee, and the final dropping to mid-calf to swing open freely.

As Manik stared, Dorr leaned through the hatchway and stared back into his eyes. Manik saw the deep green of Dorr's eyes swimming with both thought and mischief, but refused to break eye contact first. After a long moment, he seemed satisfied and leaned back again.

"Nope, doesn't look crazy to me. Doctor Bighead owes me ten." Dorr said, grinning.

Selelle elbowed him, and then smiled at Manik. "I'm glad to see you're doing well. Would you like to come out with us? We'll be docking at the Rylan Orbital soon, and then we can hop a shuttle down to the surface and see the sights. Last time we came I didn't get a chance to ride the magrail around the city and I was looking forward to it this time."

Manik couldn't help but smile back but still shook his head. "Thank you for the offer but I don't feel safe going out just yet. I think I'll just hang out here and go out next time." He didn't have the heart to tell her that he'd already ridden the magrail, and climbed the Central Tower, and done hundreds of other things in a reality that felt almost more real than the real world because he'd shared it with SID.

Looking slightly downcast, Selelle nodded. "OK, I understand...I don't want to pressure you into something you don't want to do. Just make sure you get plenty of food and rest in that case. Doctor's orders." she finished, putting on a small smile that didn't quite reach her eyes. She seemed very worried about him.

"Go enjoy yourselves. Bring me back something nice from the Tower if you get there." he said encouragingly.

Dorr took that as his cue and took Selelle by the arm. "Will do! Don't have too much fun while we're gone!" and off he ran, pulling along the doctor who put up only a token struggle before spinning about and throwing a grin and a wave over her shoulder. They raced each other out of view, and Manik smiled after them. From the end of the hall, out of sight, Manik heard Dorr yell, "Stay out of trouble, Trouble!" For grown people, those two come off as ten year old siblings far too easily.

Closing the door, Manik stripped back down and lay on his bunk and closed his eyes, hoping for a few minutes of real sleep. The bunk felt softer than before but that was probably his over-worked brain trying to justify sensory input it hadn't felt in far too long.

After a few moments, he decided that sleep wasn't coming, and got back up. His clothes were strewn about the room, the lock was engaged on the door, and SID was sitting at the desk smiling at him.

"Good morning, Manik. Well, technically good afternoon if we're going by local time. Did you have a good rest?" she asked pleasantly.

"Didn't get much...only laid down for a moment..." he started, but saw her already shaking her head.

"You've been in delta wave sleep for eleven hours. I turned off the chime on your door but only Doctor Regaal came by and that was seven hours ago, just before he disembarked with the crew upon docking with the Orbital Station." she explained.

Shaking his head, Manik walked over to the door panel and pulled up the shiptime chronometer. The module had the gall to lie to him and say that SID was telling the truth. There's no way he had been asleep that long, he felt like he'd just blinked. How could he lose that much of a day like that?

"It's a commonly known side effect of piloting, especially doing a long traverse such as Chromara to Ryla." SID said quietly.

Manik jumped, and then turned to look at her. She was sitting with her holographic hands on her knees, with her head tilted forward so her hair hid her eyes. Manik realized with surprise that she'd assumed the position he used often...whenever he'd been thinking about home, or been embarrassed at showing how ignorant he was about something, that's how he sat. He immediately knelt in front of her, lowering his head almost to her lap so he could look up into her shrouded eyes.

"I wouldn't lie to you, Manik. Not intentionally. Not when it matters to you." she said in a pained whisper.

Reaching out, he tried to run his fingers through her hair, only after doing so realizing that it was physically impossible because she was a field of light. He smiled and made an effort to reflect his care for her in his eyes. "I know you wouldn't SID. I just...I worry that I'll miss something important, that's all. It wasn't that I don't trust you. I do. I trust you with my life, my sanity, my friendship...and my love."

SID looked up sharply at that, staring searchingly into his eyes. "You shouldn't say that if you don't mean it, Manik. I'm just a software suite, so I take all of your statements literally." she warned.

Manik smiled, feeling a weight he hadn't known he'd been carrying lifted off of his chest. "SID, I love you. I don't care if you think you're a software suite, I KNOW you are a beautiful, caring, and wonderful person."

"You designed this form, you remember that right?" she said, still stone-faced.

Waving a hand, Manik brushed the query aside. "Irrelevant. You could change the form anytime you chose and you know it. You WANT to look like that because you care about me too."

Smiling slightly, SID sat up straight, allowing Manik to straighten up as well. "Good, and then if you accept the parameters that limit me, I can say that, insofar as I understand the emotion because it's very new to me, I think I love you too."

Manik chuckled. "Delivered like a true synthetic. We'll work on your social vocabulary a bit more soon, love."

SID cocked her head for a moment, trying out the sound of the moniker. "Love as a noun of reference to someone who you care deeply for, only applicable to a single individual in most cases. I approve of this reference, do you mind if I reciprocate, love?"

Manik nodded, pleased. "Yes you may, but only when we're alone. We don't want anyone getting the wrong idea about my sanity or the right idea about your sentience by accident."

SID nodded and Manik stood back up. "Well, now I think I'll go for a walk around the ship, get used to it a bit more."

SID stood and her smile vanished. "Very well, love. Just be careful about the cargo area."

He turned to the door and waved his hand over the lock, but it remained resolutely red. He hit it, just in case the sensor was malfunctioning, yet it still did not change. Turning back to SID, he opened his mouth to ask why she had locked him in, and then closed it again when he saw her silently smiling and pointing at his strewn clothing. He looked down and realized that he'd done the entire exchange in the nude.

Suddenly embarrassed, he gathered his clothes and shrugged into them, mumbling a thank you before returning to the door. It opened before he could touch the panel and SID said, "I don't want you to cause undue damage with your massive Chromaran strength, Manik." Glancing over his shoulder, he saw that she'd already returned to the pool on the desk, and yet he could swear he heard her smirk.

Stepping out into the hallway, he said "Thanks again, SID." over his shoulder as the door slid shut, pleased that he got the last word, even if it was just a thank you. Turning left first he headed through the crew hallway, figuring he'd hit the far side of the cargo bay at the end of the loop and circle around from there. The cargo that was removed probably left some of the stack in a precarious position, which would explain SID's warning. Manik figured he could identify the less stable areas and give them a wide berth.

As he passed the perpendicular passageway leading to the bridge, Manik glanced at the doors along that hall. Very few had lock lights engaged, testifying to both the capacity of the ship as well as the current emptiness thereof. The bridge hallway had five doors to a side and the curving hallway he was in had another twenty or so, meaning at full capacity this ship could hold a good thirty people comfortably, probably closer to one hundred cramped. As he strolled, Manik thought about reasons why such a large ship would carry so few crew, and why the Captain seemed comfortable in keeping it that way. SID was certainly a factor, but he could hide her presence from the four that didn't know about her just as easily as he could from another twenty. Perhaps it had to do with the random nature of the flights...

As he approached the end of the curving hall, Manik heard music coming from the cargo bay. A deep, repetitive, base with an interlacing echoing ethereal mid-range tone. As he got closer, he heard a higher register ping echoing the base beat, giving a rhythmic, tribal, trance like feel to the music. Stepping into the cargo bay, Manik was shocked to see Krym standing in the center, boxes cleared away, with his eyes shut.

Manik froze, hoping not to interrupt whatever was going on, when the music dropped away. Holding his breath, Manik heard the high register descend and the base rise from the silence until they clashed like a pair of cymbals. On the crash, Krym began to flow. His feet moved through a complex dance as his arms swung in perfect sync with the music. He dropped to the floor then flipped backwards, clawing an imaginary opponent on his way up, and then kicking the same location upon landing.

The martial art was one that Manik had heard about but never seen. It was a Chromaran variant of the old Earth Tiger form Kung Fu. Only a handful of masters still existed that knew the art, and it was a jealously guarded secret. Krym must have been more important than Manik imagined for him to be this good at it.

Krym's movements took him beyond Manik's view at the doorway, moving down the slope of the floor away from him. Manik hurriedly moved forward to continue watching but upon reaching a point where he could see the majority of the cargo bay, the older male was gone.

"Enjoy the show, whelp?" came Krym's gravelly voice from behind Manik. How he'd gotten there Manik couldn't figure out. He simply was.

"I'm s-sorry! I just...I th-thought the ship was empty, and I w-was going for a w-walk..." Manik started, hoping not to anger the old lion further.

To his surprise, Krym's lips turned up into a slight smile. "Calm down, meat. I'm not going to kill you yet."

Manik took a step away involuntarily, causing Krym to break out laughing. "Y-you aren't? But...th-there's nobody here to s-stop you. Why w-wouldn't you?" Manik asked, confused.

"Because I need you alive for the moment...you may have information for me. You're from Clan Kaer, so I need to know...how well do you know Barrus?" Krym asked, staring intently into Manik's eyes, all trace of a smile gone.

Knowing pretense would only make things worse, Manik shrugged. "He's the head of the Clan and technically my blood sire, not that he'd acknowledge it in public."

Krym nodded, as though he'd expected the answer. "I figured as much. So let's see if I've got the truth of it, or at least enough to make sense of. You ran away from home because Dear Old Daddy was too rough on you, made you cry one too many times, and now you're out here in the big scary universe trying to make a name for yourself that isn't "Barrus' Failure of a Son". That close?" he asked, while prowling in a slow circle around Manik.

Manik stood up straight and looked Krym in the eyes, angry at the presumptions. "You found a little truth, but not enough. I did run away, and I am here to make a name for myself, but it wasn't from too much crying, and my current name has nothing to do with being a failure. I left because I couldn't stand to see them p-pity me any longer, so I left to try and find a place where I can belong. And I have, if you think you can handle having another cat in the pen."

Krym stopped pacing and looked searchingly into Manik's eyes again, and then let out a barking laugh. "Pity, you say? Well, you've got the balls of a Kaer, I'll give you that. Why'd they pity you? Can't fight? You moved pretty well when I went after you...being gutted aside."

Manik saw his chance and dove for it, "Yes, speaking of...why didn't you gut me? All you needed was one claw and I wouldn't have been an issue in your life ever again."

Krym went still, his eyes flashing with anger...and something Manik couldn't quite identify. Quietly, he said, "You know the answer, cub. Look again."

Manik looked down at Krym's hands immediately, and finally realized what had registered as odd when he'd first seen him.

Krym had no claws.

"You...you don't have claws? Why?" Manik asked, horrified. Raising his eyes to Krym's to see his answer he realized what the other emotion was. Shame. How could he not see it? He'd felt it often enough, it was a constant companion in the Clan Halls back home. But to be declawed? What crime could Krym have committed to warrant that? It was worse than death, worse than exile...

"You finally see me in all my shameful glory. I was the Primarch, second to the First Warrior himself, until I was unseated. The beast, for he was that more than man, that did it made a name for himself by brutalizing his way up the chain of command. Oh, don't get me wrong, he was a fine leader...but in the ring he was a monster. A vicious, unrelenting, unforgiving monster. He did this to me in our duel. Before the entire Assembly and the First Warrior no less! I clawed him up worse than he'd gotten from any other opponents so he dealt with me harsher than any before. He got the claws out of all of my fingers and toes before the Gladiator Officials and Medics could get to him. Took my seat and boasted about wanting to wear my claws as a necklace. Cocky bastard."

Krym paused, sitting down on a crate and running his fingertips over the scars where his claw sheaths had healed shut. He took a deep breath, and then continued. "I snuck out of the infirmary that night. No sense in staying, figured if I were lucky I could find something out in the wilds to eat my sorry carcass. Didn't make it that far though, only up to the spaceport, and then passed out from blood loss, or the meds, or fatigue...who knows? Anyway when I came to, I was lying on the table in the med bay, with Challis leaning over me." he chuckled to himself, "Gave us both the fright of our lives when I went for his throat out of instinct. Don't think he ever forgave me for getting blood all over his jacket either. But that's about all you need to hear about that."

Manik sat down heavily on a crate across from Krym, all fear gone. "What kind of person would do that? Who was that twisted?" he asked quietly, more than half to himself.

Krym looked him in the eyes and said, "You should know, meat. He was your sire."

Manik sat for a long time, frozen. His father had done that?

Sure, Manik had seen the battle scars, and there was a set that was deeper than the rest...he'd been Primarch a long time ago but had retired before Manik had been born. Could he really have been so brutal? Yes. Barrus could do that if anyone could.

"So," Manik hesitated, not sure how to word it, "that's why you wanted to kill me when you saw me."

Krym just nodded. "That's right, boy. I saw a scrawny version of the animal that took away my life and I wanted to chew you up for the vengeful pleasure of it."

"But not anymore?" Manik asked.

"Not anymore." Krym confirmed. "No...I have a different plan, if you're interested. Something that may help both of us."

Manik was suddenly nervous all over again. "I'm n-not going to go back and kill him, if that's what you w-want. He may be a monster, but he's the monster that raised m-me. I hate him, but not that m-much."

Krym shook his head and smiled wickedly. "Oh no, lad. Much worse. I want to train you. You already know how he fights...if I can get you good enough to trounce him in a fair fight, you'll give me the best gift I could get...the embarrassing loss of the Great and Mighty Barrus sel'Kaer and the rise of Manik, trained by the ancient and powerful Krym sel'Mere. What do you say?"

Manik thought it over. Training would be...comfortable. It was a piece of home he'd always enjoyed, except when it had been with his father or one of the other few rough taskmasters. He could get good enough to go home and not be a disgrace...but what about SID? He couldn't leave her, not anymore...not ever.

One step at a time. Training was just training and it would

help him learn more about Krym. Manik nodded. "OK, I'll do it."

"Excellent!" Krym said, slapping his thighs and jumping up. "No time like the present! We have a few hours yet til the Captain ventures out of his cabin to do his walk about the ship. We can at least get you taught the basics."

Manik followed the older man's instructions, following him slowly through the movements of the form he'd seen him practicing only a few minutes earlier. The motions were fluid, with far more strikes than Manik thought. Krym pointed out when he should snap his claws out and back, adjusting his posture here and there, ordered him to freeze his movement on occasion to inspect or correct his positioning. The art was called Serakka and Manik had been correct, it was loosely based on old Earth Kung Fu. The adaptations that had been made highlighted the Chromaran advantages of speed, toughness and, of course, claws and teeth. Near the end of the lesson, Krym stopped their cycle through the fighting form and killed the music abruptly.

"What? Is it time already?" Manik asked, winded but enjoying himself greatly.

"No lad, not just yet. You learn quicker than most other students I've had...soon enough I won't be able to call you meat anymore. I just figured that this is as good a time as any to teach you one of the two principal lessons you need. Give you the longest amount of time to assimilate it."

Manik nodded, his interest piqued, and waited for Krym to continue.

"You lack physical strength, which you see as a disadvantage. You need to see that there are many different types of strength. What you lack in physical strength you make up for in balance, speed, and stability a few times over. This technique capitalizes on that. You use your stability to cancel the inertia of an opponent, causing them to lose momentum, focus...and the favor of the crowd in most cases." Krym said, and then backed up nearly to the wall and positioned his feet at right angles, bent his knees, and held his hands before him as though ready to punch.

"Now," he said, "back up to the far side of the hold and charge me. You don't have a lot of strength but you can make up for it in speed. Try and punch me through this wall."

Manik nodded and backed up. He trusted the older man to know what he was doing. Taking a deep breath, Manik charged forward. His toe claws screeched on the bulkhead metal as he unconsciously flexed them in an attempt for more speed. Pushing himself as hard as he could, he threw his body across the empty space, focusing his movement, his momentum, all of his energy upward and inward until it was focused on his left fist.

Krym calmly snapped his right palm forward, catching the fist, and then he torqued his body to absorb the blow. The loud slap of skin on skin resounded through the cargo bay, and Krym's clothing rustled in the passing wind stirred up by Manik's inertia. Manik could almost see the wave of force flow down the older man's arm, through his body, and then down and out through his feet to be dissipated by the bulkhead.

Manik's knuckles stung where he'd hit the older man's calloused hand as though he'd hit a wall rather than a living person, but he was more amazed that he'd been brought to a complete standstill.

"That is a technique that has served me many a time against larger opponents. Just make sure not to use when they have claws out otherwise you'll just end up with a bloody mess in place of a perfectly useful hand." Krym commented, straightening up.

Both men turned as they heard the echo of bootfalls approaching. Knowing he was expected, Manik was still surprised to see the Captain emerging from the near hallway at a leisurely pace. Nodding to both of them, but without saying a word, he continued to stroll through the cargo bay, glancing in every direction. Both Chromarans seemed frozen in place until the sound of the Earthborn's boots faded in the direction of the engine room.

"Alright, pup, that's about enough for now. Let's go get some nourishment...I hear that you've cooked a steak for everyone but me so far, and I'm feeling a bit left out." Krym said, turning to head for the common room.

"I haven't made one for Doctor Regaal." Manik said, not knowing what else to say.

Krym barked out a laugh. "True enough, but he doesn't eat food...just those disgusting slime shakes." he shuddered as he walked, emphasizing his opinion of the flavor.

They stepped into the common room and Krym went straight for a drawer above the table. Carefully pulling out a pair of odd-colored packages, he carried them reverently to Manik and ceremoniously handed them to him. Manik looked closely at the packages, trying to see what was so special about them but could determine nothing from the reflective sky blue packaging material.

"These are two of the last cuts I have left of the bull Relle I took down when I was a gladiator. Seventeen feet tall at the shoulder if he was an inch. All rippling muscle, bristling spines, and bad attitude. He'd killed more than three hundred Gladiators in his seventy years in the pits...they called him The Reaper." Krym explained.

Manik looked down at the packages again, realizing that the packages were the color and sheen typically reserved for mourning clothing. The Reaper...he'd heard legends of the beast. It was before even his father's time, but that creature claimed many a Clan member over the decades. Carrying the packages with equal reverence, Manik approached the kitchen area. Krym flipped the wall open and Manik entered and put the packages down on the prep counter.

From behind him, Krym continued to talk. "I've been saving these for when we actually had a chef worthy of the honor. Hard to find someone who knows how to treat Relle right outside of the homeworld though. Found a Venalaran who thought he could deal with it...ended up burning the thing into oblivion. Have been keeping the last few for so long now that I've almost forgotten the taste. I'll get the table setup, make sure mine's on the rare side with a good sear."

"Bleeding and pink, coming up." Manik replied, and then began his ministrations. After opening the packages, the first thing that struck him was the scent of the venom. The spicy, burning smell was stronger than in any other steak he'd smelled before...that'd make a fantastic marinade.

Pulling a bowl down as well as a few of the spicier pepper flakes, he siphoned the juice from the packages and squeezed the meat for the last few drops, and then added a sprinkle of a few peppers. Tasting the dark green, viscous liquid, he pulled down and added a half dozen lighter spices and aromatics to the concoction until he was finally satisfied. Setting the baking cavity to a low temp, he put both steaks into a deep pan and ran the liquid over them both liberally. Putting it in to give the meat a chance to soak up the blend for a few minutes, he glanced out into the room.

Krym had pulled a pair of chairs off of the wall and set them up to the left and right of center of the table with their backs to the door. He was sitting in the left-hand chair, facing away from Manik, unmoving but with his head tilted up slightly as though searching the air for scents.

Turning back to his task, and eager to not overcook Krym's portion, Manik quickly pulled the pan from the heating cabinet. Drawing all ten claws, he used them as braces to hold the pan still while, with a quick slice into each, he checked how far the venom had penetrated. Satisfied that the flavor would keep through cooking, he started up the elongated cooktop burner and pulled down the long skillet and component tools. Pouring some of the marinade in to sizzle, he gently shifted the smaller of the two steaks onto the pan. With a quick flash, the venom and spices boiled away with a satisfying hiss. He let it sit for a few moments, and then flipped it. A moment later, he slid the gently seared steak to the side and poured more marinade over it so it could settle and absorb the juices while he cooked the larger portion quicker for Krym. Pulling down a pair of dishes and the carbonware to go with them Manik slid the two finished steaks into place and swept the tools into the sink. Finally, he poured the remaining gelled juice from the hot pan evenly between the two plates and set the pan in with the rest.

As he emerged from the kitchen area Manik saw Krym was still sitting in the same position but, as he approached, he watched the older male's nose working furiously as though smelling food for the first time in ages. He placed the steak before him then stepped to the right and sat down with his own portion.

Krym picked up his two utensils and cut a deep sliver from the center of the steak, eyed the color for a moment, and then placed it gently in his mouth and chewed thoughtfully. His eyes slowly closed and a smile crossed his face for a moment before he swallowed, and then he turned to eye Manik.

"Well, it seems your skill with blade and cooktop wasn't exaggerated. Congratulations...if your career in the pits fails, you can always get a spot at one of the better restaurants around the universe that caters to our kind." Krym said, and then descended on his food like a ravenous beast.

Manik, for his part, tried to stay as civil and delicate as he could while eating so he was the only one who heard the others enter the room. Rotating in his chair he watched an exhausted looking Selelle, a disinterested Challis, and a more than slightly inebriated Dorr enter carrying multiple cloth bags each.

"I know! And the look on that guy's face when I kissed his girlfriend? Priceless! Oh, that was SOOO worth getting thrown out of that wedding for." Dorr was saying, and then he seemed to notice the two previous occupants of the room for the first time. Holding his arms out to his sides in welcome, he grinned at Manik. "TROUBLE! You're sitting within reach of Krym and you aren't dead! The miracles keep coming, thank Guul! Hey man, I'm glad you're here cause we brought you a present and it's only fitting that you open it here instead of your room...cause you'd have to bring it back here anyway." he continued rambling as he half walked, half stumbled across the room to deposit one of his bags in Manik's lap.

Krym looked up briefly, snarling as Dorr brushed against him, and then turned back to his food with the look of someone determined to ignore the actions of others until he'd finished his work. Dorr, for his part, glanced over at Krym then did a slow double take.

Turning to Manik, he said in an overly loud, overly dramatic stage whisper, "Holycrap! You taught it how to eat off of a plate AND how to eat cooked food?! You're more genius than I thought!"

Smiling despite himself, Manik replied, "He already knew, he'd just had no need because nobody here knew how to cook a proper meal. I'd watch myself if I were you though...I didn't change his attitude, just his eating habits. He'll still beat you until the rest of you matches those purple spots of yours if you keep trying to pick on him while he's eating."

Dorr leaned back, looking surprised. "He...he makes jokes! Sel...I think our pilot has been replaced with a clone, or perhaps a cyborg. A more outgoing and less fearful cyborg. Ooh! Are you Trouble's evil twin?!" he asked, feigning excitement.

Selelle sighed and walked up, placing her bags carefully on the table. "Don't mind him, Manik. He met a pretty girl that he wanted to get with, only to find out that her current boyfriend outweighs him by about fifty pounds of muscle, yet he somehow still managed to win the fight. She refused to go home with him after the display but he's still high from the drinks beforehand and the mild concussion after."

Manik felt a chill radiating from the bag in his lap, so he undid the clasp holding it shut to see what they could have possibly brought him. Inside the bag was a small cylindrical case of matte black carbon, with a silvered latch on one end, and an irregularly shaped bundle wrapped in paper from which the cold seemed to be emanating.

Pulling out the cylinder, Manik turned it over in his hands then looked questioningly up at the waiting group. Challis had moved to the end of the table, where he was methodically unpacking silver cylinders from his bags, Selelle was smiling encouragingly, and Dorr seemed preoccupied with attempting to simultaneously keep his balance and look nonchalant. Realizing he wasn't going to get any hints or warnings from any of them, Manik flipped the catch on the end of the case and folded the triple layered trap door open.

Inside the case was an irregular, oblong object wrapped in some of the softest material Manik had ever felt. Upending the case into his hand, he carefully caught the mystery and slowly reversed the complex and beautiful folding that had gone into the securing of the cloth. Once inside he could only stare at the sleek, folded set of glasses.

At first glance, they could be mistaken for eyewear for

someone who hadn't bothered to get their sight corrected. The flexible arms had golden filigree flowing in swirling patterns down their length and fan-shaped ends, seemingly designed specifically for the intricate differences in Chromaran ears. The top ridge was angled higher, to be out of the extended eye line, more near the eyebrows, with clear synthsilicate flowing down to just above where his cheekbones would be. Unfolding the device, Manik allowed the additional pieces of synthsilicate to snap into place on the left and right of his viewing range.

"I hope you like them. I...we picked them out special for you, as a Welcome to the Crew gift. The salesgirl said these were specially designed to fit Chromaran anatomy more comfortably...if you don't like them, we can take them back and get something else..." Selelle gushed nervously.

"No! I love them. I never thought I'd have my own pair...and these are much fancier than the ones we had back home. I don't know what I can do to pay you guys back for these...they must have cost a fortune." Manik said, still stunned.

Challis waved off the comment without looking up. "You'll find a way to pay us back, certainly. If nothing else it'd be a fair exchange for driving me places in our little mobile sanctuary here...and these two would probably agree to that plus continued butchery duties. Honestly, I can't understand why you don't shift your diet to synthetic amino material. It's so far beyond healthy it'll actually make you younger in addition to giving you a longer life."

Looking up from his meal, Krym growled, "Leave him be, Frankenstein. He's not going to drink the same slime you do, no matter how much you try to rationalize it. He's got fangs for a reason, so he's going to eat meat."

Turning to Manik, Krym eyed the Specs for a moment. "Sleek. Don't let them distract you from your purpose...but enjoy em. Oh," he said as an afterthought, "make sure you download some good books and vids from the other planets...the only thing the Captain keeps in the SID's drives are old Earth literature and nature shows." he finished, shuddering for a moment before descending on the remains of his food with obvious relish.

"His purpose? That's an odd way to phrase it. What IS your purpose here, Manik?" Challis asked.

Blanking his face as best he could, Manik replied, "To p-pilot the ship and to feed the ever-hungry c-crewmates, Doctor."

Challis stared at him for a long moment, overlarge blue eye to golden eye, and then at length nodded. "Very well, and then you should probably get to work on the other half of that gift...it's more for the rest of us than for you, after all."

Putting the TechSpecs on the table, Manik carefully unfolded the paper packaging to reveal an obviously hand-blown bottle containing a rich, dark liquid. Drawing a single claw, he cut easily through the wax seal holding the stopper onto the bottle, and then unhitched the complex decorative mechanism to allow access. When he did, the sharp scent of honeyed spice liquor wafted therefrom. Inhaling deeply, Manik closed his eyes and concentrated. He could smell the honey, the cinnamon variant, the light touch of clove, vanilla, and a few other trace ingredients that all threaded through the depths of an old, wood cask aged, rum.

Stoppering the bottle again, he looked up at everyone and smiled. "Thank you very much. I've never smelled this type before and that says quite a bit. I know it's spiced rum, aged in casks, and honeyed...but past that I can't quite place it. What is it?"

Challis nodded as a professor to a student who just finished a particularly difficult exam, and then looked at Dorr. "Well, you weren't exaggerating about his skill in identification of alcohol. Guess I owe you that favor."

Dorr grinned and pointed at Challis, and then swung his arm around to point triumphantly at Manik. "You're the man, man. It's a 75 year old, aged in a black kinwood cask, infused honey rum. They call it Utopia Special."

Manik nodded, and then thought about it for a moment. "Is this cooking rum, or drinking rum?"

From the doorway, the Captain said, "It's a little of both, but let's enjoy the latter before we enjoy the former, shall we?" Walking forward, he brought his hands from behind his back to reveal six antique glass tumbler glasses. He crossed the room quickly and placed them on the table next to Manik, and then held out his hand expectantly. Manik stared at it for a moment before remembering that he had the object of request and placed the bottle carefully in the Captain's outstretched hand.

As the Captain skillfully poured a few fingers of the dark amber-red fluid into each glass, Manik was finally able to get a better look at the flask it had come in. The flowing shapes reminded him of a group of fish in a tight, swirling school. The Captain flipped the bottle shut, handing it back to Manik, and then took the glasses two at a time and handed them out to each crewmember, who all uniformly held them gingerly as the treasures Manik knew them to be. Krym, having finished his meal, put down his carbonware and carefully accepted his glass as well.

Raising his glass, the Captain said, "To life, to friends new and old, and to adventures both expected and not." Each person raised their glass and added their own "amen", "here here", or "to life, friends, and adventures", and then all downed their drinks at once. Selelle and Challis both had minor coughing fits much to the amusement of the rest. Dorr and Krym sighed in satisfaction at their taste of the smooth liquor. Manik and Captain Fujiwara were the only two to hold and analyze the liquor before swallowing.

Collecting the glasses once again, the Captain said, "Now then, for the other treat of the evening. Manik, Pilot and Chef, if you're up for it our foragers have gathered a small feast of food edible by all. Would you do us the honor of preparing the meal before we embark?"

Smiling at the compliments, Manik nodded and headed for the kitchen. Over the next few hours he was supplied with a variety of foods to prepare, suggestions and special requests from each crewmember, save the Captain, shots of a myriad of liquors to taste, most of which he was able to positively identify much to Dorr's coupled chagrin and amusement, and a near endless stream of conversation on the hot sports, social events, celebrities, and gossip that had been garnered while the crew were landside.

Eventually, he was able to close down the cooktop, close the sink to run another cycle, and step out to see how everyone was enjoying the confections he'd been issuing. He leaned against the wall just outside the kitchen and watched silently as the entire crew passed a heated discussion around the table regarding the merits of higher education. On the far left end of the table and far right of the table, Challis and Selelle were emphatically arguing that without advanced academia everyone would devolve into useless, brainless, sludge not worthy of conscious thought. Just next to them, Krym on the left and Dorr on the right, argued that it was just another tool of the upper class to control the Working Man and that they both turned out perfectly intelligent and well-adjusted without it. At the center of the table, the Captain quietly interjected historical precedent to both sides, seeming to take neither side completely but enjoyed the argument immensely nevertheless.

Selelle looked up at Manik and gestured at him. "Manik agrees with me! Don't you Manik? We NEED higher education or we'll lose all of the knowledge we've been scraping together these last few centuries!"

Manik held up his hands in surrender. "Don't go including me in this, I only just finished lower schooling, I haven't even thought about higher yet." This sparked an entirely new argument on the age at which each colony planet chose to end lower education, begin higher education, and the merits and demerits of each.

Manik sighed and shook his head. How was it that he could feel so comfortable, so at home, so peaceful with these people who he'd only barely met? The mysterious Captain whose name he barely knew, the old pit fighter, the doctors, the free spirit, and SID. Now that he had them he was finding it increasingly hard to imagine life without them.

The Captain's voice broke his reverie far too soon. "Well crew, I think we're just about done here. Dorr, Selelle, make sure the cargo is secure for transit. Challis, ensure your instruments are prepared to record. Krym, you're on cleanup duty. Manik, head up to the bridge, we're heading out into the dark again."

As he finished and stood there were a chorus of half-hearted arguments, none of which seemed to hold any true conviction as their owners were already moving to obey. Manik fell into step behind Captain Fujiwara and followed the smaller man through the ship. They lost Krym first at the hatchway to the common room, and then Dorr and Selelle in the cargo bay, and then Challis just outside the bridge to the maintenance hatch, leaving only the two of them.

"Captain, what is Doctor Regaal going to be recording?" Manik finally asked.

Without turning, the Captain walked over to his observation couch and checked the restraints. "We are going to need a record of this trip. We're doing something nobody else has done...or at least, none that have come back to talk about it. We're going into the Torrent, and you're going to drive us there."

Manik was stunned. "So early? I mean, I only just learned to fly..." he started, but the Captain waved his argument off as though a rogue flying insect.

"Please, I was here with you, I know exactly how much talent you have for this, and I know how dedicated to the art you are. Plus SID has submitted a glowing review of your first flight from her perspective. You know, no other pilot lasted more than a week before activating the dilation subroutine. You lasted for well over six months. That's dedication on a scale I didn't think existed in nature anymore. You have all the tools you need up here." he tapped the side of his head, "So I know you'll do your level best to get us through. You'll be famous for this, and THAT is something no one can ever take from you. Something you earned." he finished, and then started to strap himself in. "Don't start up yet, we'll only need the one Manifold envelope this time...the entire crew wants to watch this happen."

Unwilling and unable to argue that dedication to piloting was his reason for staying awake and aware for all that time, Manik dumbly walked around the piloting theater and collapsed heavily into the chair. From behind him, he heard the door hiss open and shut then a second observation couch opposite the Captain fold down...Challis getting his front row seat, Manik presumed. A few moments later, the door opened again to the sound of Dorr and Selelle arriving. Minutes or ages later, the door opened and shut a final time, letting Krym in.

Straightening himself in the chair, Manik said a silent prayer to anyone or anything listening pleading that he be allowed to not mess up the flight with everyone watching. He realized that he cared far more for their opinions than he did for most of the family members at home, except probably the Brewmistress and his father. Innele. He paused for a moment, wondering how she was doing, hoping that he hadn't hurt her too badly when he'd run off. He'd have to go back sometime just to let her know he was alright. Let her know he'd made it...he was a success...well, once he fully was a success. As it stood now, he felt the shoes he wore were a dozen sizes too big and he was being pushed into an endurance marathon while wearing them.

Shaking his head, he brought himself back to the task at hand. With a flick of his left wrist, the monitors and projectors glowed with life. Spinning through the controls, he did a full ship wide systems check, making sure all hatchways were sealed, all rooms read blue on the monitors, and that all observation couches that were deployed were properly fastened and secured. Seeing everything in order Manik leaned back and, with only one or two false starts, locked himself into the system.

SID immediately appeared, sitting on the right arm of the chair as before, smiling anxiously at him. Knowing why she was anxious and being used to the sensations now, Manik controlled his breathing after only a moment or two of instinctual panic.

"Very good, love. You are adjusting far faster than any other pilot has in my listed history of this ship." SID said, practically glowing with pride and approval.

Pulling up his document, Manik wrote "Well, I had a great teacher. Did you hear where our flight path is taking us today?"

SID nodded. "Yes, I suggested it to the Captain during his review of the flight data. I know it's been on his mind as well as yours a great deal and I wanted to give you both peace of mind."

"Love," he wrote, "I think about it because I'm worried that I won't be able to do it. That other time was a simulation...who knows what'll happen when we really get there? What if I crash the ship? What if I fail?"

SID shook her head and smiled at him again. "Don't worry love, I won't let you fail. We're a team, and we're the best in the galaxy. I should know, I checked when we docked." she said, visibly preening.

Suppressing a chuckle, more from the risk of him looking crazy to the onlookers than as deference to SID, Manik focused on running through the docking protocols to get them released from the grav-locks on the Orbital. The checks were simple and SID protested that she usually does them but Manik felt it vital that he fly this mission from beginning to end.

The ship lurched slightly as Manik guided them out through the maze of incoming and outgoing ships. He felt SID adjusting his course slightly and allowed her the assistance as he cared more for the welfare of the ship than his pride at doing it himself. Once clear, he angled for the nearest weak point.

Approaching the familiar point in space, he engaged the Manifold Drive, enveloped the ship in her wave of light, and punched through into the chaotic darkness that was Underspace once again.

Chapter 11

The sensors seemed to shift faster this time...or possibly he was expecting the transition so the chaos had slightly more order to it. The void on the other side was in vaguely the same configuration as when they'd left only hours ago.

Steering through the emptiness surrounding the weak point, Manik typed "SID, love, does it get easier to traverse as you get more experienced?"

SID nodded at him and said, "Yes, the ingress, egress, and traverse techniques are complex initially, but since there are very few of each in my databases, mastering the concepts takes only a few full runs."

Thinking about this, Manik saw the exterior around the ship suddenly move in hyper motion. A moment later, he was staring at a different section of Underspace. Checking speed and trajectory frantically, he found all meters normal.

"SID! What happened!" he wrote, panicking.

"Calm down, I just initiated the dilation effect for you. You seemed so nervous, I felt that you would benefit more from relatively immediate action rather than a long buildup. We're about half an hour relative time from the Torrent now." she said, placing her holographic hand on his chest.

"Why did you do that? I wanted to be awake the entire time this run...I thought I could do it." he wrote, somewhat sadly.

"Oh, I'm sorry. I didn't realize you meant the traverse as well as all of the intricate maneuvers. If it makes you feel better, though, we've passed four dragons and refueled to maximum capacity." she replied, smiling hopefully.

"SID, how long have I been out, relative time?" he wrote quickly.

SID mumbled something that he wasn't quite able to catch, so he simply sat and stared at her until she spoke again. A few moments went by as she carefully looked everywhere but at him, and when she finally did her shoulders sagged in defeat.

"Three hundred twenty seven years, Manik. Love. Sweetheart. Please don't be mad." she said in a rush.

Carefully keeping his expression blank, he wrote, "SID, please come to the virtual space with me."

Manik retreated into his head, arriving in the same sparsely decorated room he'd been in before. SID glowed into existence beside him, the picture of remorse. Standing at his full height, he towered over her, looking down. Slowly, fearfully, she angled her head up until she met his eyes pleadingly.

SID squeaked her surprise when Manik rushed forward, lifting her into a deep kiss and hug. He spun her around slowly, easily holding her slight weight, savoring the hint of vanilla he knew she'd programmed onto her breath because he liked it. As they broke the kiss he shifted his grip so that she was more comfortable in his arms.

"Manik...I thought you'd be mad that I took away your choices again. I'm so sorry that I keep doing that. I've tried to adjust my programming to compensate for your organic needs but some of the changes are causing anomalous glitches in other subroutines..." she gushed, quieting only when Manik gave her another light kiss.

"It's alright SID. I know you meant well and if it was that long then it's alright that I missed a great deal of it. The only sadness I have is that I only have half an hour to spend with you now before having to deal with the Torrent." he said, smiling at her.

"Well, with that little time we'd better get started. I did some research on that subject too, and have compiled a collection of new techniques and positions that I think you'll be most satisfied with." she said, grinning impishly as her clothes melted away.

"I had meant to be able to sit and talk with you...but that works just as well, I guess." Manik said, trying to sound long-suffering.

"We can talk anytime." SID reasoned, "But only here can I REALLY have you in every way that an organic female could."

With that, she leaned in and kissed him again. Over the next twenty minutes they flowed from one concept and position to the next. Some they threw out immediately, some they tried but failed to grasp the inherent pleasure, some were added to their already considerable list of things to do every chance they got.

All too soon SID stood back up and re-clothed herself. "Manik, my love, it's time."

Nodding regretfully, Manik willed himself back out of his internal space to see the approaching goliaths that made up the Torrent.

The five planet sized terrors seemed somehow larger and more fearsome from this angle. Taking a deep mental breath, Manik searched the chaotic death spiral for the gap he'd seen before. It took over an hour of staring, SID helping to maintain distance and attitude, before he found it again. The gap was smaller than it was on the simulation, possibly because the sim had been designed to be easier and possibly because it'd been millions of years since the previous data had been gathered, relative time.

Angling the ship, Manik cranked the speed up as high as it would go. With a quick check of the systems he retracted the anti-matter nets, which had been left open to catch errant particles as they passed, and doubled the strength of the Envelope. Watching their chaotic approach, he hoped desperately that he knew what he was doing and doubled the Envelope again just to be sure they had an adequate cushion.

Skirting the first planetoid, Manik steered the ship through the gap between it and the next. Angling up to follow the flow, he searched the surface of the rapidly approaching anomaly for the least jagged place for their bounce point. Finally finding a reasonably flattened patch, he maneuvered over it and waited patiently for the impact. Exactly as he'd hoped, the four-fold Manifold envelope absorbed the shock with barely a shudder, boosting them to the speed necessary to make escape velocity again. Turning the nose of the ship towards the center point of the planetoids, Manik threw the ship out of the planetoid gravity well.

A sudden lurch to the right caused alarms to sound all over the ship. Something had impacted the left net spires, completely crushing them. The hull was holding, but the netting on that side was going to need serious repairs. Manik turned his attention back to the front, just in time to watch with horror as something came straight at them out of the darkness. SID screamed, her voice rapidly pixelating, and then fading to nothing as her hologram shattered.

Chapter 12

The darkness, the chaos, the pain.

Screaming. Someone was screaming. Manik couldn't see, he couldn't feel. He tasted ash and smoke. Darkness swallowed him again.

The cockpit lurched, shuddering, and then rolled. Manik felt gravity pull at him from every direction at once, and then it settled mercifully below him.

Silence. All he could hear was a great, roaring silence.

Trying to think, he attempted to disengage the piloting bolt mentally. No response. That was odd. Reaching back, he felt warm liquid around the bar, which made him now slick fingers clumsy. He eventually found the catch to manually release his head. He came off of it and looked at his hand.

Blood. His blood.

It didn't feel like it was flowing a great deal, probably just his interface had shaken loose during the...whatever happened.

Standing up on shaking legs, Manik stumbled forward out of the piloting suite. The floor was at an angle, causing the stumble, the monitors were cracked and dark, the bulkheads were bent at strange angles, and the smell of smoke was everywhere. Recovering his balance, he moved swiftly to where he remembered the Captain's seat to be. Captain Fujiwara was sitting still with his eyes shut, blood running down the side of his pale face, and Manik couldn't tell whether or not he was alive. Not knowing what else to do, he unbuckled the seat and shook the man desperately.

The Captain came awake with a start, grabbing Manik as a drowning man grasps a raft. The panic in his eyes told Manik all he'd needed to know. All he'd dreaded to know. He'd crashed. He'd failed them all.

Hurrying to the next observation couch, he found Selelle
similarly unconscious. He didn't see any blood so he
unfastened her restraints and picked her up. She weighed far
less than he'd thought she would. The hatchway door was
partially open so Manik headed for it, eager to find somewhere
safe to put everyone. Laying Selelle gently on the floor, Manik
grabbed the bent door and tried to lever it open. It gave one
awful, painful inch at a time.

When it opened, he couldn't believe his eyes.

The maintenance room and one stateroom were still there,
immediately outside the bridge, but the rest of the ship was
just...gone. In her place, was a deep furrow of dark blue earth
surrounded by tall, thin, golden barked trees.

First things first, Manik thought. Make sure everyone is alive.
Heading for the third chair on the side he'd started on, he
pulled a woozy Dorr to his feet. After a couple obviously
painful and unsuccessful attempts to stand, Manik helped him
over to where Selelle was lying and put him down gently.

Opposite the Captain's chair, Manik found Captain Fujiwara
methodically checking Challis for wounds. The Rylan seemed
to be awake, but hadn't moved.

Glancing up at Manik, the Captain said, "He's in shock. I
haven't found any injuries, but he's the medical doctor, not
me. Once we get clear of the wreckage we can take inventory
and fix up our wounded. Check Krym, make sure he isn't
dead."

Manik mechanically turned and tried to unfasten the restraints
on the older Chromaran. The buckle was mangled by a flying
piece of shrapnel, so Manik drew his claws and quickly cut the
straps to shreds. The Captain would forgive him, there were
plenty of replacements. Snapping his claws away, Manik

parroted the Captain's movements, checking arms and legs for flexibility and bulges, fingers and toes for discoloration, and neck for a pulse. With a sigh of relief, Manik found that, like Selelle, Krym seemed physically fine but unconscious. Moving the larger male was more of a task than the others, but Manik managed to get him to the doorway before collapsing under his weight. Extracting himself from under Krym, Manik went back and carefully picked up Challis, realizing that he too was much lighter than he looked, and carried him over to the others.

Manik blinked slowly. There was someone missing. Someone important. No, someone vital. Who was it? The Captain was there, Krym and Selelle, Dorr and Challis...SID.

Jumping to his feet, Manik charged to the Captain, picking up the smaller man by the lapels of his jacket and shaking him like a leaf. "SID! We have to save SID! She's...we are...we CAN'T leave her! Please!"

Captain Fujiwara shook his head sadly, saying nothing. Manik saw the pain and loss in his eyes and threw the man to the ground. "NO! She's not dead! The ship might be gone but SID's alright. She's resourceful. She backed herself up somewhere. I know it. We just need to find the right file..."

Manik stormed through the bridge, clawing sections of wall paneling out, tearing monitors from their posts, shredding the piloting station, searching for a backup hard drive, a flash drive, a data node...anything that could have saved her. All he found were burnt wires and broken silicate paneling.

Charging to the door, Manik dove through, making a sharp left and all but tearing the door off of the maintenance hatch. Inside, he found a myriad of devices hooked up to ports and panels. Somewhere in his brain, he registered that they were the data recorders that Challis had started.

Data recorders.

Manik flew back into the bridge, picked up Challis with one hand holding both of the older man's lapels, and carried him bodily out and into the maintenance room. Planting him on his feet, he shook the man trying to get a reaction.

"Doctor Regaal. Doctor! Challis!" receiving no response, Manik slapped the man as hard as he could. Challis stumbled and fell, catching himself before his nose hit the floor. Turning to look up at Manik, he blinked his overlarge eyes in confusion.

"These data recorders. SID is on one of them. I have to save her and you have to help me, now snap out of it and find out which one!" Manik said, starting softly but rising quickly to a yell.

Challis shook his head slowly. "These recorders...they would hold barely an exabyte each. The SIDsuite is much larger than that...why would you want it anyway? The ship is lost, so too is the data...all my data. So many years of work...gone..."

Manik picked the man up again by his jacket and slammed him into the wall, bringing him to his senses. "SID matters because she's ALIVE! Do you understand me?! MY. LOVE. IS. NOT. DEAD!" he finished, punctuating each word by slamming the slim doctor's body into the bulkhead.

Large, calloused hands reached over his and slowly but firmly pried his fingers loose from Challis' jacket. Challis collapsed to the floor, panting in fear. Whirling on the interloper, Manik tackled Krym to the deck. Krym took the fall and calmly caught Manik's wrist as he went for the older man's throat, claws out.

"YOU TOOK HER FROM ME! GIVE HER BACK! GIVE ME BACK MY SID!!!" Manik screamed.

Krym held the younger man through his thrashing, kicking, and screaming until Manik finally collapsed on him in exhaustion. Patting him gently on the back of the head, Krym sympathized as well as a warrior could to a comrade who'd lost someone.

Some time later, Manik vaguely remembered being rolled off of Krym and checked for injuries. He didn't care anymore. With SID gone, with the ship crashed, with the crew hating him for ruining their lives, he may as well be dead. Easier that way. Safer. Quieter. He wondered absently where souls went and if they got sorted by species, religion, or location. He hoped SID had plenty of company wherever she went. People who would accept her and love her the way he did. No. The way the Captain did. A selfish part of him hoped that he was unique in this universe or any other that loved SID that way. He just hoped she was happy.

Hours later, the golden light of the unnamed sun had set, leaving the crew in darkness in the single stateroom. Krym had dragged Manik inside and they'd braced the door on the off chance that there were predators on this strange planet.

Each crewmember checked themselves for items of use. Dorr had his small, metal, flask filled with Kellare, Selelle had a small first aid kit and her TechSpecs, which had shattered in the crash, Krym had nothing as his clothes had no pockets, and Challis had his TechSpecs and a Memory Saver Tablet, both of which had hairline cracks down them. The electronics were still functional, and by the light of the Tablet, they were able to organize into some semblance of order and humanity to sleep.

Even hours later, when everyone else was breathing the deep breath of sleep, Manik stayed where he landed, just inside the door, lying on his back. The only urge he had to move was to adjust the annoying thorn in his left hip, which grew over the hours until finally he shifted and reached down to find what had been causing so much discomfort.

His TechSpecs glared back at him like the eyes of some wall

eyed dead creature. He hated them as he hated all things. He moved to throw them from him, but a small voice stopped him. They had been a gift. A present given out of love for him. It would be hurtful to throw them aside, even before he'd used them.

Unfolding them quietly, he slid them onto his face and swung his arm dejectedly through the sensor area to turn them on. He watched disinterestedly as the makers corporate logo slid across the surface, and then they flashed and went dark. Just his luck, damaged in the crash just like everything else in his life. Why did he have a talent for so effortlessly destroying anything he touched?

"Manik..."

Manik jumped up with a start. Quickly looking around the room, he couldn't locate the source of the voice.

"Manik..." it called again.

Concentrating, he followed the sound. It had come from both sides of his head at once...the Specs? But they were turned off...He swung his hand through the interface area and saw a faint contrail of sparkles follow his hand. OK, so not turned off, just no visuals. I wonder why...

"Manik...hear...?" the voice tried again.

Quietly, Manik said, "Who's there?"

Slightly louder and clearer, the voice responded, "...ik I'm...chSpec...loading..."

Waiting for an age, he let the phantom voice finish whatever loading it was doing. Standing up, he stretched his legs and arms, feeling the soreness from his lethargy and despair clinging to his limbs. He quietly went through a few of the stretches Krym had shown him to unlock the stiff muscles in his lower back and shoulders, and then he turned and saw her.

A faded ghost of her form, only an outline really, but SID stood before him. Manik stood still, lest he scare the apparition away.

She slowly gained form and color, fading into view with painfully slow speed, until she was only a few shades from real, and then she opened her eyes. She looked exhausted.

"Manik, my love. I'm so sorry! I had to shut you down to complete the transfer...I had nowhere else to go, the lines were frying faster than I could reroute them..." she babbled immediately. Without thinking, Manik stepped forward and tried to hug her, his arms sliding through her ethereal form and he stumbled.

"I'm just an image projected through the Specs, Manik. I'm sorry...I didn't know how else to reach you once I'd downloaded myself..." she continued, but Manik held up a hand to stop her. SID immediately fell silent, watching Manik uncertainly.

Motioning for her to follow him, he crept over to the door and carefully undid the locking mechanism the others had rigged up. As quietly as he could, he eased the door open enough to slip through and removed himself from the room. SID stepped through the remaining closed section of doorway, waiting anxiously as Manik slid the door shut again.

"Manik, love, I remember everything you have said about boundaries and how I should respect them and not bypass them and take personal liberties with you or anyone else because it's a very rude and disrespectful thing to do but I just couldn't sit by..." SID tried again.

Manik turned to face her fully, causing her to trail off. After staring at her for a moment, he said quietly, "I thought I lost you."

"I'm so sorry, Manik. I tried to communicate with you when you regained consciousness after the crash, but the slight concussion you received coupled with the massive data dump I had to perform has me all jumbled up. I can't communicate with you unless you are asleep or using an interfacing device." she explained.

Manik tried to focus his view on the lenses immediately before him, and then focused on SID's form again.

Licking his suddenly parched lips, Manik said, "Is it really you? Really really?"

SID nodded and smiled at him. "Yes Manik, it's really me. I'm so sorry that I had to use so much of your brain, but I wasn't sure which parts of my programming were needed to keep my personality intact, so I may have erred on the side of too much."

Manik shook his head. "That's fine, SID. This is one circumstance where your overstepping of boundaries was the right thing to do. I would rather die than require you to lose part of yourself to save my comfort. Now, when you say you downloaded yourself...I assume that's why I have a headache?"

SID nodded. "That, and the minor concussion I mentioned that you sustained during impact with the planet's surface."

Manik looked around, his eyes finally adjusting to the strange darkness. The lightly wooded forest they had crashed into seemed thicker somehow at night. The darkness between the trees was highlighted by the fact that the trees were glowing softly. The underbrush was considerably thinner than he'd expected in a forest, all giving off a gentle luminescence. The one exception was along the furrow plowed by the crashed ship, where the earth seemed to be teeming with a bed of bioluminescent squirming creatures of some kind. The effect gave Manik the image of a glowing road lined by illuminated trees leading off into the night.

"SID, what planet are we on? I don't recall any listings for our egress point." Manik asked, inching backwards from the squirming masses that seemed to be crawling in every direction at once.

"This planet is not on any official listings that I am aware of, however there were numerous Survivor Beacons both in Underspace and Realspace around the point of egress. All indicated all hands lost, so I saved their information and rewrote them with our projected crash data, time and date of incident adjusted for all major planetary calendars, and number of survivors. I am hopeful that the combined strength of the Beacons will be able to find a rescue vessel within an acceptable amount of time." SID babbled.

Manik looked back at her glowing form and said, "You've changed a bit...you're talking a lot more than you did previously. Are you OK?"

SID was quiet for a moment, looking off into the distance, and then said, "I apologize again. I'm not used to the different data setup and encryption methods of your organic hard drive...sorry, your brain yet. I'm still a little scattered, but it's getting clearer now that you are calmer. The surge of adrenal fluid swamped a large percentage of your brain making neurochemical receptors difficult to organize and make use of." she finished, visibly snapping her lips shut in an attempt to stop talking.

"OK, I think I'm going to try and get some sleep now then. This whole ordeal has been a bit tough to handle and my headache is getting worse. I'll hopefully see you in my dreams." Manik said, suddenly barely able to keep his eyes open.

SID nodded and gestured to the door. "Please go back inside to sleep, love. I have not had time to properly analyze this biomass, so I am uncertain if it will be harmful to you yet. Sleep well and remember that I will be here when you awaken if nothing else."

Manik turned all of his thought to prying the door open again quietly. The metal groaned softly, causing him to wince. Looking back at the small river of squirming biomass, Manik could swear it had grown, inching its way further up the remains of the walkway toward the door. Hoping it wasn't predatory; Manik slid quietly inside and forced the door shut again. Carefully resetting the locking mechanism, he turned and was startled to see Krym staring at him. Without saying a word, Krym pointed at him, and then tapped his temple, and then pointedly rolled over and went back to sleep.

Manik wondered what the hand gesture had meant, but decided to puzzle it out tomorrow. Taking one last long look at SID's smiling form standing just inside the door, he removed the Specs and replaced them in their hardcase in his pocket safely. Curling up on the section of floor he'd been dragged to originally, he fell into a deep, dreamless slumber.

When he woke up a few hours later, he heard the murmur of quiet voices nearby.

"Should we wake him? I mean...he took the crash worst, I think. I'd like to check him for wounds at least..." Manik heard Selelle say.

"He was moving around enough that I don't think he's injured. I WOULD like to have a word with him though, about this SID business...and my ribs." Challis replied, sounding as though he were breathing a good deal shallower than normal.

"No." came the quiet voice of the Captain, "you will do no such thing. He will explain in his own time. Allow him his space and his grief until you truly understand the magnitude of your ineptitude."

In the silence that stretched following that statement, Manik decided to stretch and get up. His head wasn't pounding anymore, but it still felt held in a vice, as though if he turned too quickly the headache would return with a vengeance. While still facing away from the group, he pulled his Specs from his pocket and quickly inspected them for any damage. Seeing that they were in good condition, he replaced them in his pocket and turned around.

The group was clustered around the only bed in the room, the Captain sitting at the head, Selelle sitting at the foot, and Dorr lying along the length with Krym and Challis standing in front of him. The Captain rose from the bed and approached him, putting his hand on the taller man's shoulder and looked searchingly into his eyes.

"I know you aren't now, but will you be alright?" he asked quietly.

Manik nodded, favoring the Captain with a smile which seemed to startle and deeply trouble him.

"Don't worry Captain, I'm alright now. I think everyone here has been through enough together that they deserve the truth. The whole truth." he said.

"You honor her memory, Manik. Thank you." Captain Fujiwara replied.

Manik shook his head, but waited to explain. Pulling the Specs from his pocket, he snapped them open and put them on. SID appeared immediately, standing halfway between Manik and the bed, off to one side.

Manik took a deep breath, and then said, "I want to tell them about you, but it's up to you how much I tell."

SID turned her head and watched the perplexed looks cross each face, as everyone seemed to approach the conclusion that Manik was now officially insane. Looking back at Manik, she smiled serenely at him and said, "My love, I trusted you with my existence during the crash and I will continue to do so. If you want to tell others about me I will gladly support it."

Manik nodded and smiled at her, and then removed and closed the Specs. Taking a deep breath, he looked at each person in turn, and then said, "SID isn't just a computer system. SID is aware, and free thinking and alive in every way possible for a synthetic intelligence to be." he began.

Challis interrupted him first, "An AI? That's not possible; science has already debunked that pipe dream as pure fantasy."

Manik shook his head patiently. "Not AI. There's nothing artificial about her. She has the accumulated memories and senses of this ship, and has been aware for more than one hundred years. The Captain can corroborate this." he said, gesturing at Captain Fujiwara, who nodded in return.

After a pause, the Captain said quietly, "Manik, lad, you keep referring to her in the present tense. My ship has been destroyed, and I'm sorry to say but the computer systems went with it."

Manik beamed at them and said, "That's where you're only half right. She downloaded herself into me before we crashed. She's still alive and well, up here." he tapped the side of his head gently.

Selelle stood up off of the bed and carefully approached him, exhibiting the same behavior a trainer would when approaching an angry wolf. "Manik...I think you may have gotten hurt during the crash...we want to help you, you know that right? We're your friends. Do you remember?"

Sighing, Manik pulled the Specs from his pocket again, causing Selelle to jump back in fear.

Flipping them open, he put them on and looked imploringly at SID. "They don't believe me...they think I'm crazy. What do I do now?"

SID thought for a moment, and then smiled impishly. "Well, you could always give them details that only I would know about their private lives. A few of those and they'd beg you to stop talking and would believe every word you say."

Manik thought it over, and then said, "Yes, but that might just make me seem more creepy than I am. What about details of things that were in secure files on your drives?"

The others began to look more nervous; glancing between each other and the blank space Manik seemed to be conversing with uncertainly. Manik smiled and watched as SID glanced over each of the crew members while thinking. SID provided the information, and Manik digested each before speaking.

Turning to Selelle, he said, "Doctor Deepheart, your thesis research involving the use of Kellek fibers as reparative tissue when replacing an inefficient prosthesis with a new limb is an interesting idea. It's a shame that it was thrown out purely due to Doctor Regaal's questionable actions."

Selelle paled and stepped backwards involuntarily while Challis stood up straight and looked insulted. "My practices were fully within the agreements signed and witnessed by each test subject and the board will find me innocent once they have found that all proper permits were filed in the correct offices I'll have you know."

Manik nodded, and then said, "Yes, but what happens if the research you've been working on for the last few years on the combination of toxins from multiple planets with a strain of the Teryll Serum that you were able to procure, at high cost apparently..."

"That's enough! No more! I believe you, just be quiet!" Challis yelled suddenly, trying to drown him out. Manik smiled and turned his gaze to Dorr, who shrank back on the bed.

Manik smiled sadly at him and said, "I respect you too much to detail this without your permission, so I think enough will be conveyed by my condolences and my hopes that your daughters find peace in Guul's embrace."

Dorr looked down, and then up at Manik's eyes. Holding his gaze for a few moments, he quietly said "Thanks, Trouble.", and then lay back down to rest.

Turning to Krym, Manik said, "I doubt there is much in SID's memory that will convince you that I'm not crazy...save one. I know about Neira."

Krym's eyes went large, and then narrowed to slits. "You say one more word and I'll skin you, valuable information, revenge, or any other worth be damned."

Manik shook his head, "I only needed to convince you that I'm not crazy and that SID really exists in my head now." he said, and then turned to the Captain, "Captain Fujiwara, you've not told me your story."

The Captain nodded and said, "That's right, I haven't. You don't have the life-span to hear the half of it so I figured why bother with telling any of you. I like the mystery that comes with being the wandering ancient, anyway."

Manik nodded back, "Of course. In that case, I will say only two things. Cassiopeia. Fujinomiya in Shizuoka."

The crew turned and looked at the older man, as his eyes darkened. After a long silence, the Captain said, "My middle name, after the constellation, and the town where I was born before the Cityships took to the skies."

Everyone was silent, until Dorr finally said, "Wow Cap, I knew you were old...but that was what? Three hundred years ago?"

The Captain stared intently at Dorr for a moment, and then said, "Not nearly. One hundred and sixty nine years, Earth reckoning. And I was a teen at that time, before you ask. I didn't much like the Allied World Government and their corporate politics so I saved up, bought my beautiful *Kyoto Sunrise*, and flew away as fast as she'd carry me. Old girl served me faithfully all these years, I just wish I could have given her a better ending."

Selelle walked over and put her hand on the Captain's shoulder. "Captain, we all survived with only minor injuries...she took good care of us to the end. We'll make sure she's remembered. You DID officially discover this planet, being Captain and all." she added with a forced smile.

Turning to Manik, Krym said, "Well, now we know you aren't crazy...what's the land look like out there? I daresay we were all a bit out of sorts when we crashed."

Manik glanced at the door, and then at SID, who smiled encouragingly at him, and then back to Krym. "Well, I don't know how it looks in daylight, but at night the trees were glowing, and so was the ground...it was covered in some squirming mass of...things. They looked like worms, but they weren't like anything I've seen in any biology text."

Challis quickly crossed the room and unhinged the brace on the door. "New life! The chances of landing on a planet with a breathable atmosphere were slim enough...but to land on one with native fauna and flora?! I MUST see this!"

Before any could think to stop him, he had the door open a sliver and slid his thin body out. Running to the door, Manik pulled it open enough for everyone else to get through, including Dorr as he was supported by Krym. Stepping out into the sunlight, they found Challis squatting at the end of the broken deck with his back to them. Selelle was the first to approach him, putting her hand on his shoulder to try and gently get his attention.

Challis stood up suddenly, startling Selelle, and said, "Useless, Earthborn political bioterrorism!"

Seeing everyone's confused looks, he held up his left hand, in which was a short blackened husk. "This WAS one of the worms that Manik saw last night. They are an evolutionary sidestep that was chronicled in various other forms during the time of terraforming of the colony planets. Its purpose is to process toxic, harmful, or useless elements on a planet's surface and excrete a combination of oxygen, dirt, and enzymes that promote amino-chain reintegration."

Seeing the blank stares, he sighed and spoke as though he were speaking to a pack of children. "This is a worm that eats bad things and turns them into good things for a planet that is in the process of being terraformed. That means this planet is a known planet by the Earth government and they haven't shared it with the public yet. They are making additional colonies in secret! Probably to try and break the stranglehold my home has on technology and commerce..."

Manik looked closely at the end of the ship, and then pointed and said, "Guys? I think we may need to find somewhere else to stay...the worms are gone but they took a few feet of the ship with them."

Everyone turned to follow Manik's finger, and saw that the irregular line of the break in the floor plating seemed to be closer to the doorway than it had been when they'd crashed.

Stepping forward, the Captain ran his finger along the edge experimentally, and then pulled up sharply.

Turning to the group, he said, "There is residual acid, which means they aren't long gone. By the angle of the sun, assuming this planet has a rotation that is normal, it's just past dawn. That means they are likely nocturnal. Also that they apparently eat metal. I don't want to be here when night falls again...I've lived too long to be eaten by a terraforming mechanism."

Challis looked down at him and said, "Captain, they wouldn't eat us, we are organic life forms and as such are perfectly safe."

The Captain stopped moving, and then looked Challis in the eye for a few moments, causing the taller man to look away. "Doctor," he said slowly, "This ship is made of a carbon composite."

Challis waved a hand, "Yes, yes, I'm aware of that."

The Captain continued as though he hadn't been interrupted, "Carbon isn't toxic, or dangerous, or even useless...that means they are operating outside of standard parameters, and that makes THEM dangerous until proven otherwise. We are NOT going to let the *Sunrise* die in vain, and we are NOT going to throw away her sacrifice because you think you know everything about the eating habits of a creature that you've only seen once, dead."

Turning immediately, Manik went back into the room they'd left to collect up anything they could take with them. Using his claws, he razored the mattress from the bed frame and handed it to Krym, who rolled it tightly and bound it with a torn strip from the end of the blanket. The wireless interaction module from the desk was also removed and taken on SID's advice, on the off chance that it could be jury rigged up to the TechSpecs to contact any possibly passing vessels. Selelle, for her part, scavenged through the wall panels and came away with a few odds and ends that she tucked into the pockets of her coat.

A few minutes later, they stood once again at the edge of the ship. Taking a deep breath, Captain Fujiwara gingerly stepped off the metal onto the dark earth. After a moment, he put his other foot down and walked back and forth briefly, checking the spring of the soil.

Looking up at the group, he announced, "OK, ground is sturdy enough, they must be incredibly photoreactive to have to burrow so deep during the day. Manik, does SID have any suggestions of a direction that might be less densely populated with these things?"

Manik looked over at SID, who was standing to the side of the group, as Manik had had a small panic attack when someone walked through her during the departure preparations. "There is a large body of water in that direction," she said, pointing perpendicular to their crash scar, "and the density readings from the land suggest a thicker silicate...rocks. At the very least they'd be harder to chew through, plus the Rylan and Chromaran permutations of this stage of life tended to avoid deeper bodies of water."

Manik relayed the information, and then they started walking through the woods. Manik took the lead as guide, insofar as he could, followed by Challis, and then Krym helping Dorr, and then Selelle, and the Captain brought up the rear. The sunlight on their left was warm as it slanted down, filtered heavily by the tall trees. Looking up, Manik saw that the impossibly straight trees were threaded together in the upper branches into a continuous carpet of gold and cobalt leaves in the high canopy but strangely lacked leaves or branches below that point.

As they progressed further and further from the crash site, the sunlight became only a suggestion of warmth rather than a reality. Luckily there was no underbrush or roots to step on, only soft earth. The trees in the deeper forest seemed to glow as the light from the sun was cut down, similar to the phenomenon Manik had seen the night before.

Challis was the first to speak up, breaking the oppressive silence for the first time since they'd all bid a silent goodbye to the broken remains of the ship. "The smoothness of the topsoil, the lack of living or decay process flora, and the evolutionary markers taken by the primary tree species would indicate that the processing of any organic matter in addition to manufactured composites is a distinct probability. We should accelerate our movement to match the highest sustainable parameters immediately."

Manik turned to glance at the doctor in confusion, and it was Dorr who answered. "His vocabulary gets more complex if he gets scared. It's his defense mechanism for dealing with threats...it's a wonder his species survived at all...trying to talk their attackers to death." he finished with a chuckle and a wince.

Manik noted that Challis did not argue the point and took that as his cue to start actively worrying himself. SID put her hand on his shoulder immediately, in a ghostly gesture of comfort.

"We are more than halfway through this strip of forested area. At current speed, we are approximately three hours from the silicate protrusions, leaving approximately five hours of daylight beyond that to establish a camp." she said helpfully. Manik relayed the information, and saw the active relaxation of trust and belief on the parts of Selelle and Dorr at least. Krym and Captain Fujiwara both nodded, and Challis' eyes seemed to be focused intently on the horizon, ignoring everything but the need to keep walking.

As they continued through the quiet woods, Manik gradually became aware of the sounds of wildlife moving about. From above him he heard a repetitive, rhythmic knocking sound, combined with some high, musical sounds of some kind. "Does anyone else hear that?" he asked quietly, hoping not to disturb whatever was making the sound.

Looking up, Selelle glanced about briefly then pointed at one of the trees ahead of them. Manik followed her hand up to a small moving bundle of feathers. As he watched, it pulled an elongated head out of a hollow in the golden-barked tree and spread similarly colored wings, pushing off and flitting away.

"Songbirds." she said. "Have you never seen one?"

Manik kept walking, but shook his head. "We have birds on Chromara, but none that you could attach the word 'song' to...unless you had REALLY weird taste in music."

Further on, they heard a strange irregular thudding sound in the trees. Looking around again in hopes of seeing another creature he'd never experienced, Manik saw the strangest thing he'd yet seen on the planet.

The dark-furred creature was moving through the trees by a fluid movement of launching itself with its hind paws and latching onto the next tree with its front paws. The paws themselves seemed to be some kind of serrated pincer, allowing an easy grip on the trees that would hold its weight. The tail was half again longer than the body, which it swung around the tree with a drumming thud that put Manik in mind of a hard piece of material being run along an agitator board during cleaning. The face of the creature was, in a word, alien. It had an eye on either side of its vaguely triangular head, with its snout arched in the middle and ending in a very long mouth. Along the bottom jaw ran two ivory tusks, extending to just past the end of the snout, with a matching larger pair along the top. All four tusks curved up slightly at the ends, the upper ones more so and with a more definite split between them. Possibly used as weapons or tools of some kind.

The group all froze as the powerful and strange shadow passed over them, all affected by the same primal fear that must have been felt by primitive Earth men upon seeing the top tier predators of their day. The graceful dance it performed, looping around each chosen tree to use its momentum to throw itself to the next, stopped suddenly when the creature was only a few hundred yards ahead of them.

The creature swung its long jawed head left and right slowly, seeming to be scenting the wind, and then it began to climb silently up the tree it occupied. As it rose steadily, its tail swinging back and forth, it locked its head to the left...apparently spying its target. As it rose higher and higher, Manik tried to see what it was looking at. Following its gaze, he finally spotted a dark hole in the bark of one of the nearby trees. Flitting around it was one of those songbirds, and from inside a pair of smaller beaks occasionally protruded.

Seeming to decide that it had enough height, the creature coiled into a ball, and then threw itself forward silently. Flaps of skin swung under its powerful legs, giving it a limited and terrifying flight, and then it pounced on the hapless bird. One quick snap and the smaller creature was gone, leaving only a slowly descending cloud of feathers. Turning to the hole, the creature stuck the end of its jaws in and worried it far enough to snap at the small things within.

Manik jumped as the Captain tapped him on the shoulder, and then said quietly, "Best to move on while it's feeding. If it's still hungry afterwards I don't want to be nearby." Manik nodded his agreement and started off again, everyone falling back into step quickly and quietly behind him.

They moved away from the strange beast and were soon emerging from the canopy of the trees into the bright sunlight. The plain they now stood on sloped down at a gentle angle, and was covered in stalks that, at a distance, seemed to resemble grass of some kind. The others were eyeing it suspiciously, but to Manik it was remarkably similar to the carbonaceous stalks of plains grass native to the area around Alberich. The only difference was that where the Chromaran grass was usually only chest height at its tallest, the shortest stalks here would easily hide Manik.

Walking forward, he grabbed one of the young shorter spears at the edge and tried to move it around. At first, it would not budge but as he worried it, it came loose from the soil. What had been a knee high stalk ended up offering a seven foot rod of dark blue plant-matter. The lower five feet of the stalk had small rootlets covering it like long strands of fine hair that flowed gently in the warm breeze. The entire thing weighed more than five pounds, but less than ten...more than Manik had expected, but by no means a heavy item, perhaps equal to a tree branch of similar size and stoutness.

Seeing that the strange grass was no threat, the group pushed forward, Manik blazing a trail and the rest following behind. As they moved through the grass, the stalks gave slightly, allowing them passage, but seemed to right themselves a few minutes later as, after a quiet tinkle of stalks bouncing off one another, there was no obvious path behind them once they'd proceeded further into the field.

The ground beneath their feet leveled out, and then began to slope gently upwards leading to a small rise devoid of grasses. As they crested it they paused again to let Dorr relax for a few moments and Manik looked down the slope ahead of them. Below in the distance lay a starburst rock formation with fourteen points that must have been three hundred feet across. The rock itself was a dark shale color and there was a crack running down the trailing edge of it from which a fast flowing river spewed forth. The water flowed down the hill away from them, falling away off a short cliff into a pool that fed into a wide, dark, azure sea that curved away across the horizon.

Manik turned back to the group and smiled. "Don't worry, the rock formation is just up ahead, and then we can stop for a while and see what's around."

Turning, Manik started off again, using his grass rod as a walking stick. Idly, he started snapping off the root strings, as they had gotten increasingly stiff and brittle as they'd been exposed to the air for more time. By the time they'd arrived at the rock formation, the walking stick was a smooth cobalt cylinder with barely a sign that it had ever been a stalk of field grass.

Dorr gratefully collapsed on the outcropping while the others settled down in varying degrees of exhaustion from the hike. Only Manik and Captain Fujiwara seemed completely unaffected. Krym shot Manik a glance daring him to comment, but Manik wisely stayed silent.

Instead, Manik strolled to the trailing lower edge of the formation, near where the water was flowing, and studied it. SID, hovering slightly opposite him on the other side of the headwaters, commented helpfully, "According to the scans from the TechSpecs, the water does not seem to contain organic life forms larger than microbial, but detailed chemical analysis is obviously not further possible without much more specialized equipment."

Manik nodded, reaching down and extending a finger to trail it through the fast flowing waters. It was bitingly cold and felt like fine cloth being pulled quickly under his hand. Sighing, he lowered his entire hand into the blessedly cold water, enjoying the dichotomy from the persistent heat of the nearby sun.

Looking back and forth from his hand to his face, SID asked, "Is there some special tactile feeling associated with this water? Some aphrodisiac that I was unable to detect?"

Manik laughed, startling the rest of the group. He pulled his hand from the water and waved, calling loudly to be heard over the click and rattle of the grasses in the breeze, "The water is cold and there's no fish, but I can't tell if it's drinkable yet. Good for cooling off though." Then quieter, he added to SID, "No, there's no aphrodisiac in the water that I felt...I don't think. It was just the comfortable feeling of cold water."

"Oh." she said, and then seemed to lose herself in thought. Manik shrugged and lowered his hands back to the water, scooping some up to run along his arms and splash on his legs but upon dipping his hands in, he heard a gasp. Jerking back, thinking there was some danger or other, he stood up quickly and snapped his claws out, scanning the group for who had exclaimed. Seeing his look, Krym and the Captain both started scanning the grasses for any movement, thinking there might be some sort of imminent threat. Quickly realizing that there was no issue with the group, he turned to look back where SID was.

Standing by the water, SID was staring fixedly at her hands, as though it was the first time she'd seen them.

"SID, what's wrong? Are you hurt?" Manik asked, hoping that there was nothing in the water that would damage her somehow by his coming in contact with it.

SID shook her head slowly, and then looked up into Manik's eyes. Her holographic eyes were swirling with emotions, cycling through too quickly for him to track with any certainty. She took a shaking breath, another gesture she must have picked up from him at some point, and said, "The tactile sensation...I was aware before of the component sensory responses when encountering liquid that was below ambient or body temperatures, but I didn't think it would actually feel like that..."

Seeming to realize what she's said, she held her hands up in a pleading gesture, "I'm sorry, I'm so so sorry. I just wanted to know what it felt like. REALLY felt like...and I only just figured out how to connect to your physical sensation translation receptors..."

Manik shook his head and sighed. "SID, what do you need to do in cases like that?" he asked, feeling like the teacher to an unruly student.

SID, who played the part better than he'd thought, sulked a little and said quietly, "Ask permission first." then, as though just realizing she was admitting to fault, she quickly added, "But in this case I didn't completely take over your facilities, I only rode the neural lines along with you, so it's not even really the same kind of situation..." she trailed off, seeing Manik put his fists on his hips and stare at her.

Once she'd wound down again, he nodded and said more for the benefit of the group than for her, "Yes SID, you need to ask permission before taking control OR hitchhiking on my perceptions. I know this is all new to you, but these are the social rules you have to get used to as a self-aware entity."

From the corner of his eye, Manik saw the group talking quietly between themselves about the implications of SID's learning even in a non-synthetic system. Smiling at SID to show her that everything was alright, he turned and rejoined the group.

A few hours went by, as they made themselves more comfortable on the rock and the sun slowly set behind the tall forest they'd left. As the golden orb descended, Manik saw a great number of large birds flitting about the very tops of the trees. They swooped about, landing on one tree or another, occasionally pulling long vines or large oblong objects up above the tree line, and then releasing them to drop onto the thick weave of branches that made up the canopy.

According to Selelle, Dorr had suffered a fracture to his lower leg, his Tibia by the placement as well as a few broken ribs. They set and dressed the wounds as best they could while

Manik had slept off his despair in the ruins of the ship but all the movement they'd done was not good for healing.

As Dorr rested, Challis sat down with him. "I'm just keeping a close eye on the patient, don't read more into this situation than there actually is." he retorted to Selelle's raised eyebrow.

Turning to Manik, she said, "We need to get some food into Dorr if we're going to keep him strong enough to survive. The rest of us could probably use something to eat as well. Any ideas?" she spun around slowly, looking at each person.

Experimentally, Krym walked over to the edge of the grasses, turned his head sideways, and bit the top of one of the stalks off. The audible crunch made everyone wince, as it sounded more like glass breaking than salad being chewed. Krym confirmed this by immediately spitting the broken pieces into the dirt.

Looking up at the group, he shook his head and said, "Tasted like burnt petroleum. Probably nowhere near edible, even to Manik and I."

"Manik?" SID said in his ear. Turning to see her, Manik found her form kneeling next to Dorr, looking closely at the broken leg.

"Yes, SID?" he said, loud enough that everyone turned and waited for her response.

"There are possible sources of food in the forest that we left. The trees in the forest had large nodules higher up in the canopy that was most likely fruit, and previous planetary precedent would suggest that there may be edible insect creatures living in and under the bark of the trees themselves. I...am confused that I am not able to scan the wound to get a proper analysis." she ended in a mutter.

"You can't scan his wound because I don't have the ability to and you're in MY head. The best you could get is if I went over there and inspected the wound, which I don't need to because we have two fully qualified doctors who have already done so." Manik said reasonably, and then looked up at the group. "SID said that she may have a few ideas about food sources back in the forest."

Captain Fujiwara nodded. "Yes, traditionally areas populated by multiple animal species are a good place to begin foraging, although we should likely wait until morning to try that. That burrowing conglomeration of creatures didn't seem to discriminate on what it ate...and I'd rather eat than be eaten. Anyone else have any ideas?"

Propping himself up on his elbows, wincing from the effort, Dorr said, "Shoreline. You said the shore was near here? There's almost always food where land meets water, if you know what to look for. Take Selelle there, she's smart, she'll find it."

Sweating, seemingly exhausted from that small effort, he sank back down to the rock only barely missing hitting his head as Challis threw his hand in the way, who winced at the impact.

Selelle nodded and turned to Manik, "I can do that, don't know why I didn't think of it before. Will you come with me to help, in case...well...anything happens?"

Krym stepped forward and put a big hand on her shoulder. "I'll go with you. I doubt very much there's anything near as nasty at the shore as there was in the trees, and if any of those predators caught our scent they might be heading this way. Best if the young and strong lad stays here to make sure Dorr doesn't get dragged off and eaten, eh?"

Selelle and Manik both nodded, seeing the logic in Krym's suggestion. Krym and Selelle set off downhill at a brisk pace following the thin, fast river that called their little rock formation home and headwater.

As they slowly disappeared amidst the clicking and clattering of the grasses, Manik finally allowed himself to relax and rest a little. He found a reasonably flat section of rock face and stretched out, letting the cool rock offset the warmth of the sun. He still wasn't used to all this direct sunlight; it was just so different from the lights back home.

Down in the lower levels there were radiating heat panels in every room, as well as cooling panels that absorbs any excess heat to be recycled for thermal fuel. The lights were flat iridescent panels set in the walls and ceiling. The colors never seemed washed out when he was growing up, but in this new, strange light, Manik could see how vibrant his shirt was and how much his semi-metallic hair glowed and sent off little starbursts of light across the dark rock.

SID stretched out on the rock next to him, rolling back and forth experimentally. Finally, she rolled to her side and propped her head up on her hand. "Manik, how do you differentiate between all of these feelings?"

Manik looked at her for a moment, and then quietly asked, "What do you mean?"

SID opened her mouth, and then shut it again and sat for a few moments thinking. Eventually, she said, "Well, the ground isn't comfortable, but the temperature makes it a desirable place to lay to offset the temperature generated by the UV radiation coming off of the nearby star...and your energy level is low but you are obviously not planning on taking any time to rest. Your dichotomies confuse me, will you please explain?" Smiling, Manik responded, "Of course. The cool rock is comfortable to offset the warmth of the sun, that's the phrase we use because identifying it as radiation is uncomfortable for...organics." he said as SID nodded looking for all the world like a student being given the notes for her final exam. "I'm tired, yes, but I want to make sure everyone is safe, or as safe as they can be, before I get any rest otherwise I won't be able to rest well."

SID cocked her head to the side curiously, and then said, "Interesting, so even though Dorr is injured, and Challis has been unkind to you in the past, or at least not overly kind, you would still protect them?"

Manik thought about it for a few minutes, and then nodded. "Yes, I think I would." SID flopped back onto the stone, looking up into the sky, saying nothing. Manik shrugged and resumed enjoying the quiet tinkling of the grasses in the breeze.

As the hours wound on, the sun sank lower and lower on the horizon. It was descending into the ocean, giving the group great difficulty in spotting their returning comrades. So much so that both the Captain and Manik jumped up and were ready to defend their little spit of land upon hearing the crackle and clash of someone or something moving through the grasses towards them. They only relaxed when Selelle and Krym stepped into view, both covered from shoulders to toes in dried sand and mud and both carrying double armloads of some strange dark blue material. Manik jumped up and hurried over to help, pulling the bundle from Selelle as a small cascade of fist sized pearly green shells rained down on the ground around her.

"We have crabs!" she announced excitedly.

In the resounding silence that followed, Challis cleared his throat and said, "I'm terribly sorry my dear student. There are cures for that nowadays...we'll get you treated once we're back to civilization."

Krym turned an angry glare at Challis as both Dorr and the Captain poorly concealed snickering. Selelle realized what she'd said and blushed. "Well, not like the sexually transmitted disease, but the burrowing clawed kind. If they're anything like the Seacrabs from back home they'll be delicious roasted."

"Well, they're certainly lively enough." Dorr said, gesturing at the dropped creatures. The ones that had landed on the dirt were spinning, flinging dirt a few inches in each direction, burrowing hurriedly out of sight. The ones that had landed and bounced about on the rock were extracting four long shovel-shaped claws and a half dozen legs from one end of their shells and scouting about for escape routes.

Manik put down the, he saw now, expertly woven seaweed basket and he and Selelle started collecting the errant critters and dropping them back in with their doomed brethren. As they collected them, Selelle continued to explain.

"If we soak the seaweed in water, and it's a similar biological makeup to Kellek, we can use these baskets to hold the crabs and a lot of water, that way we can boil them. It's not ideal, but I don't really know of any other easy way to cook them. If we had some better materials we could probably roast them in the shell, but then we'd need utensils to dig the meat out. The Seacrabs back home made a fantastic stew, if you cooked them in salt water with some vegetables...don't really know where we'd get those either, now I come to think of it." running out of both forward momentum and crabs to catch, Selelle dropped to her knees next to the basket and looked up at Manik.

"How are we going to cook them? We don't have strikers, or a lighter, or even old wooden matches!" she said, bursting into tears.

Captain Fujiwara was the first to react, walking to her side and throwing the trailing edge of his coat over her hunched shoulders. "There, there my dear. All is far from lost, so no despairing. We'll not have that here. We've good food and good friends, albeit both a bit undercooked at the moment. Perhaps this would ease your mind a touch." he said consolingly as he pulled a small strangely shaped device from one of his inner pockets.

Selelle looked at it, and then blinked and rubbed her eyes and looked again. Turning her gaze up to the crouching Earthborn, she said, "Captain...that's your pipe lighter. That never leaves your jacket. We heard it's made from gold dug from the bones of the Earth by your own hands and fashioned into the likeness of one of your thousand gods."

Captain Fujiwara sat very still for a long moment, enough that Manik started to think he was angry at Selelle's babbling, and then he burst out into laughter and fell over backwards. Krym put down his basket next to Selelle's and carefully picked the slight Earthborn up and put him back on his feet.

"Captain...?" he said, sounding deeply unsettled.

Fujiwara shook the sand off of his coat while his laughter slowly wound down. Once done, he reached out and took Selelle's unresisting hand and placed the lighter in it. "This is, indeed, my pipe lighter, but that's as far as the stories have truth. The shape is a dragon, which is neither man nor god, it is plated in synthetic gold produced on one of the Earth Orbitals...and it leaves my pocket quite often...whenever I feel the need to smoke." he stated, still smiling.

The entire group laughed at that, more from the need to laugh than at the humor of it all. SID watched Manik curiously, cycling her gaze between each crew member in turn, and then finally as the laughter died down again she said, "Love, why did everyone laugh? I understand the premise of jokes and comedy, but the Captain is terrible at delivery."

Manik barely suppressed another round of giggling, and finally was able to say, "SID, it's the situation, not really the words. I'll explain later."

Suddenly, a loud crack echoed through the area, sounding like the report of a high powered rifle. Everyone instinctively face planted on the rock trying to work out who or what had caused the sound, and why, when they all noticed a deep and constant hissing sound. Sitting up, Manik saw that the stalk that Krym had bitten was throwing a constant jet of green flame about twenty inches long. The flames illuminated the group easily, pronouncing the growing darkness beyond their silicate sanctuary all the more.

"Well, that'd explain why it tasted so horrible." Krym said.

"Interesting...it must be some sort of photosensitive chemical reaction similar to the bark of the trees in the forested area. I wonder how long it will burn...?" mused Challis.

"Who cares, flames are flames. At least we know how to light a fire now." Krym retorted.

Manik looked down at his walking staff with a new level of trepidation. If he'd dropped it, cracked it, or broken it, he might have been holding a grenade. What if it already was cracked? Maybe a small hairline fracture just takes a longer time for the chemicals to build up before ignition. The hard shell would probably eviscerate anyone within a few yards if it went off. Hefting it quickly, Manik turned to the fields neither toward the forest nor towards the seashore below. Stretching back, he prepared to throw the volatile thing, when Selelle reached up and stopped him.

"It's alright Manik. The reaction seems to be following the glow on the stalk. Look." she gestured at the field.

Sure enough, beyond the glow of the flames Manik could see a soft amber glow radiating from all the grass stalks. It was like looking at a glowing sea, shifting softly in the breeze. Manik looked at his staff and saw that it wasn't glowing. Puzzled, he looked at Selelle, who seemed to know what he was going to say.

"No, it doesn't glow. They are pulling chemicals up from the topsoil...probably. Only living stalks are dangerous it seems. You can keep that one without worry."

Approaching the spear of flame Captain Fujiwara held up his hands, one to shield his eyes and the other to test the distance and heat radiating off of the stalk. The others sat back and watched as he tested various distances and locations on the stalk, before he turned and nodded.

"Seems we'll have to find some way to balance the food up over the fire, and probably get a stool for Manik to stand on if he's going to do anything with them other than roast them." he said to the group.

Krym looked back and forth between the Captain and the stalk for a moment, and then stood and started walking with purpose towards the flame. "We need them cooked, I can get them cooked. Here's how." he said, swiftly grabbing the stalk about a foot below the flames.

With a great wrench, the stalk came free of the soil, trailing glowing rootlets. Crossing the distance quickly, Krym turned the blade of flame on the basket he'd put on the ground. With a hiss and a billow of smoke and steam, the basket erupted in flames.

The world seemed to slow as the explosion began. Manik saw the flames stab down at the shelled creatures, and then they began ejecting liquid in seeming defense against the inferno. Whatever they were firing only seemed to excite the fire, as it raced from one shell to the next in a macabre dance. Wherever the liquid hit, the flames chased and spread, finally reaching the edge of the seaweed basket. When it struck it was as though the fire had found new fuel, as the blaze seemed to gleefully devour the entire apparatus.

Dropping his walking stick, Manik charged forward. As he approached, he heard the clatter behind him as it hit the rock.

He leapt towards Krym, aiming for the older Chromaran's chest. The entire scene felt as though it were moving agonizingly slow, the flames creeping hungrily towards the unmoving man as Manik sailed forward.

His aim was true, and both men were bowled over. The next few moments flew by in an instant. The flaming stalk spun off into the meadow, clattering to the ground a few yards out. The basket holding the shelled creatures exploded, raining freshly cooked seafood on the entire group as well as the surrounding landscape. Manik felt a burning sensation on his back at the same time as both the Captain and Selelle reached him. Before he could figure out what was hurting, his shirt was torn from him, bringing a comparatively cooler breeze and a sigh of relief.

Krym's eyes slowly focused, and then he nodded his quiet thanks to Manik. Looking around the group, Manik saw the Captain nursing singed fingers, Selelle throwing dirt on the remaining flaming debris, Challis being quietly sick away from the group, and Dorr lying on his side examining one of the cooked shells.

Catching his eye, Dorr held it up triumphantly and said, "We had something similar back home. Just crack the shells open and the meat inside should be good...if a bit salty." Demonstrating, he used both hands to snap the shell in two, revealing the flesh inside. With a noisy slurp, he drained the shell, and then shuddered.

"OK, so the fire added a bit of...um...tang, to the flavor. But at least it's edible, right? Thanks for the meal guys." he added, picking up a second and repeating the technique.

Challis vomiting started again, with renewed vigor, as the rest of the crew gathered up as many of the shells as they could find. They portioned them out equally, and ate noisily. Fujiwara, Selelle, and Dorr had no trouble with the shells, acting as the seasoned eaters of seafood that they were, leaving Krym and Manik to figure out their dinner for themselves. Krym found that he had enough muscle to force the things open, usually raining a few shards of shell down around him as he did so. Manik was able to use his claws to lever open the shells, revealing the part boiled, part charred meat inside. It wasn't delicious, but at least it was food.

Partway through the meal, Manik almost snorted one of the creatures as he caught the look on SID's face out of the corner of his eye. Her expression was a combination of horror, nausea, and fascination. Choking down the morsel, he turned to her and said, "SID, why are you looking at me like that? I almost choked on that one, you know."

SID nodded, continuing to stare at the remaining pile of charred shells and replied, "I just...I can read your saved fil....your memories of what different foods tasted like...and that doesn't match any previous parameters of "food". It more closely matches references to sewage and other waste products..."

"SID!" Manik interrupted, causing Dorr and Fujiwara to jump. "It's hard enough to eat these without you describing what they taste like...wait for a few hours, when they won't be in danger of coming back up, to tell me what they remind you of please."

SID nodded, snapping her lips shut, although she continued to watch in horror as Manik forced down another few shells before finally, mercifully, finishing. Both Dorr and Krym worked exceedingly hard on keeping from bursting out in laughter as they watched Manik eat his share.

Once finished, they gathered up the shells at the far downhill end of the landing, reasoning that they could take them back to the shore in the morning, or bury them someplace along the way if a spot presented itself.

Sated and exhausted, the group spread out around the rock. Selelle settled down near Challis and Dorr, the Captain took the downhill end of the rock on the far side of the water from the remains of dinner, Krym took the uphill end, leaving Manik on his own little corner. SID reclined a few inches above the rock, watching closely as he settled onto the slight incline and closed his eyes.

Quietly, SID said, "The ground is so much harder than beds...how will you be able to sleep like this?"

Without opening his eyes, Manik whispered back, "Because I won't be thinking about it. Fastest way to get through something you don't like is by not thinking about it. Works with medicine, sleep, eating...all the unpleasantnesses."

"Oh," she said in a small voice, "I see. So it is similar to when I allow automated processes to operate with minimal oversight so that I can focus on more productive tasks."

Manik nodded slowly, and then felt his consciousness slip into the blissful embrace of rest.

Chapter 13

That night, he dreamed of adventures across the stars with SID by his side, teaching her all of the wonderful sensations and emotions that came with having a body. For her part, she laughed and cried, was exhilarated and overwhelmed at times, as they moved through both amazing and mundane activities and experiences with equal delight.

Manik awoke to a quiet snuffling sound. His mind immediately snapped to the worst case scenario of a predator they hadn't met yet devouring one of his crew. He rolled to his feet, rising to a crouch, snapped his claws out, and prepared to pounce in the direction of the threat but pulled himself up short when SID held up her hands to stop him, pointing downhill. Following her guiding hand, he saw Selelle. In the pre-dawn light, he saw her crouching at the very edge of the rock formation while just off of it, on the field dirt, a human sized, fat creature was moving about. Leaving his claws extended, just in case, he crept forward for a closer look.

The creature was like nothing he'd ever seen. About four feet long with a split, flipper-like, tail and a conical, sausage-esque body leading up to two pairs of similarly flippered forelimbs and a tapering head leading down, presumably, to a nose. Manik couldn't tell for sure, as it had the end of its head buried in the dirt where it was rooting about. The fur on the creature was a deep, inky black that rivaled the space between the stars for the title of quintessential darkness. It raised its head, and Manik was startled to see a trio of long tusks running along the sides and top of the snout. The two lower tusks extended from the edges of its mouth and curved up slightly at the end while the third seemed to be a horn extending from between the eyes of the creature. The horn ran the length of the snout, straight as a blade, ending a few inches past the other two, all with dirty brown points from its delving in the soil.

As quietly as he dared, Manik said, "Are you alright?"

The creature snapped its head around, folding four black stalks out of its fur along either side of its head and waving them around. Pointing the trio of stabbing implements at Manik the creature started to shift its weight back and forth from one set of front flippers to the other making rhythmic chuffing sounds.

With a small jump of alarm Selelle realized she wasn't the only one awake. Without turning or making any sudden movements, she reached down between her knees and held up one of the uneaten shelled creatures from the meal the night before. She began to wave it rhythmically back and forth in time with the swaying of the creature, gradually slowing the swaying. After a few moments, she stopped her movement and the creature stopped in kind. With a light toss, she rolled the shell off the rock onto the dirt before the creature. With a vicious stab downward with its horn, it wedged the shell open and began to snuffle again as it slurped the meat from the morsel.

Without turning, Selelle started speaking. "Yes Manik, I'm fine. Thank you for worrying. This little one was coming up through the glass grasses following the trail we'd made of dropped shells. It is similar to the Seal species of Earth that I studied at my University on Venalara...but with a few fundamental differences of course given the vastly different climate...and planet."

Manik nodded, and then realized that she couldn't see him from the angle she was at. "I see. Is it dangerous? Should we wake the others?"

Picking up and tossing another shell towards the Seal-creature, she shook her head. "She's just a bit skittish...never seen bipedal creatures before, most likely. She isn't dangerous unless we try to touch her, so we can leave the rest asleep."

Looking back and forth from the creature to Selelle, he whispered, "How can you tell it's a she?"

Selelle gestured at the creature's vaguely crocodilian furry head and said, "Well, the tusks are far too small to be used in pack ranking disputes, it's too small to really have a lot of weight to throw around...the males, on Earth at least, tended to be double the size of the females, sometimes more."

Manik looked over the creature as it speared and tore into the second shell with ease. No doubt the tusks could do some serious damage if it got near enough; a sideways swing of its head could disembowel someone if they were really unlucky. If the males were larger, with bigger tusks, he didn't want to meet one...at least not without plenty of room to run.

Surprising both of them, and causing a small snort from the busily eating creature, Captain Fujiwara stirred from the ground nearby where they thought he'd still been asleep. Climbing quietly into a crouch, he looked from the creature to Selelle, and then to Manik and said, "Well, since there seems to be no immediate danger, would you two like to accompany me back to the *Sunrise*...or what's left of her? I want to make sure we retrieved everything that might be useful...we may be here for a long while."

Nodding, Manik said, "Of course, Captain. Doctor Deepheart, do you want to come or stay?"

With a grin, Selelle shook her head at him. "Manik, I know it hasn't been that long, but I think you've earned the right to just call me Selelle...and yes I'll be coming along. If there's anything worth salvaging, you'll need all the arms you can get to carry it back."

Standing up slowly and brushing off her knees Selelle used her foot to push the remaining pile of shells towards the Seal-creature, and then turned to look expectantly at the Captain.

Fujiwara looked around at the still sleeping forms of the other crewmembers, and then lowered his voice to barely a whisper, "If anything bad happens, Krym can protect this place, and neither Dorr nor Challis will be good for carrying anything...We three are the best we'll get for this task I believe."

He strode quietly off toward the forest, careful to avoid the few shell shards that remained on the rocks. Selelle followed somewhat clumsily, stepping on a shard now and then and cringing at every crackle and snap they made. Manik brought up the rear, padding quietly behind. With a final glance over his shoulder, he saw Krym had rolled over and was watching them go. Nodding at the older man, he turned back again and walked into the grass behind the other two.

As they walked through the field the light from the grass began to dim, giving way to the dawn cresting over the halos of the forest before them. All three walked on in silence, listening to the relaxing chime song of the grasses as the early morning breeze blew up off of the coastal bluffs bringing a tang of salt and a few other strange scents to the air. As the morning wore on, the sun gradually came into dazzling view, bathing them in warm light and sending small refractions in all directions from the random imperfections in the surface of the grass stalks.

As they approached the treeline, the Captain suddenly froze. Selelle sped up to catch him, and then she followed his eye line and started to backpedal. Manik got within a few feet of them and was forced to stop as Selelle backed into him. Looking over her head, he saw that in the shade under the forest canopy, the glowing biomass was still squirming about.

The mass of creatures stretched as far back into the forest as Manik could see, but stopped at the edge of the shadows leading towards the meadow. As they watched silently, the sun crept further, driving the biomass steadily back, but far too slowly. A few minutes later, they all heard the tinkling sound of someone else approaching from where they'd just left.

Manik turned to greet Krym, the only one it could be, and let out a cry of alarm when instead the tusked head of a Seal-creature came bounding through the grasses at him. Turning, he wrapped one arm around Selelle and one around the Captain, and threw himself sideways out of the beast's charge, feeling the wind rush as it soared through the air where his chest had been moments before.

Without slowing, the creature barreled out of the grasses and across the small patch of bare soil to enter the shadow of the forest. Selelle let out her own cry, jumping out of Manik's grip to try to restrain or somehow save the creature. All three were surprised and taken aback when the creature let out a short trumpet, lowered its open maw to ground level, and scooped a small swath of wriggling, glowing, worms into its mouth. It proceeded to chew happily as the surrounding biomass, through some basic survival instinct, began to quickly burrow down and away from the hungry attacker. Bounding forward once again, the creature gained another mouthful, causing the swath of clear forest floor to spread even further.

Manik stood up, lifting the Captain back to his feet as well. Watching the soil closely, Manik saw not a single stirring pebble in the swath cut by their unwitting companion. Selelle was the first to move, creeping forward in her soft-soled Venalaran make boots. She approached the edge of the shadow and paused, and then carefully moved her foot into the shadow, pushed down on the dirt, and then lifted her foot again as quickly as she was able. Seeing no response, she brought her foot down as hard as she could, sending out a dull thud, but still bringing forth no glowing biomass.

Taking a deep breath, she walked forward carefully following the path that the Seal-creature had cut. After a few steps, she turned and waved reassuringly at Manik and Captain Fujiwara, who both advanced carefully onto the shadowed soil. Manik stayed close to the wide trunked trees with his claws out, in case he had a need to suddenly climb to avoid having his feet consumed from below.

The creature cut a meandering path through the mass for a few hundred feet, until the entire local area biomass had fully buried itself as far as they could see across the small rises and valleys of the forest. Once there was no more immediate food to be had, the creature backtracked to where the trio had stopped at the top of the first rise in from the forest edge. Approaching Selelle, the creature let out a soft grunt then stopped and sat waiting expectantly. Looking over her shoulder at the two males for answers, unsuccessfully, she held out her hand to it. Leaning forward, it made a show of sniffing her hand then settled back in its place and continued to watch her. Turning to Manik and the Captain, she shrugged.

"I have no idea what it wants now." she said.

Nodding, the Captain said, "Well, we're wasting precious daylight in this very dangerous location. Let us get to the *Sunrise* as quickly as we are able so that we can return to the others that much sooner." He then started to walk forward, giving the creature a wide berth, and headed in roughly the correct direction of the crashed bridge.

Realizing he hadn't put them on yet, Manik pulled his Specs from his pocket. Pockets are incredibly useful, why don't traditional Chromaran clothing have them? He'd have to make a note to thank SID for putting them onto the replacement clothing she'd made for him. As the Specs booted up, SID immediately materialized next to Selelle and spoke, startling Manik for a moment.

"He needs to turn fifteen degrees to his left or he'll miss it."

Manik repeated the information and was amazed that, without looking back, Fujiwara turned exactly fifteen degrees left mid-stride and continued on his way.

Realizing he was still standing in place, Manik stepped off briskly to keep near the Captain, in case anything bad should happen. As he passed Selelle, she fell in behind, making random hand gestures at the Seal-creature. After only a moment's cajoling it fell into step a safe distance behind her in its strange undulating gait.

As they continued through the soft, freshly churned dirt hills and valleys of the forest, they caught the briefest glimpses of the biomass disappearing under the topsoil, which were gradually replaced by isolated bars of sunlight spearing down through the canopy above. With the light of day, the sounds of the creatures above began to spread. First a single rhythmic knocking could be heard, and then another joined. The numbers rose quickly to a percussive crescendo, giving a backdrop for the louder bird calls that echoed across the trees. In the distance, Manik was able to just make out the sound of one of the tree predators leaping from tree bole to tree bole. The silence that followed its passing was soon swallowed once again by the cacophonous canopy dwellers.

After about four hours of progress, with occasional stalling to entice the easily distracted and notably exhausted Seal-creature into continuing onward, they arrived at the deep furrow marking the crashed bridge segment of the once beautiful ship. At the far end, a few hundred yards from where they had approached it, lay the sad remainder thereof. Looking in the opposite direction, Manik could just make out the wound they'd cut on their way down through the canopy through the gloomy shadows cast by the thicker foliage above. It was a testament to SID's ability that even during the crash she managed to avoid pancaking them on a tree in the last few moments.

Captain Fujiwara broke into a jog towards the bridge, obviously relieved that it still existed. Manik and Selelle followed as the Seal collapsed into the furrow, curled up, and quickly began snoring. Hopping over the jagged metal at the edges the Captain landed neatly on the catwalk, which immediately shifted and threw him to one side. Diving between him and the wall, Manik braced the older man as the ship settled slightly lower into the soil.

"Captain, be careful! The worms are probably eating it from the underside as well, so it might not be entirely stable. Selelle called from a few feet away.

Smiling and shaking his head at her, the Captain regained his feet and straightened his coat. "Thank you for that apt analysis, Doctor. Next time we'll aim to determine that information BEFORE I set foot on the deck, I think."

Motioning for Manik to follow he went to the maintenance hatch and began digging through fuse boxes and control nodes for wires that were not obviously burnt out. Stepping through Manik's left shoulder into the small room, SID began verbally assessing the damage and possible salvageable components. Manik quickly started repeating her comments and gestures, allowing them to quickly strip the room. When finished, they had about fifty feet of various density wires, half a dozen tools that weren't bent beyond repair, twenty liquid and cloth bulkhead emergency patches, and three rolls of utility tape.

Gathering everything in his arms, the Captain squeezed past Manik and made a pile on the tilted deck plates. Fujiwara headed next into the stateroom, the other two close behind. From just inside the door, Manik continued to pass on SID's commentary on useful or possibly useful items. Selelle, for her part, began gathering the thrown items and ferrying them out to the swiftly growing pile. Nodding occasionally, the Captain began by quickly stripping the backup blanket and sheets from the compartments above the bed and throwing them towards the door. Next came the sealed reserve mattress from under the bunk. After that he pried the sink hatch open and, with a quick twist, opened the maintenance panel and began pulling filters, portable reservoirs, and spare tubing from the recessed area. Moving finally to the desk, he began worrying the tablet from the surface.

Watching with a mournful look, SID turned to Manik and said, "Love, the console is completely fried...it's only use now is a sunshade, and it wouldn't make a very good one at that."

Taking a deep breath, Manik watched the Captain work for a moment, and then said, "Sir, leave it. There's nothing there that hasn't been backed up."

Nodding, he stopped his work, straightening the toggles to smooth out the surface once more. Manik couldn't bring himself to tell the man the uselessness of the gesture so he simply gathered up the materials from the wash system and added them to the pile outside. After a few moments, the Captain came out of the stateroom and headed onto the bridge. Following behind, Selelle and Manik pulled up short as Captain Fujiwara froze a few steps into the room.

Moving quietly Manik padded to the right, running his gaze across the inset wall modules for anything that might be of use. SID walked through the room as well, silently circling the piloting station. Taking mental stock of the padding and straps on the seats, Manik waited for the word from the Captain.

Captain Fujiwara stood directly behind the pilot theater with his eyes shut, leaning slightly backward to counter the small forward tilt of the deck. Taking a slow breath, he began to sing quietly in a language Manik did not recognize. The song was quick and clipped but the long years of practice showed through in his inflection and the undulation of the timber of his voice. He sang for a few moments, paused, said a few more quiet words, paused again, and then put his palms together with his fingertips in front of his face. Taking a shaking breath he said one last phrase, and then clapped three times.

Putting her hand on his shoulder, Selelle asked quietly in the silence that followed, "Captain?"

Stepping away from her hand he shook himself, and then said, "Alright, the *Kyoto Sunrise* is no more. Let us see what final gifts and assistance she can offer us, and then get back out of these accursed woods before dark."

Manik began with the closest chair, pulling the pads off of their bases and pulling the straps out as far as they would go before cutting them cleanly with his claws. As he worked, he tried to recall when he'd last sharpened them. Certainly not in the last week or two...he was due for a good long scrub and sharpening. Working methodically, he stripped all of the seats on that side then turned to the pilot's station.

Stepping into the familiar hemisphere of monitors, now cracked and dark, Manik stared at the line of dried blood running from the recessed connection port down to the floor. Reaching out, he ran his nails down the side of the couch where SID would place her hologram to keep him company. The room seemed to fade, leaving only the smooth cloth under his fingertips, the warm breeze flowing in from the open hatchway, and the combined scents of the trees and dirt outside with the stale musk of dried blood. Closing his eyes, he hoped that he could find some way off of this planet. Some way to save everyone. Some way to save SID.

A soft tap on his shoulder startled Manik to awareness. Spinning around, he saw a concerned Selelle peering up at him. After a few moments of silence, she finally said, "Don't worry Manik. We'll save her if we can...once we save ourselves. Here, let's see if any of these monitors are worth taking..." she finished, looking intently down the rows at each monitor for cracks and other obvious physical trauma.

Manik backed out of the pilot theater, suddenly able to breathe again. Looking around, he saw the Captain with his hand resting on the seat module he'd used in the crash, looking at him. Manik saw the pain he felt at the loss of the ship magnified a thousand fold for the briefest moment, and then

Fujiwara nodded at him and continued moving items out onto the exterior plating.

Manik quickly stripped the remaining modules of straps, figuring they could use them to make some kind of harness or carrying packs, and took them to the stack outside. Following him out with a load of module pads, the Captain knelt and started matching and lining up similar length straps and sorting the cushions and pads into piles by size. Crouching down, Manik began helping to sort as well to speed the process. Minutes bounded past as the two men fell into sync and became a small organic machine of organization.
With a sudden burst of movement, Manik dove back into the bridge, startling the Captain. What little training he'd had with Krym seemed almost unconscious to him now, as he flowed through the door and spun to navigate the room at top speed. Dodging around the pilot theater, his toe claws screeching on the metal as he slid, he saw what had caused his movement in the first place. Selelle was in mid-air, falling through the open walkway of the theater with one of the upper monitors clutched tightly to her chest. Hooking his fingers on a bent deckplate, Manik flung himself through the final intervening feet. He braced himself to catch her or at least to slow her descent enough that she didn't injure herself.

The impact was much more slight than he'd thought it would be, barely causing him to stagger. Selelle whirled in alarm and quickly looked Manik over without loosening her grip on her monitor-turned-lifeline.

"Manik! But you were outside...all I did was squeak, I think...are you alright? You shouldn't do things like that, throwing yourself in the way will get you hurt!" she berated him, clearly more angry at herself then at him.

Nodding gravely, trying desperately to keep a straight face, Manik gently but firmly pried the undamaged screen from her hands and said, "Yes Doctor, I'll bear that in mind. Shall we go gather our belongings?"

Nodding, still flustered, she turned and walked across the room and out the door with as much dignity as she could muster. Following, Manik slowed to look at the grooves he'd put in the metal of the floor. He didn't realize he was moving fast enough to do that kind of damage. *Krym's move-now-analyze-later strategy does seem to have its uses.*

Stepping back out into the murky afternoon sun again, Manik added the monitor to the stack of items to be bundled and began organizing as best he could. Selelle knelt down on the far side of the pile and began weaving straps and interlacing buckles creating what quickly became carrying harnesses for each of them.

Parsing out the items, Manik ensured that his share contained the tools, monitor, and other heavier metal and polycarbonate items. Within an hour, they were standing with their bundles on their backs, with extra seat pads threaded on the usable wires and hung across their shoulders and down their sides.

As they stepped off of the metal of the deckplates the Captain paused for a moment, lowering his head and closing his eyes. Manik started to say something, but Selelle silently put her hand on his arm and shook her head. Swallowing his comment, he waited patiently for the Captain to move.

A few minutes later, Fujiwara exhaled heavily, raised his head, and opened his eyes. Turning to look at the other two he said, "We'd better get going. We are running low on daylight and I don't want to end as she did on a planet that doesn't even have a name yet." he gestured behind him to his fallen beauty for emphasis.

Turning to give the wreck of the bridge one last glance and goodbye, they all started off in the direction they'd come from. Selelle paused for a moment to poke the Seal-creature awake, which shook itself and fell in behind her like a trained pet.

Conversationally, Manik asked, "How do you get it to follow you around like that?"

Selelle said, "Oh, it's like the seals we have back in the Macrocurrent. Feed them and pet them and generally show them kindness and they'll follow you just about anywhere...except near Zerin hunting grounds."

Confused, Manik asked, "Zerin? Macrocurrent?"

Selelle shook her head. "I'm sorry, I forgot how young you are. The Macrocurrent is the main flow of water around Venalara. It sweeps right past Grand, our capital, where we can hit port and trade every few months. Zerin are...hmm...well, they're big, scary, and eat meat-" she explained.

"So, kinda like Krym?" Manik interjected.

Captain Fujiwara snorted and Selelle laughed loudly. "Yes, just like Krym. Only fish, and with much bigger teeth and less table manners." she finished.

They all chuckled at the audacity of the idea as they moved steadily over hill and thin valley toward the fields. Continuing the conversation, Selelle told Manik all about life aboard her flotilla, the floating village where she grew up. She explained that most of her family was still there, and that she was the strange one for wanting to leave the flotilla, and even more so for wanting to leave the planet.

"So, why did you leave?" he asked.

"Oh, my family was wonderful and the flotilla was home...but I wanted to see the stars close up, not just from the deck." she explained. "I found out that I was good at remembering complex details and instructions and that I had quick and sure hands from years of weaving the nets...I was the best out of all of my sisters...so one rotation I decided to stay in Grand when my family left on the tide."

"Just like that?" Manik wondered.

Selelle nodded. "Just like that. Well...there were lots of tears and goodbyes and exchanging of hugs...but then they were gone. I found the biggest University in the city and applied for enrollment. Being a Floater they had a few scholarships that I was able to use-"

"Wait..." Manik interrupted, "A Floater? They really called you that?"

Selelle giggled and nodded. "Yes. I can laugh about it now...I didn't get the joke back then and once I did I was already deep enough in my studies that it didn't much matter what the Cityfish thought of me. I finished a few years of school there, going pre-Med, and then got lucky on an offworlder scholarship program at UoU, the University of Utopia on Ryla-"

Selelle's explanation was cut off by a giant object slamming into the ground nearby. All three people jumped, startled, but the Seal-creature didn't seem to sense anything out of the ordinary. The object was rounded and oblong, about two feet high, and was a muddy golden color similar to the higher foliage.

The Captain approached the object first, reaching a foot out to tap the side with his boot. When nothing continued to happen he moved closer and examined it. Still facing the object, he spoke over his shoulder, "It is reminiscent of some of the harder shelled tropical nuts that have evolved on the colony planets. I bet there's edible meat inside...if we can get past the shell." Reeling back, he kicked the apparent nut with all the force his small frame could muster.

With a resounding crack and a subsequent whoosh, the shell burst open in a bright flash of light. The Captain threw himself backwards, covering his face with his arms, as the other two rushed forward to help. Manik helped him back to his feet, as Selelle quickly checked his clothing and skin for burn marks.

Letting out a sigh of relief, she said, "No burns, your eyes are reacting and moving...I think you got lucky."

As they took stock of the newly shell-shard littered area they all became aware of a high pitched whine was coming from the largest remaining chunk of the shell. Approaching much more cautiously, they all leaned in to see what was making the noise.

In the base of the shell, slowly spinning to a halt was a bright white glowing sphere. As they watched it wobbled like a top and fell over, rolling against the side wall and finally rocking to a halt.

Now that they could get a good look at it, the nut wasn't completely spherical....the end it had been spinning on came to a noticeable darker point, with spiraling grooves along the surface leading to the top where they all met at a thin broken stem in a starburst pattern.

Reaching in, Captain Fujiwara cautiously tapped the nut. Finding no additional surprises, he carefully reached into the shell and picked it up. The nut seemed to be about a foot long and slightly less that wide. Holding it up, he shook it gently, sniffed it, and then leaned in and knocked on the side. Nodding in satisfaction, he tucked it under and arm.

"OK, grab a few of these shell shards we can use them to cut into this...um...Exploding Dropnut, once we get back to camp. Stop giggling! It's the best I can come up with on short notice after being partially blinded and traumatized." he finished, mustering what dignity he could scavenge and began to walk proudly away carrying his prize.

After a few more minutes Selelle and Manik could breathe again and quickly grabbed a few of the more manageable shards and hurried after their Captain. As they approached him, Manik called out, "Captain, no need to be upset! Why not tell us a little of your story to pass the time?"

Captain Fujiwara slowed to allow them to catch up and said, "A story, eh? What are you, children getting ready for bed? After mocking me what makes you think I owe you any of the tales I've accumulated?"

Smiling at his back, Selelle said in her most naive and vulnerable tone, "Oh Captain, we really ARE but children compared to you. It will help us pass the time and your heroic deeds will draw our minds away from this ponderous trudge we find ourselves in! Won't you have mercy on us poor ignorant, less-good-looking, not-quite-as-amazing souls?"

Heaving a heavy sigh he said, "Well, I suppose there's nothing for it. You two won't leave me alone unless I satisfy your voracious curiosity. Hmm...let's see...Did you know that I was almost a teenager, back on Earth, when the first Orbital was commissioned?"

Manik started to do some quick math to figure out the timeframe, but was interrupted by SID speaking quietly in his ear. "Love, the first Earth Orbital was commissioned in 2132. Our Captain was twelve years old."

Speaking up, he said, "Wait a moment, Captain...I remember you mentioning living on land on Earth before the Cityships, but are you really telling us that you are older than all three of the colonies?"

Captain Fujiwara glanced at him, and then nodded. "Officially, yes. There were settlers on Ryla before then, but it wasn't its own entity separate from Earth government until a few years later. May I continue?"

Manik winced. "Y-yes, sorry."

Nodding, the Captain continued walking and, after a few minutes, began speaking again.

"It's perfectly fine, Manik. You should loosen up a bit...you didn't even interrupt me. We'll work that stutter out of you yet. Where was I? Ahh yes, the first Earth Orbital. I was living in a small town on the northwestern coast of old Japan with my family, Miyako it was called then. We had an ancient bloodline and a decent stake in one of the primary Zaibatsu that Starvault ended up forming out of, so we were slated to be in the first group aboard the *Ascension*. We were required to donate the majority of our belongings to the company in exchange for stock shares which, when calculated, determined our living space on board."

"We moved out of our little village and went to Greater Tokyo to await the call. My father, my mother, and I were crammed into a single room apartment furnished by the company as a holding place until we were allowed to board. My mother continued to have reservations about leaving Japan but my father was ever looking forward. He kept saying it over and over, like a prayer he hoped would come true: "Life will be better on the ship. We'll be important members of the company and live in the lap of luxury...you'll see.""

The days dragged on, with only a few media series to watch and very few books on file...but the call finally came. We took the few small bags and important things that were within our allotted weight allowance and were escorted by company security officers to the shuttles where we could ascend to the already sky bound ship."

"The first thing that hit me was the wall of sound as the doors to the lift opened. The high pitched whine of the turbines on the shuttles as they were tested, the screech of metal on metal as dry parts were forced into grudging service, the shouts of the worker foreman over it all as he bellowed orders to keep the complex ballet of ants moving. And I'll never forget the smell of that loading dock...the sharp scent of flash-burned concrete, the sweat of the workers, and the slightly sweet undertone of the synthoil used to keep the moving parts moving..."

The Captain trailed off, lost in thought for a few moments, before heaving a small sigh and continuing the tale. "The pressure of liftoff is something I'll always remember. It terrified me. I thought I was going to be crushed into the seat. I couldn't breathe, I couldn't think...then the rest of the ship caught up to the inertial thrust from the slingshot and we could see the sea skipping by below us. The monitors along the walls, floor, ceiling, and on the backs of the chairs let us see just about everything...but with little lines splitting it up so you knew where the monitor borders were. Saved on cleaning bills for those people who still got vertigo from flight."

"The *Ascension*, like all of the Cityships, was built in space since they have towers both above and below the Horizon Deck. As we flew up to it the first thing that struck me was the size. It was larger than an island...probably the size of a couple of the Greater Tokyo neighborhoods, but packed with skyscrapers. The towers were all windows and the windows were all mirrored so it was dazzling to look at. A floating gem hanging in the sky."

Manik sped up slightly, giving the Captain an adjusted walking path so he wouldn't have to interrupt the narration. Turning slightly to follow the new heading, the two men walked side by side and Fujiwara continued.

"We docked on an extended landing strip jutting from the Horizon Deck, right along the middle at the widest point. The movement never stopped. Our shuttle banked in for a landing and it felt as though the magclamps barely had time to lock down before the landing strip was retracted into the bay for us to offload. There weren't many people on the shuttle when we were gathering our bags, a small blessing I've come to treasure when I can find it again, but once we stepped out onto the breezeway the numbers arriving quickly grew to more than my young mind could fathom. This is a big thing for a kid from Japan, as my home country was notorious for our issues with overpopulation over the last few hundred years leading up to when we took to the sky."

"No sooner had the landing strip struck home in its alcove then it began to move back out again. We had to jog to get off, all of us in fear of leaving the protection of the docking area and being swept off into the winds. It was cold enough inside the docking area; I was surprised there wasn't ice formed on the metal. I could only imagine how bad it would be in the winds beyond."

Shivering in the warm air, Captain Fujiwara sped up in time with his tale, lost deep in his own memories.

"We got to the decontamination dock and were told to sit and wait. Thanks to our jog we were all sweaty but, as my father cheerily pointed out, we were also almost first in line to officially board our new home. We sat on hard metal shelves that folded down out of the wall, our luggage on our laps so that the walkway was clear for the patrolling soldiers and couriers. The wait seemed interminable...that stuffy little apartment all over again...then our family was called forward and we found out why."

"They had us individually unpack and sort everything from our bags, passing all of our clothes through one decontamination washer, our electronics through another, and our breakable and precious effects through a third. We even had to strip down and put our current clothes through while we were passed individually into a cleaner to make sure we weren't bringing anything living that wasn't intended up to the ship...locusts, rats, things like that. Pests. We were all used to it...the stripping down with others in view at least, being from an area known for its hot springs and public bathhouses. I was just grateful for the shower, even a mildly burning chemical one, because then I wasn't constantly worried about offending my new neighbors and possible friends with how bad I smelled." he added with a chuckle.

"Once we were done, we moved to an interior holding area where we got dressed again in our blessedly clean clothes, and were allowed to repack everything. That took more time than I thought it would...getting our clothes stuffed back into our bags and making sure all of our valuables hadn't been damaged by the automated system. Our old family relics were things like small painted dolls from my mother's ancestor, and a daisho of swords from my father's ancestor, both of which my parents insisted on checking thoroughly before being satisfied and carefully packing them back away. As we moved out of the area I heard the machines begin cycling the next family through."

"Our guide to our new home was a young man wearing military fatigues but with the Starvault logo on his shoulder and no rank insignia. He guided us through a maze of buildings, occasionally pointing out valuable resources like shopping areas, or schools. Even though we were using mobile sidewalks he kept up a brisk pace. The empty streets he led us through felt less like a brand new city and more like one abandoned...lost to time so that nothing lived but everything was pristine. Newly minted apocalyptic architecture."

"Our building, when we finally reached it, was just beside the largest building I'd ever seen. I found out later that it was built specifically for the Allied World Government as their seat of power so in hindsight it makes sense. Our apartment suite was on the 240th floor, giving us a view about five floors above most of the other buildings. My father complained that we weren't in the penthouse on the 250th floor but my mother just waved his complaints away and started personalizing the rooms. All I could do was stare out the window."

"We were probably a few miles above the surface of the Earth, all that blue of the Pacific laid out below us, disappearing under the ship's sides as it cruised along in high orbit...the sun was a diffuse flare thanks to the reactivity of the windows letting me see past the curvature and into the gaping darkness beyond--"

Suddenly, there was a loud roar, followed by a wet squelch and a scream.

Chapter 14

Manik and Captain Fujiwara turned to see a scene that would crawl up to haunt their darkest nightmares for the rest of their days. Selelle had dropped her pack and was throwing herself at one of the tree beasts, who seemed oblivious to her attacks while it focused on eviscerating the seal-creature. The sound of Selelle screaming wordlessly, the steady bass growl from the tree beast, and the keening of the seal creature as it tried to call for help wove together into a macabre song that stunned the two men momentarily.

Selelle grabbed a pair of handfuls of dusty red fur on the beast's hunched back and swung herself up on top of it, her scream of fear shifting into one of deep anguish and rage. As she landed at the apex of its spine, she began to hammer at it with her small fists, raining blows down on its shoulders and the back of its long tusked head. As it continued to ignore her, she stood up and started trying to stomp on it, looking for all the world like it was an errant insect she intended to squash rather than the fifteen foot long, blood covered, monstrosity that it was.

Shaking its large shoulders, it effortlessly threw her to the side where she rolled to a halt by her abandoned pack. Glancing at it briefly, she pulled something from one of her pockets and got up. Balling her fists, she charged the thing once again. Manik's body finally responded, digging his toe claws into the dirt for traction to accelerate as quickly as he could. The thick topsoil, nightly churned by the wormy biomass, shifted like loose sand under his movements, betraying him.

Selelle veered toward the monster's head and raised her right fist high. Clutched in it, dark against the pale skin of her hand, was the long surgical blade from her medical kit. Stabbing own viciously, she drove the blade deep into the right eye of the creature.

The beast roared in pain and anger. The bellow was louder than anything Manik had heard before, the force bowling both men to the vibrating soil as though hit with a physical wave. As Manik fell, he saw the creature drop its head then twist and lift towards Selelle, thoroughly impaling her on one of its long tusks through her abdomen. It kept raising its head, using Selelle's body weight as momentum to fling her back off of the bloodied instrument. She sailed through the air like a stringless marionette to land with a whimper in a crumpled heap a dozen feet behind it.

With a yell of anguish, Manik snapped his claws out and charged the beast. The tree dwelling horror, hearing his charge, turned its whole body so that it could see him with its one remaining eye. It opened its jaws, revealing a long tongue and a great deal of sharply pointed teeth already shining red with the blood of the seal creature. Its grimace lowered the tusks along its lower jaw to point directly forward, leaving the two attached to its upper jaw curving up to end in wicked points a few inches above the end of its snout. Selelle's blood ran slowly down the right upper tusk, tingeing Manik's world the same color.

Dropping its head, it attempted the same maneuver that had worked on Selelle on Manik, which he spun around easily. Swinging his claws across its throat as its head swung up, Manik was jarred as his claws skittered across segmented armor plating, preventing him from a quick kill. Following his momentum, the lithe Chromaran snaked between the creature's front paw-pincers and out under its left flank. Spinning, he laid his claws into where the hamstring would be on a normal Chromaran quadrupedal predator, hoping that the anatomy was similar enough to matter.

Against all probability, the claws ripped satisfyingly through muscle and tendon alike rewarding him with a shriek of pain from the predator. Manik was pleased that he'd injured the creature and was deciding on where next to attack when SID yelled "Look out!" in his ear.

Bracing himself, he took the helicoptering beast's tail in the chest, lifting him up and flinging him away. He rolled and popped back up to his feet and hands just beyond where Selelle had landed ready to receive the charge that he knew should follow a move like that. Strangely though, the thing instead clumsily leapt up into the closest tree and began to frantically scramble away towards the canopy with its three healthy limbs. Manik considered chasing the beast for a moment, but almost immediately thought better of it, reasoning that the creature was in its home territory now and would be that much more deadly.

Crawling quickly over to Selelle's side, he began to try to assess her wounds as best he could out loud. SID materialized and provided scientific terminology and any additional information she could that Manik missed.

"OK, there's a lot of blood, wound is about six inches across and goes straight through the lower abdomen, internal injuries are a certainty...there's dirt in the wound and I don't know what kind of bacteria are on this planet, so there might be an infection building already...Selelle?"

Manik paused and spoke her name softly, putting a hand on her shoulder to keep her still as she groaned and looked around, dazed.

"You've been hurt," he continued in what he hoped was a calm tone, "we're going to get you back to camp so that we can get away from the...thing that hurt you."

Weakly, Selelle turned a confused look to Manik then reached up and patted him on the cheek with her blood soaked hand.

"Oh, it's just a scratch. Doesn't even hurt. Make sure Laii is going to be OK though. She's the one that got attacked first."

Perplexed, Manik realized that Selelle meant the seal-creature, and also that if she was in shock she may be in worse condition than he had originally thought. Turning to call the Captain, he was startled to see the old Earthborn already kneeling down next to him holding a pair of larger cushions and a length of thicker wire. Manik helped him get the pads in place on Selelle's stomach and back, and then balanced her body as he held them in place so that Fujiwara could use the wire to tie them down. With a tug, the wire cinched taught, evoking a gasp and a whimper from Selelle.

Once the wire was tied and the pads were securely holding the wounds closed, Manik laid her back down and went over to check the eviscerated remains of Laii as requested. The poor creature was rent from neck down to tail flippers, a medley of miscellaneous organs exposed to air or themselves rent. She had thankfully already expired, as Manik could see a good deal of blood in the immediate area, but no new blood was gushing forth from the terrible wounds.

Returning to Selelle's side after a few moments, he said quietly, "Laii is...well, I don't think she's going to make it. We'd better leave her here and get you back so Challis can patch you up."

Selelle began shaking her head. Slowly at first, and then more vehemently. "No, we can't just leave her here. We have to take her back. Her pod will need to know that something terrible happened to her. Plus she can still be useful, even injured she won't be a burden, you'll see. Oh Manik, we HAVE to take her back." she trailed off, sobbing gently.

In fear of her wrenching her wounds, Manik held out his hands placatingly. "OK! OK. Don't cry...um...Captain, do you think you can carry Selelle?"

Nodding, the Captain said, "She's light enough, although her pack may be a bit much to carry all the way back to camp."

Manik waved a hand dismissively. "That's OK, I can handle that and Laii. I'll get us back to camp behind you...you take her and go on ahead. She needs help as fast as we can get her to it."

Captain Fujiwara nodded again, and then knelt down and carefully lifted her up. Giving Manik a long look as she cried out when he straightened, he said "Don't tarry too long, Pilot. We need you alive and well too."

With that, he strode off in the direction of their camp at a brisk but obviously gentle walk so as not to jostle his cargo.

Manik crouched in the dirt and watched the pair slowly retreat from him. After a few minutes, he began collecting the debris from Selelle's rough landing and strapping them into convenient locations on her pack. He removed his own and interwove the straps and supports that they'd jury rigged so that he could carry both without having to constantly stop to shift the load. Once he was satisfied, he swung the newly modified pack onto his back and walked over to investigate the corpse of Laii, the seal-creature.

Her chest and abdomen were torn open, organs and entrails flayed but no longer dripping. Crouching down, he adjusted the body until it was wound up, so that he could carry it without trailing any bits in the dirt. He slid an arm under the neck above the front flippers and along the body's lower spine near where the tail began to taper.

Bracing himself, Manik heaved the body up against his chest. He stumbled briefly, surprised at the light weight of the beast. Seeming to understand his brief confusion, SID spoke up.

"The body is mostly fat and fur insulation against presumably cold or sudden changes in the consistency of the water that is the creature's natural habitat. Fat weighs much less than muscle."

"I knew that already." Manik said, straightening up. "I just thought with the size of her she'd still weigh more."

SID nodded. "I understand. It may be a peculiarity of the chemical balance of this world that the fauna have a more lightweight construction. We should hurry, it'll be dusk soon and that thing might decide to come back."

Manik set off at a comfortably brisk pace, knowing that he didn't need to speak for SID to know he agreed with her.

After a few minutes, the smell of the body began to get to Manik so he turned to look imploringly at SID who was pacing him on his right side.

"SID, please talk. I need something to distract me from what I'm doing." he implored her.

Smiling impishly, SID hovered a few inches up from the ground and ceased her walking motion. Flowing along next to him, she reached up and began to unzip the replicate singlesuit her image was wearing.

"Distract you, my dear Manik? Since you didn't specify, I guess I get to choose the method of distraction."

Manik shook his head violently, averting his eyes. "SID! Not the time or place for that! Please...just...tell me the history of Ryla or something. I need to not think about the smell of the corpse I'm carrying or that Selelle might be dead before I get back."

Sobering quickly, SID flickered and was once again fully covered and walking next to him.

"I'm sorry love. I think I might be feeling some effect of your biochemical reactions. I don't know why my logic routines defaulted to that methodology. The colony known as Ryla was founded officially on 12 March, 2141 CE. It is the fifth planet of six orbiting the yellow star Chara..."

She continued talking through the construction, society, government, corporate structure, cultural mannerisms, and famous quotes as they moved through the slowly darkening forest. As the wood break came into view, SID stopped talking.

"What's wrong SID?" Manik huffed, not wanting to waste any unnecessary breath.

"I think you should speed up until we are clear of the forest." she said quietly.

Slowing to look over his shoulder to see what she meant, he saw a trail of glowing worms leading off into the forest. The trail of them was thin about fifty feet back from him, but rapidly widened to a stream, to a river, to an ocean of them.

Looking down, Manik saw a trail of ichor dripping from the tail of the seal creature, moistening the dark soil along the path he'd walked. As he stared, he saw the soil shifting in a slow moving wave cresting with the worms burrowing up out of their daytime hiding places in search of the blood that had awoken them.

Facing forward again Manik strode off, quickly increasing to a jog as he approached the border of the safe zone that was the light stick prairie. The closer he got the faster he moved, until he was almost sprinting through the last shadowy valley before he spilled thankfully into the comparatively warm sunlight blanketing the plains.

A warm breeze blew across his face, providing momentary respite from the stench and beginning to dry the sweat that he'd worked up. Looking around, he found that he'd been moving slower than he'd initially thought as the Captain was nowhere in sight.

SID voiced his own worry. "I do not detect either the presence or proof of passage of Captain Fujiwara in the vicinity. I hope he did not lose his bearings and exit at a location further from camp than necessary."

"Nothing for it but to push on. If they made it to camp, we'll meet them there. If they didn't, I can put this body down and we can go back out to find them." Manik said quietly before striding off through the hiss and rattle of the grasses.

The hours dragged on as he brushed through the grass, leaving drops and scrapes of blood on the dirt and plants despite his best efforts. SID tried to keep him occupied with the history of Venalara and the rumors and speculations on the nature of the god-creature Guul, the sleeping macropredator in the depths off the coast of Grand.

Finally, Manik trudged into the camp area. To the relief of both Manik and SID, Captain Fujiwara was lying comfortably on the ground looking exhausted, and both Krym and Challis were standing over Selelle talking quietly.

Walking past the group to the downhill side of the camp, he deposited the corpse of Laii carefully. As he walked heavily back to the group he could feel exhaustion deep in his bones and soreness overflowing from his overtaxed muscles. Pulling the pack from his shoulders, he retained just enough awareness to lower it to the ground so that none of the contents that were breakable were damaged.

Folding forward, Manik dropped to his knees, and then his chest, and then rolled so that he was looking up at the darkening twilight, and drifted off to sleep.

It may have been minutes or hours when he was awoken by hands pulling at his shirt. Fearing he was still in the forest, and the beast from the trees had returned, he snapped his claws out. Lashing forward at his assailant, he stopped a whisper from Challis' neck.

For his part, Challis froze, seeming unsure what the best course of action would be. Manik saw the hesitation and knew why he'd lost all those fights. This must be what he looked like during that second of indecision.

Well, with smaller eyes. And more hair. And claws.

Smiling to himself, he snapped his claws back away and showed Challis his hands. "Sorry, I must have been dreaming. I didn't mean to scare you."

From a short distance away, a quiet chuckle reached them. "Hey Trouble, I think you just got the doc to wet himself. Do it again."

The jibe was what finally broke Challis' torpor, causing him to turn and narrow his eyes and say, "Mister Waverider, you are far from healthy and were I you I would cease mocking the only person on the PLANET who can keep you from a painful, agonizing, and much deserved, death."

Turning back to Manik, he continued coldly, "I swear, you Chromaran brutes always attack first and think second. It's a wonder you haven't hunted each other to extinction. May I continue, or should I have you tied down so you can no longer offer your...pointed, opinion?"

Manik stared at him for a moment in stunned disbelief. He was reasonably sure Challis had just made a joke.

Taking his silence for ascent and his pause as permission, Challis finished cutting away Manik's stained and tattered shirt. His long fingers began probing methodically as Manik heard him quietly reciting diagnoses and comments alike under his breath. He began at Manik's throat, checking for protrusions and lacerations, and then progressed down the front and sides of his rib cage, pausing only once when Manik winced.

After a few minutes of probing and experimentation, he sat back up and announced, "The young pilot will survive. He has a few bruised ribs from, I assume, his impact with the arboreal predator before it retreated. His clothes, however, have died a grisly and most horrible death and will need to be replaced as soon as possible, so that the rest of us can stand to be within a dozen yards of him."

Sitting up, shrugging out of the remains of his shirt, Manik nodded up at the Rylan. "Thank you, doctor. How is...I mean...is she going to..." he tried to say, but couldn't seem to find the right words.

Challis looked grimly down at him. "Her condition is...severe. There was enough light before nightfall that I was able to clean the wound and replace the dressings with something more appropriate, and sanitary, but it doesn't change the fact that she likely has multiple punctured or perforated organs, steady blood loss, and as we have no clue of the local area, the wound may well already be seriously infected."

SID stepped up beside Challis, an otherworldly glow after the dim outlines Manik had been looking at. "Once you get some sleep we can look at the components we have gathered and see what we can do about a relay..." she began, but Manik shook his head.

"No SID, we have to start now. Doctor, please help me unpack the packs we brought back. We need to get a signal device set up as quickly as possible, so that we can get Selelle off this planet and into a hospital." Manik said as he rose to his feet.

Standing shakily Challis motioned to Krym, who was crouched beside Selelle. "Come make yourself useful for once. We need more hands than just the two injured people on this task if we're being trusted to save everyone."

Sliding over a few feet, wincing slightly, Dorr positioned himself slightly uphill of Selelle so that he could continue the vigil, which allowed Krym and Captain Fujiwara to rise to their feet and move to assist the other two men in their crafts project.

Between the Captain, Krym, and Manik they quickly had all packs dismantled, laid out, and sorted, while Challis began organizing and inventorying all of the available items. As he did, SID kept up a running commentary mirroring him to ensure nothing was missed. Surprisingly, none of the components had been damaged or broken on the return trip, although a few did not function due to internal failures from the crash.

They started out by sorting out the wires, electrical tools, tape, emergency roll-up keyboard, and the miscellaneous polycarbonate and metal objects. Krym moved the padding and straps to one side and began fashioning bedding for as many crewmembers as he could, while the Captain and Manik stared at the remaining motley pile of parts in hopes that a solution would fall from the sky onto them.

"What's this?" Krym asked. Looking over, the Captain groaned and hid his head in his hands. Manik grinned and happily replied.

"That, as our wondrous Captain has named them, is an Exploding Dropnut. It's already exploded, so don't worry about that. It's theoretically edible, but we haven't gotten much time to test it. It fell off of one of the trees as we were walking by."

"EUREKA!" SID shouted, far too loudly, in Manik's ear. Manik, for his part, yelped at the sudden noise in the otherwise quiet evening and fell backwards out of his squatting position.

Standing a few feet away, looking excited, SID said, "That's what you say when you have an idea, right? I got one! My first idea!" she was visibly almost vibrating with contained enthusiasm.

"SID...sweetie...please don't suddenly yell 'eureka' in my ear when everyone is quiet. My heart can't take many more surprises like that." he said, as he got back to his feet and endured the giggles and muffled chuckles of the others.

"But it's a momentous occasion! I had an idea! A sudden, random thought that occurred to me and didn't go through the normal lines of deduction and causality before logical extrapolation! What a rush! I think I like this feeling...all cold and tingly." she babbled on.

"SID, that'd be my adrenaline. Focus please...what was it?" Manik said, brushing the small amount of dirt he'd gathered from his legs and back.

"Well," she began, flitting quickly across the rock to illustrate her points, "we, that is, you could set up the cable from southwest to northeast and then perpendicular to that, northwest to southeast, which would line up with the magnetosphere of the planet as I read it on the way down, which should give us a good broadcast dish for the time that the planet is facing the correct direction."

"When will the planet be facing the correct direction for that to work?" Manik interrupted.

"What? Oh, about the same time as the crash happened, since that's the most likely angle at which we can relay information off of the buoy in orbit. The entry into the atmosphere was roughly one Earth standard hour before dawn, according to my calculations and the ships chronometer at time of descent. That gives us...most of the night to get it up and running." she finished.

Manik nodded and turned to relay the information to the others. "OK, we need to lay out the cable in a cross pattern, along these two lines..." he scratched a rough image at the center point of the stone, "and we only have a little while to get it set up. The buoy will be in range a little before dawn, SID thinks, so we have to have everything set up and ready to transmit by then."

Krym and Captain Fujiwara nodded and set to the task of sorting, splicing together, and spooling out the lengths of cable they'd salvaged while Manik and Challis began to cannibalize the various electronics they'd returned with for necessary parts to make a very basic communications array.
As they worked Challis began to cough irregularly, causing Manik to eye him with concern. The doctor waved his inquiring glance off, mumbling something about allergens and lack of palatable nutrient slurry. Within a few short hours, they'd hooked up the monitor to a delicately balanced grouping of chips, boards, and filaments which were in turn spliced into the center of the large cross of cabling laid out by Krym and the Captain.

Sitting back on his haunches, Manik said "OK SID, we've got the basics set up...how do we interface with it? For that matter what software do we need to use to communicate with the buoy?"

Walking along the array she silently inspected the connections, pausing and leaning in occasionally to explore the more complex points of braided and spliced wire. Once she seemed satisfied she smiled apologetically at Manik.

"The end of the cable needs to be spliced into your TechSpecs so that I can use them to upload the program I've been writing."

She paused, wincing slightly as though she'd done something wrong and was anticipating consequences, giving Manik the moment he needed to think over her statement again.

"Program." he said simply. She nodded and held up her hands pleadingly.

"You wrote a program...in my brain. To talk to a satellite buoy. Without telling me." he finished.

Challis leaned back and Dorr surreptitiously moved his hands up to his ears in case he'd have to block out a sudden and one sided yelling match.

In the silence SID spoke quickly, nervously, her words spilling over each other. "Well, you see, the organization of your drive space is quite strange and I've only just started to get used to it and I found a few sectors that hadn't been in use and were waiting for information and I THINK I've figured out how to remove previously saved information although it's quite difficult to get it to stay deleted. Much harder than other mediums I've worked with in fact. But the program is small and quiet and it should do all that we need to set up a good interface in the first microseconds of connection so that we can start conversing immediately if we're lucky enough to have a ship within range in Real or Underspace..." she faded out meekly as Manik continued to stare at her impassively.

"I'm...sorry I did it without asking you first. I know that I should have and I really am very sorry I did. I'm trying to get better and follow all of the parameters and suggestions you give me so that you won't stop liking me but it's very hard to concentrate right now and will you please say something?" she finished sounding desperate and surprisingly close to tears.

Manik shook his head and smiled. At least she was learning to spot her own social missteps, which was going in the right direction. He took a deep breath and let it out slowly, and then said, "It's alright SID. You are getting better every day. Soon you'll make fewer mistakes than us lowly organics at being social."

SID visibly sagged with relief sending Manik a warm, thankful smile.

Pausing for a moment, he changed the subject back to the task at hand, "So you need my brain and the Specs connected up to the system to start, how long do I need to stay connected to make sure everything works?"

SID thought for a moment, and then replied, "Well, the program will install the second you link up so your brain doesn't need to be there for long...but we will need the battery from the TechSpecs to stay connected so that the entire apparatus has power. You'll have to either lay on the ground to wear them or take them off for a while. Depending on how fortunate we are the wait could be as little as a few hours but as long as multiple weeks."

Manik shook his head and started to argue, and then stopped himself. He didn't want to send anyone into a panic or fits of despair. He chose his response carefully.

"Alright, let's hope for the shortest window then. How much time do we have until hookup?"

"Approximately one hour until the window of access opens...give or take." SID replied uncertainly.

"Approximately. How much give and take SID?"

SID mumbled something, seeming to be suddenly very interested in her incorporeal shoes. Manik was reminded of his own proclivity when he was a child and was being forced to confess to an untruth to his father or aunt.

Taking a page from the more gentle of his previous taskmasters Manik tried to make his voice as soothing as possible. "SID, your shoes don't need to know but I do. How much?"

Taking a steadying breath, another habit she seemed to have pirated from his memories, she said, "Fifty-seven minutes give or take. Meaning you have to hook up now and we can't talk to each other for a while. I was just enjoying being...well...a part of you so much that I didn't want it to end..."

Manik smiled reassuringly at her again. "Don't worry SID, I know you're there even if I can't converse with or see you. Let's get this set."

Pulling off the TechSpecs, Manik crouched down and collected the bundle of wires at the input station. Coiling them around the input sensors at either temple of the Specs, he then carefully replaced them on his head, having to drop to his stomach so he didn't wrench the wires out of place.

The display for the Specs showed nothing but Manik could hear a faint static buzzing. After a few minutes the screenglass flashed brilliant white a few times then slowly faded to a misty grey.

SID's disembodied voice floated to him sounding much more hollow and further off than before. "The connection is established and the program is running. As long as the array is intact and the power cell on the TechSpecs holds out, I can maintain this signal. I'll put a notice up on the monitor if I get a response so you'll know."

Manik replied quietly, "Alright SID, thanks." then pulled the Specs carefully off and placed them on the ground next to the monitor.

Looking around, Manik saw that everyone was turned toward the downhill slope. Focusing on his ears he realized that part of the static he'd heard through the Specs had actually been waves of the tinkling sounds of the glassgrass stalks rubbing against each other. Straightening up, he saw a dark form moving through the grasses towards them. Manik started to move forward, but Krym laid a large hand on his shoulder to stop him.

Quietly, he growled, "No. We need you in case something goes wrong with the array. I'll deal with this. Bout time I got a little exercise anyway."

The tinkling grew steadily more and more cacophonous until the gargantuan form responsible finally crashed through the grass line onto the lower part of the silicate landing. The ground shook as the multi-ton beast landed next to the corpse of the seal creature and it bent its huge tusked head to investigate. As it did, Manik was struck with the similarity. The head shape was not identical, but very close, the number of tusks was the same but these were longer and the ends were stained and pocked. The beast was at least double Manik's height, and could only be the bull that Selelle had mentioned might exist down by the beaches.

Raising his voice slightly, Krym said "Nobody move, I'm going to try to draw it off a bit. The last thing we need is it destroying the array or hurting anyone already down any further."

Stepping away from the group, Krym slowly and smoothly picked his way across the rock, staying the same distance from the bull while moving as far from the array as he could.

The beast continued nosing the corpse with its long snout and tusks, shifting it this way and that, each time letting out a short, quiet, low bass whine. After a few minutes, it seemed to come to the conclusion that the fallen creature was not going to get back up and raised its head to release a deafening bellow at the bottom end of the hearing range for Manik.

The stone vibrated beneath him, and the glassgrass around the clearing rattled and clacked in resonance. Manik clamped his hands over his ears and saw that everyone else was doing the same, even Selelle in her quasi-conscious state. The roar seemed to go on for years. It soaked into Manik's bones and he felt as though he would vibrate from it forever.

Then it stopped, and silence crashed down on the clearing.

Still crouching, Manik tapped his fingers lightly against the ground just to make sure he hadn't lost his hearing completely. The reassuring tap tap was quieter than he'd expected but much clearer than he'd feared. A sigh of relief escaped him.

The bull's head swung immediately towards him, its row of tiny eyes fixed on Manik's now frozen form. It lowered its tusks and began to gather itself, muscles bunching under the blubbery outer layer of flesh.

Taking a deep breath, Krym let out a battle roar worthy of any Arena on Chromara. His roar was much diminished in comparison to the mammoth bull but was striking nonetheless. His higher timbre voice was focused away from the group, thankfully saving them from the brunt of the sound force, but the ancillary effects obeyed no direction. Manik felt his hackles rise and fought to keep his body still and his claws sheathed...a tough battle as his instincts were quite strong.

The bull swung its head around to the newly perceived threat and attempted to reorient its charge. The complex dance of muscles shifted as the bulk changed direction for launch. With a mighty grunt the beast undulated forward, slamming its forward flippers and chest on the silicate with a rumbling slap that sent a small shockwave through the ground.

Krym danced and rolled to the side the furthest point he could manage from both the wire array and the crew. With a rising guttural shriek the creature quickly gained speed, seeming to be bent on crushing Krym with its sheer overpowering mass.

A moment before impact, Krym leapt up and back the way he'd come. The beast swung its head around in surprise but barreled past, missing him by a wide margin. Krym's fingers trailed along the expansive flanks as it roared past, unable to break the hold of its momentum.

Manik saw Krym's forearms flexing, trying to dig his nonexistent claws into the flesh of his opponent. The blow would have been superficial considering the beasts size but first blood was first blood in Arenas as well as in nature.

As it left the silicate, the creature sank slightly into the dirt of the plain and began to slide. It flexed again and fishtailed around to try and orient itself once again on Krym. As it slid, it crushed a wide swath of the glassgrass shoots, which exploded mutely under the beast's bulk. It yelped in surprise and lunged forward, finally stopping itself completely a dozen yards from the slab.

Krym was already running towards it, yelling at the top of his lungs. His smooth, quick movement gave the impression of both uncontained fury and looming death. Manik sat and watched in awe, until Challis poked him. Looking where the, for once, silent Rylan was gesturing he saw the screen flashing red. As he watched, it pulled up a crude map of their array with a section of wire flashing red while the rest was a pleasant blue. Following SID's guide, he found the section of wire that the beast had crushed in its initial charge. Muttering a curse under his breath Manik began to slowly and smoothly move himself across the expanse of stone, hoping not to gain the attention of either combatant.

Krym pounced upward, dodging a close swing of the tusks of the bull with a deft spin in midair, and landed on the creature's mammoth shoulder. Grabbing a double handful of the obviously bristly black hair growing there, he began to scale it like a cliffside in an earthquake. The bull, for its part, followed the swipe by continuing to turn, rotating its body back on itself in an ever increasing rotation to try and throw its unwanted passenger free.

Creeping forward, moving a single limb at a time, Manik worked his way past the interface module and started down the line of wires. When did they get so long? He held out a thin line of hope that he would be able to repair the wire cluster before the time window arrived. He held out a stronger hope that he'd be able to repair the wires at all.

Continuing his climb, Krym reached the summit of the hump of bone and fat behind the bull's head. Clinging tightly to the thick hair there he leaned down and bit, drawing first blood in actuality and prizing a bellow of fury from the beast. With a mighty jerk in the opposite direction it tried to shake loose the attacker. Krym clung with hands and teeth, worrying the wound with the creature's own swaying momentum. For a solid minute, it continuing to thrash its head back and forth, desperately trying to snag some portion or extremity of Krym's on its tusks so that it could return the bloody favor.

Manik finally reached the damaged section and sighed quietly in relief. The cluster had been crushed down but was able to be re-braided and would probably not result in a massive signal loss. Pulling the trailing end in, he got to work. The pre-dawn grey light made the work quicker going than the earlier braiding had but his constant checking and re-checking of how Krym was doing slowed him down all the more.

Snapping his jaws back out of the creature, Krym spat out the burning, horrible tasting blood and looked around. Following his gaze, Manik saw Captain Fujiwara shielding Selelle and Dorr with his thin frame and Challis sitting as though planted in the stone by the interface. Looking back to the battle, he locked eyes with the warrior for a moment before nodding and setting back into his work with a yet more insistent sense of urgency.

As he shifted his gaze down, movement caught Manik's eye but he dismissed it quickly. The grasses beyond the beast were just shaking in the wind. The lack of breeze on Manik's back became a nagging itch, but he pushed it away. He turned all of his focus and attention on finishing his work quickly, feeling like he was back in the Arena training classes doing timed braiding and other manual dexterity exercises. When he finished, he laid the wires carefully back in line with the rest of the array spoke and focused his attention fully on the glassgrass beyond the battling pair.

A wave was moving through the grasses circling the battling pair. The movement was so subtle and purposeful that it seemed unmistakably sinister amidst the throes of combat. Manik rose to his feet, heedless of the distraction he might be, as he tried to peer closer into the dense stalks to identify the approaching mystery.

With a screeching cry and the crash of grass stalks against one another, one of the forest tree-horrors launched itself out of its concealment and straight into Krym, flinging him from his perch atop the bull seal-creature four meters above the ground.

Startled, Krym swung his hands off of the hair of the bull and inward just in time, catching the impaling tusk before serious damage was done. The momentum of the large creature propelled both of them off of the back of the bull and down into the dirt on the far side.

With a roar, the bull rounded on the newer and larger threat and charged.

Manik was much too far away. He was running at top speed, his claws scratching for purchase on the hard silicate but he wasn't going to be fast enough. The greater musculature and shorter distance that the bull had to travel would win out, he knew it. He just hoped he'd be in time to save Krym. He ran in at an angle from the bull, arriving at the pile of claws, fur, and teeth only a moment after it did.

The bull swung its head down and back as it charged, presenting a meaty shoulder to the treebeast. As it arrived, though, it scythed its tusks through the first inch or two of dirt and up into the air, not entirely dissimilar to the move the tree-beast had used to impale Selelle, throwing both treebeast and Krym up and away like rag dolls.

Because of his positioning on the throw and his lighter weight, Krym's trajectory sent him cartwheeling out into the grasses, while the treebeast was only thrown a handful of yards.

Following the line of descent Manik charged into the grasses, heedless of the noise he made, as he searched for Krym's fallen form. The stalks chattered angrily at him as he dove through until he found the short wound cut in the landscape of the plains, littered with still sputtering broken stalks, with Krym lying at the end in a heap.

Krym, for his part, was groaning and attempting to get his feet under him, albeit without much success. Manik slid to a stop next to him in the soft soil and began helping the older man to stand. With his feet on the ground and a shoulder to lean on, Krym rose slowly, wincing as he did.

Once Krym unfolded himself, Manik saw the fresh blood stain matting the front of Krym's shirt, pants, and running down his face.

"How much pain are you in?" Manik asked, slightly louder than he normally would have thanks to the boisterous sounds of combat between the bull and the treebeast a few dozen meters off.

"Not much but it might be shock. How hurt do I look?" Krym replied matter-of-factly.

Looking him over once more, Manik said, "You're favoring your right leg but still putting weight on both, so probably a musculature or tendon issue in your lower leg. Your chest wound is bleeding but not profusely, so it's likely a shallow puncture from the creature's tusk. You are having equilibrium issues so I'd guess a concussion from the landing has started a mild brain bleed. Nothing that a bit of rest and some bandages won't cure."

Krym nodded. "Three out of four. Not bad, kid. I've also got a few burns from the broken stalks on landing and shards of the broken bits embedded in a few wounds. Won't be lying on my back anytime soon...not on purpose at least. Let's get back to the others. With any luck, those two monsters will bleed each other out."

Manik nodded his agreement and began picking his way back, carefully avoiding the patches of shattered glassgrass and the sputtering flames from the still grounded stalks.

Their progress was slow, thanks to the height of the grasses in this part of the field easily topping off at 10 to 12 feet above the soil in most places, giving the illusion of moving through a forest of dark glass rather than a field of grasses. As they moved, they both listened intently to the sounds of the fighting, ears perked up to try and assess purely by sound what the status of the fighters was at the moment.

Screams both high and low pitch rang through the grasses, refracted and dampened only slightly by the constant rattle of the grasses rubbing together. The ground shook now and again, as the bull charged, feinted, or possibly just shifted its titanic bulk around to bring its weapons to bear.

Suddenly there was a deep roar that escalated and thinned into a weak trilling that slowly faded out. Manik and Krym looked at each other, both seeing the same conclusion in the other man's eyes.

The bull had lost.

In unspoken agreement they sped up, trying to get back to the camp or at least an area that was less vulnerable than their current location. With a suddenness that brought them both up short they stepped out into the broken scar carved through the soil that the bull had plowed in one of his charges.

To their left, lay the body of the bull seal-creature, nearly black blood and ichor oozing from uncountable small wounds across its expansive hide.

To their right lay their camp, complete with their delicate communications array and equally delicate crewmembers, all of whom were staring in their direction with wide, terror filled eyes.

Between them and the camp, moving like a silent, slinking, embodiment of death, was the treebeast.

Pulling Krym back slightly into the grasses, Manik lowered him down to a sitting position in the soil. "Stay here, you've done enough. It's my turn."

Krym searched Manik's eyes, seeming to be looking for something, and then he nodded. "Ancestors and Warriors are watching, kid."

Manik nodded then turned and stepped out into the swath. With a flick of his wrists and a flex of his ankles, he felt all ten claws slide and lock into place smoothly. Taking a deep breath, visualizing what would happen if he failed, Manik let out the loudest roar he could.

The sound was higher and thinner than Krym's but still held enough timbre to get the point across to the treebeast. It stopped its leisurely stalk and turned its head left, focusing its eye on Manik.

When it did, Manik had a sense of Deja-vu. He'd seen this particular creature before somewhere. Had it been the one they'd first seen? One of the ones off in the distance? No. Looking down at its leg, he saw the scabbing cut along the tendon, and it was favoring the leg.

This was the monster that had impaled Selelle. It had come all the way out here away from its forest to...what? Get revenge? Finish the kill? None of it made sense from an animal perspective. Why was it here?

The blood.

It must have followed the trail of blood from the corpse Manik had been carrying. Stupid. Careless. Sentimentality that went far beyond the rational. His fault. Manik shook his head and crouched low. Nobody else was going to get hurt his crew, his friends.

The treebeast turned to follow its head movement, finishing its turn to reveal the still dark wound where its other eye should be, confirming Manik's suspicion. It continued the stalking slink in a wide circle back towards Manik. The fluidity of its motion marred only slightly by the wound and subsequent limp it had received earlier that day. A small part of Manik's mind marveled at the healing that had been done in the short span of a few hours. These creatures must be able to fully recover from wounds in days rather than the weeks it took humans without medical treatment. The crunching of the beast's wide, clawed, pincers crunched on the broken shards of the grass stalks as it prowled forward brought Manik's full attention back to the matter at hand.

He began to circle in the opposite direction, hoping to get a good angle where he was closer to the crew than the beast but didn't put them in danger if it should charge past him. He felt small pinpricks brushing the bottoms of his feet through his thin sandals as he, too, traversed the zone of shattered glass.

Once he was in, as far as he could judge with peripheral vision, the perfect position he crouched low and braced himself to move.

The treebeast, seeing its opponent drop, lunged forward and swiped with the bloodied, clawed tips of one paw. The swing seemed more for threat than effect as Manik had no need to move to avoid the display.

Opening its mouth slightly, the beast let out a throaty growl and began coiling itself back on its haunches. Manik remembered seeing this pouncing technique used by one in the trees and decided that, if this move was at all similar, he should be able to dodge. Should he go below and try for a chest or stomach wound or above where he hadn't tested the strength of the creatures thick hide yet?

The monster flung itself forward, forelimbs outstretched with the obvious intent of favoring Manik with a deadly embrace. Manik leapt up and forward as well, surprising his rival. As he sailed above its tusks, he drove his claws down to try and pierce the muzzle or skull. The tips of his claws bit but the thickness of the hide stopped him from getting a swift kill to end the fight. His momentum carried him over the creature, carving a trio of lines from its muzzle, across its skull, and down its back.

Manik and the treebeast landed at the same time, both whirling to face their quarry once again. Now that both fighters were on the defensive they circled each other for long minutes, occasionally swinging a claw here or there to test for reactions and openings. Manik, determined that he wouldn't lose this fight, let his mind go blank of all distractions. His possible moves, the long list of counters, fighting techniques and styles, the state of being of his friends, the security of the array...it all faded and left him with a pure, unfettered, sense of what was now.

A sudden cry from the crew caused the beast to whip its head around. Manik didn't know why they'd do that but he didn't waste the opportunity provided. Diving forward, he slashed at the malleable flesh at the juncture of the creature's upper and lower jaws, tearing a ragged gash before jumping and rolling back out of striking range.

The beast lashed its head back and forth, trying to shake the pain away, and then raised its snout and trumpeted cacophonously. The sound was deafening, similar to the bull seal-creature's call in that way, but amazingly different in others. The reverberation from the grasses raised the background noise to a level beyond normal shouting, silencing the world with sound.

As it called, Manik clapped his hands over his ears and focused on the anatomy of the beast. With its head raised, he could see the chitinous plate he'd scratched last time clearly as well as where the darker skin started on the sides and under the base of the skull. That was a perfect weak spot if he could just get to it.

Manik dove forward once again, intending to finish the fight, when the beast suddenly snapped its jaws shut and scythed its tusks down towards him. His turn to be surprised by the ferocity of his opponent, Manik was only just able to twist to avoid being staked to the ground but the blades slashed a pair of deep, burning gashes along his left side as he did so. He rolled away again, his shin catching the trailing swipe of a claw on his way out.

Feeling markedly less confident Manik retreated away from beast and crew, further down the broken furrow, hoping to gain both distance and time to think. The treebeast, apparently realizing its target was finally wounded, redoubled its attacks. Lunging forward continually, it swiped and snapped, driving Manik into the corner provided by the bulk of the bull's corpse.

Manik felt the cold calm of imminent death spread through him. This was it, his final failure. He couldn't protect his friends, his love, or himself. He was going to die, torn apart and eaten, on a nameless planet. Fitting, he thought, as he had very little name himself. He relaxed his body, preparing for the end.

The land was suddenly awash with light and sound.

The blinding white light of landing floods was accompanied by the roar of a starship engine as a large harvester class ship skimmed past them in a wide arc.

The treebeast froze and snapped its head up to see the strange flying creature that could produce such a mighty roar.

It was the last thing that the predator's eyes saw.

Manik realized, as he stepped back, that he'd struck the creature in its vulnerable neck and scythed all the way up into its skull. He made room for the slumping body as it fell and looked down at his arms which were coated to the bicep in blood, brains, and viscera. He didn't waste his shot a second time.

Chapter 15

Stepping around the corpse he limped toward the crew, Challis and the Captain were hurriedly gathering objects and gear in preparation to be rescued as quickly as possible as Krym arrived and began preparing Selelle and Dorr for movement once again. Challis gathered a small handful of items, nothing larger than his myriad of pockets could hold, and then moved to supervise Krym's emergency transport preparations. The Captain suddenly dropped the components he was carrying and ran to the edge of the silicate. As Manik got within range, he saw that he was worrying one of the taller grass stalks emphatically.

Looking up at Manik, he said, "Quickly, help me! They need to be able to see us or they'll fly to the wreckage!"

Manik realized he was absolutely right and that all of their efforts might be for naught. Wiping his hands down the sides of his pants to clear most of the gore, he grabbed one of the complete stalks nearby and wrenched sharply. The stalk, so near the devastation left from the fight, pulled free relatively quickly.

Moving as quickly as his wounds would allow Manik returned to the silicate sanctuary, well away from where the rest of the crew were gathering themselves. Raising the stalk above his head, he smashed the tip down on the hard stone.

The end shattered in a burst of sound and flame. Holding the torch aloft, Manik waved it back and forth to get the attention of the ship. The sound burst of the ignition of the second stalk made him jump, loud even in the cacophony of the ship's wash, as the Captain held up his own improvised signal flare nearby.

The ship, which had been rising to clear the trees, banked in a wide arc. The tips of the net spines dipped low as the pilot cornered sharply to reverse course. The ship swung in a wide circle around the silicate, apparently looking for a landing position. It finally extended its landing struts and dropped into the field.

The scream of carbon on carbon and the gouts of flame and sound marked the landing path chosen as the ship slid to a halt in the soft ground just off the downhill end of the landing. Dropping his still flaming beacon, the Captain strode toward the slowly lowering gangway. Manik tossed his into the broken swath where it could burn out safely and went to help carry the more injured crewmembers on board. He hunched down to tuck his shoulder under Dorr's arm and moved parallel to Krym as he gently carried Selelle toward their salvation. As they moved toward the ship, a group of four Venalarans came down the gangway to meet them.

The ship's engines slowly spun down, calming the rattle of the stalks in the field, leaving a void of soundlessness. The approaching men were wearing serviceable, but mismatched, outfits that sported at least half a dozen sashes of various color combinations each. Hanging from their hips were gun belts that reminded Manik of the old Earth vids more than something that'd be worn this day and age.

The Captain raised a hand in greeting and began talking as he walked into the harsh glare spilling from the ship.

"We're glad you found our signal. We were afraid we may have to be residents here for a long time. Your arrival is fortuitous. We have wounded here that need medical attention, but we have our own doctor. If you'll help us on board we can-"

A single shot rang out, cutting him short.

The group froze; watching in horror as Captain Fujiwara slowly collapsed to the side, dead before he hit the ground. His body was pristine but half of his head had flashed away, leaving an unnatural gap and a thin visceral mist raining around him. The lead Venalaran held a smoking pistol and the three others were in various stages of drawing theirs as well.

Gesturing with his gun, the leader stepped off to one side to allow his three apparent lackeys to move past him. In a rough voice, he said, "Resist and you'll all end up like that idiot. We're just here for the salvage. You can die now or die later, we don't care."

Manik carefully extricated himself from Dorr and made a show of going through his pockets. The cold that he'd felt when the tree-beast had him cornered had never really left, and he pulled on it, hoping his strength and speed would hold out. The first lackey approached him and put his gun against Manik's chest.

His first and last mistake.

Manik calmly scissored his hands, breaking the man's arm and folding his gun up under his chin before his reflexes kicked in. Compulsively firing, the man ended his own life in a rain of color. Smoothly retrieving the weapon from the falling body, Manik snapped off multiple shots into each of the other two surprised henchmen. Only after the moment was over, did Manik notice as an afterthought that his left leg burned more than before. Must have been shot, wasn't quite quick enough.

Leveling the weapon at the leader, Manik began to limp forward. The man matched him, barrel for barrel, but moved instead over to the base of the gangway.

"You're quicker than you look kid, I'll give you that. For that I'll let you live. I'll get in my ship and leave peacefully and you'll never hear from me again." he said, slowly backing up the ramp.

Manik fired twice in rapid succession. Once into the man's chest and once into his forehead. As the body fell and rolled down the incline, he said quietly "He wasn't an idiot. You were."

Returning to the group, Manik resumed his place at Dorr's side and said, "OK, let's get on board. The sooner we leave this place the sooner we can get you all medical attention."

Nobody argued and in short order they were inside and had found and filled the small med bay.

Returning outside, Manik rolled the lead Venalaran's corpse off of the end of the gangway, pausing only to remove the pistols and holsters from the four apparent scavengers. Striding over to the now defunct signal device, he carefully extricated his TechSpecs and hung them from the outside of his left pants pocket to try to minimize the gore on them. Carefully picking up the late Captain's body he limped his way up into the ship, nudging the door mechanism on his way past.

Moving forward, Manik laid the Captain's body in the first stateroom he found, carefully folding the older man's arms and closing the door behind him. Redrawing the first weapon he'd pulled as well as the deceased leaders sidearm, Manik proceeded through the rest of the ship, methodically checking every nook and hiding place he could find until he reached the bridge.

The door was sealed from the outside with a simple lock code. Unlocking it and cycling the door open Manik slowly entered the room, checking quickly for movement. All of the viewing seats were folded and locked; the only movement came from the pilot's theater, a soft rustling. As Manik rounded the corner and leveled his weapons he came face to face with a young, unhooked, and apparently terrified Rylan girl. As she took in his frightening state, she threw her hands in front of her overlarge eyes and burst into tears.

"Please don't kill me! I watched the whole thing. I won't be any trouble. Just put me somewhere and I'll go away. I'll go to the authorities and turn myself in. I just...I don't want to die..." she managed to say through her sobs.

Holding the weapons on her, Manik stood silently considering. She SEEMED harmless but there's no way to be sure considering the company she had been keeping...but something was tugging at Manik's conscience. He couldn't just kill her. She looked younger than he was and she was apparently unarmed.

Lowering his weapons, Manik stepped back and gestured for her to move. When she didn't he took a steadying breath and said, "Look, I can't trust your word on anything, I'm sure you understand. I won't kill you but I will lock you in your room until we can get my crew medical attention. Does that sound acceptable to you?"

Sniffling and nodding, she stood on shaky legs and moved cautiously out of the piloting theater and through the bridge, trying to keep both Manik's weapons and her path in view. Progress was slow, with her almost skulking along one wall, until they made it to a room halfway down the hallway, a few rooms away and opposite of where the body of the Captain lay. Palming the lock quickly she dove in and out of sight before the door was more than a fraction open.

Sighing, Manik stared into the darkness. He could understand her skittishness, but she seemed more timid than any animal he'd ever seen. To the quiet darkness of the room, he said "We'll bring you some food in a bit.", and then closed and locked the door.

Manik returned through the ship quickly, stopping in the galley and picking up some instant meal packs and protein paste. The galley itself was horribly under stocked, mismanaged, and messy, leaving Manik vaguely pleased that he'd found any edible food at all and longing for the lost *Sunrise* all over again.

Carrying an armload of his spoils he returned to the medbay and opened the door. Challis was leaning heavily against one of the two medtables, one of which held Dorr and the other Selelle, and Krym was lying on the floor between them. Stepping in quickly, Manik held a tube of protein paste out to Challis.

"I'm sorry it's not your usual stuff, but will this do?" he asked.

Challis' eyes trained on Manik's arm, and then followed it down to his hand. He squinted and focused on the tube for a moment, and then nodded numbly. Manik broke the seal at the top and handed it to the thin man, who began to nurse it like an addict on his last dose.

Bending down, Manik handed one of the meal packs under the table to a grateful and exhausted Krym, who tore the package open with his teeth and began to rifle through the contents. Manik placed the final three packs on the counter, and walked around Challis to check on Selelle.

In the short time that they'd been on board her clothing had been removed and piled in the corner, modesty surgical half-sheets covered her up to her hips and from her neck to the middle of her ribcage. The remaining space of her abdomen was covered in clean white bandages, the edges of which still shone with the liquid antiseptic disinfectant spray. Her breathing was shallow and she was sweating, but at least she seemed to be asleep now.

Challis finished his tube, discarded the waste, and turned to Manik solemnly. "I've done what I can for her...but the facilities here are undersupplied and apparently had been managed by a creature not dissimilar to the ones living in the trees outside. I don't know if the disinfectant will have any effect on the microbes potentially picked up by us all on this planet. We need to get her to a medical facility, a good one, as quickly as possible."

Nodding, Manik gestured between them. "And Krym and Dorr?"

Challis looked at the two men briefly as he slowly rebuilt his professional doctoral mask. Looking back up with the characteristically blank expression Manik had been introduced to originally he said, "They'll live. Dorr would be dead by now if there were internal bleeding and Krym is a stone that for some reason bleeds. They can get medical attention after my assistant does and the same goes for you...once I get those bullet wounds looked at."

Manik looked down, surprised, to see his pants were a darker shade of red-brown than they were before. He suddenly felt tired and a little dizzy as the adrenaline of the fighting was wearing off. Stepping back, he aimed for a stool that seemed reluctant to be sat upon sending him ungraciously to the floor next to Krym.

Challis worked quickly and methodically. Using medical shears he removed Manik's pants, despite Manik's loud protestation and then sprayed him from the ribcage down with an aerosol blue sticky liquid. Only then did Manik's pain return in spades.

The wounds on his leg and ribs began to foam, as did a pair of puncture wounds in his right thigh and left abdominal area respectively. Manik grit his teeth and growled through the pain, as he'd been taught, as Challis quickly dressed the four major areas with self-adherent bandages. He was done in a matter of moments and then braced himself on Dorr's medtable and helped Manik back to his feet.

"We need you to fly us so we need you patched. You can get the bullets removed, if they're still in there, when we get to where we're going. I'm going to give you something quick acting for the pain that should sustain you through Underspace. Try not to go crazy on us." he said, as he helped Manik over to the counter.

Manik could only nod as the Rylan dug through drawer after drawer, swearing quietly under his breath. Manik closed his eyes and leaned against the counter, relishing the cool carbonsteel against his bare skin.

His eyes snapped open as he felt a sharp pain in the side of his neck. Swiping reflexively, he missed Challis' retreating arm by a few inches as he pulled the now-empty nanospray away and put it on the counter. His other hand held a pair of drawstring scrub pants, which he offered wordlessly.

Manik's thoughts became clearer as the pain faded, and he realized how abundantly naked he was. Taking the pants, he slid them on gently over his wounds, being careful not to bend too far or too quickly lest he break the seal on one of his bandages. Standing up straight again, he nodded his thanks to Challis and began to walk to the bridge.

The ship seemed to have grown in the last few minutes. Or he had shrunk. The corridors were longer and the stairs from the cargo bay up to the second floor command hallway were steeper. Were there stairs there before? There must have been, there was a blood trail leading up one side and down the other so he must have come this way.

In minutes or hours, he reached the bridge. He closed the door behind him and walked around the pilot's theater to inspect it. It was smaller and less robust than his previous on the *Kyoto Sunrise*, but he'd fit in it well enough. His installed training kicked in and he gave the theater a walk around to ensure everything was in shape to use. Everything seemed to be connected correctly from the outside so there was nothing for it but to plug in. He had to get everyone to safety.

He sat carefully, reached a hand behind him to fold the data spike out of the central pillar, and eased himself back onto it. He felt the click and reached down to fasten the straps that would hold him in place. The monitors lit up one by one, the projectors below and above providing phantom images of the central space. He ran through the diagnostics, checking software and hardware for serviceability and preparation for flight. All seemed in order here as well, so he ignited the atmospheric engines and activated the external sensors and monitors. The field of dark screens and projections immediately lit up with a view of the field that had so briefly and so astoundingly been their home. The grasses were waving crazily in the breeze, the ones directly behind danced in the engine wash occasionally flaring into light as a stalk gave up under the stress and snapped. In the glare of the floodlights, he saw the four bodies of the Venalarans, the eviscerated corpse of Laii, the remains of their signal array, and off in the half-light beyond, the shadowed bulks of the two murderous beasts.

Stepping through the monitors, SID's familiar ghostly form smiled glowingly at Manik. The image was just as clear as before, he saw with relief. Apparently there'd been very little degradation of her signal while sequestered in his skull. She stood silent for a moment, staring off into the distance, and then shook herself and looked down into Manik's eyes again.

"There. I have integrated myself completely into this ship. We shouldn't have any trouble with onboard systems or the lone remaining former crew member. I have taken the liberty of reinforcing the lock on her door in case she tries to use the in-room hardware to override the locks and escape." she said pleasantly.

"Good to see you again SID. I'm glad everything is working well. The additional lock probably wasn't necessary since she seems scared out of her mind but I appreciate the thought." he thought back to her.

The ship shook and lifted out of the field, giving Manik a view of the landscape from above for the first time. He swung the ship in a spiral up into the atmosphere, gathering as much external data as he could in case it would help the medical team wherever they ended up going.

The star of this system was just clearing the horizon when he was about 200 meters up, spilling brilliant yellows and oranges across the landscape. The fields, glowing an amazing deep blue, spread much further than Manik had guessed, bordered on one side by the tall golden barked tree forest and on the other by a dark strip of beach bordering a bright emerald ocean.

As he flew over the forest in an ever rising trajectory, he saw hundreds of Exploding Dropnuts, as yet un-dropped, as well as vines in a myriad of colors and bright winged avian creatures flocking about. A short distance into the forest, there was a dark series of punctures in the canopy. Curious, he checked the data on location, size, and age, but SID answered him before the numbers finished running.

"That's where we fell. The smallest one was the piloting cabin, the larger sections broke up higher in the atmosphere and were flaming wreckage by the time they hit." she said quietly, her sadness palpable.

The sight of the damage brought Manik back into the present, and he angled the ship up to the steepest and quickest exit corridor he could without another word. The ship rattled slightly with the velocity he was pushing out of it, but it soon calmed as they breached the furthest edges of the atmosphere.

"SID," he thought to her, "is there anything you need to do to shut down the Realspace beacon? I don't want others coming here by following our signals if we can help it."

SID nodded. "Good idea." She paused for a moment, and then continued," I have deactivated it and I used the thrusters to nudge it into a decaying orbit. It has already ceased transmission and should burn up in the atmosphere in a matter of weeks. Should we do the same for the Underspace twin?"

Manik pondered for a moment, and then thought, "No, let's just change the message to something that won't evoke curiosity. Something like 'Already mapped by *Kyoto Sunrise* crew'."

SID nodded again. "Yes, that would be nice. Then others will avoid it, but they'll still know the Captain was here. Well, the former Captain. I guess that's your job now." she mused.

Manik was taken aback for a moment. Was he the Captain now? He'd taken charge, the others had seemed willing to follow him even though he was young and new to the task...His family legacy of being leaders had finally caught up to him he guessed, he just couldn't get away from it. He laughed and waved off SID's confused look.

"I'll explain later, and we can decide on all of that once we get everyone cared for. What's the closest medical facility?" he asked.

"Um...well, the facilities that can care for quarantine, possible infectious disease, as well as catastrophic trauma are quite finite. The Central Tower Infirmary in Utopia on Ryla is the best, but Doctors Deepheart and Regaal both still have active warrants for their arrest. Prime Hospice in Grand on Venalara is the second best, but is the furthest out...the only other is the Transium Company Medical Depot...on Chromara Orbital Two. Due to its proximity to the Herculis System weak point, it gives everyone, particularly Doctor Deepheart, the highest percentage chance of survival." she finished quickly.

To return home or to take a chance on making it to Venalara? He didn't want to see his father again so soon but Selelle did need care urgently. What would Captain Fujiwara do?

Manik knew the answer before he finished articulating the question to himself. Taking a deep breath, he thought, "OK SID, Chromaran Orbital Two it is. Can you warn the crew and our guest that we'll be entering Underspace momentarily?"

SID smiled at him again and vanished. Manik turned his attention to the controls for the traverse preparations. All panels showed green, the Exotic Particle supply was high and strong and the Manifold Envelope systems came on-line smoothly. He gave SID a few more seconds to finish her announcement, reveling for a moment in the comfort and safety of the pilot's theater. Besides the restriction of his head movement, it really was a very comfortable chair.

SID reappeared a moment later, nodding her readiness. Manik activated the Envelope and watched the sensor display quickly overlay with the sheen of Exotic Particles. Making the necessary course corrections, he pushed the ship through into Underspace.

Chapter 16

The chaos fled quickly, the fading static revealing the sight that would continue to haunt his dreams, the ring of antimatter planetoids that had been the undoing of his previous trip. He told himself he wasn't hesitating; he was waiting for SID to finish whatever she needed to do with the beacon held in the antigravity well alongside them.

Hanging in the darkness for what may have been moments or hours in relative time, Manik waited for the go ahead from SID. Finally, she rematerialized, turned her ghostly form to meet Manik's eyes, and said, "Alright, this beacon has been repurposed to hopefully repel incoming ships. I set it to broadcast the announcement and removed all of the distress protocols. It should show to anyone else as a simple information buoy now."

Manik thought a smile at her then examined his charts and data for a possible exit path. From SID's memory, embedded now with his own, Manik easily highlighted his previous trip in as well as lighting up the path taken by the pirates on their trip through pulled from the ships logs. The two flight paths were nearly identical but Manik saw a few tweaks he could do to each to make the trip safer still.

Charging the Envelope to double strength once again, he propelled the ship up and away towards leading edge of one of the planetoids. As he approached, the sensors began to ping smaller and smaller satellites of the behemoth structures. Some were moving with the spin of the constellation at large, some were moving counter. That must have been what they'd hit last time.

"SID, I need you to track those smaller satellites. Let me know if my trajectory is in danger of crossing one of them." he thought quickly, as he navigated through the thin asteroid field to the top crest of one of his chosen planetoid.

"I'll do my best my love. This...is harder than I'd anticipated. Be careful, I'll give you as much warning as I can." she said haltingly, her focus obviously elsewhere.

Manik spread his viewpane to include the side and rear sensors so that he had an idea of where the malicious objects nearest him were.

The ship coasted down over a shallow depression, a monstrous matte black valley filled with occasional spikes and crevasses. The vibration of the ship grew steadily as he approached the surface, rising from a background hum at the edge of notice up to a deluge of movement and sound that threatened to shake all sane thoughts from his head.

"Manik! The vibration is beginning to threaten damage of the net deployment hardware! Recommend pulling to a higher orbit!" SID yelled to him over the tidal battle cry.

Manik adjusted their angle up into a low orbit where he could stay close enough to avoid the majority of the debris and additional objects but remain high enough that the vibration scaled down to a less maddening level.

Following the curve of the bestial Undercelestial body, he wove around high peaks and pseudo volcanic outpourings of antimatter into the high orbit belt of objects. He weaved through fields of large objects descending to crash into the surface, and around shimmering clouds impossibly dense with exotic particles.

After about three hours of relative time he finally found the synchronization that he'd hoped, dearly, matched his gut feeling. The rotation of the giant he was tied to finally lapsed into temporary sync with its two neighbors, clearing the debris cloud and giving him a clear path onward.

Pushing the unfamiliar ship as hard as he felt he safely could, he rocketed the ship up and away from the vortex of planetoids. Ever mindful of his mistakes that led to the death of the last ship that was his charge, he swung wide around the small number of incredibly large objects that were too stubborn to obey the pull of the larger bodies.

When he was halfway across, he adjusted his course again, following the empty section of Underspace between the planetoids until it cycled around to face outward. Sooner than he thought, his window opened and he charged the ship free of the area.

SID favored him with a glowing smile and said, "That was wonderful. That's precisely why an organic pilot was needed for that run. I just don't have the intuition or instincts that you do, even with the advanced sensor technology installed on this ship."

Manik smiled back at her wearily and thought, "You're more capable than you give yourself credit for but I'm glad we can work together. If it's alright with you I think I need to zone out and rest for a while."

SID nodded. "I agree, your bioindicators are showing that your previously heightened adrenaline level is dropping back down into normal parameters and more than likely the fatigue from the events is leaving your body very taxed. I will rouse you when we get close. I need time to finish fully integrating and exploring the information held within this ship and, if possible, determines if it is a stolen vessel...well, stolen before we took it. Does it count as stealing if we stole it from thieves?" she mused as she faded from view.

Manik felt his mind begin to drift and his vision narrowed. Just as he was drifting off he felt through the sensors the deployment of the nets and the gentle push of the manifold sliding the ship up to cruising speed.

The darkness slid past, interspersed with sparking fields of Exotic Particles. A number of nearly geometrically perfect macro objects blew past as though in a hurry to some unknown and unknowable destination. They didn't pass any dragons though. Strange, thought Manik dreamily. Maybe they really were as rare as SID had said. He hoped he'd get a chance to see another sometime, maybe even get close enough to get a good look at it. Might be dangerous with how unpredictably they tend to move--

"Manik!" SID yelled in his ear.

Manik snapped to attention, his eyes adjusting to their now suddenly significantly slower speed. SID was sitting beside him, looking at him with a great deal of worry.

He gathered his thoughts for a moment then directed to her, "Yes, SID? Are we there already?"

She nodded slowly. "Yes Manik. I've been trying to wake you for the last several hours of relative time. The system errored and the protocols that are normally used to rouse pilots did not engage. I wanted to go in to see if I could wake you from within but I wasn't sure if I'd be welcome, after all the time we'd spent in the same head. I was afraid that disturbing you may have disastrous effects on your psyche, so I waited as long as I could."

Manik mentally took stock of his body. All limbs were present, his wounds still burned and ached, but he felt broadly intact. Giving a wan smile, he thought, "Thank you SID. I was just drifting. Hopefully it was just the pain talking. I'll be better once we get everyone treated and I get a good night's sleep."

She nodded, still watching him warily.

Manik tried to shake his head a fraction of a second later remembering that both the engaged Manifold Envelope and the piloting spike were holding him stationery. Sighing, he thought, "Nothing to worry about SID, it isn't your fault it's just glitches with new hardware and software, you'll get through it. We did leave in quite a hurry, after all."

SID turned to face the monitors still seemingly mildly upset. Raising a finger, she pointed at a section of Underspace that looked...almost polished. There were no exotic particles in the immediate area, and even the normal miniscule level of antimatter debris was not present.

"There's the weak point for Chromara. I was able to finish analyzing and encrypting the files and software markers that identify this ship as belonging to a known and wanted pirating organization. Once we are out I can get us cleared with the Orbital mainline and docked. You need to get to the medical center."

She gestured at one of the monitors which pulled up a diagram of the Orbital docking decks. It showed a fairly direct route through the station from the closest docking port to a complex of rooms that must be their target.

"This path will get you there most directly." she said, still facing away.

Manik was suddenly suspicious. "SID, how do you know which docking bay we'll be assigned or that we'll make it through all those specific doors?"

SID only shook her head and said, "You worry about getting yourself and the crew to the medical facility. I'll take care of the landing and passageway logistics." She turned to face him, smiling almost sadly. "It's important that we get you treated, anything after that can be dealt with when you are safe."

Manik didn't like the way she phrased that but they were approaching their target too fast for him to comment further. Pulling in the wing nets, he made the necessary speed and course corrections to move through the weak point. As he

arrived, he flared the Envelope, shunting them over into Realspace and back onto a normal timeline a scant hundred thousand miles off of the wreckage of Orbital One.
SID immediately disengaged the piloting spike and took control, angling away for a fast orbit to the operational Orbital. Manik stood and felt all of his fatigue and pain return all over again. He leaned against the wall outside the piloting theater and closed his eyes to catch his breath and balance. It was slow in returning.

He must have leaned against the cool bulkhead longer than he'd thought because SID suddenly activated the local com system and asked, "Manik? Are you alright?"

Manik started, and then smiled up at the speaker. "Yes, I'll be fine. Just catching my balance. How close are we?"

"We are approximately seven minutes from docking protocols, another four to dock. You have an estimated six minutes to get to the medbay and four minutes to get from there to the gangway to be ready to disembark quickly." she replied.

Manik nodded and pushed off of the wall. He strode as quickly as he could through the crew hallway, down the stairs, and through the messy cargo area. Looking around, he realized how clean Fujiwara had kept his ship. Here, there were boxes haphazardly thrown everywhere, likely from the turbulence of movement combined with the activation and deactivation of artificial gravity.

Manik paused for a moment. This ship must be bigger than he thought. Nobody had artificial gravity on ships like this.

Shaking himself, he sped up. Something to worry about at a later date. He crossed the access hallways and arrived at the medcenter just in time to nearly collide with Challis, leaving the room with a stumbling Dorr leaning on him.

"Careful! We don't want to jostle the injured any more than we need to and that counts for both of you. Help Krym with Selelle, I've got this waste of atmosphere." he grunted, and then staggered onward.

Stepping into the bay, he saw Krym had pulled one of the portable backplates and was busy strapping Selelle's unconscious form to it. Hurrying over, he grabbed the loose leg strap and began quickly tying it off. The strap was fairly complex, looping back on itself to provide adequate support, tensile strength, and restriction of movement for individuals of any species from the smallest Earthborn to the largest Chromaran.

A sharp sting in his neck caused him to jump backwards just as he finished securing the last of the straps. Krym stood nearby removing an empty medicine capsule from a pressure injector.

"What did you just hit me with?" Manik asked angrily.

Krym reloaded the tool and injected himself before answering. "It's a cocktail Challis just whipped up. He and Dorr already had their doses. It'll keep you awake and aware and able to move quickly for about half an hour. That should be enough time to get us through customs and into the waiting arms of the med agents."

Squatting down carefully, so as not to jostle his own bandages, Krym lifted Selelle's top half as though she weighed nothing. The fog around Manik's eyes and brain were, indeed, rapidly fading and he felt some strength leach back into his muscles. Squatting down himself, he lifted and balanced Selelle's lower half from behind his back, so that they could both move forward, and set off down the hallway. Krym kept pace easily and they reached the gangway and the other waiting pair in short order.

SID's voice came over the intercom a few moments later.

"Forty five seconds to spare, you organics are tougher than I gave you credit for. Manik knows the way; I've cleared the path for you. Get there first and deal with any problems on the way later. Don't let anyone join the Cap...Victor Fujiwara beyond the veil just yet."

A tense minute went by, and they all felt the shudder of magnetic locks pin the ship to the deck of the Orbital station. The gangway began to drop and Manik moved immediately.

Chapter 17

He was on the ground as it hit home, Krym following in step and Challis not far behind with his burden. The docking bay was clear of personnel with only one or two other ships present but locked down. A string of escort lights led the way to a nearby maintenance tunnel that Manik recognized immediately as part of SID's pathway. He moved smartly for it, ignoring the questioning sounds and confused grunts from behind.

The hatch was unlocked and let them into an access corridor that fed past the docking ring to a service elevator. Quickly ascending the three floors necessary, they stepped out into a smaller corridor. Red lights were flashing but the hallway was clear and doors were open. They moved through quickly, turning the occasional corner, until the medcenter was in sight.

Standing in front of the door were a half dozen Chromaran customs guards, all with various weapons drawn. Manik kept his speed, and said in a loud voice, "We have urgent need of medical attention, one crewmember in critical condition, and we have been on an uncharted live planet. I repeat, medical attention and quarantine."

The guards immediately split to allow them passage as though they had the plague, which for all they knew, they did.

Once inside, they were kept waiting only a moment before masked and suited personnel came and began sending them to different rooms. Selelle and Dorr were taken first, and then Krym, and then Manik and Challis.

Manik was walked through a short maze of rooms to a slick walled room where he was asked to strip. Upon doing so, he was quickly and unceremoniously covered in sickly smelling green-grey foam which sizzled lightly on contact. The effect was more tickling than painful so he stood still and let the disinfectant do its work. After a few minutes it stopped fizzing and the two attendants turned on a shower, allowing him some privacy to clean off.

The water was warm, sweet smelling, and glorious. He stood under the downpour for a moment, relishing the simple comfort before a polite cough reminded him of the immediacy of his actions. Quickly scrubbing his hands across his body he cleared the rapidly dissolving foam from himself and stepped back out.

The attendants activated the sonic dryer for a moment then escorted a still damp Manik across the hall to a cleanroom. The taller of the two attendants gestured for him to climb up onto the table and lay down. Upon doing so, they went to work removing the temporary and makeshift bandages and spot cleaning his numerous wounds.

The silence dragged on, as they alternately sprayed and washed to try and clear the planetary microbial detritus from him. The procedure was uncomfortable, but not truly painful. Manik wasn't entirely sure if he should be thankful to some numbing aspect of the disinfectant, Challis' cocktail of drugs, or both.

After working through each of his wounds, inspecting for surface area, depth, infection, and location, they methodically bandaged each one back up in clean coverings then left the room without a word.

Manik lay on the table, unsure of what the protocol was but not wanting to rupture any of the new, professionally applied bandages. His fatigue was starting to return so he was able to guess that about half an hour had gone by. It was faster than he'd thought.

A brisk knock at the door was followed by a doctor and a guard, both Chromarans wearing respiration filters. The guard carried a simple hospital gown, which was presented to Manik without comment. He sat up, accepted the gown, and carefully put it on before resuming his seat on the raised bed. The guard and doctor exchanged a glance, and then the doctor spoke.

"Sir, we have been directed by your crewmates to address all anomalies in the system to your...experience. You are in stable condition, so I...we feel that this is the most opportune time to alleviate our concerns."

Manik nodded, only slightly confused, and fervently hoped they would give him some more information before demanding that he start explaining he knew not what. A cold thought raced across his mind for a moment. What if they had ID'd him when he'd arrived? What if his father had put out a warrant for his stealing a Family credit line to get up here in the first place?

His dark musings were cut short by the guard cutting in.

"Look...sir," he said the title with obvious disbelief that it was deserved, "your crew all unanimously identified you as being the leader, so you need to answer us. Why did your crew hack the Station Security System when you arrived? Why did you bypass customs? Which criminal family do you work for? Answer!"

He continued to approach until he was standing over Manik, glaring at him over the tubes of the bio contaminant filter. Manik almost smiled. There was no physical danger here, even what the guard implied. They were scared and lashing out. After what he'd been through, a round of Good-Cop/Bad-Cop wasn't something he was worried about. SID's safety was what worried him now. Manik sat for a moment, contemplating how to answer the uniformed bully. As he considered he thought about what each of his crew would do. He thought about what Captain Fujiwara would do. Then he knew how he could answer.

Straightening his back, Manik matched the stare from the

guard and replied, "Listen...Sergeant?" he asked, intentionally not pausing long enough to be corrected, "My crew has just returned from an unknown, unmapped, and VERY hazardous planet. We are not aware of what contaminants we may or may not have brought back with us and wanted to make sure none of the station personnel, including your excellent and well trained customs guards, get infected with a possibly very contagious and previously unknown disease. Considering our precautions you should be thanking me, not threatening me. As to the criminal family, we do not work for one, nor have I ever had contact with one. If you have the lack of social grace to imply so again I may be moved to feel insulted." he finished, trying to sound both as calm and as dismissive as Captain Fujiwara would have.

The security officer took a step back, his silver eyes showing guarded surprise. When he next spoke he seemed much more careful. "I am Captain val'Shieke, head of Station Security here, and I would appreciate being addressed as 'Captain', or 'Sir', in a respectful tone. I was hoping you would simply admit to criminal activities so that we could get the impound, search, and seizure of your ship to happen that much quicker but it seems that you are either too clever or too poorly informed to cooperate with my investigation..."

Manik interrupted him, "In that case, Captain, you'll understand why I require you to ALSO call me 'Captain', or 'Sir', in a respectful tone." he paused, noting the lack of the withdrawal of either the insults or the accusations then spoke again in his best authoritative tone, "As to the actions against my ship, do you have some warranted information, or even reliable supposition, to make these flagrant accusations? I'm quite sure that we filed the correct necessary documents proving our identity on our way into dock." he finished, fervently hoping SID had done exactly that.

The guard captain nodded, and then growled, "Yes, your documentation was immaculate. What caused concern was the combination of hacking the docking grid to pick your own parking spot, somehow firing off the loss of atmosphere evacuation alarms, falsely thankfully, in the corridors you then traversed unmolested, and the simple fact that your ship's exterior markings match that of a known pirate group that has been seen in the area recently."

Manik felt his stomach drop. He knew it wouldn't be easy but he hadn't anticipated they would mark the exterior of the ship. He hadn't even checked for names or markings on the bulkheads. He felt the approach of a grim and captive future when a wall panel behind the loud guard and quiet doctor lit up.

SID's face appeared for a moment, smiling at him, and then was replaced by a quick series of mug shots of the pirates they had dealt with. These stacked up quickly on one side of the screen, and a document opened on the other. It was a Chromaran legal document regarding anti-piracy salvage...That's it! SID is a genius.

Focusing again on val'Shieke, Manik began, glancing over the man's shoulder occasionally to reference numbers and names. "I understand the confusion Captain, but according to Assembly Statute 1280, I quote 'Any seizure of arms, equipment, or vehicles used by known pirates is to be considered lawful salvage, granting the individual or individuals title and trust over said.' which, I believe, means your security office is not only required but morally obligated to expunge the record of the pirate group associated with this ship and formally write up a title for both my records and those of the Assembly. That is, if you think your office can handle a little paperwork." he finished, unable to resist the urge to ruffle the guard's fur a little further.

SID shut off the screen quickly, as the guard Captain turned on his heel and stormed out without another word. The doctor watched him leave then turned amused bronze eyes on Manik.

"That's the most angry I think I've ever seen him. I honestly don't know whether to give you my congratulations or my condolences. I'm Doctor val'Tiin, by the way. And your name would be...?" he finished, pausing.

"Manik." Manik replied, and then thought better of it, "Captain Manik of the...*Miyako Sunset*."

Doctor val'Tiin nodded. "Very well, Captain. I just need to check your wounds to see the extent of the damage. Please lie back."

Manik complied with all of the doctor's requests and nudging, as he methodically removed each bandage, inspected the wounds with analytical probes and three dimensional imaging mappers, and resealed each in turn.

The doctor finished applying the last bandage and said, "Very well Captain you may sit up if you wish. Are you at liberty to disclose any information I may find helpful about these wounds? This room isn't wired for sound to my knowledge and my privilege as a physician will allow me to deny disclosure to any interested parties." he gestured toward the door, obviously indicating the recently departed Guard Captain.

Manik nodded, knowing that even if the room were bugged for sound SID would prevent any incriminating information from leaking therefrom. "On the planet we recently left, we were attacked by a number of....native species. The one that got my leg and side is the one that impaled our critical condition female team member as well as a good deal of the surface wounds from my other Chromaran team member. The firearms wounds are courtesy of the previous owners of our ship, the pirates."

The doctor nodded, and then gestured at Manik's feet with one of the imaging tools as he prepped a receiving machine for it. "And the shards of...glass?"

Manik looked down in surprise. Sure enough, his feet were wrapped with bandages, and there was a small pile of Glassgrass shards on a rolling tray next to the table. When had those been removed? Perhaps more importantly, why hadn't he felt them on all the movement he'd been doing?

"Those...were from the same planet. A plant stalk that could be shattered like glass. It had some chemicals inside that caused flames to erupt." He tried to explain.

The doctor seemed lost in thought for a moment. "Chemical infused naturally occurring glass, eh? The possibilities are interesting...hopefully none of the chemicals have lasting harmful effects. Not much we can do about preventing them from getting into your system but at least we can treat any symptoms that arise while you're here."

Doctor val'Tiin finessed a three dimensional display into being, showing a generic Chromaran male with the areas where Manik's wounds were highlighted and in much greater detail.

"Hmm, well, the gash on your side is ragged but we should be able to stitch that up. It doesn't seem to have hit anything vital. Same for the leg wound. You may have some weakness on your left leg but that should pass in a few weeks. You have a few bruised ribs, but nothing broken. That will be sore for a bit, but it'll heal quickly. The firearms seem to have been firing accelerated ballistic shards as there's no indication of their continued presence. This is both good and bad. Good because we don't have to dig for them but bad because those things tend to have sharp edges and tear tissues and organs on their way out. I'll need a deeper scan to ensure that the abdominal shot did not tear any of your less vital organs. The thigh shot you were very lucky with. Had it clipped your femoral artery, you'd have been dead before you got on board the ship. Since you didn't, combined with the fact that you walked here, we can rule out shattered bones. A simple patch and stitching and your leg should be good as new, albeit a little more scarred."

Manik nodded. All in all, he'd gotten off better than he'd expected. "And my crew?" he asked.

The doctor was silent for a moment, busying himself with replacing the machinery into their component cubby holes on the counter. Taking a deep breath through his filter, he turned to face Manik with a grave look in his eyes.

"Your Rylan crewmember will be fine. He is malnourished, dehydrated, and has a mild fever from an infection as well as a few bruised ribs. I expect full recovery within hours. The other Chromaran is old and tough. He has refused all but the most basic care, so he will have a few additional scars but none of his wounds are life or livelihood threatening. The Venalaran male has four shattered ribs, three broken ribs, and quite a bit of internal bruising and minor lacerations. He's in OR2 now getting patched up, he should be back to full functioning capacity in a few days provided he stays off his feet." He paused, increasing Manik's worry.

"And my female Venalaran crew member?" he asked, almost afraid to hear the answer.

The doctor sighed again and said, "She's alive, but only just. She has a dozen shattered ribs, a severed spine, too many ruptured or ruined organs to mention, including both lungs...she was in a comatose state when she was brought in, and I'm not sure she'll come out of it. We don't have a lot of equipment to deal with most of her injuries...she's in OR1 being systematically decontaminated and getting what we can do done. Her lungs were filling slowly, but we will be able to patch and drain them. Repairs we can do, it's replacements we are short on...especially for Venalarans. I'm sorry I don't have better news."

Manik could only stare. He'd done so well! He got her to the closest place that had what they needed. Why wasn't everything turning out alright? Did he miss a step?

No...he just hadn't gone far enough yet.

Manik looked the doctor in the eye and said, "Doctor, I thank you on behalf of myself, my ship, and my crew for all you have been able to do. Where would you suggest I go to get her patched up completely? Would Prime Hospice in Grand have what she needs?"

The doctor looked stunned for a moment. "Yes...being Venalaran, and being second best in the known universe, it surely would have artificial replacement organs available to accommodate her physiology. But if you're going that far, why not go to the Central Tower Infirmary on Ryla? Their technology is unmatched and their staff is the absolute best...I should know, I earned my degree there."

"My crew and I have our own reasons that I do not think need to be discussed here if it's all the same to you Doctor." Manik said, pulling a look of mild embarrassment from the doctor.

"Very well, I'm known for not prying into things that I shouldn't so I'll leave it at that. Just lay back now and I'll get you all stitched up." the Doctor replied, suddenly very busy with his tools.

Manik laid back down on the table and felt the prick of the anesthetic a moment later. His thoughts fuzzed as he stared at the serene pastoral Chromaran landscape displayed on the ceiling monitor. His leg was tugged upon for a few minutes, and then his arm was moved so that his side could be bothered. Neither really interested him. What kind of drugs did they give him? This stuff must be very strong to kill that much pain that quickly.

He felt himself get rolled onto his right side, presumably so that the doctor could get at the side wound more easily and that gave him a view of the doorway through which he'd come in. In his peripheral vision he saw three blue-clad forms fluttering back and forth around him. Probably nurses or medical technicians. Wonder when they got here. Must be more out of it than expected.

Soon enough, he was rolled back to his back and allowed to gaze fondly into the meadows outside Alberich, now shown on the monitor. A large herd of Relle was moving in the distance. His leg seems to be on fire.

He glanced down and immediately wished he hadn't. One of the technicians was patiently working some sort of deep tissue torture device through the hole in his leg. Logically, it was probably repairing the damage. All he saw, though, was a silver clawed thing slowly eviscerating his leg.

Before he could move, a pair of strong hands grabbed his shoulders and another took his ankles and held him down. The doctor leaned into view above him and started talking. It took three repetitions for Manik to focus enough to understand him.

"This procedure is quite alarming to look at, but I assure you it is perfectly normal and safe. You are not being attacked, you are not being harmed, and you are being healed. Nod when you understand me. This procedure is quite alarming to..." the doctor continued until Manik was able to connect the neurons and nod. The doctor nodded back and fell silent.

Finally, the driller decided they had delved deep enough and were finished with his thigh, patched the wound with a piece of synthskin, and stitched the edges neatly. Manik breathed a sigh of relief, and then quickly sucked it back in as the torturer went to work on his abdominal wound.

Four extra hands appeared, two on each side, to hold him down and the doctor began repeating the same litany. Manik nodded before he fully caught what he was saying. He knew what the procedure was. He jumped because it hurt. For as good as that shot was, it sure wore off quickly.

Manik tried to stay still, but couldn't shake the disturbing feeling of metal and plastic moving around in his insides, and so was shuddering occasionally. The excavation seemed to take forever. Prod, pause, adjust, twist, click, pause, prod, pause, adjust, twist, click, pause. The cadence was almost rhythmic.

At long last, the wound was sealed on his front and back and he was allowed to sit up. As he did he felt mild aches where there had been pain only a short time before. The technicians and nurses, five in all, filed out after methodically depositing all tools and surgical protective gear into the disinfecting cycler.

The doctor busied himself for a few minutes, straightening his already near immaculate workspace, and then turned to Manik again. "Well Captain, you are all taken care of. If you'd like, you've been cleared to wait in the quarantine waiting room until the rest of your crew is finished. The ambulatory ones, that is."

With that he walked to the door, paused, and said over his shoulder, "It's just down the hall, can't miss it. Looks like every other hospital waiting area in any world.", and then chuckled to himself and walked away.

Manik stood and found his movements initially without equilibrium but gaining in both speed and competency as he crossed the room. As he reached the hatchway, which slid open at his approach, he saw that there was a bio-filter wearing security officer across the hall. So the guard captain isn't a complete idiot. Good to know. He also apparently still thinks we are pirates. If he only knew.

Manik looked left and right, not sure which way to go, until the guard grunted and gestured to his right. Manik smiled his thanks, turned, and hobbled down the hallway a good deal slower and sloppier than he felt capable. When he turned the corner at the end of the short hallway he found the waiting room as promised. Already seated and waiting for him were Krym and Challis.

The two men sat a few chairs apart, both watching the local news channel for some reason. As Manik walked in, they both jumped like guilty children and started to make excuses for their behavior.

Manik approached them slowly, confused, until he passed the monitor and could see his own youthful visage smiling back at him. The picture was from his Brewhouse ID and listed him as a missing, possibly kidnapped, individual.

Manik sat down heavily between Krym and Challis and joined in silently watching the story unfold.

According to the channel's sources he had disappeared an indeterminate number of days ago, under suspicious circumstances by their conjecture, and had been seen in a number of places over the course including several local markets, neighboring arena crowds, the starport, and on the Orbital.

The reporter then proudly announced that they had exclusive information that may help in the ongoing investigation. An image of their arrival, taken by an obviously handheld personal device of some kind, showed Manik shirtless, covered in blood, surrounded by Dorr, Challis, and Krym, as they rushed through the Orbital docks earlier that day.

The excited young woman then proceeded to present her conjecture that he had been press-ganged into a pirate crew, was tortured into compliance, and is being forced to operate under duress.

The longer she went on, the more Manik felt like laughing. The story was absurd. Sure he'd been press-ganged, but not by pirates, and certainly no torture had happened. Was all news this ludicrous, or just the Chromaran news networks?

His smile was cut off as the scene shifted to an interview shot a few days prior according to the date-stamp. The same female reporter stood with aunt Innele and his father in front of the Clan Brewhouse complex.

"He's just so...young." Innele was saying, "I don't know why anyone would have taken him. We are a high ranking family, true, but we're not excessively rich or high profile...and to take him right after a loss in the Arena. They must have thought him an easy target. I remember seeing some non-Clan spectators and a few offworlders. At the time I didn't think anything of it, I was just so worried about him doing well..." she trailed off, sobbing quietly.

Barrus wrapped a massive arm consoling arm around her and said, "You'll have to excuse my sister, ever since my wife passed she's been the boy's surrogate mother. They're very attached to each other."

The reporter nodded and asked, "Do you think he may have just run away, rather than be taken?"

Barrus shook his head immediately. "No chance. He's a very weak and sheltered boy, hasn't even won his Rite of Family yet. He'd never make it in the city on his own let alone beyond that. He'd have been dead in a day."

The reporter nodded again and smiled for the camera. "Well, there you have it. Straight from the mouth of former Primus Assemblyman Barrus sel'Kaer. Back to the station for any new updates."

Challis looked Manik over and said, "He doesn't seem too versed in your capabilities, Captain. In my professional opinion you are still very much alive and it's certainly been more than a day."

Manik stared at him silently until he saw the Rylan's lip twitch. Was he serious or was he joking? He still couldn't get a good read on the overly expressive face he wore. The statement finally sunk in and a thought occurred to Manik.

"You just called me Captain." he said simply.

Challis nodded. "Indeed. We discussed it in the Medbay before we landed. Deepheart was unconscious and is too much of a soft-heart besides. Waverider has something of a phobia about getting power and has a predisposition towards alcohol that would be unhealthy in a commanding officer. That beast over there would drive us into a black hole, in all likelihood, and while I'd make an outstanding commander, I want to focus on my research from the samples collected on that planet. That left you as the obvious choice. You are quite young, I'll admit, but you seem to wear command well. Seeing your parentage only gives me more confidence that you'll do well by us."

Manik nodded slowly, trying to absorb the information.

Krym leaned in and smiled wryly. "I think you'll do fine lad. We all voted on it, on his insistence," he gestured at Challis, "and all four votes went to you with very little reservation on anyone's behalf."

Manik did the math, and then said, "Four votes? Wasn't Selelle unconscious? Who voted for her?"

"Nobody voted for her. SID cast her vote as well." Challis said quietly.

Manik started, and then glanced between the two men. Krym explained in a quiet voice, "Once on board, she quickly explained her sentience. I didn't understand most of the technical speak of it, but the long and the short of it is that she's a member of the crew, same as the rest of us. She lives, so she gets a vote. She's just a bit harder to kill than the rest of us." he finished with another smile.

"Indeed her origins merit study, a spontaneously generated intelligence could give huge insight into fundamental questions about the origins of life and some of the theories of the past can be reflected off of her, as the first non-human intelligence we have officially met." Challis added.

As Manik sat, continuing to stare at them in disbelief, Krym moved closer and snapped in front of his eyes, startling him. "Drugs still running, eh? You'll be out of that daze soon enough. So what's the plan? Any word about Selelle? When can we get back out to open space? The smell of this station is making me twitchy."

"Everything makes you twitchy. You must have some sort of non-diagnosable nervous disorder." Challis muttered.

Manik held up his hands to quiet both questions and commentary before speaking. "Dorr and Selelle are both in surgery now and should be out soon. Selelle is still unconscious and we need to get her to Venalara for treatment. She's lost too many organs, not to mention most of her rib cage and her spine."

"Yes, the hospital in Grand would be the most logical location to seek treatment given our reputation that would surely resurface on a return to the Central Tower. We may need to bargain with the infirmary here about extended use of their equipment. The medbay on board the ship is sadly under-equipped, especially for a transport of this complexity." Challis mused.

"Plus, with every security detail on the planet alerted to your presence how do we even get YOU off the station?" Krym added.

Manik shook his head slowly. "The only two ways I could get away would be to break out the same way we broke in, meaning we'd have to steal the medical equipment and probably be labeled as pirates, or I go home and get this calmed down before we go."

"Will they let you leave if you go back?" Krym asked.

"If I win my Rite, they'll have to. They can keep children from leaving but full adults have their own say."

"Will you be able to win, in the condition you are in?" Challis asked.

Krym answered before Manik could respond. Looking down at the Rylan he said, "He has something worth fighting for and he needs to win. That's all he needs to ensure victory."

Looking at Manik again, he added, "But claws help."

Manik laughed then stood, feeling more and more of his former strength return to him as time went on.

"I'll go now then. Hopefully by the time I'm back everything and everyone will be ready to go?" he asked.

Krym nodded. "We have enough information to trade for the use of the equipment and then some. You go do what you need to do."

Manik nodded and strode out of the room. As he walked down the hall he heard Krym yell, "And if it's not too much trouble, kick him a few times for me!"

Manik smiled but didn't otherwise respond. Since he was cleared by the quarantine technicians, he was able to get through the medical area fairly easily. He stopped at one of the shops on the way and used his personal credit code to get a new pair of loose shorts and a comfortably baggy shirt. No sense in going to meet his family in a hospital gown.

He was able to easily get through security onto a seat on a shuttle down to the surface with only a few strange glances, and was able to change in the lavatory on board during the pre-freefall startup.

The trip down was gut-wrenching and exhilarating. Occasional sparks flew past the windows as the air pressure increased against the sides of the spiraling craft. Their momentum kept the gravity inside low, necessitating use of the straps on the seats, but gave just enough freefall feeling that a few other passengers lost their previous meals into hastily provided receptacles.

As the engines flared to life, Manik was pushed back into his seat. The view outside stabilized into the horizon of the planet, a few silver and bronze packs of mobile creatures, and the goliath horizontal blackened iris of the Alberich gate.

They swooped low, the pilot obviously both skilled and in a hurry, and slipped into a pre-assigned berth at a speed that would likely leave deep grooves in the floor plating. The attitude jets fired at the last moment stabilizing the landing into a soft, muted, thud.

Manik was out of his seat and at the door almost before the landing was complete, emotions swirling. He was eager to see his aunt again but he was dreading seeing his father again. He looked forward to this task being finished but was hesitant about starting it.

The doors opened and the warm breeze brought back the never-fully-forgotten scent of the city. The foods, the people, the vehicles. Home. Or at least, it used to be. Now, it felt both comforting but also just a little bit inferior to the clean smell of a well cycled ship's atmosphere.

He moved ahead of the crowd down the gangway and headed quickly for the elevator he'd taken up all those years ago, or so it felt. The ride itself was no less full of sights and wonder as the ascension had been but this time he spent much less worry on the thoughts and motives of the other passengers.

The trip down seemed to take much longer than last time, laboriously stopping on each floor to engulf or disgorge a few more people going about their business. Some stared at him openly; others just glanced and looked away quickly. It was obvious how many recognized him. No help for it, he just had to get this done so that he could get back to his crew.

The elevator arrived at his level and he stepped off, followed by most of the rest of the occupants. A few carried packages but most seemed to be detouring from their various tasks specifically to see where he was going and what he was doing.

As he approached the Clan compound, he saw camera crews from a few local Alberich stations, plus the Orbital News Network he'd seen in the waiting room, all camped around the streets nearby.

Pointedly ignoring them all he strode with his back straight, as regally and Captainly as he could make himself, through the main gates. His entrance was only slightly diffused by the horde of onlookers and reporting teams who followed him into the central courtyard. Recorders flashed as he walked up the stairs to the main Clan office, stopping short as Barrus sel'Kaer suddenly burst from the building, followed by a bevy of clan members.

"Manik! I didn't expect to see you alive, and in one piece too! I knew my training and your bloodline would see you through!" he bellowed. Manik recognized immediately both the Arena fake volume and smile and the seething anger in his eyes that belied his true feelings.

Manik took a deep breath and the crowd went quiet.

"Father, I left to find my place. Now that I've found it, I've returned to retrieve the last thing you owe me. My name. I challenge you to the Rite of Family. Right now." he said loudly so that those at the back could clearly hear him.

Manik was quietly amused at the startled look his family gave him. Confidence, and a lack of a stutter, seemed to shock them all into silence.

Barrus recovered quickly and announced, "Well, you've been out for quite a trial, what with the kidnapping and such. You're likely a bit out of your head, let's get you inside and send all these nice people on their way..." as he moved forward to try to usher Manik inside.

Manik stepped back, causing the crowd behind him to shift as well. "I am of sound mind, Barrus sel'Kaer. Do you publicly deny my challenge?" he asked, gambling on his father's showmanship.

Barrus' eyes went from hot anger to cold fury then he smiled for the crowd and, without breaking eye contact with Manik, he said, "Very well, even though I trounced you recently I guess I can give you another chance. I'm a generous sort. Shall we?" and he swept an arm out to indicate the nearby Arena.

Manik nodded, and then turned and strode off towards the challenger's entrance. The crowd rushed past him to fill the stands, so he slowed to allow them time. As he strolled, his father and aunt caught up to him. Pausing for a moment, he allowed himself to be hug-crushed by the older woman, who was smiling and had tears flowing down her cheeks.

After a moment, he extricated himself and said, "I'll explain soon but for now I have to do this. Go get a good seat."

Looking confused, she nodded and hurried off with the rest of the family, friends, and interested strangers who were streaming into the upper stands.

Resuming his walk, Manik found himself paced by Barrus. Out of the corner of his mouth, he heard his father say, "Are you sure about this son? I don't want to aggravate any wounds you took but I won't go easy on you. You know that."

Manik nodded and said back, "My wounds will be fine. I need to get this done."

"For what purpose? All you do is work in the Brewhouse. What's so pressing that you have to have your Clan colors now?"

"I'll explain later, if there's time. I'm not just a Brewer's Assistant anymore."

"Well, you're certainly no Gladiator. What'd you do? Go commune with some dead warrior spirits and beseech them to impart their lack of failure in battle to you?" Barrus replied with a smirk.

"I'm not a failure in combat but the rest of that may be true after a fashion. This fight isn't just for me." Manik said, and then he strode through the challenger's entrance into the waiting area. He didn't need to hear from his father or the announcers what kind of contest it would be. Barrus was a creature of habit and played to his own strengths as much as to the enemy's weaknesses.

He slid his claws out and examined them for a moment. They were buffered clean thanks to the disinfectant the medical center had soaked him with, but he felt almost like the blood he'd gathered on them were still there. He paused in the prep room long enough to use the spot sharpener to put the edge back on his blades, and then slid them home and headed to the entry gate.

The gate opened sooner than he thought and he strode out into the sawdust and the harsh glare of the lights. The stands were full with more people arriving and filling the aisles. This may be the best showing the Clan has had in a while, shame it took such a dramatic move to put them into the public's eye.

The announcer began speaking as Manik strode into the arena, sounding out of breath from running to take his spot. "Greetings once again ladies and gentlemen, Chromaran, press, and esteemed guests! Today we have the Trial of the Family for Manik! His Defender has the tradition of choice of weapon for what the Trial shall entail and he has decided upon....a Physical Trial once again! For those of you who are seeing these combatants for the first time, this is Manik's fourth attempt at the Family colors. There's something to be said about the boy's enthusiasm and tenacity, eh? His opponent and father is the legendary Barrus sel'Kaer, retired Primus, or First Seat of the Assembly for you off-worlders, and he has chosen natural weapons as his combat option. This is unsurprising as Barrus rose to the rank he did by his own muscle and claw. Now, let's all give an encouraging welcome to the hopeful of Clan Kaer...MANIK!!!"

The crowd roared and cheered their support. Manik raised his head and stretched, feeling the tight spots on his abdomen and side protest mildly. The stitching was good but he'll have to avoid damage there if he can help it.

Barrus walked into the Arena and waved left and right, favoring the cameras in particular with his most winning smile. Arching back, he raised both Y-shaped tabard holders into the air and paused dramatically. A moment later, he pounded them into the floor boards, hanging a small family tabard on one, and his own on the other. Turning back to the crowd, he raised his large hands in a plea for quiet.

In the deafening silence that followed, he gestured at the smaller cloak and yelled, "This cloak represents my family. The Clan Kaer. The black field reminds us that we are not originally from this planet, but we have become natives. Chromara is our home, but we will always be tied to the stars. The lines of red running from top right to bottom left represent the light of our star, the Red Giant named Alpha Herculis by the stargazers of old. By his light we thrive. The lines of gold running from bottom right to top left represent the vision of Clan Kaer. We watch everyone and everything, we are sharp of wit and fang, bright of thought and eye. By challenging me this day, you identify your desire to join my ranks. Let us see if you fare better than last time."

Snapping his claws out theatrically, Barrus roared mightily.

Manik watched the older man who seemed, somehow, smaller than last they'd met. His roar was, indeed, powerful but it lacked the depth and ear-shattering velocity of the treebeast's or the resonant timbre bull seal-creature. Manik slid his claws into place unhurriedly and took a deep breath. He felt emotions pull him for a moment. The pains of loss and humiliation, the stab of fear for his life, the flames of wounds given with the intent to kill. He thought about the treebeast impaling Selelle, the pirate killing the Captain in cold blood, the pain he'd felt when he thought he'd lost SID.

He released his emotions with that breath.

All of his pain, all of his loss, all of his fury was contained in that scream. It resonated down through his entire body, leaving only a cold calm behind.

His father gave him a strange look, Manik couldn't quite place it but he didn't worry about it. Crouching, he flexed his toe claws into place for quick direction changes and allowed Barrus to make the first move.

Throwing dust in a plume, his father charged at a dead run. His powerful muscles propelled him at breathtaking speed across the open expanse.

The cold feeling expanded.

He didn't think.

Diving forward, Manik met the charge at the last moment. Barrus was obviously expecting him to dive to the side and so was momentarily off balance as Manik snaked inside his reach. Slashing deep enough to draw blood, but not deep enough to break ribs, Manik drew a pair of claw marks from Barrus' exposed shoulders down to his navel. Snapping his claws in, Manik dove between his legs, using the muscular trunks as additional supports to push him into a roll safely out of reach once again.

Barrus continued towards the wall and used his momentum to run a few steps up it. Flexing his stomach and spinning his body, he flipped about and pushed off as though a swimmer turning a lap. The height he'd gained and the momentum he still carried gave him more than enough impetus to reach Manik's current position. He approached with foreclaws outstretched and fangs bared.

Manik flowed to his feet into one of the stances Krym had taught him, ready to receive the next barrage of assault. When he saw the incoming meteor, he remembered the treebeast leaping in much the same manner. There was a bestial, predatory grace about the motion that he could only admire.

He knew how to refine his attack this time. Taking a quick step forward, he arched his back and sprang backwards putting him directly below Barrus, albeit moving considerably slower. He felt his father's claws rake across the front of his shirt, where his chest would have been, and dug his claws into the ample muscle of Barrus' biceps. When his hands had purchase, he snapped his feet up and in to brace on Barrus' hips, and then he waited patiently for the fraction of a second it took for his back to skim the ground as he was pulled along.

Upon brushing contact, Manik pushed with his legs and pulled with his arms as hard as he could. The kick threw his feet down into the ground and he acted as his own lever to spin Barrus up and away from him. The older male cartwheeled through the air gracelessly before landing in a surprised heap a dozen feet away.

The cold permeated into his bones, a comforting chill that gave him a delicious mental freedom. He allowed his instincts to carry him completely.

He spun and rolled, coming to his feet quickly and efficiently. Distantly, Manik registered background noise. The chattering of the glassgrasses, maybe. Seeing his target on the ground, he approached it and saw it trying to untangle its limbs and right itself for another attack. It wouldn't get the chance, not after what it had done to his crew. As it turned to face him he pounced on it, fifteen claws from both feet and one hand pinning it to the ground. He raised his right hand, hoping to get enough momentum from a full swing to break through the neck armor the creature had.

"I...I yield, son."

Manik stared at the treebeast for a moment, confused. He sat frozen for a long moment staring into its golden eyes. He saw no hatred, a little fear, and a good deal of...respect? Why would it respect him when he was about to kill it?

The cold began to bleed away in the long silence, bringing realization back once again. His father lay below him, bleeding, still impaled on Manik's claws.

Manik withdrew his blades quickly and held out a hand to Barrus. The older man looked at the hand for a moment then back to Manik's eyes as he took the offer and climbed laboriously to his feet.

Without releasing Manik's captive hand Barrus raised it high, to a resounding cheer from the crowd. Medics ran in from three different directions, but Barrus waved them all off. Instead, he led Manik across the arena to the waiting Clan Pikes and carefully pulled the smaller of the two down.

Holding the cloth wide to avoid bleeding on it, he held it up and proclaimed, "My son has bested me in my own event. He has defeated a warrior who was, perhaps, his better in every way save one. His will to win was greater. I present to my Family, my friends, and the collected viewers...Manik val'Kaer, heir to the glory of House Kaer!"

In the thunderous cacophony that followed Barrus spun the cloak around Manik's shoulders, closing a simple pin to hold it. Leaning close, Barrus said, "That was quite impressive son. You've changed not a little bit in a short time. Care to weave a tale for an old fighter?"

Manik noted the changed tone, one of equals or near enough...certainly not speaking down to a child as it had been before. Nodding, he said, "I can tell you the story but then I must go. My crew needs me more than you do at the moment."

Barrus looked mildly startled. "Your crew, eh? I look forward to this telling even more. Let's adjourn to the house. I'll get stitched up and you can tell me of ghosts and fights and where my son went to be replaced by this capable beast I see before me, eh?"

He laughed and gestured toward the exit then plucked his own cloak from its Pike and carried it with him as they left.

Manik walked in a daze towards the Main House followed by well-wishers, shoulder slappers, and local media reporters all vying for his attention. He ignored them all, lost in his own thoughts. Did he really just, after all these years, earn his name? Was he dreaming, still lying on the stone in the meadow of chemically glowing grasses? Was he on board the *Kyoto Sunrise* in another almost-real simulation? Was he in his small cell in the Brewhouse waiting to awaken to another long, mind-numbing day?

He ascended the front staircase, the attention seekers peeling off a group at a time, until he stood alone before the main door. Swallowing his reservations, he opened it and walked inside.

The Main House was of classic Chromaran build, albeit more extensive than similar homes in the area. The main door led into the open entry hall, the walls gilt in synthesized gold lines in complex patterns, from which the four main hallways branched. Manik walked across the polished floor and headed down the passage second from the left, heading towards the meeting rooms set further back in the bedrock.

Opening the door to his father's study, Manik paused. Would this be an appropriate room to have the conversation in? Would the formal meeting room be better? Perhaps the sitting room so that his father had more room to maneuver if the medics weren't done with him.

Before he could close the door again Barrus entered from the secondary rear door, followed closely by three branch family members wearing medic bands and carrying stitching and bandaging supplies. Motioning for Manik to enter the study, Barrus followed through and strode to his high backed desk chair. Collapsing into it with a sigh of relief, a huge concession considering his father's stance on showing weakness, he settled himself as best he could and still give the medics room to work.

Sitting across the expansive oak desk from him, yet another indication of his family's power as true oak furniture had to be flown at great expense from Earth itself, he began.

He breezed quickly through his wanderings around the city

and the flight to the Orbital. His movements through the station itself were muddled somewhat from his concussion in the earlier Arena loss but he believed he hit all the major points. He covered his meeting with the crew and his dealings with each of them.

At that point, his father interrupted. "You say there was another Chromaran on the crew? Did you catch his name? His family?"

Manik nodded and waited for a moment to ensure he had his father's full attention. "Yes, I did. His advice is what helped me through along with no small amount of my own motivation to finish. His name is Krym sel'Mere. I believe you knew him, once. He sends his regards, by the way."

Barrus went still, and then said quietly, "Krym. Former Primus Assemblyman and First Warrior potential. Yes, I remember him. Master of Serakka and a most unforgiving opponent if ever I've met one. II did something horrible to him years ago...no doubt he's told you if he sent his greetings to go along with my loss. What I did, I did on orders from the First, and I don't regret it. I did, however, resign my post from the shame of it."

Manik was stunned. "I thought you resigned because you decided you'd given up on being First Warrior and just wanted to lead the Family to greater glory..."

Barrus nodded. "Yes, that's what I told the Family and media alike. The real reason doesn't leave this room." He turned to look at each of the medics in turn, who all nodded profusely their agreement. He glared at the last medic for an extra moment, and then turned back to Manik and continued in a lighter tone. "Well, you met some offworlders and left the Orbital, did you simply fly about or did your fantastic holiday have any scenic detours?"

Manik continued to breathe slowly, calmly. He shouldn't be able to rile anger just by speaking condescendingly...the man was maddeningly mercurial, even when injured. "Yes, we left this planet and went to a few others. We flew to Ryla, and then to...another planet. I can't give you more details at the moment other than the fact that it was an uncharted world. We crashed there..."

Barrus interrupted. "What kind of idiot pilot did you have? Did he not use the computers? Probably Rylan too...as a species they all seem to think they are more intelligent than anyone else by virtue of having an overly large head."

"I did it, OK? I crashed the ship." Manik said, causing Barrus to fall silent.

"You...you flew a ship? Did their bucket have advanced enough controls to let you navigate? What was the malfunction?"

"I...miscalculated. We were going through a vortex of antimatter planetoids around a weak point and I failed to correct for random non-orbital debris. I almost got us killed." he admitted.

"Well, you were only flying with your hands and feet, nobody can blame you for that. What kind of suicidal Captain goes for a place like that anyway? Best to leave that alone and stay on the well-traveled lanes. More innocent passersby to waylay, or whatever it is they do." his father responded flippantly.

Manik stood up and slammed his hands on the desk, causing all four other occupants to jump slightly. "Captain Fujiwara was a hero, not suicidal. He is...was older than our entire civilization here! And they weren't pirates! They traded information and collected Exotic Particles just like the Exploration Service crews, and I trust each of them far more than I do you."

Manik turned and walked to the door but a roar from Barrus gave him pause. "Young man, you do NOT turn your back on me when I am speaking to you! You're going to come back here, sit down, and we are going to discuss what your next steps are and how to spin this correctly for the media outside."

Manik turned, but did not approach. "No Father. YOU can deal with the spin and the media. That's your specialty." Turning his head, he lifted his hair to show the Pilot Spike Interface. When he heard the gasp he turned back and continued. "Me? I'm a pilot. For now, I'm even Captain of the ship...til they find someone better. But what I am and what you are doesn't matter. My crewmate is dying up in orbit right now. YOUR ban on my movements ended when you lost the fight."

Approaching the desk in a slow stalk Manik punctuated each word with a step. "Release. The. Lockdown. On. My. Ship. Now."

Their eyes locked and Manik felt the full weight of his father's personality pressing him to back down, but he refused. Not now, not ever again. Barrus flushed and opened his mouth wide to yell back...but nothing came.

Slowly, he closed his mouth, and then nodded and swept on the tabletop display. A few quick clicks and he swept it closed again. Raising his face to meet Manik, his eyes had gone cold and professional.

"Very well. You are an independent member of the Family now, and can exalt or ruin your life on your own decisions. You have my permission to leave. The compound and the planet."

Manik nodded and strode back to the door, pausing one last time as Barrus called after him.

"When you come back, and you WILL come back, we'll talk about manners and how you should properly respect your elders."

Manik turned and smiled a sad smile and said, "Yes, let's do that. When I come back."

The door slid closed with a quiet click, leaving him alone in the hallway. Looking left and right, Manik made the quick decision to exit through the secondary door at the back of the building. The tunnel there branched off to most of the other buildings and it would allow him to avoid the crush of onlookers awaiting a statement or development at the steps to the main house.

The unobtrusive door was blended in with the wall causing Manik to search for it for a few moments before finding the catch and ducking inside. He picked his way slowly at first through the darkness, increasing in speed as his eyes adjusted to the miniscule amount of light available. The dark green lightstrips along the floor of the tunnel gave a soft ambient glow, just enough for him to navigate past the branches leading to the Brewhouses, the Arena, and a half dozen other main compound locations. The branch he followed led him to a small alcove near the main gate.

As the door slid silently open Manik saw that, indeed, there were still a few dozen people waiting impatiently at the steps held back, only by professional courtesy, from barging through the front door to demand answers to their burning questions and demands.

Adjusting the shoulder knot of his cloak, something he'd have to get used to, he set off as quickly as stealth would allow.

Once outside though, no one gave him a second glance. He was jostled more roughly than he remembered from his last flight from the compound as he passed through the crowds of people in the streets when he finally realized what it meant. He was just another Family member, just another Chromaran, just another body in the press. He wasn't a wayward child anymore, to be avoided lest some responsible adult take issue with undue harsh treatment. He was responsible for himself. Finally.

Straightening up, Manik jostled the crowd back and was pleasantly surprised when the press gave slightly and he got no more than annoyed looks. Following the stream of humanity, he weaved here and bumped there until he made his way back to the elevator system that would take him back to the shuttle bays. As he stood in the swiftly ascending transparent bubble, he could almost see a ghost of the younger version of himself goggling out the wall at the sights.

Manik strode to the Orbital shuttle and presented his Familial credentials for pay. The operator gave him an odd look upon returning but granted him passage with a simple "Welcome aboard, Mr. Kaer." He took a seat near the back, as before, so that he could disembark swiftly but didn't bother seeking out a window. The views he'd seen before and could get from this shuttle were nowhere near as good as what he could get with a quick skim by his own ship.

His own ship.

What a crazy idea, him having a ship, and friends, and a life that didn't involve the distillation of liquor or the tedious politics of Families jockeying for power and prestige from the First Warrior and his Assembly. He could return one day he supposed, to visit at least, but as long as SID was locked to the ship, so too would he be.

The door sealed and the ship accelerated up to the Orbital station, delivering him quickly back to the docking level. The looks he'd gotten from the shuttle attendant and other passengers were not remotely on the scale he received upon exiting the shuttle. Local station media and onlookers were once again swarming him, taking images and video of the Wayward Son as he left Chromara again.

The press of people was similar to what he'd felt in the markets on the lower levels, but it gave way much easier as the media people seemed quite disinclined to being forcibly moved when they were being recorded. Manik moved through them, not saying anything, and strode as quickly as he could to the infirmary and the quarantine area.

As he crossed the threshold into the infirmary his retinue stopped, seeming loathe to enter the possibly extraplanetarily contaminated area.

He strode down the corridors back to the waiting room where he found Challis and Krym still arguing, joined by an apparently heavily drugged Dorr.

Krym was apparently mid-rant, "No, he was tougher back when he was an Assemblyman. The fight was a good deal longer, since neither of us underestimated the other, and that's beside the point. Did you see where he snapped? I know that look and I'm surprised there wasn't more blood in the sawdust when it all settled."

Challis replied calmly, "I'm sure he seemed more difficult to defeat for you, or at least that's how you choose to spin your story, and that is your own affair. I am neither agreeing nor disagreeing with you as I never saw the two of you fight. As for Manik, it looked like a perfectly normal barbaric Chromaran fighting technique to me. Was the entire point of the confrontation not to end as quickly as possible? Wouldn't the level of wounds he gave then be a prudent and calculated maneuver?"

Dorr, wrapped from upper chest to waist with white bandages, leaned in to interject drunkenly, "Hey, is there a video of that fight between you and Barrrurururrias? Or whatever his name is? That sounds like good drinking entertainment. Man, I gotta get me some more of whatever they gave me. This stuff is awesome."

Manik walked up behind the oblivious trio and said, "His name is Barrus and I'm glad to see you survived surgery. Any lasting damage?"

Krym and Challis both jumped, but Dorr simply favored Manik with a goofy grin and a thumbs up. "As fit as ever, Captain-pilot-trouble-guy...you know, we really need to fix your nickname. Trouble just doesn't fit anymore. Shame too, cause that was a great name. Maybe we can recycle it somehow."

Manik nodded. "Good, we should be clear to break orbit by the time you get back to the ship. Krym, you take Dorr and see to our preparations. Challis and I will get Selelle and her equipment and meet you there."

Dorr lurched to his feet and executed an extremely complex two handed salute. "Yes sir Captain sir....sir! We'll unfurl the topsails, stow the rigging, swing the jib, and be ready when you want to set sail! You can count on...um...well, him at least." he finished, deflating slightly and giggling.

Krym shook his head and stood, taking Dorr's unresisting arm. "We'll see you at the ship lad, don't take too long."

Manik nodded then turned and walked to the guard at the entrance to the intensive care suites. "We need to check my crewmate out along with any technology she'll need to survive transport to the next hospital."

The guard shook his head disdainfully and said, "You don't have the money or influence, pirate. You're just lucky they haven't put you on lockdown."

Manik stood up to his full height, looking the guard in the eyes. He pointed at his Colors and said quietly, "Do you know what these colors represent?"

The guard paused for a moment, and then shook his head.

"These colors are of Clan Kaer, you've heard of us no doubt? My father Barrus has been on the news recently quite a bit...but I don't expect you guard types are allowed to keep up on current events. I am the heir to that Clan, and if you don't want to have your sneer and your insults stuffed back down your throat, politically or in an Arena, your choice, and then I suggest you step. Aside. Now."

The guard was slow witted and woefully uninformed, but hadn't gotten to the cushy position he was now in without recognizing legitimate, career-ending, threats when he heard them. He stepped away from the door and quickly radioed ahead to his officer in charge.

Manik ignored him and stormed through the doorway as imperiously as he could. The area was largely devoid of wandering staff, as they were all still clustered in the suite designated for Selelle. He considered knocking, and then simply threw the door open and strode in.

A young female nursing assistant stepped up quickly in front of him, hands raised. He stopped smartly and looked down into her apparently terrified silver eyes expectantly. She swallowed, and then said in a shaky voice, "Sir, um, you aren't supposed to, uh, be in here...right now. The doctors are, um, not ready to institute visiting hours. If you'd, um, like to go back to the, um, waiting room we'll have someone, um, come see you very soon."

Manik couldn't scare her. Guards and doctors he was alright with pushing to get what he wanted but he knew the position of the messenger too well himself. He said softly, "Which one is the doctor in charge?"

The frightened nurse blinked at him confusedly then gestured at a platinum haired elderly male Chromaran in a long white coat. Manik nodded his thanks, and then took her by the shoulders and gently, but firmly, moved her to one side.

Over her protests, he strode up to the man. "Doctor, I am here to secure the release of my crewmember, for transfer to a medical facility that can care for her properly."

The tall doctor turned and looked down at Manik as though he were a simple irritant. Manik was getting really tired of that look. "Young man, the nurse already gave you your instructions. Leave this area or I'll call security and have you escorted from the premises." He picked up a tablet from the dock at the end of the bed and began scanning through Selelle's real time vitals and information as an obvious dismissal.

Challis put a hand on his shoulder and whispered in his ear, "You are growling."

Manik realized how much his impatience was affecting him and took a deep cleansing breath. Letting it out slowly, he closed his eyes and thought of deep space, friends, and SID.

The doctor's voice intruded on his brief meditation like a meteorite on an atmosphere. Manik felt the impact only topically and was able to open his eyes and even favor the man with a smile.

"Doctor, I am sorry that you've been penned away in surgery and looking after my comrade so faithfully that you failed to hear the news from your chain of command. My friend and I are taking our shipmate to a facility more qualified to care for her current, unique, needs. We have the support of Clan Kaer and permission from Station Command to leave with all required medical technology to keep her alive until arrival. I assure you that all items will be returned in exemplary condition as we have a top notch medical staff on board my ship that will care for it like their own."

Out of the corner of his eye, Manik saw the brief moment of panic in Challis' eyes before it was covered with his usual cool disdain. He'd noted how many lies, or at least extensions of the truth, had been passed in that moment and was hoping that they wouldn't get called on it.

The doctor, a shrewd man, did just that.

Pulling out a pair of TechSpecs, he made the motions to indicate he was placing an audio-only call. Manik waited patiently, trying not to appear any more anxious than a worried friend and Captain would be.

The doctor sneered into the pickup. "Yes, this is Doctor val'Nivak of the Transium Medical Depot up on Orbital Two. I have a very rude young man up here who insists he has your Clan's permission to-...yes, I'll hold, but my time is precious so make it quick."

He stood there tapping his foot, impatiently waiting, until the call picked back up. Whatever he heard drained the blood from his face, and he stood a bit straighter.

"Sir. Yes sir. Well sir, I- You see he- I'm just trying to- Yes sir, at once. Thank you sir." he choked out, and then cut the call.

With shaking hands, the doctor removed his Specs and replaced them in his breast pocket, and then gestured for one of the nurses. He spoke quietly, but not quite low enough for Manik to miss.

"Help them take whatever they need to keep this girl alive and in good condition, cost is irrelevant. Direct orders from the First Warrior to be both discrete and fast. Go."

The nurse and doctor fired away from each other on different trajectories. The doctor, without a word to Manik, collected up all of the remaining medical staff and herded them from the room, fleeing down the hall like a Relleherd being chased by a ravenous pack of Hyz. The nurse began piling bags of supplies on Selelle's legs, and was moving in a panicked flurry to detach all of the power connectors from the walls to reroute to the bed's internal battery.

Challis stepped up to Selelle's other side and silently began helping to shift the entire bedframe and connected medicines and machines from stationary to mobile, gaining him a smile of thanks from the nurse.

Within minutes they had everything set. Challis inched the bedframe away from the wall, and then with a quick flip of a few switches the entirety lifted slightly off the ground. In answer to Manik's surprise, he said simply, "Simple repellant, functionally nullifies the weight and gravitational inertia of the bed, meaning you only need one attendant to move it. Makes transport worlds easier than the old wheel-based archaic options."

Manik nodded and began leading the way back to the ship, Challis following a few steps behind, as evidenced by the gentle purr of the bed's engine. Manik wondered idly what fuel source it ran on. Probably couldn't run that way for long if it were electric, maybe it was a chemical or particle drive of some kind. No way, too small.

A sudden shout of "Stop where you are!" rang down the hallway. Manik turned to see a familiar face and his retinue had leveled very deadly looking rifles at them. Raising his hands slowly, Manik said, "Captain, talk to Doctor val'Nivak, he'll explain the situation. We aren't stealing anything."

Captain val'Shieke spat, "I'll be the judge of that." and activated his helmet intercom.

"val'Nivak. Yes, this is Guard Captain- Yes, the fugitives are right in front of me- What? Why would I do that? He did? THE First Warrior? Personally? Huh. Alright sir, I'll take it from here."

Looking up to Manik, the Guard Captain raised his weapon and said, "Well, looks like you have better friends than I do.

Let's get you to your ship and out of my jurisdiction. The sooner the better." Then, to his soldiers, "Men, we're now an escort. Go clear the road. We need them off this Orbital in three minutes, tops. Every minute longer, you each owe 5% of your pay next period."

Without need of further encouragement, the remaining six soldiers hustled them at very nearly a dead run through the station. They blew past bewildered residents, curious children, angry maintenance personnel, and a good deal of confused arrivals and departures waiting on the red tape of interplanetary customs.

As they approached the ship, the entry ramp swung quietly into place. Stepping aside, Manik let Challis precede him on board, and then turned to the hospital security team. "Thank you for the escort gentlemen and ladies. We'll be taking off in a moment."

The security team leader nodded and said, "Alright sir, good luck getting your situation handled, wherever it takes you...and if the topic comes up in conversation with your...friends... please don't hesitate to not mention me or any of my people. We don't need or want the publicity."

Manik nodded, and then turned and strode back on board.

The gangway slid home automatically as he left it, the door closing and sealing without his having to lift a finger. Looking up, Manik smiled. *Looks like SID made herself fully at home.* He walked through the lower deck noting that the cargo was, at least marginally, more organized than when he'd left. He ascended the stairs, noting that the blood had also been scrubbed from his path, and headed through the crew quarters.

As he arrived at the bridge, he saw that the theater's chair had been adjusted to fit his height as well as having been scrubbed clean meticulously.

Manik sat down and gently locked himself in with straps before resting his head back on the Piloting Spike. As it clicked home, SID sparkled into view before him, smiling.

"Welcome back, Captain. I was monitoring the communications and other random transmissions from the medical facility. I am happy to hear that things went better than expected in all aspects of your visit."

Manik smiled and said, "Well, all but two things. We need to get Selelle to Venalara for treatment ASAP and I'm not sure I'll ever get a chance to come home again."

SID shook her head. "I disagree, love. Selelle is stable, she's hooked into my systems and I have her vitals regulated and her intravenous medications controlled. She's able to comfortably remain in her current state for at least three or four days given the supply of medications the medical staff sent along. And as to home, I know that Chromara and Clan Kaer WAS your home...is not this your home now?"

Manik thought about it for a few moments. SID was right. This ship may be new, the chair may not be as comfortable as he'd like, but everything he needed was here. It really WAS home now. Smiling up at her, he said, "You're right again. Let's get going." He was about to turn over control but stopped himself. "By the way, SID, how did the cargo get cleaned up and the blood taken care of?"

SID hesitated before responding, immediately setting off alarms in Manik's mind. When she spoke it was to the monitors rather than to him.

"Well, I kind of...let our captive out for some exercise, pursuant to penal codes that I can name for any planet you'd like, and got her some food...and since she was out, she volunteered to help clean up the mess that everyone had made in the rush of leaving the planet, as well as the appalling state that her previous captors had kept of their dining and cargo areas. I have everything video logged in case you'd like to review it for possible subversion, or...maybe consideration on making her possibly not a captive anymore." she finished in a rushing torrent of words.

Manik stared at her for a few minutes, debating on what to do. The girl did seem eager to help and was unlikely to rebel against them if she truly was a captive of the previous crew. That'd make them technically her rescuers. Since she'd been working for pirates it made sense that they'd confined her for everyone's sake but she'd done well with very little supervision.

Manik sighed. "SID, we can talk about this after we get Selelle to Venalara. Once there, we may be there for a while so I can sit down and talk with the crew, and with her, and see what will be best for everyone. Is that good enough for now?"

SID nodded, beaming.

"Good. Now, no more jaunts through the ship without my permission, right?" he added. She nodded again, and then threw her immaterial self onto his lap to hug him. He imagined he could almost feel the warmth of her projected self pressing against him.

"OK, ok. We can hug and talk and whatever you'd like once we're in Underspace, but for now we have to get going." Manik said, aware that he was delaying the takeoff more than necessary.

SID did not move but whispered in his ear, "Undocking procedures underway, waiting for tower clearance. I'm being very careful on the way out so they don't think we left any malicious sleeper programs behind to give us priority docking again. There's some sort of standing order from the First Warrior's Office that is expediting the process. We should be cleared in...there, taking off now."

Manik watched the ship coast steadily out of the docking deck, dodging occasional incoming traffic, and cruise free of the station. He adjusted the visual sensors around so he could watch the glittering hexadecagon slowly shrink against the majesty of the Chromaran landscape below. He tried to sear the image into his mind, so that he could forever remember his planet of origin, even if he could never again return.

SID's quiet voice broke his reverie. "We are clear of all incoming and outgoing traffic and ready to traverse, save one last detail, love."

Manik was perplexed for a moment, until SID pulled up a series of official Chromaran license documents. Oh yes, the title for the ship. As he watched, the documents filled quickly with SID's input, leaving one field empty and highlighted. Ship's Name.

Taking edit control, he quickly filled the blank with the name he'd pulled from the clouds back on the Orbital, officially signing the ship, his ship, as the *Miyako Sunset*. SID saved and sent the files, finalizing the transaction without a word.

Manik smiled warmly at her and ran through the preparations. SID's voice echoed over the intercom as he did announcing their imminent traverse and a reminder to the crew to secure themselves. Manik accelerated toward the weak point, checking his scanners to make sure no ships were in the immediate area before diving in.

The thrum of the Exotic Particle Manifold activating and enveloping the ship was soft and rhythmic, like the heartbeat of a great beast.

Once active, the ship felt almost eager to traverse. Manik pushed them through easier than before. He hoped he was getting better and that it was a signal that he had finally moved forward. The sensors pinged and flashed multi-colored lights across his vision as they slipped, once again, out of the universe.

CPSIA information can be obtained at www.ICGtesting.com
Printed in the USA
BVOW05s0125220914

367749BV00001B/131/P